TREOIR DRAGON HOARD

THE
BELADOR
SERIES

BOOK TEN

DIANNA LOVE

TREOIR DRAGON HOARD
The Belador Series, Book 10

Copyright © 2018 by Dianna Love

978-1-940651-64-4

Printed in the USA.

Cover Design and Interior Format

PRAISE FOR THE NEW YORK TIMES BESTSELLING BELADOR SERIES

BELADOR COSAINT

"Wow! I'm not real sure exactly how to describe how fantastic this book was. It takes a special kind of writer to be able to take a series to nine books, and still have it going strong." ~~ Heather, Amazon

"Hat's off to Dianna Love for another thrilling and gripping action packed story that I just couldn't put down until I'd finished it." ~~ Clare and Lou's Mad About Books

"Dianna Love takes her latest Belador release to new heights..." ~~Always Reviewing

"Another great read in a fantastic series!" ~~Amazon review

DRAGON KING OF TREOIR

"Once again, Dianna Love gives us another fantastic story that keeps us glued to our seat, unable to put the book down."~~The Reading Café

"...an ongoing fantasy series, and definitely not the end, nor is it a cliff hanger. I loved the ending and can't wait for the next book to come out."~~ Madison Fairbanks, Amazon

"As much as I am impatient for each installment these stories are so worth the wait." ~~ Rosemary, Amazon

"Dianna Love has created an extremely diverse group for her Belador series, and seeing if they can overcome challenging issues makes her stories continuously riveting." ~~ Always Reviewing

"What a ride!!! This series keeps getting better and better." ~~ Gaby, Amazon

ROGUE BELADOR

"When it comes to urban fantasy stories, Dianna Love is a master." ~~A. Richards, Always Reviewing

"This adventure win or lose is going to change things for Evalle and her friends. Brava Ms. Love for another fantastic ride." ~~ In My Humble Opinion

"It was worth every day of waiting." ~~ J. Cazares, Amazon
"As always, Dianna Love delivers another sensational story that will blow your mind," ~~ Barb, The Reading Café

"Keep them coming and I will keep reading. Thank you for another awesome adventure." ~~ Candi, Amazon

WITCHLOCK

"Fans of Rachel Caine's Weather Warden series will enjoy this series. I surely do." ~~D. Antonio, In My Humble Opinion

"Every scene in WITCHLOCK is absolutely spellbinding...This remarkable author repeatedly leaves you wondering if there truly are happenings on earth of which we are not aware..." ~~Amelia, SingleTitles.com

"I LOVE THESE BOOKS! I wait impatiently for every book to come out and have never been disappointed." ~~Elizabeth, Reader

DEMON STORM

"..non-stop tense action, filled with twists, betrayals, danger, and a beautiful sensual romance. As always with Dianna Love, I was on the edge of my seat, unable to pull myself away."~~Barb, The Reading Cafe

"There is so much action in this book I feel like I've burned calories just reading it."~~D Antonio, Goodreads

"...I have to thank Dianna for keeping this series true to the wonderful world, witty dialogue and compelling characters that I have loved since the first book." ~~Chris, Goodreads

RISE OF THE GRYPHON

"...It's been a very long time since I've felt this passionate about getting the next installment in a series. Even J. K. Rowling's Harry Potter books. It's a story you don't want to end and when it does, you can't help but scream out 'No! NO THEY DID NOT JUST DO THIS TO ME!! NO!!!!'" ~~Bryonna Nobles, Demons, Dreams and Dragon Wings

"...shocking developments and a whopper of an ending... and I may have exclaimed aloud more than once...Bottom line: I really kind of loved it." ~~Jen, Amazon Top 500 Reviewer

"I want more Feenix. I loved this book so much...If you have not read this series, once again, what are you waiting for?" ~~Barb, The Reading Cafe

THE CURSE

"The Beladors series is beloved and intricate. It's surprising that such a diverse and incredible world has only three books out." ~~ USA Today, Happy Ever After

"The precarious action and genuine emotion in THE CURSE will continuously leave the reader breathless..." ~~Amelia Richards, Single Titles

"If you're looking for a series with an epic scope and intricate, bold characters, look no further than the Belador series...This new addition provides all the action and intrigue that readers have come to expect...a series to be savored by urban fantasy and paranormal romance fans alike." ~~Bridget, The Romance Reviews

ALTERANT

"There are SO many things in this series that I want to learn more about; there's no way I could list them all... have me on tenterhooks waiting for the third BELADOR book. As Evalle would say, 'Bring it on.'" ~~Lily, Romance Junkies Reviews

"An incredible heart-jolting roller-coaster ride ... An action-packed adventure with an engrossing story line and characters you will grow to love." ~~ Mother/Gamer/Writer

"An intriguing series that has plenty of fascinating characters to ponder." ~~ Night Owl Reviews

BLOOD TRINITY

"BLOOD TRINITY is an ingenious urban fantasy with imaginative magical scenarios, characters who grab your every thought and more than a few unpredictable turns ... The meticulous storyline of Book One in the Belador series will enthrall you during every compellingly entertaining scene." ~~Amelia Richard, Single Titles

"BLOOD TRINITY is a fantastic start to a new Urban Fantasy series. The VIPER organization and the world built ... are intriguing, but the characters populating that world are irresistible. I am finding it difficult to wait for the next book to find out what happens next in their lives." ~~Diana Trodahl, Fresh Fiction

"BLOOD TRINITY is without a doubt one of the best books I've read this year... a tale that shows just how awesome urban fantasy really can be, particularly as the genre is flooded with so many choices. Brilliantly done and highly recommended." ~~ Debbie, CK2s Kwips & Kritiques

TREOIR DRAGON HOARD: BELADOR BOOK 10

Two thousand years ago, someone stole the king's treasure from Daegan's father. An unexpected enemy uses this hoard to set Daegan on a path to his ultimate demise by dangling the one bait everyone knows the dragon king can't ignore—protecting one of his own.

While racing to help a friend, Evalle lands in a trap where she's given the unimaginable choice to either destroy her dragon king or condemn everyone she loves to die. Even her Skinwalker mate, Storm, has no way to track her this time.

Friendships and alliances are tested as Atlanta erupts with preternatural exposure. Who will join Storm and Daegan to go where, even for a dragon, the chance of survival is nil? With the enemy willing to gamble everything to take down her dragon king, Evalle makes up her mind to accept her destiny, but on her terms. She never wants anyone to see what she's become, especially Storm.

Destiny is not a choice, but a summons. The hourglass favors no one.

"The Belador series is beloved and intricate."
—*USA Today*

"*When it comes to urban fantasy stories, Dianna Love is a master.*"
—A. Richards, Always Reviewing

—————◆—————

For signed books, bookplates, and swag, visit
www.DiannaLoveSignedBooks.com

DEDICATION

*Thank you to Jennifer Cazares
for all your support over the years.*

PRONUNCIATION GUIDE

Note: A complete guide of unusual names, places and terminology is located on any Belador book page at *www.AuthorDiannaLove.com.*

Abandinu - AH ban DEE noo
Brynhild - burn HILD
Casidhe – CAH sih duh
Cavans – cah VAHNS
cockatrice – CAHK ah trees
Dragani – drah GAHN nee
Eógan – Oh un
Germanus - Jur MAN us
Halcón - al KOHN
Gruffyn - GRUFF in
Ixxter – ICK ster
Jennyver - JENN uh vir
La Cuchilla – LAH coo CHEE juh
Lann an Cheartais – lahn nah KAIR tus
Lann na Fírinne - lahn nah FEAR in yah
Lann Saoirse – – Lahn SEER shuh
Lugisech – LOO gi sehk (g is hard like 'egg')
Misstag – Miss Tog
nisse – NIS uh
Nunc aperta – NOONK uh PAIR tuh
Ossory – AH suh ree
Piri Barajas - Pi ree Buh RAH has
Rias – REE uhs
Scamall – SKAH mull
Seanmháthair Piritta – SHAN mwuh her pe REE tuh
Tuatha Dé Danann - TOO uh huh DAY DAN uhn

CHAPTER 1

County Kilkenny, Ireland

*D*UNMORE CAVE IS TOO POWERFUL *for even you!*
His mother's words kept playing over and over in his mind. She would not be happy with him if she lived today. She had nicknamed him *La Cuchilla*, The Blade, because he had been her favorite child. Neither sibling had his gifts, nor understood that with great power comes great expectation.

For him, that expectation meant he would rise above all others who had come before him. By ten, he'd proven to be more deadly than the sharpest blade. His mother would whisper her special name for him when calling on the powers of her ancestors, who went back to days of the ancient kingdom of Ossory, now known as County Kilkenny in Ireland.

He used La Cuchilla as a code name these days, as none could link it to his face, but one day, once he rose to the level of the most powerful beings, that name would be known—and feared—by all.

To his core, he was La Cuchilla and no human man. He refused to fear any ethereal presence living inside this cave.

You promised, La Cuchilla!

His mother's words hammered his conscience.

He'd sincerely meant the vow he'd given to her at ten years old when he promised to stay far away from this treacherous location.

Now, at thirty-four, he realized how naïve he'd been to utter those words. If his mother still lived, he hoped she'd understand, because he'd been inside Dunmore Cave for over an hour, waiting for staff to close the place to visitors.

That had happened ten minutes ago.

This wasn't actually the area she'd warned him about, where all but one soldier of an army had met their end many generations ago. He waited in a part of the cave that had become a museum for humans to wander through and admire, clueless about what lurked deeper inside, behind thick walls.

Shrouded in darkness, he gathered himself for the task ahead as the staff cleaned up after another day of sightseers.

Today's humans were curious of the past, but lacked the ability to truly appreciate stories they considered little more than myth. Most of these puny humans toyed with electronic devices while wandering through the cavern. No respect for those who died here.

Some came only to see if Dunmore Cave was truly haunted.

Wouldn't you expect a place where a thousand women and children had been murdered to house a few spirits?

Allowing another minute to be sure all workers were gone, he moved quietly through security lighting, but he was invisible to any video monitoring. He'd learned how to cloak himself by the age of twelve. All three children of the famed Piri Barajas had inherited her gifts, but as the middle child he'd shown far greater ability than the other two.

He'd also worked harder than his brother and sister.

"You are special, La Cuchilla," his mother would say.

It was true. Not ego so much as confidence.

Some might call him a warlock or sorcerer, but his mother had been the first to refer to him as a mage. He'd hidden his abilities from others when necessary. His mother had taught him that showing off his gifts was to invite his death.

Moving quickly, he chose his path through the narrow walkways carefully. This place smelled too clean, too new for an ancient burial site. His mother's voice continued to harp at him to turn back.

He had heeded her advice his whole life ... until now.

He had an opportunity to gain immortality.

That had to be worth the risk of entering the Cave Of The Damned, as those in his mother's secret coven had referenced it in hushed conversation.

His heart hurt when he thought of how disappointed she would be, if she still lived, at him breaking his word. But she was long gone, as were his father and two siblings.

Of his two parents, his mother had possessed by far the greater power.

She'd carried the blood of the witch Seanmháthair Piritta, his Celtic, many-times-great-grandmother, who had lived during the time of the Viking raids on this land. Piritta's village had been near this cave when the area was still known as Ossory.

Poor Piritta had been only fifteen when she arrived too late to save her child from dying with many others in here.

Piritta raced to the cave when she heard the Vikings were raiding her village. Another woman had been watching her baby while Piritta cooked. She and the other mothers had agreed that if danger came to their home and their men were outnumbered, they'd hide all the children in the defensible cavern.

With a severe downslope to the narrow entrance, the women believed they had the best chance at killing the heathens in small batches by using the cave mouth as a choke point.

In 928, hulking Vikings, both men and women, from Dublin had been on their way to attack the Vikings in Waterford. The Vikings of Ireland were not at all united back then. The bloodthirsty pagans lived for a brutal battle and to bludgeon all who were of no use to them, but they captured women and children as slaves.

Upon discovering where their future slaves hid, the Vikings decided to force the captives out of hiding by setting fires near the cave entrance.

Unfortunately, a thousand innocent women and children died of asphyxiation.

Coming upon the scene, Piritta lost her mind, screaming at the Vikings and racing out into the open to save her child.

As her captors dragged her away, she cursed them.

According to his mother, Seanmháthair Piritta eventually escaped the Vikings, married again and had more children, then lived to well over a hundred.

But she never forgot her murdered child.

She spent a year perfecting a spell that pushed the King of England to slaughter young Dane males of fighting age. That campaign was now known as the St. Brice's Day massacre, and those Danes would have been the next generation of Vikings.

The bad blood between Vikings and England lasted for over sixty years.

La Cuchilla chuckled to himself. Piritta knew how to dish out revenge.

A bird caught inside the cave fluttered and chirped, pulling his attention up. He smiled, recalling how he'd studied many birds growing up, but his favorite would always be the Halcón Peregrine, a magnificent falcon. He'd been sad over his prized bird faltering with age until inspiration struck and he realized how his falcon would become even more valuable after death.

He'd possessed more than one peregrine falcon over the years, but the one he had now would become a truly exceptional creature if his mission today were successful.

Now was not the time to allow his thoughts to wander if he intended to survive, and he did.

In spite of archeological explorations of this cave, the spirits prevented discovery of one particular pile of bones that lay beyond a tunnel, which dwindled until it appeared to terminate.

He remembered every word his mother had shared about her ancestors. She'd passed them down only to her most powerful child, but even so, she had not told him everything. Some things he'd discovered on his own.

When he encountered a printed sign ordering him to go no farther, he slipped by and continued to the tunnel he'd waited his entire life to enter.

Deep inside, the narrow passage split off in two dark directions. Opening his hand, he whispered words and a flame appeared above his palm. Now he discerned that the arched ceiling of the left side had a dip in the center.

That was the marker.

His heart thumped loudly in his ears as he headed down the left vein. The deeper in he traveled, the lower the ceiling of the tunnel became until he was on his knees.

He kept placing his left hand against the short wall, beginning to worry when he continued to encounter no indication of an opening.

On the third try, his fingers tingled.

Taking a deep breath and swallowing hard, he killed the flame and closed his eyes, then spoke the words he'd found in his mother's journal. She probably never expected him to translate the odd text passed down from one generation to the next.

Nothing happened.

Sweat beaded his upper lip. He repeated the words two more times, then his fingers pushed through the wall as if it had turned into a cloud.

No going back now.

He twisted his body and wiggled his way through the ethereal opening. Energy sizzled across his skin.

Once everything stilled, he reached his arm outward. Was he on the other side of the wall?

His heart thumped so loudly the sound should be echoing in here. This place was darker than the souls of those Viking raiders.

As he stood, he called upon his majik. A glow grew around his feet and climbed toward his face, spreading slowly until the soft light reached the walls on each side of him. He glanced up to find a ceiling that soared two stories. As the light expanded and touched the upper walls farther back, he estimated this room stretched at least eighty feet.

The sound of something moving drew his eyes down to find a thin vine snaking slowly from the dark floor, which his light had failed to conquer.

Was something, or someone, blocking his majik?

The vine moved slowly toward him.

He smiled and kept his voice calm as he spoke. "I am a descendant of—"

A thicker vine shot out from behind him and wrapped his throat, choking him. He grabbed at it, fighting to pull away something with the strength of steel.

That's when light rushed through the room and he finally saw the entire floor of skeletons covered in vines with glowing, red-orange flowers the size of his hands. The stalks had thorns as long as his fingers.

His chest heaved for a breath. He squeezed out, "I ... am ... blood kin."

The neck vine would not let up.

Panicking, he clawed at the plant strangling him. He'd been told to never call up his majik here, but he had no choice. He had to break the living rope trying to kill him.

Squeezing out hoarse words, he fought to keep from passing out.

Smoke boiled around his face.

The killer neck vine hissed.

His eyes filled with tears and his chest wanted to explode.

A small plant at his feet lifted into view, stopping when it had grown much thicker and reached waist high. The stem divided into two offshoots.

A flower blossomed at the top of each one.

What did that mean?

Thorns sticking out just below the flower grew and extended six inches from the stem. The vine whipped back as if yanked away and came flying forward and down, hitting him square in each thigh.

He screamed in his head, because his tongue bulged in his mouth. Tears poured from his eyes.

Agony lashed up his legs and through his body.

Everything spun into a blinding red haze. He could see nothing else though his eyes were open.

Then, all at once, the thorns retracted from his thighs.

He heard a hissed word being repeated, but not in a language he knew.

The pressure around his neck released just as quickly.

He doubled over, hugging himself, coughing as he slid down the wall to sit. His mother had been right when she told him that to come here was to ask for his death.

Blood trickled from his mouth.

"You are not welcome," whispered viciously through the air, then more voices echoed the words over and over.

He blinked.

Plants rose, along with spirits, above each skeleton lying prone on the floor. The spirits stared out through huge, dark eyes and had black holes for mouths. Their filmy bodies were dressed in clothes from the era in which they'd died.

His body ached from head to ... hell, his legs felt numb. "I ... am family," he wheezed. He coughed and spit up blood.

A small female spirit from the center of the room glided over plants that moved gently in her wake, as though she were nothing more than a summer breeze.

When the girl reached him, she said in an emotionless voice, "I know your blood. Not you."

He caught a breath. "Please don't kill me. I'll explain."

She waited there, weaving back and forth. Was this Seanmháthair Piritta's child? Her black mouth opened with another question. "Who are you to come here?"

He cleared his ravaged throat and spoke. Giving any being of power your real name was never wise. "I am called La Cuchilla by my mother. She was a descendant of Seanmháthair Piritta, who I believe was *your* mother. My mother was named Piri after her."

The small child's head tilted in confusion.

Rather than waste this chance, he kept talking. "It's true. I am descended of your blood." Then he considered something they might not know. "Do you know that your mother lived long, and made Vikings regret killing you?"

The image wavered back and forth as if the child's spirit was anxious. "How?"

That had to be a good sign, yes? He told her of her mother's life and of the St. Brice's Day massacre.

For a moment, none of them made a sound.

Then the most horrible howling erupted.

His ears hurt, but he feared moving and ending up stabbed or strangled again.

Hold everything. This racket was a good sign.

The spirits were actually cheering.

Moving his hands to the holes in his thighs, he covered the wounds, hoping to heal them. But when he moved his hands, thick black blood oozed and smelled disgusting. He had to stop that before his damn legs rotted off.

If they allowed him to leave soon, he could heal, but that was a big if, after the reception he'd received.

When the noise quieted, the child spirit's voice returned to sounding flat and empty. "Why are you here?"

He'd originally thought to tell the truth, that he wanted their plant majik for his own use, but he was rethinking that plan. This group of spirits had once wiped out almost an entire army sent by a goddess. From what he knew, no one from the preternatural world had dared to visit this tomb again.

Gathering his courage, he said, "I wish to ask a favor of you."

Hissing echoed.

He held his breath, but the small spirit lifted a translucent hand.

Once peace settled again, he continued. "Your mother made the Vikings pay in her day, but I have encountered their descendants. They do not deserve to live. I have done my best to rid the world of them, but I am not your mother. I have some gifts and only ask humbly for help in destroying the rest of your enemies."

That eerie quiet descended again.

Could this child spirit know he lied?

She said, "I will grant you this aid one time if you do as you say."

Fair enough.

He could find some Viking descendants and kill them to make good on his offer. "Thank you. I require only a small plant."

More hissing. Another ghostly hand signal.

She said, "That is the same as taking a limb from one of us."

Was she really going to give him the plant? "I understand and will not let you down."

"The last person to steal a plant did so without giving an oath. We are stronger now and will not allow that again. You swear on the blood of our family to do as you say and also harm no female or child."

That was not a question, but a demand.

He hated to swear anything to a supernatural being, but what was the consequence of crossing this spirit? If he asked, she'd probably refuse to give him a plant. Besides, if her reach went beyond this cave, wouldn't she have gone after the last person to steal a plant?

She must have taken his silence as confusion. "Break your oath and you will join us for eternity."

Once he left this place, he'd never come back here. Just standing here had his skin crawling. His plan was simple and he answered to a powerful goddess. Once he succeeded at what he had in mind, though, he'd never need this kind of magic from anyone.

He'd be immortal.

Nodding, he said, "I swear on our family's blood to do as you request."

"Not a request. An order."

A sharp curse sat on the tip of his tongue for this mouthy brat, but he was too close to pulling this off. "My mistake. I swear on our family's blood to use the plant you gift me as you expect."

Floating back, she lifted a plant ten inches tall and carried it in her open palm. When she reached him, he took the offering.

As soon as he did, her tiny hand disappeared.

Damn, that was weird.

But he lived in the world of weird.

Ready to get out of there, he tried to push up to stand, but his legs wouldn't work. What the hell?

He asked, "Uh, will you allow me to use my majik to heal my legs?"

"No. Your legs carry your oath."

This might not turn out as he'd hoped after all.

"Close your eyes," she instructed in her monotone voice.

Should he do that?

Was she jerking his chain and intending to finish him off? What could she do once he closed his eyes? How was he going to reach the door between the museum area and outside? He'd placed a spell on the door to open when he was ready to exit, but he couldn't move his legs even to crawl.

"Do you wish to stay with us?" the child asked, sounding genuinely curious.

"No." He probably shouldn't have said that so loud. "I mean, no, please. I want to go, so that I may fulfill my duty."

When she said nothing else, he gave up and closed his eyes.

The red haze returned, but it was inside him.

He twisted and turned in a whirling ball of writhing energy that seemed to go on forever, then suddenly stopped. Dragging in deep breaths, he opened one eye to peek.

Nothing but darkness.

Had she fooled him after all and locked him in with the rest of them? His heart beat crazy and blood rushed through his ears.

Then he felt ... grass beneath the fingers on one hand.

Opening both eyes, he moved his hand again, happy to feel more natural terrain around him. He looked up to see a bare outline of clouds hiding the sliver of a moon.

"I'm outside," he whispered in a thankful voice. He tried moving his right leg. No pain. He breathed a sigh of relief.

Calling up his majik, he created a tiny glow to keep from drawing any attention until he figured out exactly where he sat.

A hint of moonlight slipped out to shimmer across the top of the hill overlooking the cave.

"I'll be damned." Had the little child spirit teleported his body out here?

That was some kind of power.

"Wait!" He looked around frantically, then saw the plant she'd gifted him.

The stem moved gently, waiting patiently as a puppy, with an open flower turned to stare at him.

"Hello, baby," he whispered and reached to stroke the petals.

The flower hissed.

He snatched his hand back and reminded the plant, "She promised you'd help me." Drooping over, the flower seemed to sigh.

That was more like it.

He hadn't gone through all that to get a pure Noirre plant for it to misbehave as soon as he touched it.

CHAPTER 2

EVALLE FELT EYES ON HER as she maneuvered her Suzuki GSX-R motorcycle slowly through a dark, wooded area off a paved road. Her crotch rocket hadn't been designed for off-road riding, but she'd taken it through worse places.

The last town she'd noted as she'd cruised southwest of Atlanta had been Whitesburg.

Dead-quiet streets. Not that surprising for a Saturday night before Memorial Day. Some schools were out for the summer and families had headed to the beach. Might be a bit chilly down on the Gulf Coast, though, with this late cool front rolling through the southeast.

She doubted anything preternatural was going on out here in the country and so far from Hotlanta, some days known as demon central. But she had no complaint about a relaxing bike ride down back roads with temps in the low fifties.

Dry skies would be nice. *Can't have everything.*

If a demon or some other predatory supernatural being really was out here harming innocents, she'd introduce it to her spelled blade. That would kick her holiday off.

Rain continued to drizzle, unable to make up its mind to get serious or quit falling.

She parked and fished a flat aluminum disc the size of her hand from her tank bag, then dismounted. The disc prevented her kickstand from sinking into the wet ground. Her black bike jacket kept her top half dry and her boots were waterproofed, but her jeans were soaked. She replaced her helmet with a black ball cap and pushed her soaked ponytail over her shoulder.

Hairs tingled on her neck again.

That feeling had stayed with her since leaving Atlanta a half hour ago.

Did she have her own private stalker?

Does he, she or it think I'm vulnerable right now?

That brought a smile to her lips.

Darkness encroached from every direction, but the moon kept slipping out from behind the scattered clouds to offer a dusting of light before hiding again.

She pulled off her special sunglasses, which protected her uber-sensitive eyes from bright lights. Her natural night vision was a benefit of being a half-breed Belador, better known among other preternaturals as an Alterant.

The low rumble of a high-performance engine approached.

Evalle stilled. If she turned, the headlights washing past her body now would blind her.

The engine silenced and the lights disappeared.

She spun around as the female driver stepped out and closed the door to her badass black car that looked capable of doing a million miles an hour.

Adrianna Lafontaine wore a denim jacket and black jeans like a runway statement. Her long blond hair had been pulled back into a single braid and covered with a black cap.

Closing the car door, she said, "I thought I was meeting Tristan. How'd you get stuck with this gig?"

Evalle grumbled, "He guilted me into it. Said his girlfriend was back in town and started pointing out that I get to see Storm every night, blah, blah, blah, whine, whine. I finally told him I'd take this VIPER assignment just to shut him up." Giving the hot car a second look, Evalle asked, "What are you driving?"

"McLaren 720 S." Stepping past the front of her car, Adrianna said, "I've been meaning to ask Daegan why we're supporting VIPER again after they turned their backs on the Beladors last month."

Evalle had wondered the same thing when Daegan announced that the Beladors would resume handling assignments from VIPER, a coalition of preternatural beings tasked with protecting humans from their kind. Those same humans were unaware they received this security, or that it was needed, since only a very small number of them knew Evalle and others like her existed.

Sitting back on the seat of her Gixxer, she explained, "Daegan thinks the bounty hunters VIPER hired to replace us when we pulled back to protect our people could end up being a threat to Beladors and our allies if we don't step back in to hold a position within the organization." That made sense and Evalle was glad for allies like Adrianna, a Sterling witch who wielded an ancient majik.

Evalle trusted Daegan the way she'd never trusted their last leader, a self-serving goddess.

As a two-thousand-year-old dragon shifter, Daegan had proven his ability to preside over and protect the Beladors.

"I can see his point," Adrianna said. "Okay, what are we looking for tonight? The voice mail I got only said to meet at this coordinate to investigate a disturbance reported by a troll."

"Right. That troll is a friend of Tristan's who stays out of preternatural politics, but evidently is well connected inside the Atlanta troll community and beyond. He didn't want to give the name of his informant, but said if we walk a hundred feet northwest of this location, the informant would find us."

"That sounds like a trap."

Evalle had echoed the same thought earlier. "I'd agree, but Tristan trusts his friend and vouched for this not being a setup."

The witch shrugged. "Fair enough. Tristan wouldn't make the assertion knowing he'd have to face Storm if anything happened to you."

Evalle chuckled. She could handle herself in battle and shifted into a ten-foot-tall gryphon, but she liked knowing her sexy Skinwalker mate had her back. He'd had her back ... and her front ... in the long shower they'd taken before she left.

Adrianna snapped her fingers. "Mind back on task. What kind of disturbance is it?"

Ready to get this done and go home, Evalle got serious. "Not sure, only that the informant said it sounds like something wild in the woods and believes it's unnatural because it doesn't sound like any animal he's ever heard. Being that the informant is very likely a troll as well, we have to accept that he should know."

"Lovely." Adrianna had been standing with her body loose, but she became very still and slowly gazed right then left. She whispered, "Do you sense anything?"

Nodding, Evalle kept her voice down. "I've felt eyes on me since I left the city. Somebody must feel the need to get their butt kicked tonight." She lifted her sunglasses and slipped them in place. "Ready?"

Adrianna opened her hand where a tiny ball of light spun above the palm. "Some of us need a little light."

"That's the smallest I've seen you contain your Witchlock power. Are you gaining better control?"

"I think so. I haven't had any way to test it recently."

"Let's hope you don't have to tonight."

"Agreed."

Leading the way, Evalle pushed past branches and weeds to find a narrow footpath beaten down.

That had to be encouraging, right?

She opened her empathic senses to search for anything beyond herself and Adrianna, which the witch would be doing, too. Her mate, Storm, was a powerful empath. He'd been training her to better utilize her gift.

After a moment, she picked up on a preternatural presence nearby. While also trying not to catch a tree root with her toe and fall on her face, she focused hard and pinpointed the presence as being off to her left and behind her.

Not exactly correct. It felt as if the presence was *above* her.

Was it in the trees?

She didn't hear branches rattling, but then she didn't hear any other sound besides her, Adrianna and the rain.

That was probably the informant, right?

When they reached approximately one hundred feet, Evalle stopped to search the area. Through the trees, she saw an opening and headed that way. When she stepped out of the thick tree cover, she stood in front of a pile of boulders fifteen feet high.

Nothing about that seemed natural since they weren't in the mountains and these were the only big rocks she'd seen since arriving.

It was as if some giant baby had been stacking them like alphabet blocks.

She crossed her arms and remained thirty feet back to allow herself a good view of the area, but kept sending an occasional glance at the pinnacle of the rock pile.

Adrianna stepped up next to her.

They made an odd-looking pair with Evalle so tall and Adrianna barely over five feet.

She didn't care what they looked like to anyone else. She and Adrianna had started off on the wrong foot when they first met, but this witch had fought beside her in many battles.

Adrianna whispered, "Think *that's* him?"

Evalle followed Adrianna's gaze to the top of the boulders, where a three-foot-tall figure now stood. If she had to guess, she'd say he was a cross between a garden gnome and a lizard troll because of his bushy beard, short tusks poking through that beard, pointy ears and gray-green skin on arms sticking out of overalls.

Rain seemed to avoid him.

She murmured, "Looks like a farmer gnome."

"Not gnome," he corrected in a rich baritone, which didn't fit the image.

Adrianna murmured, "Maybe a miniature troll?"

He snapped, "Not *troll!*" His gaze switched from Adrianna to Evalle. "Which one Tristan?"

Evalle started explaining, "He's not here, but I'm—"

The little guy's eyes got wide. He took a step back and pulled a tiny sword out of somewhere on that outfit and pointed it at her. "Is *trap!*"

That sword might be little, but Evalle knew better than to discount any weapon in the hands of a supernatural being.

Holding up her hands with palms out in a nonthreatening way, she said, "Not a trap. Please, wait. We're Tristan's friends. He couldn't come and asked us to help."

Adrianna hadn't moved a muscle and Evalle now realized the witch had doused the Witchlock power ball at some point. Good thing or the little guy would be freaking out over that, too.

He moved another tiny step back. Skittish, but at his size she might be just as wary.

What could she say to convince him not to run? "Otto will vouch for me." She had no idea if Tristan's troll friend would do such a thing, but bluffing was all she had.

The little guy kept a grim expression parked on his face and gave her a long look.

She was not the people person of the two and gave Adrianna a how-about-a-little-help glare.

Offering the irritating little guy one of her signature sexy smiles, Adrianna asked, "What's your name?"

"Why?"

Evalle almost laughed at the grumpy reply instead of the tongue-dropping male reaction the witch usually received.

Undaunted, Adrianna said, "I like to know who I work with on a job. My name is Adrianna and this is Evalle."

"Otto vouch you, too?"

Evalle held her breath, but Adrianna said, "Of course. Think about it? How would we have found you if Otto had not shared this location?"

The not-a-gnome scratched his gray beard. He made the sound of a quick inhale and stared at them as if he'd replied.

Was she supposed to infer his reply from any of that? Evalle asked, "What does that mean?"

He sighed and shook his head, muttering something, then said, "*Ja*. I said *ja*."

When had he spoken the word *ja*?

Adrianna offered, "His intake of breath is how they sometimes say yes. It's ingressive phonetic speech."

He nodded with another quick inhale.

Unbelievable. Evalle mentally cursed Tristan. Was she supposed to interpret miscellaneous sounds as words? Getting tired of staring up in this drizzle, she tried to be conversational in hopes of getting him to talk.

"I'll make a wild guess that you're from Sweden."

He nodded this time. Was he running out of air for his ingressive whatever?

Done with meet and greet, Evalle suggested, "Why don't you tell us what the problem is so we can take care of it and move on?"

"Much screaming. Three nights. Not natural."

"Where?"

Using his thumb, he pointed behind him, which could be on the other side of the rocks or ten miles in that direction.

"Have you gotten close enough to see anything that would help us determine what it is?"

"Why I do that?" He pointed at his chest. "Not VIPER agent. Not killer. Your job. I pass word to troll. He tell Otto. He tell your kind. Is enough."

"*Our* kind?" Evalle asked in disbelief. As if he was any more human than her? At least she *looked* human.

Irritated at being labeled unfairly, she straightened him out. "If you mean Beladors, we're not killers." Her mind was jumping around with frustration, which caused her to drag up a bad memory of trolls and Sweden. "We only kill to protect others, not like those cold-blooded assassin Svart Trolls who came to Atlanta from *your* country."

His face registered shock when she mentioned the Svart Trolls. Huh.

She asked, "Hey, is that Svart bunch friends of yours?" She seriously doubted it since he was adamant about not being a troll, but she wanted to push a button that might result in more than choppy and vague answers.

He lifted his little hands and grabbed his head as if this whole line of discussion was giving him a migraine. Growling as he answered, he said, "Not friends. I hide and travel here with them. Nothing more."

She hadn't seen that coming. "Let me get this straight. You're *not* a troll, but you traveled with that bunch of assassin trolls. Why would you associate with them?"

Frowning, Adrianna asked, "What does it matter?"

"Because he could be setting us up for some trap. Tristan trusts Otto and Otto must have trusted the troll this guy talked to, but that could mean Otto might not even know about this guy."

"You've got a point." Adrianna arched a no-longer-friendly look up the tower of rocks at the informant. "Enough of this dancing around. What's your name and why should we believe you?"

Crossing his little arms, he sent an equally stubborn look right back. "No name. I give message. Is enough."

"Fine." Evalle shrugged. "Good luck with whatever is terrorizing the woods here and finding anyone else to help you once we leave. The minute I get back, I'm informing my people there's a Svart Troll supporter in these woods."

"*No!*"

She gave it a moment then said, "Tell me why I shouldn't."

"I have family. Is why I need beast killed."

There were more not-gnomes?

Keeping her voice calm, but full of warning, Evalle said, "I have family, too. Svart Trolls tried to kill me and people important to me." Rain slid over the brim of her cap and down her face in a stream. She didn't want to leave a beast of some kind running loose in these woods, but neither would she let this little guy off the hook without finding out his tie to the Svart Trolls.

He muttered something, shaking his head and kicking at a tiny bit of gravel. Finally he said, "I am born to troll father and nisse mother."

"What's a nisse?" Adrianna questioned in a gentle voice while flashing a cut-him-some-slack glance at Evalle.

"Is small people in same homeland as Svart. Live in secret on farms." He raised his chin and pushed his chest out. "Help good humans many generations."

"Small people like you?"

Now he looked insulted by Adrianna's question. "Me big. Like father."

Evalle rolled her eyes. Men.

That explained the tusks and leathery skin of a troll, though. She said, "I'm still confused. You have troll blood, but you claim to not be friends with the Svart."

"No." His voice turned sad. "Trolls hate me. Father's family try to kill me many times. I find nisse wife and we leave."

Adrianna pointed out, "You still haven't given us your name."

He strutted back and forth, clearly deliberating then turned to them. "Only if swear to keep secret."

Evalle arched an eyebrow at him. "I am not swearing anything to a nisse-troll."

"Not *troll!* Must keep name secret."

"Fine, fine, fine," she snapped. "I give you my word that if you harm no humans and none of *our* kind who don't first threaten your life, that I won't share your name. That's it."

Adrianna gave the same agreement and added, "We keep secrets all the time. We have no reason to share yours unless you give us reason to do so. What's your name?"

He studied his hands, muttering again, then raised eyes ringed in misery. "Misstag."

"Huh?" Evalle looked at Adrianna who hadn't gotten it either.

"Is name," he whispered, sounding embarrassed. "Mean

mistake. I am mistake. Not nisse. Not troll."

Well, hell. Evalle had a soft place for outcasts, having been one since birth. She groaned out a sigh and glanced at Adrianna.

The witch cut her eyes at Evalle. "Sounds believable, but a good lie always does."

"No lie," he argued. "Why lie? You send more killers."

"We're not killers, dammit," Evalle snarled.

He did that whole raise his arms in exasperation thing and stomped around. This time he spoke more clearly in what Evalle guessed to be Swedish.

Probably cursing.

Evalle just had to be the nice person and take Tristan's place tonight. "Never mind, Misstag. Just please get to the point. Tell us everything you know, such as the exact location where you heard this screaming. Anything that would help us."

He scrunched up his wrinkled little face at her. "Is long walk that way." He pointed over his shoulder again. "Rip deer in pieces. Rip us or human next."

Showing more patience than Evalle felt, Adrianna pecked away at their informant. "What makes you sure it's not natural?"

"Smell scent. Not human. Not animal."

Evalle perked up at some decent intel. "Demon?"

"No. Smell odd."

And she was back to getting better answers out of a toadstool.

Misstag ordered, "Call Tristan. More men. Not good for you."

Evalle started to argue that only minutes ago he'd called her kind killers. She quipped in Adrianna's direction, "Listen to that. He's worried about us and thinks we should call in some great big men to back up us women. What do you think?"

Adrianna met Evalle's gaze for a brief moment before they started laughing.

The witch said, "Oh, yes. That'll be the day when you and I call in reinforcements to investigate something like this." Wiping her eyes, she told Misstag, "We've got this. Show us the way and you can go back to wherever you live."

He vanished without a word.

"Are you kidding me?" Evalle shouted.

Misstag stepped from behind the stack of boulders, but on the same level with them. He had his hands over his ears. "Too much mouth."

Adrianna found that hilarious.

Misstag took off, not allowing Evalle a chance to counter his insult. She caught him immediately, "Slow down so Adrianna can keep up."

That made him happy.

Whatever stroked his ego for the moment.

They trudged through trees, over a creek, up a hill, down a hill and back through more trees, then stopped at the edge of the tree line. A wide space of gently rolling ground spread beyond this point. With a little grooming, it would be a pasture.

Wasn't this area near the Chattahoochee Bend State Park?

"See?" Misstag said, stepping to the side then pointing at the ground.

Evalle told him, "No, I'm not Superman with x-ray vision. I can't see through dirt and rock."

She got a pint-sized glare for that. He pointed harder and ordered, "Look."

Giving in, Evalle and Adrianna moved closer to Misstag, who pulled out his sword and made a circular motion with it above the ground.

A circle of light an inch tall glowed around a two-foot diameter area.

Inside that, Evalle now saw a footprint she seriously doubted anything natural had made. Whatever it was had some wicked claws and ... crud. That looked suspiciously like her beast footprint before she evolved into a gryphon.

She suggested, "Misstag, can you track that—"

Her voice faded as she turned to find the spot where he'd been standing empty. "Misstag? Misstag?"

"He abandoned us," Adrianna groused.

"You hear that?" Evalle murmured.

"Hear what?" Adrianna asked. The witch opened her palm and Witchlock swirled, growing to the size of a grapefruit as the witch powered up the ball of majik.

"Silence?" Evalle replied. The trickle of concern climbing her neck was not due to Misstag having obviously left them on their own, but the sudden stillness of the woods.

Just as quickly, the dead quiet gave way to something large

crashing through the woods behind them ... and coming in their direction.

"Get ready," Evalle snapped, spinning around to face the threat.

"Can't get much more ready than this."

Evalle glanced at the glowing ball of Witchlock. "Why isn't it any bigger?"

Louder pounding approached.

Adrianna scowled. "I can manage this size. Things get hairy when it gets twice as big."

"We may need hairy if that thing coming this way is Misstag's monster. It sounds the size of an elephant."

"You can't handle an elephant?" Adrianna challenged, splitting her attention between the spinning ball of energy she held and the noise in the woods.

"Maybe not if the elephant is jacked up on demon power," Evalle shot back. She prepared for an attack and raised her hands to wield her kinetic ability.

A tree thicker than her body snapped and fell straight at them like it had a rocket booster.

CHAPTER 3

EVALLE SHOVED ADRIANNA TEN FEET away and fell backward to the ground with her hands up.

She flashed up a load of kinetic power seconds before that massive tree trunk crushed her. If not for keeping Adrianna safe, Evalle would have used her Belador speed to outrun the tree.

She hoped she hadn't broken any witch bones, but injured was always better than dead.

Struggling to keep the tree far enough above her that what was left of a jagged, broken branch didn't impale her, she strained even more when something caused the weight to bounce up and down.

Slapping branches, Adrianna complained, "Can you get this thing off us?"

"No, what about you?"

"I can do it, but with hitting something so close I might set the tree on fire. I'm pinned between two branches."

Gritting her teeth and grunting, Evalle pushed her way up to a sitting position. The minute she did, the creature made a hideous roaring noise and stomped on the tree trunk again.

Evalle's arms shook.

Misstag had been right.

That was no natural animal or she could have pushed it off by now.

She told Adrianna, "It's standing on the tree. I'm going to give it a good push, which is probably going to piss it off, so be ready to move if I can get you clear." Evalle pushed her power hard and shoved the invisible field up. Something crashed when she did that and the tree got lighter. "Can you get out now?"

For all her primping and put-together look, Adrianna was a solid combat partner. She twisted around and got on her knees then started pushing through the mass of branches surrounding them. Evalle was starting to get to her feet when the tree suddenly lifted up.

That would seem like a good thing, but she knew better.

"Look out, Adrianna, its ... " Evalle shoved her hands back up as the tree crashed back down with more force. She fell to her knees, bent backward and straining every muscle.

Adrianna said, "I'm out. Hang on and I'll ... umph."

Evalle fought for air. "Adrianna?"

What had it done to the witch?

"What are you doing?" an angry female voice yelled.

That was not Adrianna.

The creature roared and stomped on the tree again. Dammit.

Evalle had to do something, because if that was a human she'd heard, the woman would end up dead. Sucking in one last chest full of air, Evalle yelled at the stranger, "*Run! Get out of here!*"

"Is someone under that tree?" the voice demanded again, and this time Evalle thought she'd heard it before.

The creature grunted something.

Misstag failed to mentioned an insane human out here.

The female voice said, "Move it. Now!"

The tree lifted another time and Evalle held her arms up. She might not be able to survive being hit with that tree again.

Thankfully, the thick trunk and all the branches still on it continued to lift away, then dropped to the side where the tree got caught between two others that were still standing.

That blocked Evalle's view of the woman and the beast.

Since the creature had obeyed the woman, Evalle turned to check on Adrianna, who was out cold with blood seeping from her head.

"Adrianna?" Evalle scrambled over to her just as the witch opened her eyes. "Are you okay?"

"No. I got knocked over like a pin by a Fred Flintstone bowling ball."

Evalle helped her sit up.

"What are you two doing here?"

Evalle and Adrianna turned to see Kit Nyght climbing over debris to reach them. Behind her stood a ten-foot-tall monster with claws curled from four fat fingers on each hand. Shaggy, gray-black hair covered its body below a slick head with jaws wide enough to snap off a human head.

At one time, Evalle had shifted into something just as hideous, but her eyes glowed green, where this monster had human eyes as dark as two coal pits.

Kit stormed up to them, face covered in worry lines. "You're bleeding, Adrianna. Do you think you have a concussion?"

"If I do, I'll live."

Kit swung her harsh glare at Evalle. "What were you doing wandering around out here? He could have killed you."

Why do I feel like I'm in trouble? Evalle explained, "We got a call to check out an unnatural threat in this area, which clearly there is ... wait a minute. Is that ... Jasper, the Rías?"

"Yes. He would not have hurt you, but you probably scared him."

"We didn't scare him," Adrianna argued, then grimaced and held her head.

"You didn't mean to, but I told him not to let any nonhuman get a jump on him." Kit frowned. "Actually, it's my fault he hurt you. I'm sorry. Let's get you fixed up. He'll apologize as soon as he shifts back. I know he feels bad about hurting you." She offered Adrianna a hand, which she took.

Evalle leaned past Kit to look at Jasper-the-monster, who stood with his head hanging. She got to her feet. "You're lucky he didn't hurt you, Kit."

"Luck had nothing to do with it. I've been training him."

"Now I really have a headache," Adrianna muttered. "Have you forgotten how Isak freaked out when you and the twins were captured by those pseudo-Beladors?" Kit started to speak, but the normally reserved witch wouldn't allow Isak's mother to get a word in, and kept ranting. "Because I still remember Isak clearly saying he did not want his mother around any of our kind, as if we're all a bunch of killers threatening humans. How can he be such a hypocrite to let you come out here with something that shifts into a ten-foot-tall ... danger?"

Kit had given up trying to talk and stood there with her arms crossed. Since she was just as short as Adrianna, they were having a glaring contest at eye level.

"Are you done, Adrianna?" Isak's mom asked.

Evalle had never seen Adrianna lose her cool like that, but Isak had really hurt Adrianna when he'd said those words specifically to her. Until that moment when he warned all of them to stay away from his mother, Evalle had been pretty sure those two had been swapping spit, if not more.

Sounding chagrined, Adrianna held her head and said, "Sorry, Kit, but this blows my mind. I'm trying to figure out how he's going along with this."

"He's not."

Evalle and Adrianna gaped at her.

"Close your mouths." After that order, Kit explained, "My son would pop a vein if he knew I was out here with Jasper, which is why he doesn't."

"Really?" Evalle questioned. "Isak has the largest human intel network I've ever known about. He probably knows more than Santa Claus."

That pulled the start of a smile from Adrianna.

Kit's eyes lost their worried-mother look and twinkled. "He'd like to think he is all-knowing, but I've been around a lot longer than he has and I've owned this property since before he was born. He doesn't know about it." Kit turned to Jasper. "Your clothes are where I always leave them. Want to go shift and change?"

He nodded and made a soft grunting sound.

"Good boy," Kit praised.

When Jasper pounded away, Kit returned to their conversation. "We held Jasper in nice quarters after he shifted and attacked Evalle in the warehouse, but it's still a jail cell when you have no freedom."

"Jasper attacked you once before?" Adrianna said to Evalle. "When did that happen?"

"It was the first time I went to the Nyght headquarters. Jasper was working on a forklift and he had no idea he was a Rías until that moment. Remember when that funky energy cloud came over cities around the country and forced Alterants and Rías to shift, even if they'd never shifted before?"

"Oh, yeah, that's right."

"Jasper was just another unsuspecting soul during that time." Evalle said to Kit, "I still don't understand what you and Jasper are doing. How have you trained him not to attack?"

"I spent a lot of time talking to Jasper. He almost shifted once when he got upset talking about how he turns into a monster. That's when he told me I should go ahead and hit him with one of our demon blasters, because he didn't want to hurt anyone. I refused and he asked me to not come into his quarters again. He said the longer he stayed in there, the more upset he got and he might not be able to keep from attacking me the next time."

"He sounds like a good guy," Adrianna said.

"He is," Kit confirmed. "A wonderful man, but Isak couldn't get past the fear that Jasper would hurt me. I suggested asking Evalle about training him and that set my son off. So Jasper and I came up with a plan. The next time Isak was gone with his men, I helped Jasper escape and brought him here where he'd have plenty of room to move around when he shifted."

Evalle brought up, "We could have been hunters or hikers who ignored the restricted area signs."

"They would have been safe. Jasper won't touch a human, but he fears nonhumans after Evalle blasted him."

Kit did have a point. Evalle murmured, "Sorry."

"He knows you were only protecting everyone, but it got his attention. He kept obsessing about a nonhuman finding him and attacking because he can't communicate in that form. He didn't want to shift until I agreed to carry one of our Nyght weapons set on heavy shock. The first time he lost control, I hit him with a blast that knocked the starch out of his shorts."

"Poor guy," Adrianna sympathized.

Kit sighed. "Yes, because it took about eight times for him to begin gaining control."

"You used shock therapy and it worked?" Evalle couldn't believe it, but more than that she was thrilled to think there would be a plan if they found more Rías. Getting shocked hurt, but in her beast form she could have handled it.

Given a choice between that or being caged or killed, she would get trained with a blaster.

Kit sounded sad. "It did work, but it was killing me to zap him." She took a deep breath and let it out, sounding relieved to be at this point. "He hasn't lost control since the last time and that was ten days ago."

Scratching her head, which was covered in leaves and dirt,

Evalle said, "Okay, I think that's amazing, but why are you training him? You can't keep him at Nyght headquarters around Isak, can you?"

"I'll answer that," Jasper said, walking up to them in a gray T-shirt and jeans, just as wet as everyone else. He had a friendly voice. "Sorry about attacking you two. As for the training, Kit wants to hire me as her personal nonhuman bodyguard."

Kit grinned and gave Jasper a loving look that a mom would cast. That Kit took everyone under her wing, including the twin nineteen-year-old male witches living in Evalle and Storm's building, was a testament to the strong woman she was, who called her own shots.

Isak's mom was both a born nurturer and tough as nails.

Adrianna brushed dirt off her sodden clothes. "Why would you need a bodyguard when you're not allowed to be around nonhumans anymore?" That had come out sounding disappointed.

"To quote a favorite line of mine, 'Isak is not the boss of me'," Kit replied. "But I understand his fear of losing both parents to nonhumans. A demon killed his father years ago and an Alterant killed his best friend. When Isak saw me captured by that crazy bunch of bad Beladors, he snapped. He'll come to his senses, Adrianna."

Kit's comment about bad Beladors referenced the Laochra Fola, warriors that were part of the original force of Beladors created by a god called Belatucadros.

Evalle had picked up bits of Belador background from time to time after joining their warrior force as a teen, but she'd never been given the entire history. The goddess Macha, former ruler of the Beladors, had been tight-lipped about everything before Daegan showed up to boot her off of Treoir Island. She'd also been stingy when it came to giving aid when needed. Like when Kujoo warriors from thousands of years ago carried forward a grudge, traveling to Atlanta through a portal opened by a witch just to battle descendants of their Belador enemies. Macha and the Kujoo god Shiva had known each other. She could have helped when today's Beladors battled the Kujoo, but the goddess showed up only when she had no other choice.

Daegan knew things, though. Evalle made a mental note to ask him about the Belador past and how Macha and other deities played into all of it. That information would have come in handy recently when someone gathered a small army of Laochra Fola warriors and secretly brought them into Atlanta.

They'd captured Kit and the twins.

Something clicked for Evalle. She read between the lines of what Kit had just said. Isak's mother did not want Adrianna to give up on Isak.

Still probably too hurt to give an inch, Adrianna replied, "I seriously doubt Isak will back down from his stance against nonhumans, Kit, but for your sake I hope so."

"I'd like to think it would be nice for you, too."

Shaking her head, Adrianna said, "Whatever was going on between us in the past is over, and I've moved on."

Kit arched an eyebrow at the witch that said she didn't believe her.

Rain started coming down in earnest. Evalle made a decision. "I'm going to report that it was a demon and we disposed of him, but you've got a snitch out here."

"Who?" Kit looked around like a general hunting for a private to ream.

"He's a little guy who came over from Sweden with his family to hide from persecution. They evidently live somewhere on this property and he sent word through the trolls about a monster out here."

"I want to talk to him."

"Not sure that's possible. We had a hard time having a conversation with him. He's ornery as all get out, does not like to be called a troll and is unreasonable to deal with."

"Am not!"

Everyone turned to look up at a tree limb fifteen feet off the ground where Misstag sat with his arms crossed.

"Who are you?" Kit asked.

"No name."

Evalle groaned. "Can we not go through this again? This is Kit and Jasper."

"Monster."

Jasper said, "Troll."

"Not troll."

Jasper pointed at himself. "Not monster. I have not hurt you, and if you act right, I'll keep your family safe."

That shocked Misstag. "You protect us?"

"Depends on if you're going to be nice to Kit or not. I'm her bodyguard and she owns the land you're homesteading on."

Misstag leaped to the ground, landing lightly on his feet. He walked over to Jasper and lifted his hand. "Friends."

Jasper smiled and using three fingers, shook hands with the not-troll.

Then Misstag extended his hand to Kit. "Friends."

Kit didn't accept his offer right away. "I'm your landlord."

Misstag lowered his hand. "No money to pay."

"I don't want money. I want you to keep an eye out for anyone trespassing and alert Jasper when he's here. When he's not, I'll set up a communication where you can reach me. Agreed?"

"Yes. Yes, I can do," Misstag said, looking as relieved as he sounded.

Smiling now, Kit extended her hand. "Friends."

The little guy wrapped his fingers around three of Kit's to shake.

Evalle asked Adrianna, "You ready to get some ice on that?"

"Absolutely. Let's go."

"Wait," Kit said. When Evalle turned back, Kit swallowed and asked, "Are the twins okay?"

Offering an understanding smile, Evalle told her, "They're doing just fine, but they do miss you."

"Tell them I'll see them soon. They can take that to the bank."

"I will." Evalle had seen Kit in action and not even Isak could stop her when she had her mind made up. The woman had taken it upon herself to train a Rías. Evalle wanted to be her when she grew up.

A great idea hit Evalle. She would check with Daegan about Jasper visiting Treoir to train with the other two Rías.

Once Evalle and Adrianna left, they found a gas station where Adrianna fashioned an ice pack from a scarf. The witch would heal quickly just from possessing the Witchlock power, and she could probably do it in seconds if she didn't have reservations about experimenting with the power so close to humans.

Evalle got a text from Storm that he'd tried calling and was worried about her.

Adrianna spouted off. "You've got that stupid-in-love look on your face."

"You're just jealous," Evalle quipped, and regretted the joke when Adrianna said nothing. Seeing Kit had obviously brought up all those hurt feelings about Isak again.

"Anything important?" Adrianna asked, clearly shifting the topic as she leaned against the front fender of her car.

Evalle perched on her motorcycle seat. "Got the text ten minutes ago. He was worried because he couldn't reach me by phone. Wanted me to know he was heading out to track a suspicious being that was last seen around Woodruff Park. Quinn asked him to look into it. That's like five minutes from our place if you walk slowly. Said he should be home when I get there. I sent him a text ... "

Pausing to check her phone, Evalle said, "Huh. The text hasn't sent yet. Stupid cell service." She looked at her calls and muttered, "No missed call. I must have been in an internet black hole."

"It's nice he lets you know. I'm glad you two worked out," Adrianna said with sincerity.

"Thanks."

"You still got the tracking stone on your chest?"

Evalle laughed, touching her shirt where the smooth stone rested beneath it. "The emerald chakra stone? Yes, but not for much longer."

"Are you saying Mr. Overprotective is giving up that connection to you?"

"Yep. He explained that although we're mated, we've never gone through the bonding ceremony of his father's people. I'm okay either way, but he's determined to do the ceremony. He said he should have handled the mating better."

"Like telling you he'd taken you as a mate," Adrianna said with a teasing smile then frowned when water from the melting ice leaked down her face. She swiped it off and adjusted her makeshift ice pack.

Evalle agreed, "I think it still bothers him that he didn't ask me before he claimed me, but let's just say he was ... *distracted* at the moment it happened." Her face heated at the memory of their first time making love.

"I get the picture," Adrianna muttered, trying to sound annoyed, but failing miserably when she sighed and chuckled. "How much more can you two be bonded than you are now?"

"Storm said it would make more sense when he could show me how this works, but he told me a little for now. He said he doesn't want me obsessing about it, which we both know I will." She laughed. "What we have now is sort of like level-one mating. Once we do some ceremony, we'll have a much deeper connection where we can actually find each other. I'm not sure how that works or if I will be able to find him the way he's always been able to find me, but once we bond I won't need the emerald to give him a sense of comfort."

Adrianna shifted the ice pack. "When are you planning to do all this?"

"As soon as Brina and Tzader have their wedding at the end of this week."

Adrianna moved the pack from her head to reveal a nasty gash that was swelling. "They're finally going to get married before she pops out a baby Treoir heir?"

"Yep. Tzader is trying to be cool, but he stays in our world as little time as possible, then gets teleported back to Treoir Island. He's always there if Daegan is gone." Evalle snapped her fingers. "That reminds me. Brina wants me to ask you to attend the wedding. It'll be at Treoir Castle. She said she won't be able to send out actual invitations since no one except the inner circle knows what's going on as a precaution against attack."

Adrianna looked a little pleasantly surprised to be invited. "Please tell her I said yes and thank you for inviting me. I'm flattered to be included."

"Seriously, Adrianna? Brina and Tzader both appreciate your friendship with me, Storm, the Beladors and Daegan. You're either family with them or not." Evalle added, "Daegan would be disappointed, too, if you weren't there."

She arched an eyebrow at that. "That dragon? We tolerate each other. Nothing more."

"Yeah, yeah, yeah." Evalle rolled her eyes and laughed. "Okay, back to what I was saying about my plans with Storm. Once those two get married, I'm asking for a week off so we can go to the Navajo home of Storm's father."

"Why does it have to be there? I didn't think he had anything to do with his father's people."

Evalle shoved her phone into her back pocket. Probably not a good idea since her jeans were soaked, but it would be a good test of its durability around her. "Storm told me he's been in touch with his uncle. His father didn't hate his brother or anything like that, he was just disappointed when Storm's uncle built a casino and had bigger plans. As to the reason we're going there, Storm said the power he inherited from his father would be strongest on his people's land, which would allow him to form a bond that will last through eternity."

"Wow. That's ... " Adrianna murmured, then looked off into the distance. "That's amazing. You're very lucky."

"I am. I don't know how I got this lucky, but he is all I could ever want. I want this bond." To ease the sad look on Adrianna's face, Evalle quipped, "Besides, I'm so over having a rock majik-glued to my chest."

Adrianna grinned at that even though they both knew Evalle would happily wear that emerald for the rest of her life and beyond.

Adrianna's phone dinged at the same time as Evalle's, which meant an all-agent alert. Evalle waited for the witch to read her message. No point in pulling out her phone when they were both getting the same message.

The witch put her icepack down and said, "Something is going down at Five Points."

Alarmed, Evalle said, "That's where Storm was headed. Who sent the message? What'd they say?"

She shouldn't worry, since Storm shifted into a massive black jaguar and had majik to boot, but this sounded like more than checking out a suspicious character.

"It's an all-agent blast from VIPER headquarters." Adrianna scrolled as she shared the information. "All they know is two nonhumans are dead, five more seriously injured and they're battling to keep it shielded from the humans." Standing away from the car, Adrianna grabbed the icepack. "Sounds like chaos. I'll try to reach someone on the way and get more information."

Evalle's heart clenched.

Which nonhumans were dead?

Something odd hit Evalle. "Why hasn't Trey contacted me by telepathy?" As a Belador telepathic powerhouse, Trey could probably contact her in outer space.

"They said no telepathy. They think that's how someone in the preternatural world set up those early responders and were able to kill the nonhumans." Adrianna paused. "Evalle, Storm is fine. You know he's powerful and smart. He isn't going to fall into anyone's trap."

"I know." The problem was her heart wouldn't buy what her head was trying to sell. She started to call Storm, then realized he was very likely either in animal form or fighting. She would not distract him. She sent a quick text she knew wouldn't interfere, then put her phone away.

Opening the door to her car, Adrianna tossed in the icepack. "They're looking for anyone and everyone. I'll put my text on speaker in case I get another update."

"Good. I'll follow you then," Evalle called over her shoulder, already mounting her bike. She had no way to access her texts or phone calls while on the motorcycle. That had never been an issue, but after this she might consider outfitting her bike helmet with the voice-operated technology.

Storm would be fine.

She kept telling herself that, but the words wouldn't slow the panicked beating of her heart.

CHAPTER 4

E VALLE HUNG CLOSE TO THE black McLaren driven by a witch who could hold her own against professionals on a Grand Prix track. Chilly wind that had buffeted her hard on the ride back into Atlanta backed off as she leaned into the curve to exit the eastbound interstate. That dropped them into the south side of downtown.

She had to admit her legs were feeling warmer now that the wind had dried her jeans.

No matter how many distractions riding provided, she couldn't stop thinking about Storm.

He had to be safe.

She wanted that full bonding more than ever now.

He had the emerald on her chest to keep him assured that she was safe, but she had nothing to reassure her. Although she knew in her heart that she'd feel it if he ... died, she'd feel better with more information.

Plus, his spirit guide, who had helped Evalle locate Storm once in the past when he'd been trapped in a demonic realm, would know if anything happened to him.

She'd definitely let Evalle know.

Nodding to herself as she followed Adrianna, Evalle murmured, "See? No reason for this gut-wrenching worry."

Adrianna drove efficiently, slowing for traffic lights and speeding ahead as soon as they changed to green.

The usual late-night human activity moved in pairs and singles along the streets, but not so many groups. She caught the occasional flicker of nonhuman energy in dark spots.

That would be the harmless Nightstalkers, the ghoul informants of the preternatural underworld.

The closer she and Adrianna got to their final destination, the fewer people she passed. It might be a holiday weekend, but this city should be busier during prime rowdy hours before midnight.

She lifted her gaze to the tops of buildings, looking for any sign of smoke. The throaty sound of her Gixxer's muffler drowned out many human noises, but she should be able to hear sirens.

Had the problem been contained?

It figured that she'd worried for nothing.

Maybe Sen had shown up to lend a hand.

Heh. Maybe the VIPER liaison would apologize for being an asswipe the entire time she'd known him.

Neither one of those was happening.

If Sen happened to be on site, things had gone really bad and he would be his usual roaring-pain-in-the-ass self over having to clean up someone else's mess.

At the next corner, Adrianna took a right onto Peachtree Street—the famous road running through the middle of downtown, not one of the many other thoroughfares with a similar name.

Evalle leaned to take the turn smoothly, staying a half block behind Adrianna when she wanted to race around and get to the scene faster. But the witch had her phone on speaker and might be getting updates.

At one time, Evalle wouldn't be as willing to wait, but they'd come a long way and she now trusted the Sterling witch with her life.

Approaching an intersection near Kenny's Alley, the traffic light flipped from red to green.

She never caught this light green.

When riding a motorcycle, never complain about a green light.

Up ahead, Adrianna put her foot on the accelerator and zoomed forward.

Ready to get to Storm, Evalle caught a lower gear and rolled on as Adrianna's car reached the intersection.

Blocked from view by a building on the left, a car shot out from that side as if it was being chased, and plowed into the rear of Adrianna's car.

Stunned, Evalle watched for two seconds as Adrianna's car spun wildly and crashed into a building headfirst.

That bastard!

Evalle rolled hard on the accelerator. The front of her bike lifted up for twenty feet, then dropped down as Evalle rode beneath the still-green stoplight to reach Adrianna.

A white blur on her right snatched her attention in time to see a huge white van speeding forward.

The van hit her broadside.

Instead of skidding across the pavement, she and her bike went airborne.

The handlebars slipped out of her grasp. She had the thought to tuck her body to roll upon landing ...

One arm wouldn't work.

Her body slammed into the side of a brick building. The sound of metal bouncing over the pavement, then crashing into the building followed. She heard bones pop and break. Pain slammed her. The helmet saved her skull, but her head spun with vicious vertigo. Her eyes rolled up in her head.

Blurred sounds reached her.

She tried to grab her head to slow the spinning, but couldn't pull that off. Where were her fingers? She couldn't feel them.

Her body had gone from pain to numb. Shouldn't it hurt? She fought to keep from blacking out.

Someone unsnapped her helmet and yanked it off. Her head hit the hard ground.

Ow, dammit.

He shouted, "Hurry up... seconds ... get the damn thing."

What did they want?

Maybe he was shouting for an ambulance.

Her thoughts came and went.

Hands grabbed under her arms from the back and lifted her halfway up. Pain showed up now in a brutal wave.

She hurt everywhere and moaned, "No, don't ... "

Her shirt ripped open.

What the ...

Evalle tried to open her eyes. Warm liquid pooled in them. Blood? Maybe the helmet hadn't survived the crash.

A deep voice snarled, "What the fuck?"

"*Get. It. Off. Now!* We're out of time."

Claws dug into her chest around the emerald stone and ripped it free.

She screamed, out of her mind with pain like nothing she'd ever suffered. Someone shoved a rag in her mouth, cutting off her scream, but the howling went on in her head. She reached for her chest with the only arm that worked and it got yanked back.

Next, a sack was jerked over her head.

Agony tore through her, forcing all thought from her mind except making it stop.

An invisible force levitated her body into an upright position until she stood on her feet. She made a muffled cry of pain. Both legs had to be broken. Her body was raised a tiny bit more so that her feet didn't touch the ground, but her arms were locked against her sides by the same invisible force.

Tears ran down her face every time she took a breath. Her chest had been ripped apart and she could feel blood soaking whatever was left of her shirt.

Anger boiled with her misery. Her mind fought to clear. She was a powerful Alterant. She tried to call up her beast to heal her.

Nothing. No sign of her power.

She reached out telepathically to Trey. *It's Evalle. I'm being captured. I'm ...*

The words blasted back inside her head.

Who was doing this? What did they want?

Were they kidnapping Adrianna, too?

Not that she wanted her friend captured, but the possibility gave Evalle hope. Once she healed, she and Adrianna would put the mother of all smackdowns on this bunch.

Her mind wanted to black out, anything to get away from this raging pain. She had to stay awake even if she couldn't see.

Then she inhaled the stinking scent of limes. The worst smell of Noirre majik smoked around her, as a slimy, crawling feeling slid over her entire body. She struggled, trying to push out kinetics wildly from her fingers.

"Make her stop that," someone ordered.

A fist hit her in the wound in her chest.

She stopped breathing.

CHAPTER 5

A DRIANNA CAME ALERT, JERKING UPRIGHT in the driver's seat of her sports car. No longer a high performance car, though, with the front end, rear and both sides demolished.

Water drizzled in where the windshield should be.

Stars flickered in her gaze. Blood ran down through one eye. Her head felt like a pile driver hammered into it from every direction. Her chest hurt and face was bruised from when the airbag deployed upon impact with ... a building.

The air smelled of chemicals and dust floated around her face in a swirl. No, maybe all of her surroundings swirling was due to having her brain jarred.

Energy zapped around the inside of the car.

She opened her hand, calling up Witchlock as she did. Luckily for the city of Atlanta, she and Witchlock had not exploded.

The ball of energy shimmered to life, spinning in place.

Speaking carefully so she didn't destroy anything, she called upon the ancient power to energize her healing. Slowly, her head eased to a dull headache and her vision cleared.

Anything else could wait until she went to a place where she could push the limits of her ability with Witchlock.

Why hadn't Evalle come to check on her yet?

Looking around, Adrianna saw very little from her scrunched up position. She sent power to the fingertips of her free hand and shoved against the crumpled dashboard.

Metal screeched as the car stretched away from the building.

Once she could force her door open, she shoved it away and eased her boot to the sidewalk.

"Ouch, ouch, ouch." She was a forgiving person when it came to an accident, but she'd seen that maniac purposely accelerate around the corner.

This was no accident.

Forgiveness was not on the agenda.

Once she had her balance under control, she reached in to lift her phone off the floorboard. Everything she and Evalle had done prior to the wreck was coming back to her. She'd been in the lead so she could get updates on the chaos at the Five Points intersection next to Woodruff Park.

The stupid phone had not worked correctly the entire drive from the woods where they'd left Kit. She hadn't been able to reach anyone to get an update.

Looking around, she stared at the intersection she'd cleared right before getting hit.

Where was the crazy driver and his car?

And where in the devil was Evalle?

Adrianna's pulse jacked up.

Her friend would not have left her voluntarily.

She closed her hand, putting Witchlock away for the moment so no human would see it. None were around at the moment, which was odd. Walking back toward the intersection, she noticed the streetlights were now dark.

It wasn't until she reached the intersection that she saw a white van seventy-five yards away on her right. Heading that way, she passed debris from a vehicle.

She froze. Not a vehicle.

Evalle's motorcycle was lying between the white van and a building.

Adrianna ignored her hurting body and ran forward. She caught the scent of fresh blood first. "*Evalle!*"

What had happened?

Out of the quiet night, Adrianna sensed a powerful being approaching fast. She spun around and opened her hand.

Witchlock bloomed bright on her palm.

Terrifying snarling and glowing yellow eyes burst out of a dark shadow, racing forward at inhuman speed.

Adrianna quieted her majik, leaving it just bright enough to light the area. This was no threat to her.

A massive black jaguar slid to a stop and stood eye level to her. He inhaled deeply and roared a vicious sound.

There was no way to make this better for him. Adrianna said, "I don't know what happened, Storm. Someone wrecked me. I just got here myself."

In a blur of black fur and claws, Storm changed back to his naked human body and stood from a crouched position. The look on his face was too brutal to describe.

"Where is she?" he demanded in a hoarse voice.

"I don't know," Adrianna admitted. "Evalle was following me. Someone intentionally crashed my car into a building so I didn't see what happened after that. As soon as I came to, I climbed out and found this. You were maybe ten seconds after me."

As the best tracker the VIPER coalition of preternaturals had in the southeast, Storm's gaze darted everywhere, taking in every inch in seconds.

He looked through a window on the van then gave the bike and the wall a second look.

Adrianna waited silently for him to find out what he could, but they both knew Evalle had not left here of her own free will.

He jumped over the wrecked bike and grabbed up Evalle's helmet and stared. Then he turned his head up and released a gut-wrenching wail of hurt and fury.

Someone was going to die a painful death.

She hurried over to see what he'd found. "What is it?"

Reaching into the helmet, he withdrew the emerald chakra stone in a trembling hand. His fingers closed around it in a fierce, shaking grip. Tears poured from his eyes.

Adrianna wanted to throw up. Blood ran from the skin still attached to the emerald. Someone had ripped that stone from Evalle's chest.

Headlights glowed on the other side of the van from an approaching car.

Flicking her hand in Storm's direction, she cloaked him before the car came into view and snapped her glowing hand shut.

The driver called out, "Hey, what's going on, mama?"

Before Adrianna could answer, Storm growled in warning. His eyes hadn't lost the yellow glow.

"What the hell?" the young guy said, looking around. "You got some animal over there?"

Storm had demon blood. He might lose control, break out of the cloaking and rip everyone who came near this place to pieces.

Adrianna couldn't let that happen.

Evalle and Storm were close friends. With Evalle gone, Adrianna would watch both of their backs.

Smiling took a monumental effort when she wasn't far from lashing out herself. Adrianna told the couple, "Got a team working on special effects for a movie."

"Oh, really? What movie?"

"It's a secret right now. Come back tomorrow and you'll see the whole cast. We're just doing tech work and I have to ask you to move on or we'll get off schedule."

Thankfully, Storm's face was no longer visible to anyone but her right now. There was little humanity left there.

"Okay, thanks." The car drove off.

Adrianna dug into her jacket pocket and tried her phone. It actually worked this time. She called Trey and started talking as soon as he answered, explaining the situation and that she needed Daegan.

When she finished the call, Storm was staring at the emerald he held, but instead of bright yellow his eyes now glowed red.

Bad, bad, bad sign. Adrianna removed his cloaking and asked softly, "Storm, are you with me?"

He growled in answer and stalked away, sniffing at everything around the white van.

Streetlights started coming back on.

She heard a truck driving past the crash intersection. Two men walked along the street, pausing to look at her car up against the building. They moved closer, no doubt looking for a hurt driver.

One of the men inspecting her car had his phone out. He would be calling emergency services.

This was going to get out of hand quickly.

Power boiled next to her, close enough to send her hair flying around her face.

Daegan, the dragon king who ruled the Beladors, materialized inches from her.

She was short on patience and snapped, "Did you have to teleport in right on top of me?"

"Yes. Trey told me to locate you to find this place. What's going on?" Then his gaze dropped to take in her face. "What happened to you?"

"I'll live, but ... " She looked at Evalle's bike.

That's when Daegan noticed the busted motorcycle. "Is Evalle hurt?"

Storm came around the front of the van at that moment. Red eyes glowing, face contorted with pain and rage, he looked like some monster from a horror show.

When he spoke his words pushed out past fangs. "Someone took her."

Daegan was as old as Witchlock and could shift into a mighty dragon. He could have used his power to contain Storm, but he treated the Skinwalker as the trauma case Storm was at the moment.

"Storm, we will find her, but not if you lose control. Can you track her?"

"I could have, but they ripped this out of her chest." He opened his hand that held the bloody emerald.

Adrianna explained, "Storm had placed that chakra stone on Evalle with majik, which allowed him to find her anywhere."

Storm's chest vibrated with a deep rumbling sound that belonged in a nightmare. So did his demonic voice. "I will destroy everything in my path until I find her."

Frowning, Daegan said, "That is your right, but if you start killing without cause you force me to stop you."

Growling got louder.

Daegan kept talking in that calm tone. "I promise you when we find her, the right to punish her kidnapper will be yours."

Adrianna kept an eye on people entering the general area. Soon, more humans would show up.

A siren sounded, but was a couple of streets over and not coming this way. Maybe the men looking at her car had not called in the wreck. If they were looking to scavenge parts, they could have it.

She had bigger things to worry about.

She told Storm, "I want my pound of flesh, too, but we both want Evalle back first. I will be with you, watching your back while we hunt the bastards who did this. You're our best tracker. Please, for Evalle's sake, lock down your control."

Storm's entire body shook as he drew heavy breaths, but his eyes finally lost their glow. The black pits staring back didn't look any more welcoming, but he had returned to them.

Daegan turned, taking in the surroundings, then asked, "Would you like clothing, Storm?"

"Yes."

In the next blink of an eye, Storm wore jeans, a black T-shirt and boots. He wiped his mouth with his hand and kept dragging in deep breaths. "I smell human and no scent trail leaving the scene."

Daegan jerked back around. "Human?"

Nodding, Storm said, "But a human couldn't do this alone."

"You're right," Adrianna agreed. "Someone cloaked their scent then teleported Evalle and the humans away. Sounds pretty powerful."

"That may help us narrow our list of kidnappers."

"Maybe," Storm allowed. "But what powerful being would need the help of humans?"

"That is strange," Daegan admitted.

Sirens blared as an ambulance finally drove up to Adrianna's car. A police cruiser approached from the opposite direction.

She told the men, "We're going to be discovered any moment now."

Daegan walked halfway to her car, paused and lifted his hands above his head, then whipped them down in wide arcs. When he stepped around to return, Adrianna could see the fine film protecting them from the humans.

Impressive cloaking.

"That will give us time to search this area," Daegan said, walking back to them. "We need intel. I'm thinking the Nightstalkers in this area could be of help."

Storm swallowed and found his voice again. "Evalle has a favorite one that treats her like his grandkid. Once he learns this has happened, he'll shake down all the other ghoul informants until he gets anything that can be had."

"Evalle, where are you? Evalle?" the muffled voice of an old man called out.

"Who the devil is that?" Daegan asked.

Adrianna supplied, "Speaking of Evalle's favorite Nightstalker, from what she told me, that could be Grady."

"It is," Storm confirmed. "I've met him when Evalle and I tracked together."

Within seconds, the old guy wavered in and out of view. Grady's weathered face wrinkled with sadness and worry above the gray beard, which stood in sharp contrast to coffee-colored skin. A flannel shirt and baggy pants he'd worn the day he died hung on his skinny frame.

"Can you let Grady in here?" Storm asked Daegan.

"Sure." Daegan lifted a hand and curled his fingers closed as if calling the ghoul in.

Grady's image sharpened, though still wavering in and out of solid form. He demanded, "Where's Evalle? Who hit her bike? Where is she? Ghouls all talkin' 'bout a crazy Alterant biker gettin' wrecked down here. I knew it had to be my baby girl."

Adrianna didn't think anyone could sound more destroyed by what had happened to Evalle than Storm, but Grady came in a close second. Walking over to the Nightstalker, she spoke gently. "I'm Adrianna, a friend of Evalle's."

Grady said, "You the one stomped that evil witch Veronika."

"That's right." She caught him up on what had happened and said, "Someone intentionally wrecked Evalle, then snatched her. It appears the kidnapper teleported away with Evalle and the humans. We need any help you can give us."

Grady's face went from upset to angry when he swung to face Daegan. "You that dragon king?"

"I am."

The old Nightstalker addressed Daegan as if the dragon king were his subordinate. "I will find out who drove that van and what preternatural was here, but you got more power than me. You better handle it. No Nightstalker gets a handshake until I'm done with them. Understood?"

He was talking about how a Nightstalker traded preternatural intel with a powerful being in exchange for a brief handshake. That moment of power surge allowed the ghoul to take corporeal form for ten minutes.

Showing no sign of insult, Daegan agreed. "I can speak for the Beladors who will receive that order shortly. I'll go to VIPER next and warn them to not interfere."

"You do that," Grady said. Then his gaze moved to Storm. "She said you majik-glued a rock to her so you could find her."

Lips clamped tight, Storm nodded.

"But you ain't runnin' outta here like you can track her." His old voice turned pitiful. "It ain't workin'?"

Storm opened his hand to reveal the bloody chakra stone. "It would if she still wore this. Based on the jagged edges, someone clawed it out of her chest."

"Oh, mercy." Grady sounded like he was going to cry when he looked at the stone. "My poor baby girl is hurtin'." Looking back at Storm, he said, "I know they got to be smarter than to be anywhere close to here. I want to make 'em pay, but you have to be the one. When you find who did this, you send 'em to hell in pieces and bring her home to us."

Clearing his throat, Storm said, "Bet on it."

"I gotta git out of here and start findin' out who knows what," Grady announced.

Daegan said, "Thank you for your help. Go to your left. I've opened a spot in the shield."

Grady floated past the white van then slowly faded from view.

Storm's gaze moved past Adrianna, focusing on something and turning even more dangerous. "*He* better get the hell out of here or he's the first one I'm taking out of my way."

Adrianna twisted around to see who or what Storm referenced.

Three Hummers had spilled into the intersection.

Isak Nyght and his black ops team had arrived.

Turning back, she said, "I'll deal with him. I think we all need to vacate this spot right away."

Daegan asked Storm, "Can we move the van and Evalle's bike to your place where we can go over everything more thoroughly?"

"Good idea. Send it all to our garage. Teleport me first, then I can open the ward for all of this and you as well."

Daegan silently took in the entire scene and said, "I have it all in mind. What about you, Adrianna?"

"Go and I'll catch up to you once I deal with Isak."

Storm came over to her. "Sorry I lost my shit."

"Understandable. But we're going to do this and I'll be there with you every step."

"Thank you."

Storm told Daegan, "I'm ready." With a last glance at Adrianna, he said, "Call when you're ready and I'll pick you up or Daegan will teleport you."

"Sounds good."

Storm gave Daegan a thumbs-up.

Adrianna started walking toward her car where Isak was stomping around it. What had him upset?

With his intel, he had to know it was hers.

She was nonhuman, which meant he shouldn't be concerned, right? Yes, her inner bitch was having a Roast Isak party, but he should be glad it wasn't her outer bitch, who could actually set that party into motion. She'd been a fool to open her heart to him. A fool to trust that he would stand by his words when he'd said her being nonhuman didn't matter.

Those words had been uttered when they were physically entwined, after all, and she should've known better. Human or not, men were all alike when the little head started talking.

When she reached the outer limit of Daegan's protective shield, power rushed around behind her, then everything outside the shield came into clear view.

One of Isak's men spoke to him.

Isak whipped around and headed for her like a bull charging a red flag.

She reminded herself about maintaining control.

But if he pushed her right now, Kit would not have to worry about Isak discovering his mother was training a preternatural being. He'd be too busy trying to figure out how to find his way home from the other side of the world.

CHAPTER 6

THIS WAS WORSE THAN ANYTHING she'd ever suffered. Evalle moaned and curled into herself, holding her hands against her chest. Blood oozed through her fingers. She'd lost track of time and shivered against the cold. Probably her body fighting through shock.

Where had her clothes gone? Why was she being kept in this dark pit? Every time she opened her eyes, she saw a black wall of nothing.

She drifted in and out of consciousness, longing to stay unconscious and avoid the agony racking her body.

But she was awake again.

Her body tried once more to heal. She'd feel a trickling of power, but never managed to truly repair the damage, leaving her in this constant half-alive state.

What little energy she could drag up from her beast tried to heal the worst damage first, which would be the hole gouged out of her chest. Even now, the ravaged skin was a raw wound that throbbed viciously with every labored breath. Her right leg had partially healed, but it was not straight.

She was ready to let life slide from her fingers. Death had to be better than this.

You will not die! yelled in her head.

And now she had the mysterious voice in her head again. It had been absent since she'd finally found some happiness these recent months.

You know who I am, Evalle.

An idea had niggled at her, but she'd never had reason to believe it. Was this really her mother?

Yes. Who else would watch over you?

Evalle's throat hurt from screaming. She swallowed and croaked out a whisper. "I do want to die."

No you don't. You have too much to live for.

Was she really going to have this conversation with the woman who had died birthing her? Evalle murmured, "Is being dead so bad? You had to suffer delivering me, and then you died."

I would suffer it again and more just to have had one minute to hold you. Death is not peaceful for those of us who can't pass on. You would not be happy watching Storm grieve for you.

Tears spilled from Evalle's eyes. Where was Storm? He had never failed her, but Storm couldn't track teleporting and she was sure that's what happened when her body lifted in the air at the wreck site. "I want to go back, but I don't think I'll live long enough for him to find me," Evalle admitted.

You have to fight death with every breath.

Evalle drifted into a fitful darkness.

Wake up, Evalle!

"Leave me alone." When no sound came into her head, Evalle mumbled, "Why are you here now? I thought you were gone."

I tried to let go of your world once I believed you would be safe and loved with Storm, but then I heard you screaming. I felt your pain. I will not leave you.

A thought struck Evalle. "Do you have any power?"

No. I'm sorry. I was only a human in life. I had no powers to bring with me.

Defeated, Evalle grumbled, "You can't help me."

I intend to try.

"Do you know who took me?"

Only that he is not human.

That didn't narrow down the possibilities much, but her mother was nothing more than a spirit who could speak in Evalle's mind. The woman was not to blame for what she couldn't know.

Her mother said, *It takes a lot of effort to reach you. I can't stay much longer, but I'll be back. Promise me you won't give up.*

Her mother was actually leaving? Well, that sucked.

Evalle, please promise me.

Whispering in a dry voice, she murmured, "I'm in no place to make deals with anyone."

It's not for me. Her mother's voice drifted off, but Evalle heard her last words. *Storm is hunting you.*

Evalle blinked, trying to see, but she stared into a void.

Storm. She loved that man with all her being. He loved her just as much, if not more considering the battle he'd waged to tear down her defenses and plant himself in the middle of her world. She would fight a million battles to keep him.

What about now? Her conscience picked up the torch after her mother withdrew. Storm would be disappointed if Evalle gave up.

She'd expected him to fight with all he had when he was captured in a demonic underworld.

Shouldn't she do the same for him?

But how long could she hold on? She was lightheaded from loss of blood and not healing.

Warm liquid continued to ooze around the hand she had clamped over her chest wound.

How much blood had she lost? And why couldn't she heal? She could barely feel her beast. The hole in her chest might take all decisions away from her.

Who had done this?

For what purpose?

Power swirled around her. She hated tucking into herself like a frightened creature, but she couldn't deny the truth of feeling like one.

She waited for someone to speak to her, but instead she heard murmuring close by.

Male voices, if she had to guess. Duh, she had no choice but to guess unless someone wanted to turn on some lights.

In a nasally voice, one guy asked, "You are certain that he is hunting it?"

The other one spoke in a smoother tone when he responded. "Yes. If you want to be free of this place forever, then hand me his head."

"If all you say is true and he does show up as expected, I will keep my end of our bargain. I expect to be not just free, but immortal. Understood?"

"Yes. Why do you continue to ask me the same thing?"

"I want there to be no confusion when I claim my due," nasal voice said. "But this will not work if the Alterant dies, or escapes."

"I told you neither of those things is going to happen," smooth voice said. "Remember my demonstration earlier with the wyvern?"

"I do."

Mr. Smooth said, "Observe closely as I will do this only one more time to aid you in keeping her contained."

A soft glow broke through the darkness far away, like a pinpoint of light, then gained power as it came closer. Adrenaline surged through her body, which hurt like a bitch because it made her heart beat faster.

"Hello, Evalle."

"Who are you?" Evalle asked in a rough voice. Someone had stomped a dusty path through her raw throat.

"You have no need of my name."

Evidently she had no need to see his face, either. All she could make out was a foggy image of a dark figure wavering through the field of light.

"What do you want with me?" She grimaced, determined not to moan or whine in front of this bastard. If she planned to live, she'd do it with her ego intact.

"It's not what I want with you. It's what I want in exchange for you."

He was trading her to someone?

She snorted, but it sounded rusty. "Gonna suck when I die before you get what you want."

"I do have to ensure that you will live, although upon closer inspection, you appear to be losing ground faster than I realized."

She listened for any inflection in his voice that would give away his identity. She wanted to say she heard a soft accent underneath what sounded like a pretend voice, as if he wanted to shield even that clue to who he was.

Her mind couldn't work that hard right now.

Stick to what he *was* sharing.

He wanted to trade her? She'd have a better chance of escaping if she survived. Her mind struggled to think and come up with a way to get an edge. She dragged in enough air to say, "Something ... keeping me from healing. Free my powers. I'll heal myself."

"I'm sure you probably could, but that would be too risky. You might attack me."

Ya think? Of course, attacking him would require being able to at least stand until she had her kinetic power back.

She slumped back into herself. "Tough shit then. You lose."

"I never lose. Open your arms so I can patch your chest."

"Sure thing. You stand there and hold your breath."

"Don't be difficult."

Did he really just say that? "Listen, you piece of shit, I ... "
That disgusting Noirre odor was back. So incredibly strong, like nothing she'd ever smelled before around the Medb.

This guy had to be Medb. Was he acting on his own or supported by Queen Maeve and Cathbad? Daegan would smash both of them if those two were doing this. Evalle had to keep telling herself that for any hope of clinging to life.

Storm would make people pay, but Daegan had ancient demigod powers. He'd use them, too.

The burnt lime stench clouded around her and smothered every breath she took.

On the heels of that returned the creepy feeling slithering over her skin that she'd experienced right before she'd passed out at the crash site.

What was he doing? The dark majik pushed and prodded around her face and over her arms, which she still had tucked close.

Her arms began moving away from her body.

She fought to keep them in place, but was quickly losing a tug of war to control her arms. "No! Stop it," she snarled.

Maybe not so much a snarl as a whine.

"If I don't do this, Evalle, we both lose if you die."

His light blinked out.

She hated the dark. It reminded her of the child she'd been, locked in a basement where a man ...

Chilling majik crawled over her body, much stronger this time, wrapping around and around her until it finally burrowed into her chest.

He whispered words that blurred in her ears.

His dark majik came alive all at once, stinging her chest like a thousand bees dumped into the wound.

She screamed and screamed, wrenching back and forth to get away, but she couldn't move.

He shouted at her.

She couldn't hear him over her shrieks of pain.

Nasal voice yelled, "You're killing my Alterant!"

"No, no, no. That shouldn't have been too much. Listen to me. You have to ... " was the last thing Evalle heard.

CHAPTER 7

Downtown Atlanta, Georgia

WATCHING THROUGH THE RAIN-MISTED AIR of pre-dawn in the city, Adrianna crossed her arms, allowing her body language to warn she had no tolerance for anyone at the moment.

Certainly none for Isak, who had headed for her as soon as she stepped out of Daegan's cloaking and into view.

Her McLaren sat crumpled, with steam rising from the hot engine after someone had intentionally crashed into her with incredible force.

That move had been part of a devious trap to capture Evalle.

Adrianna kept trying to sort through the timing. That could happen *only* if somebody had a way to know the very moment she entered the intersection prior to the crash.

Definitely a powerful preternatural involved.

The level of insanity to orchestrate all of that against someone under Daegan's protection was beyond her imagination. All she cared about right now was finding her friend. Dealing with Isak would waste time.

Emergency vehicle lights flashed across the dark landscape, where humans were now busy trying to figure out what had happened. Most had their phones out to videotape the drama.

With Daegan and Storm gone from Evalle's crash scene and teleporting everything, including the white van, to Storm's place, the entire area had returned to the way it should look sans the second wreck site.

What about those cell phones? Had someone captured the before and immediately after images? Someone from VIPER would have to manage damage control with that and the traffic camera footage. She couldn't deal with the potential human fallout right now.

Isak got larger the closer he came. Next to his mountain of a body, she'd look like an anthill, but she was the deadliest being present and he better remember that.

She was in no mood for his questions or his condemnation of nonhumans.

The last time they'd seen each other, Isak made it clear he did not want nonhumans near him or his family. That had been only hours after trying to get into her pants.

Okay, in fairness, she'd put out the welcome mat for that intimate episode, but no more. He was an enemy to her kind.

"Are you okay?" he asked, sounding panicked as he closed the distance between them.

She hadn't expected those words to be first out of his mouth.

That didn't change her feelings toward him. "What I am is busy and in no mood to answer questions, Isak. Take your men and go home."

He stopped two arm lengths away. He had a hurt look in his eyes she'd never seen before, but he had no right to look hurt. She hadn't been the one to stomp on his heart.

"I just got word about your car being wrecked and wanted to see that you were ... alive," he said, sounding concerned.

How dare he act even a little bit caring after what he'd done? "As you can see, I am fine."

"Your forehead is bleeding," he argued softly.

Her chest felt like she'd gone five rounds with a professional cage fighter and one leg had been tied, but she would not allow this man to do anything for her.

Not again.

He was the only man she'd ever opened her heart to and she would not do that again.

Not for a human with his prejudice.

Cocking her head in a tart way that sent spikes of pain jabbing through it, she gritted her teeth and said, "As we both know, I can heal myself. Let's not forget that I'm not like you."

"Adrianna, I—"

He was not doing this here. She said, "Stop right there. I've got things to do. Someone will show up to deal with my car so your presence is not needed."

The wounded look in his gaze grew darker.

He was not making her feel guilty. Not one bit. And that wasn't the reason she softened her next words. "Please leave, Isak."

"I also heard Evalle's motorcycle was crashed, but it's nowhere around. What happened to her?"

So much for trying to be nice. She powered her voice enough to let him know he was poking around in the wrong area. "This is *not* human business. You made it clear that you wanted nothing to do with *our* kind. So stay out of our way. Stay out of *my* way."

He grimaced. "I know I said some harsh things and ... "

Her heart cried and beat angry fists against her chest. "Don't even go there, Isak. You have no idea the frame of mind I'm in right now. The last thing I have patience for is you."

Running a hand over his face and lowering it to his side, he said, "I'd like to talk."

"Is the word *no* not getting through to you? We have nothing to talk about and I have zero time to waste talking."

A muscle jumped in his cheek. "Okay, fine. If you don't want to talk about us—"

"There. Is. No. Us." Those words slashed across her soul, but she had to say them.

"What I'm trying to say is, I have a feeling something bad has happened to Evalle and I want to help. I have resources for tracking humans and, uh, nonhumans."

He did have an intelligence network that rivaled that of human law enforcement agencies, and even some preternaturals, when it came to ferreting out information in this world.

What kind of friend was she to turn down any help that might save Evalle?

Isak must have taken her silence as an opening. He added, "I'm willing to offer all my resources with no strings attached."

She chewed on it another few seconds.

"I only have one request, Adrianna."

Her face shifted from one of concentration to suspicion. "Not that I'm accepting your offer, but what do you want?"

"For you to be my contact person."

"Is that all?"

His face showed the first sign of hope. "That's it. I don't want anything else."

"Too bad, because I don't want anything to do with you, so the answer is no. We'll accept any real intelligence, but one of the Beladors will be in touch with you."

Power surged nearby and Daegan emerged from a shadow, striding toward her. "Is there a problem, Adrianna?"

Isak jerked toward the booming voice and what he would assume was a potential threat. Witnessing Daegan in both dragon and human forms was part of what had driven the big jerk over the edge into complete meltdown.

Adrianna said, "I'm certain you remember Daegan, dragon king of the Beladors, who helped save your mother."

Daegan looked from Isak to Adrianna, clearly confused about Isak's presence.

Adrianna explained, "Daegan, this is Isak Nyght. I don't believe you've formally met, but you saw him in the battle with the Laochra Fola a few months back."

"Yes." Daegan nodded. "While in gryphon form, Evalle asked me not to kill you."

Adrianna noted a moment of embarrassment in Isak's face. He should be. Evalle had never discounted Isak for being a mere human and neither had Adrianna.

She told Daegan, "Isak has known about nonhumans for some time. In fact, his company develops weapons to use against our kind." Daegan's eyes narrowed. An uneasy tension crackled in the air, then one of his eyebrows twitched upward and his glare grew harder.

Slashing a hard look at Adrianna, Isak said, "That's a bit unfair, wouldn't you say? I've loaned weapons to Evalle for the Beladors in the past."

She shrugged in reply, because he was right. But she'd never let emotions rule her decision-making, and clearly the emotions she still harbored for Isak interfered with her brain waves. That was unacceptable.

That was also the main reason she could not accept his offer.

She was honest enough with herself to admit she'd made a grave mistake by spending time around the nice Isak.

That made it difficult to keep remembering the jerk Isak.

Daegan wore a dark T-shirt and jeans like a native to this world, but his words still rang of ancient life. " I owe you thanks for your aid in the battle against our enemies, but what business have you *here*, Nyght?"

"I'm offering help to find out what happened to Evalle."

Before Adrianna could admit she'd refused to work directly with Isak, which would reflect badly on her for letting feelings get in the way of helping Evalle, Daegan handled it.

He said, "We want no aid from humans."

"Why not?" Isak asked, clearly confused about being turned down twice. "I'm getting the feeling that Evalle was not just wrecked, but is missing. Doesn't Evalle matter to any of you?"

Daegan's power surged so fast and hard that Adrianna frowned and Isak rocked backward on his feet. The dragon king spoke in a voice that sent chills across Adrianna's skin.

"Humans aided preternaturals in an attack on Evalle. Beladors have watched over humans for many years. I protected our humans thousands of years ago. Do not *ever* think to question me."

Isak's eyes widened at the remark about thousands of years.

Daegan seethed with anger. "Take heed, human. I will not tolerate any being, human or other, attacking one of mine. You would be wise to heed her words and leave."

So Daegan had arrived in time to hear those words? Adrianna knew without asking that he'd returned to ensure her safety, but now it felt like a show of support, which felt nice considering her bruised heart.

The same stupid heart that had wanted to warm to Isak again.

Without taking his eyes off a clearly shell-shocked Isak, Daegan said, "Are you ready to leave, Adrianna?"

"Yes."

All lights around them went out, tossing the three of them into darkness.

"Wait a minute," Isak shouted. "I'm not through ... "

Adrianna heard his words trail off as Daegan teleported her away.

She'd like to say it felt good to have had the upper hand in that meeting, but that would be a lie. Pain jabbed her heart almost as much as the night he'd walked away after she'd helped rescue his mother from dangerous preternaturals.

But after seeing Daegan's unexpected reaction to Isak, she could not allow Isak to get involved now because she feared Isak's life would be in danger as well.

CHAPTER 8

Storm and Evalle's Building in Atlanta.

STORM STARED AT THE PIECES of Evalle's GSX-R lying on the floor of the parking garage in their warehouse home. If sheer force of will could make the inanimate objects tell him what happened, those parts would be spilling their guts.

He still held the bloody emerald in his hand as if it would connect to her again.

The stone felt cold as a cadaver.

He should have had the bonding ceremony completed by now so he could at least feel if she still lived. Hell, he could probably track her with their connection alone.

It might take leaning hard on all of his skills plus a load of majik, but he could do it. He would at least be able to feel her presence still in this world.

His body was so attuned to her coming in after a night of doing her duty as a Belador, he could sense daylight coming soon.

He would ask his spirit guide, but Kai was not connected to Evalle. Now that he thought about it, would his guardian have a connection if he and Evalle bonded?

His mind rejected that outright. Not if, but *when*.

Evalle could be anywhere, but she was not in this human realm. She might not have the chakra stone, but she was his mate. Even early on, long before they'd mated, he'd been able to find her anywhere in the human dimension.

If she were still in this world, he'd know.

His demon blood surged forward, pushing him to strike out and kill everything until he found Evalle. Storm fisted his hands, took a deep breath and forced the darkness back down. His body shuddered with the effort to control his demonic influence.

That side of his genetics had been dormant since Evalle put her life at risk to enter the underworld of a demon king and drag Storm's sorry ass back after a witch doctor had led him into a trap.

Evalle had refused to quit on saving him when he'd already lost the ability to shift back to human form from his black jaguar.

He had a soul again because of her.

His father's Navajo blood now ran stronger through him, too.

Storm slowly opened his fingers. The sharp edges of the emerald had gashed his hand from gripping it so hard, but the wound healed as he watched.

He would not disappoint the woman who had stood by him in his darkest hour and given him her love, a gift beyond words.

Energy pulsed through the garage.

Daegan and Adrianna appeared. The witch normally shielded her emotions behind a placid expression, but not now. Her face held a rawness Storm could appreciate.

He had his demon blood under control and would hold that control with an iron fist ... for as long as hope lived in his heart.

Walking forward quickly in spite of her legs being much shorter than Daegan's, Adrianna asked Storm, "Have you found anything? A scent maybe?"

"Nothing useful on the van or around her bike parts beyond smelling the two human scents, but I'll be able to identify those scents forever." He took in both gazes. "Now to figure out what kind of being masked his or her personal scent at the crash site."

Daegan spoke up. "I know this is hard for you, Storm, but Evalle isn't dead."

Storm said nothing. The words piled up in his throat.

Not pausing, Daegan said, "You have to believe the person behind this had the opportunity to kill her on the spot. If that had been the motive, then they'd have left her body as a message instead of that emerald. This is a kidnapping."

"I know what you're saying and I've thought about that." Storm opened the hand with the emerald now crusted with dried blood. "But keep in mind that it took considerable power to rip this from her chest. Evalle would now have to access her beast to heal. Anyone who planned this elaborate kidnapping feared my ability to track her. They may also fear Evalle's power. If so, that makes me think they would hesitate to allow her to heal completely. She could bleed out of the hole this rock left or be slowly dying in the most painful way."

Adrianna said, "Evalle will fight to survive. We'll find her. I'm not stopping until we bring her home."

Unable to say much more, Storm nodded and murmured, "I know. I'm not giving up, just stating what is running through my mind."

Daegan walked over to the van, gave it a final look and turned back. "I don't know where this hunt will lead us, but if she is no longer in this realm we will find where she is and go there. We are not coming back empty-handed. We need to form a team of our best, but not everyone who volunteers can go."

Storm frowned at the dragon king. "What are you saying?"

"If we end up traveling to another realm, we'll all be at risk. This feels like either a trap to capture me or to rupture the Beladors." Daegan paused, then added, "None of us may make it back."

"I don't care about any life here without her." Storm figured they both knew where he stood, but he was making it clear that this would only end one of two ways.

Either he brought her home or he would unleash an apocalypse on those responsible.

The rules went out the window the second they touched his mate.

Giving Storm a nod of unity, Adrianna said, "I agree with Daegan. We need a strong team, but we keep the number small to move most efficiently."

"I can't allow Tzader to leave Treoir Island while my life will be at risk," Daegan added.

"Good luck with that," Storm said.

Daegan sounded tired just talking about that battle. "I know he'll put up a fierce argument, but he understands duty. At this moment, he is of more use to us by protecting Brina and their unborn babe."

"Quinn will want to join us, too," Adrianna pointed out.

"That will be his decision," Daegan said. "For now, we need to set up a central location to plan our strategy."

"I have everything we need right here," Storm said, leaving no question about where he wanted all information funneled. "We'll use the boardroom on this level."

Adrianna twisted her blond hair into some kind of knot that stayed put. Was that a female skill or a witch skill?

She asked, "How many beings do we know who can teleport and would risk a war with the Beladors to grab Evalle?"

"Macha or Maeve," Storm stated bluntly.

"I agree and disagree," Daegan said.

"Why?"

"Macha might be a difficult goddess, but she has never been insane enough to invite the risk of having her pantheon directly attacked. I can enter that pantheon. I might be struck down in two seconds, but that would be only if I went alone."

Storm caught Daegan's reference to his mother, a powerful being whom Daegan had refused to identify. That lack of knowledge kept gods and goddesses from attacking Daegan in his first Tribunal meeting, when they could have joined forces to kill him in their realm.

Continuing to share his thoughts, Daegan said, "As for Queen Maeve, she has clearly shown signs of control issues, which makes me think her reincarnation may have had drawbacks. She wouldn't hesitate to start a war, especially with me, but there's Cathbad the Druid to consider. Cathbad has been the queen's partner in evil for a long time. The druid made it clear he was not happy about Maeve's warlocks going after Belador human children. Why would Cathbad hand over Phoedra when he could have kept Quinn's daughter?"

Daegan made valid points. It did little to ease Storm's homicidal frame of mind.

"You trust Cathbad?" Adrianna asked with no small amount of surprise.

Daegan gave her a quelling look. "Of course not. I'm only saying Cathbad would not support this knowing I would teleport enough warriors into TÅµr Medb to decimate it."

Storm admitted, "I'm all for that."

Daegan turned a dark expression to Storm. "I will not hesitate to lead my people into an unavoidable war, but attacking the Medb realm would cost a significant number of Belador lives. Through no fault of her own, Evalle would always carry the burden of that loss if she is not in TÅµr Medb and we attack under the premise of saving her."

"True." Storm wanted answers, not more questions. "I can't think of a possible third player beyond Macha and Maeve. As for Cathbad, maybe he's not happy with Maeve now that she seems to have a control problem. What if he's trying to get her kicked out of the picture by grabbing Evalle, then making it look like Maeve was at fault?"

"I hadn't thought of that," Adrianna admitted. "But it could happen."

Even Daegan appeared to study on the possibility. He said, "If that was the case, Cathbad would come to us to negotiate our help in dealing with Maeve."

Nodding, Storm said, "This might have more to do with a power play going on inside TÅµr Medb."

Adrianna tapped her index finger on her lip. When she pulled it away, she said, "How can you go into TÅµr Medb or any other realm and survive, Daegan? Even if this isn't to trap you, they won't hesitate to take a shot at getting you out of the picture."

"I will go where I am needed. My life, while important to the safety of Brina, her family and Treoir Island, will never be more important than that of any one person who follows me."

Daegan had earned Storm's respect when he supported Evalle time and again, but knowing this dragon shifter would enter a realm where he could be subject to more powerful beings looking to kill him earned Storm's loyalty eternally if they all survived.

Daegan said, "Besides the three of us, I have to give Quinn the choice of going and I think Tristan would be an asset."

Thinking on all the skills at their fingertips, Storm said, "We need someone who can help us search for Evalle through supernatural means other than our own."

Adrianna snapped her fingers. "Reese!"

Daegan asked, "The woman Quinn brought back with him after Veronika escaped VIPER lockdown? She has those gifts?"

"Yes, Evalle told me that Reese was the reason Quinn could track his daughter from Tulsa, Oklahoma, to New Orleans and beyond."

Hope grew inside Storm and flooded his chest. "Adrianna's right. I'd forgotten about what Reese could do."

"Very well, time for action," Daegan said, sounding like he'd issued an order. "Adrianna, you should go take care of your injuries and put whatever you need in place before we leave."

"I'm good."

"No, you're not," Storm argued. "I can feel the pain coming off you. We need you healthy."

"Or I can heal you," Daegan offered.

She waved him off. "Thanks, but no. I have no idea how anyone's power will react with Witchlock. I can handle my body. I'll deal with it."

Accepting that, Storm moved on. "How long will it take you to do what you need and get back?"

Giving them both a disgruntled look, she replied, "Daegan can teleport me home. I won't need that to come back, so I will probably return by the time Daegan does or sooner."

Daegan said to Adrianna, "Once I deliver you home, can you locate Quinn and inform him of what has happened, plus ask that he bring Reese in to meet with us?"

"I can handle that."

"That will give me time to visit Treoir to explain it all to Tzader and Brina. They'll need to know how to move forward if I don't return. I'll bring Tristan back with me." Turning to Storm, Daegan said, "It may be an hour plus or minus. I will move as quickly as I can."

"I understand." Storm would rush out to track Evalle this minute if he had any hope of locating her. But hunting a kidnapper who could teleport meant Storm needed the dragon with his ability to teleport, plain and simple.

Adrianna said, "Tristan may not be in Treoir. Evalle believed he was in Atlanta visiting his girlfriend."

Without hesitation, Daegan said, "He will come when I call."

"Okay, this is weighing on my conscience so I have to bring it up," Adrianna piped up.

"What?" Storm hadn't meant to sound so harsh, but if it involved finding Evalle no one had better hold back.

"Daegan knows I spoke with Isak and he offered his resources."

Storm and Daegan shouted, "*No!*" at the same time.

"Got it!" she snapped back at both of them. "I'm just letting you know and saying if I have to go to Isak to gain more information, I will."

"Sorry, Adrianna." Storm had to get a grip or he would run everyone off who could help. "It's just that there were humans involved and I don't want anyone muddying the waters the way Isak has done in the past with his men. Thank you for offering after how he treated you."

"He doesn't matter to me anymore," she said too quickly.

As a walking lie detector, Storm caught the lie as it rolled off her lips, but would not call her on it.

She deserved to protect her pride.

"Exactly," Daegan agreed. "Humans will interfere. If I thought they could help us, I would *make* them." He paused and suggested gently to Storm, "You should also make arrangements if this doesn't go well and you don't return."

That was sobering. "I'll handle it. Let's meet back here by ten o'clock at the latest."

Daegan lifted a hand. He and Adrianna vanished.

Storm started a mental list of things to do, which was a strain when he wanted to take action.

He had to contact Rowan, a white witch who lived in Midtown and led a powerful council of white witches. She would jump in to help the teens living here if need be.

Hell. Storm had to tell Lanna and the twin boys something, but what about Feenix? Evalle's little pet gargoyle had a sixth sense about her sometimes.

Quinn's teenage cousin, Lanna, was a busybody Storm had to make sure stayed out of this. She had a streak of loyalty a mile wide, but with that came a single-minded determination to help.

Not this time.

Storm washed the emerald and placed it on a shelf while he cleaned the blood from his hands.

Evalle's blood. His mate was hurting and alone.

He clenched his hands, waited for the rage to pass so he could function, then kept moving.

When he shoved the stone in his pocket, it still had bits of her blood that were not coming off. He walked from the garage to the street-level reception area for the offices he had no plans to lease out.

Someone knocked on the front door.

Pinching the bridge of his nose, he opened it since no one could pass his ward unless he allowed them entry. He had to look down at the tiny woman no taller than Adrianna.

Maybe not even that tall.

"This is not a good time to visit the boys, Kit," Storm told Isak's mother.

Kit glared up at him. "I'm not here to visit. Get rid of whatever is pushing me away from the door and do it right now."

What the hell?

He would not harm Kit, but neither would he allow her to waste one minute of his time when every second was precious.

"You're standing in the way of getting her back, Storm. Don't you want to know who was involved in Evalle's capture?"

CHAPTER 9

S TORM SETTLED KIT AT THE giant conference table. Normally he'd offer her tea, but he could not be more social than
he was managing at the moment.

"Isak told me what happened," Kit started in. "He also said
your people are refusing his help."

Digging deep for the manners Kit deserved and Evalle would
expect of him, Storm explained, "We don't want humans
involved."

"Too late. They are involved." Kit leaned on the arm she'd
placed on the table. "That's why I'm here. You can't refuse help
when we need to find Evalle."

Was she really lecturing him? "I *will* find her."

"God save me from hardheaded men," she muttered. "You
aren't the only one who cares about her."

That just hit the wrong nerve for Storm. "Your son has no claim
to her. She's *my* mate."

"He doesn't want Evalle," Kit said with plenty of exasperation.
"He thinks of her only as a friend. My son is lucky Evalle didn't
smoke him over how he treated Adrianna, but he'll have to fix
that on his own. In the meantime, Evalle is our friend. She's *my*
friend." Tears pooled in Kit's eyes, but that woman did not break
easily and would not allow a drop to fall. Kit added, "In fact, I
saw Evalle right before this happened."

Storm sat up. "When?"

"Very early this morning. She and Adrianna came to
investigate a report of something preternatural in the woods near
Chattahoochee Bend State Park. It was Jasper."

He gave her a confused look. "Who?"

Kit explained how Jasper had been the forklift operator in their
weapons facility, and had shifted into a Rías the first time Evalle

visited.

Storm recalled that story. Yet another time that Evalle had been in danger, but still protected the humans around her.

Rushing to finish, Kit said, "I've been trying to train him so he can integrate into this world."

Storm's mouth opened and closed. "You've been ... are you nuts?"

"No. I'm actually making headway. Evalle was impressed." She shook that off. "Back to Evalle. We don't have time to visit."

With this miniature general berating him, Storm had a fleeting moment of empathy for Isak.

Wouldn't Evalle find *that* amusing? Just thinking about her being happy gutted him. *The hell with past issues.* He was not turning down help from any direction.

But he wanted to make one thing clear to Kit. "If you share information on humans involved, I can't promise they'll make it to a court of law, human or otherwise."

"If I had them standing in front of me right now they'd beg for death," she countered.

Alrighty then. "In that case, thank you for coming by. What have you got?"

For the first time since opening the ward for her, Kit's face lost its fury, but was no less serious. "Two humans were involved. Our people have been combing through the traffic cam footage. We have facial recognition software. Once we have identities, you'll know. In the meantime, Isak has everyone hunting for them. One thing though is that he can't find the white van that was on the traffic video from that location."

"That's because it's sitting in my garage."

"Hmm. We need access to the van."

Storm told her, "I've gone over it and have two human scents."

"But do you have any fingerprints?"

Damn, she had him there. "No. We don't work with fingerprints."

"We do and we're good at it. Will you let me bring in one of our team to pull prints and any DNA they can find?"

This hunt had clusterfuck written all over it, but Storm wouldn't waste time trying to turn chaos into an orderly plan. He'd just manage it so that everyone pulled in the same direction.

He nodded. "I'm not going to be here long. Your person will

have to get in and out before I leave."

"He will. Now, what are you doing about the kids?"

"I'm ... " Storm paused. What *was* he going to do?

"I know you are out of your mind worried about Evalle. So here's the plan for our teens," Kit said in the voice of a commanding officer. "You tell them whatever you want, but you're going to leave the ward open so I can come and go. They can all go home with me—"

"Quinn won't go for that for Lanna. This is the safest place for her to be and the twins won't leave her here alone."

"Good." She smiled, sitting back. "That makes me proud of those two boys. In that case, I'm staying here while you're gone. These teens will need someone to be here with them if ... this doesn't turn out well."

This woman was some powerhouse.

She'd blown in here and taken control without a shot fired. No wonder Evalle held Isak's mom in such high regard.

Now that they were no longer on opposite sides of a line in the sand, her whole demeanor had eased. She gave Storm a compassionate look that matched the empathy wafting from her.

"Evalle loves you beyond anything in this world. You look like a man who has lost everything, but you haven't. That young lady will battle to survive just to return to you. Keep your faith solid for both of you."

That sounded like what Daegan had said and words his father would have given at this time. "Thanks, Kit. Sorry if I was not exactly friendly when you showed up."

She huffed. "That was nothing. I deal with men all day long and I always get my way."

He bet she did. "Once I head out with our team to track Evalle, I don't know how long I'll be gone. I will leave all of you a way to get out in case of emergency, but this is a stronghold against almost all beings. I have an additional apartment you're welcome to use while here and all the apartments are stocked with food and other necessities. If you want to make yourself comfortable with some tea, everything is over there." He pointed to the side. "I've got to talk to the kids."

"Go ahead."

He climbed two flights of stairs, bypassing the level with the apartments until he got the most difficult visit over first. When he stopped, he was on the level dedicated entirely as a playroom for Feenix, Evalle's pet gargoyle who spent most of his time there when she was not home.

Storm and the little gargoyle had reached a point of acceptance, because they both loved Evalle and wanted her happy. Feenix had an internal clock for daylight and got antsy when Evalle wasn't home by morning.

The sun had already begun rising.

Storm stopped at the door to the playroom and dropped his head against it as a new worry drilled into his mind.

Would whoever grabbed her know that Evalle couldn't be exposed to the sun?

Storm couldn't spend minutes on what-ifs.

The faster he told Feenix that Evalle had to go to Treoir for a few days, the quicker he could get hunting. Evalle would agree with the white lie, even though Storm would pay a price for lying. His ability to detect a lie was countered by a backlash on his body when he did not tell the truth.

But for her, he would do his best to leave Feenix as at peace as possible.

Opening the door, he expected Feenix to be chasing one of the many whirligig toys Storm had created for him that ran on majik.

Or even playing with the big flat-screen television Storm had installed and customized so Evalle's two-foot-tall critter could operate it with his pudgy, four-fingered paws.

He hadn't expected to find Feenix standing just inside the door, having abandoned his stuffed alligator toy, which he'd left lying on his favorite beanbag.

Feenix's normally bright-orange eyes were dull and drooping. He whispered, "Evalle."

Oh, hell. How did this little guy know something was up?

Storm started in, "Evalle had to go to Treoir and ... "

Feenix shook his head slowly from side to side. A fat tear rolled down one green, leathery cheek.

Storm dropped to his knees. "Come here, buddy."

Standing very still at first, Feenix frowned with deep concentration, but over time he'd learned that Storm was not the enemy. Storm had created a place for Feenix to live happily with him and Evalle, but her pet did not trust easily.

The little creature waddled over to Storm and stepped into his arms. Storm had never held a gargoyle, but this one was warm and soft.

Petting Feenix on the back, Storm swallowed hard and said, "Evalle was captured."

Feenix made a sound that broke his heart. He kept explaining, "I'm taking a team of powerful friends to help me find her."

"I go," Feenix said in his tiny voice.

"No, Feenix. If I let anything happen to you it would kill Evalle."

"Evalle mine."

Storm smiled at the word that had annoyed him so many times in the early days when Feenix did not want Storm there. "Yes, she's yours, but I love her, too. Will you watch our home so I can go save her?"

Feenix sniffled, which was something, considering he could torch this room with his fiery snout. "'Kay."

"Thank you." Storm hadn't realized how much he'd been dreading this until relief swept across him from Feenix agreeing to work with him. "I'm leaving soon, but Lanna and the boys will be here. So will Kit. I think Evalle told you about the woman the boys stayed with for a while. That woman is Kit and a friend of Evalle's."

"'Kay."

The little guy didn't have much vocabulary, but he said a lot with one broken word.

Easing away from Feenix, Storm stood.

Turning away, Feenix walked with a sad gait to his beanbag where he sank into it and pulled his stuffed gator to him.

Storm could see how Evalle had gotten so attached to Feenix.

He had just closed the door and started back down the stairs to the second landing when he felt power move toward him. That would be Lanna. He'd become accustomed to the energy she exuded.

She waited at the bottom of the stairs on the next level down. "What is wrong with Evalle?" she whispered.

No secrets around here. Lanna had a crazy amount of power, and even she didn't know for sure what she was, but it was more than a witch.

For all the times he'd used gentle words with Evalle, he was struggling to keep his voice even right now. "She's in a jam and I have to go help her."

"Is not truth," Lanna accused.

"So now you're a lie detector, too?"

"Not like you, Storm, but I can tell. Evalle has been in trouble before. Is bad this time. You would not be here if you knew where she was."

He couldn't argue with that logic. "You're right. She's been kidnapped and I have no idea where she is."

Lanna's face started to crumble.

Storm rushed ahead to console her. "But I will find her." He wished he could believe his own words. Doubt was having a field day with his mind right now.

The nineteen-year-old pulled her emotions together. She'd shown scary control after having been attacked by a crazy wizard who had been determined to drain her power.

Lanna stated, "I can help."

"Can you find someone in another realm?"

She frowned. "Evalle is not here?"

"I don't think so." He finished descending the steps to stand next to her. "Best we can tell, she was teleported away and I ... " He took a breath. "I can't feel her at all. If she was in the human realm, I would at least feel her as my mate."

Nibbling on her lips, Lanna said, "You give me something very important to her and I will tell you ... what I can."

She'd stopped short of saying she'd confirm if Evalle was alive or dead.

Storm had the emerald in his pocket.

Why was he hesitating to hand it to Lanna? Because as much as he tried to be realistic about all this, he wasn't ready to hear that Evalle was dead.

The air backed up in his lungs.

Lanna reached out and hugged him. "We will find her, Storm."

He patted her on the back. When she stepped back, he sucked up his courage and withdrew the emerald.

Her eyes rounded in horror. "Is that the ... "

"Yes. The one I put on her so I could find her."

She extended a trembling hand.

He started to hand her the emerald then lifted the stone out of her reach. "Wait. This might harm you like that braided hair bracelet Quinn had that burned your hand."

Gifting him with a watery smile, she said, "It will not harm me. That emerald was bound with love on both sides."

Accepting the confidence in Lanna's voice, Storm placed the stone in her hand, then held his breath.

Sandwiching the stone between her small hands, Lanna closed her eyes and nothing happened at first. Then her whole body shook. She moaned, "No, is bad, no."

"Lanna, open your eyes." His heart thrummed rapidly.

When she looked at him through tear-flooded eyes, she said, "Evalle is alive."

He leaned over, propping his hands on his thighs to keep from folding to his knees. She was alive.

"But you must hurry, Storm."

He jerked his head up. "Why?"

"Her energy very weak. I barely feel it. She is alive, but not well. Almost like ... hurt and not healing."

CHAPTER 10

The realm of TÅμr Medb

MAEVE CAST AN EYE AT the empty spot where her dragon throne should be perched, but that miserable lizard had escaped.

This was not the way she had expected things to go once she and Cathbad the Druid reincarnated in the present day world. Two thousand years she'd been waiting, stuck between life and death in perpetual stasis until the curse she and the druid had created came to fruition.

She'd cursed Daegan's dragon into the form of her throne and had left him unable to sleep that entire time. She'd allowed him to nap a few times recently, thinking she'd found a way to manipulate him into sharing what he knew of the time before she reincarnated. He'd shared nothing of value.

That proved how showing any mercy was foolish.

Torturing Daegan for two thousand years was not enough.

He owed her far more now that he'd escaped.

A tap on the tall, double doors to her private domain in TÅμr Medb distracted her. That better be the person who'd promised he could bring Daegan down.

She glanced at the doors and they opened for her.

Outside the entrance, two guards stood at attention as a man strode through the opening before the doors closed. Based on the size of this warrior's arms and legs alone, he had inherited decent genetics. She prided herself on possessing the largest force of witches and warlocks, some who possessed powerful gifts. What abilities did this man before her possess?

This warrior could hold his own with Adonis and had come highly recommended by the head of her Scath Force unit, whom she'd already gifted with a boost to his power.

See? She could be a generous queen if people proved their value. Bowing low at the waist, he said, "Queen Maeve."

"Hello, Perth."

"I am honored to meet you in person."

This man had approached the leader of her Scath Force unit in the human realm, surprising her warlock when he identified the Scath leader's energy as one of dark nature. That had been disturbing since her special warriors could conceal their scent.

Perth had explained that he had not picked up on the scent, but the additional power from her. He then said he was also not a fan of Beladors.

She gave a brief head tilt. "My warlock tells me he explained the terms of the reward I've offered for capturing the dragon king. What makes you think you're capable of such a task?"

Lifting his head, he stepped forward. "I inherited gifts that have allowed me to outperform other bounty hunters, even those who are known to have exceptional skills and powers for their line of work. Additionally, I have resources most can't access. Plus, I am in a perfect place to gain knowledge of what goes on with the Beladors and their dragon king now that I am a contractor to VIPER."

"Oh?"

"I answered Sen's call for new agents when the Beladors left VIPER's operations crippled last month."

That vacancy in VIPER's numbers had been due to her warlocks turning trolls into demons and capturing Belador children. Daegan had taken exception and pulled his Beladors out to do his own bidding.

VIPER should have been incensed enough to banish the Beladors from the coalition again, but no. Sen, the VIPER liaison between governing Tribunals and the pool of agents, had never been one to tolerate insolence though.

He'd gained her notice by the way he made life as difficult as he could for Beladors.

If not for clearly being tethered to VIPER and the Tribunal, Sen would have a place in her organization. Her plan to capture Belador children had been working flawlessly until Cathbad the Druid interfered.

As someone she'd partnered with long ago, Cathbad's position next to her provided him certain benefits, but overruling her orders was not one of them.

That druid had become more annoying in recent days than ever in the past. His value to her dwindled each time he crossed her.

She waved a hand at Perth, dismissing information already reported to her. "Yes, yes, I was informed about the bounty hunter group that stepped in when the Beladors abandoned VIPER."

"True, but I am independent of those bounty hunters. Sen didn't care who came in as long as he no longer had to teleport all over the place to deal with problems. I am my own man."

Her warrior had shared that as well, but she would not trust any man's word. She'd ordered her Scath Force to investigate Perth further and determine for sure that this man was associated with no one else, like perhaps that blasted dragon.

Ready to determine if he would be of use to her, Maeve asked, "Back to my first question. How do you propose to win the reward?"

"As I understand it, you want the dragon captured, but not killed."

"Exactly."

"You could go on for many years, hundreds of years, without that happening. I would like to propose a different approach."

She would always allow creative thinking when it was in her best interest. "I'm listening."

"Daegan has to know he was fortunate to escape. He would not risk being captured again only to have you compel him to do your bidding, which would include sharing all knowledge he has gained since joining the Beladors. From what I've gathered, you are capable of necromancy. Considering your power, I can only believe that what *you* are capable of with a decapitated head would be far superior to any other who might attempt to compel such a head to speak."

"Of course." Maeve started seeing where he was going with this line of thought and allowed him to finish.

"Killing Daegan is considered impossible by many." He offered a smile that had her thinking about how he'd look naked in her bed, but she would not be swayed from her goal.

"You say that as if you don't consider it impossible, Perth."

"I do not. I have spent my life figuring out the impossible and have a plan for dealing with him, but I require more than the ability to teleport that you have offered your warlocks."

This one had balls. Perhaps this man could prove worthy of being the next leader of her elite Scath Force unit. "What would that be?"

"I wish to serve you for eternity. You would never have a more loyal man at your side. Before you think that I am a fool to aspire to keep you to myself, I am not. You are an exceptional beauty in addition to being a powerful queen. Eternity is a long time. I would never interfere with your decisions or complain about those you'd take to your bed. I would be the perfect right-hand man. Yes, this is a bold request, but so is bringing a dragon to his knees."

She found his confidence extremely seductive. Bedding this one would be an adventure for sure.

He was not a druid, but then she didn't need a druid these days if having one around was going to interrupt her plans.

Allowing the hint of a smile to touch her lips, she said, "You have given me something to think on. I admit that I had not considered how valuable a dragon's head might be."

"Yes, my queen. Especially in place of an empty hand."

Wise man to claim her as his queen. Was she really going to do this? What would be the harm in agreeing? He could do nothing to her if she lied to him.

"Very well, bring me the head of Daegan in his dragon form and I will grant you immortality, but I am not agreeing to more than that as yet."

With a broad smile that spoke of success, he said, "I would not expect more unless it was your desire."

She wanted this one. He had piqued her interest in ways no man had for many centuries. Cathbad could take a few lessons. The more she considered this Perth and his claims, the more she could see him at her beck and call.

He very well might end up immortal and at her side.

Careful not to allow him to believe he had any control of this meeting, she handed him a deadline. "My offer is good for only two weeks."

His searing green eyes darkened at that. "Wonderful. As I have already set my plan in motion, I need only one week. I merely wanted to reach an agreement on terms and that a dead dragon would be as much use to you as a live one."

Possibly more useful, now that he had her thinking that way. Just imagine the secrets she could pull from Daegan that would aid her in conquering Treoir while the Beladors were in turmoil after his death.

"One last point, Perth," Maeve said. She'd realized a potential flaw in his plan.

"Yes, my queen?"

"If the dragon is killed or destroyed entirely and you fail to deliver a head to me, the only reward you will receive is a slow and agonizing death." She smiled as she gave that warning.

"I would expect no less from you as that would be unacceptable for both of us."

She had to give it to Perth. No fear. "I admire your bold attitude, but how do you plan to keep up with a dragon that can teleport?"

"I will not be chasing the dragon. He will be chasing me."

Having a champion for her cause emerge from the human world couldn't be more surprising, but among preternaturals anything was possible.

For all Cathbad's ranting about the power he'd expended on Ossian, one warrior who was now gone, he could have found this Perth.

No, Cathbad had focused all his energy on turning a Scath Force warrior into a polymorph. Granted, Ossian, his pet warlock, had been able to shift into any human form, but that one had been flawed and failed to survive one simple duty she'd assigned him.

Cathbad was still upset with her over losing his polymorph.

When had the most powerful druid she'd ever known become so attached to anything? Their partnership had lasted two millennia only because she was no weak-kneed woman.

She held the power here and he had better remember that, once he got over his pity party.

Ready to dismiss Perth, she said, "Few men have surprised me. I enjoy rewarding those who rise above the mediocre and prove their potential."

"Is that so, Maeve?"

Snapping her hand in a quick move, she teleported Perth to the human world before Cathbad got a good look at her new pet.

She swung around. "Ah, Cathbad. I see you've returned from your wandering."

Cathbad eyed the spot where Perth had stood and failed to hide the scowl on his face. "Who was that?"

This druid had spent plenty of time in her bed, but that had never given him the right to question her or anyone she brought to her chambers.

She was beginning to find him boring.

Not sexually. Cathbad would never bore a woman in bed, but he took offense at the least thing these days, like the loss of his polymorph. Cathbad should have given the warrior enough power to avoid being captured and controlled by a deadly witch.

Although calling Veronika a mere witch was an understatement. She'd intended to control Witchlock and boasted she'd force everyone under her thumb.

That Sterling bitch, Adrianna, had grabbed the ancient power instead.

What a waste. Adrianna Lafontaine wasn't even a dark witch, according to what Maeve's warriors had recently reported.

Veronika might have had extraordinary powers, but she was not Maeve. She was not the leader of the Medb coven.

And she was now dead.

Cathbad's sour attitude was infringing on Maeve's upbeat frame of mind. She asked, "Are you better now?"

His gaze locked on her and stayed there longer than she'd have liked, considering the anger simmering beneath it. "What were you up to, Maeve?"

"You mean with that *young* man?" she asked, pushing hard on the word "young" as a dig even though Cathbad could appear any age.

"Of course that's what I'm askin' about," he drawled.

"You're a surly bastard these days. If you weren't so depressing to be around, I'd invite you to spend a few hours relaxing with me." She added that last line only as a taunt.

"Depressing?" He strolled around, not really walking toward her, but gaining distance each time. "We both know I'm not the sort to be depressed. I am, however, quite capable of extreme rage."

Giving him an exaggerated sigh, she said, "Can you not get over losing Ossian? These things happen."

"That's what bothers me about you these days, Maeve. At one time, you could look farther down the road and see the greater picture. Not anymore. He was not *just* a polymorph. He could have been our secret weapon in the human world for a long time. He could have handed us Daegan *and* Macha, but you were so reckless you didn't care."

Perth could turn into her own secret weapon in the human world. "When have you ever known me to be emotional about a servant, Cathbad? To care about losing anyone is not in my makeup."

His eyebrow arched. "Does that include me?"

With any other man, that question could be a positive sign, but she knew Cathbad too well. He had not meant anything personal by that question. No, this sly bastard would trick her with his words if she allowed it.

"I will be honest, Cathbad. I would miss you if you were gone."

"Such heartfelt concern," he said, his words swimming in sarcasm.

Throwing up her hands, she demanded, "What is it going to take to mend this rift between us? I won't play word games with you." She did harbor a concern that the longer Cathbad remained angry, the more she had to watch her back around him.

She trusted no one.

Definitely not an angry druid who knew many of her secrets.

"You wish to fix things between us?" he inquired.

Hadn't she just said that? "Yes."

"Then you could start by discussing your plans so that I know what you are up to in the human world. What have you got our Scath Force doing?"

"My Scath Force," she snapped, and power sizzled through the air.

Cathbad ignored her show of anger, instead pushing her more. "You seem to forget that I was the one who infused them with the power to hide their scent, among other things, Maeve."

What an ego. "If you need to take credit for that, fine. I give you credit. Happy now?" Why did she waste her time trying to deal with him when he was surly?

His eyes narrowed and he became quiet again.

She'd seen Cathbad like this right before he decimated an enemy. He was slow to rile, but once he reached his limit he became a dangerous threat.

"Have it your way, Maeve." He lifted a hand.

"Wait. Don't teleport away."

Lowering his hand, he asked, "Why not?"

Because your recent absence is suspicious. She had to think what a woman who cared would say and tried not to cringe at sounding so needy. "I want to spend time together and get back to where we were before, in a happy partnership."

His eyebrows climbed up his forehead. "Truly?"

Maybe sounding a little emotional had done the trick. She softened her voice to siren sexy. "Yes, Cathbad."

"Then you'll allow me to call in our Scath Force for a report and to answer my questions."

"No." She silently cursed at her foolish attempt to sway him.

"Very well, Maeve. You continue to put our Scath Force at risk. When they're all dead, you'll be the one to create the next ones."

"You're so pissy," she muttered. "I don't know what you want."

"It's not what I want, but what I'm due. I expect my considerations to be respected. You may be queen, but you would not be here without me."

Don't lash at Cathbad. Don't lash at Cathbad. She kept repeating that to avoid losing control of her body. He'd love to see her warp out of shape right now and she would not give him that opportunity.

She had to regain her control or he might think she was vulnerable in those moments. Drawing herself up, she warned, "Tell me where you're going or you may not be able to return."

"I am finding a way to bring Daegan to his knees. Isn't that what you want?"

"Why would you do that if you're still so angry with me?"

The muscles in Cathbad's face relaxed. "I don't care for this constant tension either. I am not just using this time as a sabbatical. I'm working on a surprise."

The man could be so confusing.

Did he mean he was trying to smooth things out with her? "Is the surprise for me?"

Offering a genuine smile for the first time in a while, Cathbad said, "Of course it's for you, love."

He lifted a hand and teleported away, leaving Maeve staring at an empty spot.

Did he think she just accepted those words?

Not for a minute.

As she had done many years ago, Maeve started thinking on a plan for the future.

One that might not include Cathbad.

CHAPTER 11

E VALLE STRUGGLED TO MOVE HER arms and fight what-ever held her down. "No! I'll kill you."

"Evalle, stop."

She heaved deep breaths and froze at the voice she'd thought never to hear again. She opened her eyes. "Storm?"

"Of course." His beautiful, naked body stretched out above hers, propped up by powerful arms. He leaned down and kissed her. "I've missed you."

She tried to call up where she was and why she'd been fighting. Squinting, she could barely make out shapes around her in the darkness swallowing them.

Was she at home? The bed felt soft and Storm was here.

"What's the matter, sweetheart?"

Relief washed out of her faster than water over a cliff. "I can't ... I don't know. Something happened, but ... "

He gave her a concerned look. "You were captured and now you're safe."

"Why can't I see our room? It's just blurry. My vision is better than that."

His big hands spread over her face and hair. "It's going to be okay. Give it time. You're having a reaction to the dark majik."

"Oh. Who had me?"

He kissed her, paused, then kissed her some more. When Storm touched her, nothing else really mattered. She joined in and wrapped her legs around his nice, taut butt. That gave her a close encounter with one of her favorite parts.

Chuckling, he asked, "Ready, are you?"

"Oh, yes."

"I don't think so." One of his hands moved down to toy with her breast, cupping it before he pulled the nipple into his mouth and sucked on it.

She grabbed a handful of his silky black hair and begged him not to stop.

He kept up his siege on her body, moving from one breast to the other and easing down as he kissed a path to between her legs. Her muscles trembled in anticipation. "Enough already."

Did that push him to hurry up? Nope.

Using his tongue, he took his time, driving her crazy. Then without any warning, he teased the one spot she was sure controlled her entire nervous system. That's all it took to uncoil the heat in her womb and shove her over the edge.

As she came down from somewhere out of this world, Storm moved up and drove into her. Wow, that felt ... incredible. She met him with every hard stroke, urging him to hold back nothing.

When he collapsed on her with a long sigh, she smiled with contentment. She lived in a crazy, preternatural world, but no matter what life threw at them, Storm was hers and she was his. They were mates.

But ... something pecked at her conscience.

He hadn't used a condom. Not a huge thing, but he'd told her they had plenty of time to plan a child and that he wanted them to bond before that happened.

Maybe he just lost track of it in the moment.

She probably wasn't ovulating anyhow.

Another thing, and maybe it was silly, but he hadn't spoken to her as much as he normally did when they made love. He'd whisper in an erotic voice that would send her reeling just as fast as his hands.

Also ... she hadn't felt his energy the way it normally surged with hers when they joined. Or maybe it was her energy that hadn't come to the surface.

She'd enjoyed everything he'd done, but this time had felt ... odd.

He nuzzled her neck and she sighed at having him close again, but she had to get her head clear first. Much as she'd love round two, she felt off balance now.

Had something physically happened to her when she'd been kidnapped? Or was this weird feeling left over from the dark majik Storm mentioned?

In fact, who had kidnapped her?

Storm snuggled next to her, probably sensing that she needed time to adjust.

He'd always known exactly what to do.

Now that the heat of the moment had passed, she returned to figuring out what had been going on. The last thing she recalled was riding her bike as she followed Adrianna on her way back to Atlanta.

Then someone intentionally wrecked Adrianna and ...

Evalle flinched at the memory of the truck ramming her motorcycle.

Storm propped himself up. "What?"

"Where's Adrianna?"

He shrugged. "Have no idea."

How could he not know? Evalle asked, "How's Adrianna doing?"

"She's fine." He gave her a little kiss on her cheek and started toying with her again.

Evalle put her hand up. "Wait, Storm. I want to know exactly what happened to Adrianna."

After a long sigh, he said, "I have no idea. All I care about is being here with you."

Something was very wrong. Evalle asked, "Who captured me?"

"Can we talk about this tomorrow?"

"No." A sick feeling started forming in her chest. He wasn't making sense to her.

She asked, "Who rescued me?"

"All of us."

"Who is all of us?"

"Why so many questions? Aren't you happy to see me?"

She shoved him off her. "What's going on?"

When he didn't answer, she searched the room that was still nothing but blurry shadows. "Where are we?"

"Wherever you want to be."

She tried to jump out of the bed to find the door, but she couldn't move.

Everything spun.

In the next second, she was sitting up with her arms locked against a wall on each side of her. She jerked back and forth.

"Storm! Get me out of this!"

He didn't answer. She looked over to find him and he was gone. Warmth soaked the front of her clothing. It smelled like blood. Wait. What clothing? She was naked a minute ago.

A pinprick of light pulled her gaze left.

Mind hazy, Evalle demanded, "What is going on?"

The light continued to grow until she could make out the inside of the room where she was clearly being held in a cell of some sort. Four walls, a floor and ceiling, no more than ten feet in any direction. Her wrists were manacled to a stone wall. Not a medieval type of manacle. These were shiny blue and glowed.

Sniffing, she recognized another odor with the scent of fresh blood ... ew, was that Noirre majik? She dropped her gaze to see a red stain spread across the top of a sack dress she wore.

Now her chest throbbed with a sharp pain.

She groaned and gritted her teeth.

The fog cleared. She knew in her heart it had not been real, but couldn't stop the breath that squeezed out a desperate, "Storm?"

"Hello, Evalle," a male voice said in that nasally tone she'd heard when half conscious.

"Who are you?"

"You may call me Germanus." He spoke with an odd accent that sounded old, like something from another time.

Her heart sank at the complete flip from being safe with Storm to realizing she was captured. More like *still* captured, now that her mind continued to pull everything together.

Germanus asked, "Did you enjoy your conjugal visit?"

What had happened hit her like a backhand. This monster had used her memories of Storm to inspire the fantasy hallucination. She snarled, "Stay the fuck out of my head!"

No figure materialized yet, but the voice explained, "That was for your benefit."

That bastard. Making her believe she'd been rescued and was at home with Storm? "My mate will find you, and when he does, I will cheer him on as he takes you apart one limb at a time."

A loud sigh answered her.

She was making no headway by yelling at him even if it did boost her spirit. "Okay, I'm here, wherever here is. You must have gone to a lot of trouble to have me captured alive. What do you want?" she snapped. Her body hurt from one end to the other. She had a crooked leg and pain streaked through it every time she moved. One of her arms had been broken when they locked her in manacles. It had also healed poorly.

But her chest leaked blood. Too much blood.

Hair hung down around her face in sweaty clumps. Everything that had happened came back to her. The hole in her chest had been left after someone clawed the emerald chakra stone from her body. That had been her closest connection to Storm when they were apart.

No connection now. Someone, this Germanus, had gone to great effort to kidnap her and leave no trail.

She smelled as filthy as she felt, but one thing was clear. They didn't want her to die or she'd be dead.

Germanus had not answered her.

Short on patience, she asked, "Why am I still alive?"

"Because I have something for you to do."

"I don't remember applying for the position. Tell you what. Have your people get with my people and work out the terms, then we'll talk. In the meantime, stay out of my head or I'll find a way to kill you myself." She grimaced over the ache in her chest, which intensified with every breath needed for talking.

"This will go much better if you do not constantly fight me. There is no way for you to win."

She cut her gaze from side to side, then up and down. "Are you so afraid of me you won't even show yourself?"

Energy sizzled and a man emerged from a blurry spot on the wall. There was no door to this cell, because preternaturals didn't always need the kind of entrance humans used.

His body came into focus from the boots up, filling out a loose pair of dark pants, then a sleeveless blue tunic with a Celtic design of braids and those interlocking shapes she never could name, but the center had a dragon face. The lack of sleeves showed off well-shaped arms, but not big guns, plus the limbs ended in hands too perfect for a warrior.

When Germanus finished coming into view, he had carved cheeks, a narrow nose and smooth lips. His dark eyelashes gave his elf-like, deep blue eyes the look of being outlined. Black hair fell in waves to his shoulders. He wore a thick gold chain with a pendant sporting the same Celtic dragon emblem as his tunic.

What cosplay event had he dressed for? She gave him her best attempt at a bored look, which was tough to do when suffering multiple injuries. "Let me guess. You're a Sir Lancelot wannabe. No, wait, maybe you're one of the alien beings from an early Star Trek show. Or ... "

With a flick of his finger, a cloth gag shoved into her mouth, a wider strip covered that, then tied behind her head.

"This is no game, Evalle. When you're ready to listen, I'll tell you what you're going to do."

She breathed hard through her nose and hoped she'd managed to jack her glare up to make him worry about ever turning his back on her.

He advised her, "I'm going to allow you ten minutes to heal. I suggest you use it wisely."

No, no, no. She strained against the gag, grunting that she was ready to listen.

He must not be fluent in grunt speech.

The bastard left.

But the gag vanished with him. She spit to clear her mouth and yelled, "You miserable shit!"

No one answered her, but a small hourglass appeared in the air in front of her at eye level. It flipped and began spilling sand.

Ten minutes was not enough time to heal everything wrong with her, but she called up her beast, hoping to flood energy into her chest first.

The flood turned out to be more of a trickling stream.

What the hell was wrong?

She directed the energy specifically to her chest. Fiery heat burned as she pushed hard to force healing power into her most debilitating wound. She arched away from the wall, enduring the pain, gritting her teeth.

Stars flew through her vision.

Don't black out, she silently pleaded with herself.

Who was Germanus? What did he want? Maybe the job he had for her was something she could do as long as it didn't harm anyone.

Exhausted from what little healing she could manage, her eyes drooped. She opened them wide in panic. She couldn't go through another round with fantasy Storm. Her heart couldn't take losing him over and over.

A new worry struck her as she played the sexy dream back through her mind.

Maybe Germanus wanted more than her Belador and gryphon powers to perform some task.

He might be able to keep her from tapping her powers, but if he tried to physically attack her, she'd make him regret being born male.

CHAPTER 12

"'TIS THE WAY IT MUST be, Tzader," Daegan argued right back. "You cannot go with me. This may not be a brief journey." That was better than admitting out loud that this team might not return. He had to tell Tzader of the possibility, but now was not the moment.

Tzader kicked a chair in Brina's solarium. "I'm tired of Evalle being screwed six ways every time I turn around. She deserves to be happy with Storm."

"Agreed, but that won't happen until we find her."

Furious, Tzader swung to face Daegan. "What about that damned stone he stuck on her? Doesn't it work?"

Sighing, Daegan explained all of what had happened.

As the truth sank in, Tzader's normally rich brown skin turned a sickly color. "They ripped her chest open?"

"Yes. That's why I don't believe she's in the human realm, but there are many places she can be. Before you start on me about the Medb being at fault, I am considering all possibilities including Macha, but someone expects us to default immediately to those two. We can't make a mistake by jumping to conclusions or we might lose Evalle."

Sounding more like the Maistir who had watched over North American Beladors before Daegan showed up to take control of Treoir, Tzader said, "We need to eliminate everyone we think isn't behind this so we can be sure where to hunt."

"Good point."

Turning a steel-eyed gaze on Daegan, Tzader ordered, "You need to go to a Tribunal and make them pull in Macha, Maeve and ... anyone it might be just to rule them out. Or to finger the guilty."

Daegan stroked the short beard he'd allowed to grow. "The

coalition does owe us at this point, in return for Beladors rejoining the agents of VIPER."

"Damn right. I wouldn't suggest you going there, but Quinn told me the way you gave them a smackdown. So you're good to go, right?"

"Is that an order, Tzader?"

Catching himself, Tzader said, "Sorry. I'm not used to staying behind."

"I understand, but there is no one I would entrust with Brina's safety, the future heir's safety and the entire Belador power base, but you. As great a warrior as you are, I am the one who has to lead this team. I'm the only one who can teleport a group anywhere."

"I know."

"When did you two intend to tell me about Evalle?" Brina asked, storming into the room and looking like the warrior queen she was even at seven months pregnant.

Tzader muttered, "Fat's in the fire now."

Daegan opened his arms. "Come here, niece." As he hugged her, he said, "'Tis bad manners to eavesdrop, niece."

"I don't care about manners when one of mine is in danger," she replied and stepped out of his embrace, then moved to Tzader's side.

Her future husband kissed her head. "I was going to tell you as soon as we were finished here."

"I should be in this meetin'." Then she flinched and twisted to the side.

"What's wrong?" Tzader demanded.

"This child is practicin' for battle." Shaking it off, Brina placed a hand on her side and asked, "Can you find Evalle through dream walkin'?"

Tzader's face lit up at that thought.

Unfortunately, Daegan had to douse his hope. "No and please do not dream walk while I'm gone. I was able to come to both of you in the dream world before I escaped TÅµr Medb, but no one knew I could reach out that way at the time. Now, anyone who dream walks could be waiting for me, or you. If I were killed or even captured, there would be no one to teleport our team. If anything happened to you in the dream realm, that would leave Brina unprotected."

"You've a good point, uncle."

Anxious to get moving, Daegan said, "I must see Garwyli before I go. I will get word to both of you as soon as I know something."

"Daegan?" Brina said, stopping him from teleporting away.

"Yes?"

"I refuse to have a weddin' without everyone and I mean *everyone*."

"I will do my best, niece."

"No, you will bring her back," Brina clarified, but her words were more worried than demanding.

"I won't return without Evalle." Daegan teleported to the center area of the castle where the entrance met the hallways. For some reason, that seemed to be the best way to find the old druid as opposed to jumping around to hunt him.

"*Garwyli!* Where are you?" Daegan shouted, adding power to his voice.

The old guy stuck his head out of a doorway halfway down the hall on Daegan's left. "Ya coulda just walked ten more steps, dragon."

"Only if I knew you were there."

Shaking the white head of hair that fell well past his shoulders, Garwyli muttered as he stepped out, then tottered down to Daegan. He was missing his cap, but he wore his standard robe. His white beard reached his waist.

"What ails ya, dragon?"

Ignoring the way Garwyli liked to address Daegan, he asked the druid, "Are you making any headway with my family's history?"

"Some, but not so much I would be ravin' about it. We have few history books here and none I would call more than random scribblin'. I do have an idea of where to search next, though."

Daegan didn't have time for one of Garwyli's long-winded visits. "You haven't determined who might have freed Lorwerth from Anwynn or how he showed up in Atlanta with Laochra Fola warriors, have you?" His uncle had been sent to the underworld realm, and he shouldn't have had any way to escape. Someone had bargained to take him out.

"Not yet, but Lorwerth was your father's bastard brother, right?"

"Yes."

"In thinkin' on that, plus the fact that Laochra Fola were created at the same time as the Belador warriors, it comes down to one simple point of origin."

"What are you saying?"

Garwyli's thick white eyebrows lifted. "That knowledge had to come from someone who knew your family history. Start by lookin' at those who were around when your father still lived."

Daegan knew this, but he hadn't really focused specifically on that since so many preternaturals in today's world were a threat. But the old druid made sense.

Based on that, it had to be Macha or Maeve. Both would have that history. Add Cathbad to that list, as he'd been around then, too.

Lifting a wrinkled finger, Garwyli said, "While I've been ponderin' your past—"

In a rush to get out of there, Daegan cut him off. "Do you have anything else that might help me find a missing Belador?"

Garwyli stopped short at that. "Who?"

"Evalle."

"No." The old druid looked shaken. "What can I do to help?"

"Nothing unless you can think of another enemy capable of teleporting and who would do this besides Macha or Maeve."

Shaking his head, he said, "I wish I did."

After the stories Daegan had heard about Evalle and how she'd been misused by Macha, Sen, and others, he wondered if she had any idea how many people stood behind her now.

"I have to go, druid. Please lend a hand to Tzader in watching over my niece and her bairn while I'm gone."

"Of course I will. I have more to tell you—"

"And I do want to hear it, just not yet. I'll return as soon as I can." Daegan teleported away before Garwyli could say another word.

Back in Atlanta, Daegan called out telepathically to his second-in-command. *Tristan, meet me immediately.*

Daegan? Where are you? What's going on?

Daegan gave Tristan his location on the roof of a building in a run-down part of downtown Atlanta where they had met before. No tall buildings stood close enough for anyone to see them blink in and out of sight.

In the next fifteen seconds, Tristan appeared with a shirt slung over his shoulder, hair askew and zipping his pants. Yanking the T-shirt over his head, he ran his hands through his tawny hair, taming it a bit.

"Sorry to disturb you on duty," Daegan said in a wry tone.

"First of all, I didn't shirk my duties. I traded with Evalle. She owed me."

"Sadly, that may be the other way around now."

Tristan hooked his thumbs in the belt loops on his jeans. "Why? What's up?"

Daegan filled him in.

"Fuck me. Storm is going to kill me when he finds out she took my place last night."

That would not help anyone and it brought up the question of whether the attack was meant specifically for Evalle, or for any gryphon.

Daegan ordered, "You will not share that with Storm. He's got a lot to deal with right now without you two tangling. We all need to work together."

"Got it, boss. I'm in no hurry to say a word about that to her mate."

"Our team will be entirely voluntary," Daegan made clear. "Are you saying you do volunteer to join us?"

"Well, yeah." Tristan scrunched his shoulders up, looking uncomfortable. "First of all, I'm your guy. You call. I'm there. In addition to that, Evalle would be jumping to the front of the line for me. I'm not giving her any less."

Here was the young man Daegan had made his *Rí Dtús*, better known as a right-hand man in this era, but Tristan was so much more. He just didn't realize it.

"What are we doing now?" Tristan asked, sounding ready to go on attack.

"Our next stop is visiting a Tribunal."

"You're really a downer today," Tristan grumbled. "Are we going to piss anyone off?"

"Most assuredly."

Tristan grinned. "Fuck yeah, let's do this, world-beater."

Daegan shook his head at the irreverent young man who had yet to truly understand his potential. As an ancient being, Daegan wasn't much for technology, especially when he could normally reach any of his people in the local area telepathically, but Storm was not a telepath as far as Daegan knew.

He instructed Tristan, "Before we go, send a phone message to Storm for me."

Tristan dug out his phone. "You mean a text, right?"

Ignoring Tristan's correction of his terminology, Daegan hurried through a message explaining where he was headed and that it would be a brief meeting.

Tristan typed so fast his fingers blurred. He tucked the phone away and crossed his arms. "Ready for takeoff."

In the next minute, Daegan stood in knee-deep grass at the base of a mountain in North Georgia. "Sen. I have a request."

Tristan appeared and asked, "Can he hear you out here?"

In answer, Sen shimmered into view and demanded in a surly tone, "What do you want?"

Daegan got straight to the point. "I wish to speak with a Tribunal."

"When?"

"Now."

Daegan fought not to smile at the appalled look on Sen's face. The VIPER liaison did not care to be challenged.

Too bad. Daegan didn't care what Sen thought.

"I'll ask if they'll make a time for you, but they're not seeing you this very minute," Sen said, taking a threatening pose with his hands loose.

Daegan made no action of acknowledgement. Instead, he told Sen, "You have one minute to arrange a meeting. When I leave, so will my Beladors and all of our support for VIPER. Be sure to relay that when they finally decide upon a time."

Sen blinked out of existence without another word.

Tristan asked, "Think he's doing what you asked?"

Daegan had no idea. He'd been broken out of TÅµr Medb while still cursed as Maeve's dragon throne, and this new world he'd rejoined had proven to be a curious place. People did not always act as if they understood how close to death they stepped.

Power belched out all around them as Sen appeared.

Tristan pinched his nose. "Ugh. Don't do that so fast. The majik stinks."

Sen sliced a look at Tristan that could cut a man in half. Then he told Daegan, "The Tribunal will see you, but they warn that it had better be worth doing it on short notice."

"What are we waiting for?"

In the next instant, Daegan and Tristan were deposited in the familiar Tribunal setting he recalled from his first visit. Same circular plane of grass beneath their feet. Same endless sky that surrounded them, similar to the glass cover on a snow globe, an odd trinket he'd found in Atlanta.

And the same raised dais with three entities standing upon it.

Unfortunately, one was Loki, the god who lived to create turmoil in all worlds. He had probably only agreed to support Tribunals for the sheer fun of causing chaos.

Next to Loki stood Justitia, goddess of justice, wearing a gold blindfold and simple gown, but holding a set of scales to one side. Assuming the blindfold meant she would not be able to know what happened around her would be foolish.

Daegan had heard plenty about her as a child.

Tinkling sounds came from a lyre Hermes strummed while staring off at nothing with a bored expression. Easy to understand, with the boring music this god played endlessly.

Why was he even in a Tribunal?

He belonged in a king's court as unnoticed entertainment for guests wandering around. Hermes had the face of a god, but he could not hold his own with others like Loki.

Speaking of the trickster god, the last time Daegan had met him in this location Loki had been in a jovial mood. Loki had enjoyed his power play until Daegan pointed out that none of them knew his powerful mother, whose identity he intended to keep secret.

Had been *sworn* to keep secret.

"What is the problem, dragon king?" Loki asked, no patience evident.

"One of my people has been kidnapped in a brutal fashion. I wish to question Macha and Maeve to see if either was involved. Doing that here where they are unable to lie would save everyone time."

"We are not expected to provide for interrogations," Justitia replied, but Loki lifted his hand to request the floor.

Just as Daegan had heard, Justitia missed nothing. She turned her face to Loki with a sour expression on her lips even though she couldn't see his hand. She returned to facing forward and Hermes kept plucking away at his strings.

Loki asked Daegan, "Why should we provide this service for you?"

"Upon VIPER's request, my Beladors have returned to support the coalition's enforcement for the past ten days. From what I understand, the Beladors have provided the largest number of warriors for many years. For that reason alone, my request should be met with the respect it deserves." Allowing a moment for his warning to get through, Daegan continued. "More than that, the time is coming that preternaturals will face exposure to humans. When that happens, you will need us more than ever."

"Too late," Loki countered. "There are reports of humans using their phones to film strange events at two vehicle wrecks in downtown Atlanta. Sen tells us the Beladors are at fault for this, yet you come here demanding our aid."

Tristan murmured, "Sorry."

Daegan would have preferred to be informed on that point before arriving here, but it changed nothing. VIPER would not hold Beladors responsible for incidents out of their control.

They had Sen to clean up things.

Daegan asked, "If that is so, why did your liaison not wipe human minds and destroy electronics that could be replaced? Seems you have the answer to that issue standing here with us."

Sen's power flushed out hard.

Daegan ignored him, keeping his attention on the three gathered on the dais.

Rather than respond to that question, Loki said, "We are busy. What do you want?"

"To locate our missing Belador."

"Who is it?"

By the sly look in Loki's eyes, Daegan knew that the god had been well informed of who was missing. "Evalle Kincaid. If Macha and Maeve play no part in this kidnapping, then they should have no problem saying so."

The irritating god made everyone wait during a long moment of decision simply to insult Daegan, who would never waste time posturing frivolously with Evalle's life at risk.

Casting a smirk in Daegan's direction, Loki said, "Macha refuses to join us. She did ask me to pass along her pleasure at hearing Evalle is captured. Maeve said Cathbad is unavailable and she refuses to join us without him present even though I assured both her and Macha they would face no penalty for agreeing to attend."

Daegan wanted to crush that god. He had not given leave for Loki to allow those goddesses the freedom to come and go if either had committed this crime.

Remaining here would only cost valuable time. Daegan said, "I have a Nightstalker actively searching for details on this kidnapping. He requested that no handshakes be shared with Nightstalkers in Atlanta until he ferrets out every piece of information we need. My Beladors have been ordered to comply until I say otherwise. I suggest you warn others associated with VIPER to also not interfere, as I will be informed immediately." That wouldn't guarantee VIPER stayed out of his way, but agents with any survival instincts would not want a dragon breathing down their necks.

In closing, Daegan said, "Loki, Justitia and Hermes, thank you for the meeting. I will not forget your aid."

They could take that at face value, or read between the lines and hear his anger over their lack of support.

Smiling as if this had turned out better than expected, Loki said, "You're welcome, dragon. Does this mean you'll be gone for some time hunting for the gryphon?"

Daegan gleaned Loki's meaning.

This group of entities thought they saw an opportunity?

Offering a warrior's face in return, Daegan said, "I'm often gone overseeing my Beladors. They are a power to be respected, especially considering our telepathic abilities. My people can reach me anywhere and anytime should they need me."

No exactly true, since even Trey McCree, the most powerful known telepath of the Beladors, could not reach beyond the human realm to a different one other than Treoir.

Daegan doubted Loki believed his bluff, but it might buy him enough time to hunt Evalle and return to the castle before someone teamed up with Macha or Maeve and Cathbad to invade Treoir.

If they made that mistake, they would all pay dearly.

CHAPTER 13

Tuatha Dé Danann

MACHA HELD HIS HEAD AT the juncture of her legs and shook with need only because she didn't want this to end soon. This man had seduced her years ago, confidently stating that he could make her see stars using only his mouth.

He'd made good on that claim more times than she could count before she broke off their arrangement when he overstepped his position.

He had to be driving majik through his tongue, the devil.

No human tongue could plunge that deep inside and emit an electric charge.

But then again, he was not human.

That same tongue had convinced her to bring him back into her world.

She arched two feet into the air off the plush lounger and rode her climax into a bath of stars. Energy spiraled around her in arcs of bright light.

His hands were on her breasts, teasing the hard tips and sending her into another wave of orgasms.

Time had no place in this realm.

She couldn't say if the climax had lasted seconds or hours, but when it was done she slowly floated down and allowed him to enter her.

That had been almost as enjoyable as hearing that Daegan was hunting for Evalle. She loved good news.

Dakkar drew her attention back to him. He had been gifted with beautiful teak skin, dark curly hair and a dick Zeus would envy.

The bounty hunter might have been born this way, but she

doubted it. As a mage, he'd gained a lot of skills and gifts, which put him in a position to run herd over an army of other bounty hunters.

But they weren't Beladors.

Dakkar pumped harder and she enjoyed the feel of him, watching with fascination as he came all on his own. He'd once tried to have her join in his climax, but she'd told him no.

She preferred being a voyeur at this moment.

She didn't want him to ever think these couplings had deep meaning.

As an immortal, she'd had many lovers over the years. He would one day be replaced by another, but it would not be easy. Dakkar had become her favorite lover of recent times.

He should live another sixty or seventy years. With his majik, he would not age beyond the way he looked right now until his majik gave out.

Dakkar expected her to make him immortal before that time.

He didn't understand that even if she were to consider keeping him longer, it wasn't as if she could use a majik wand to accomplish such a change.

While she resided in this realm, she had to abide by a few rules. One had to do with turning anyone immortal. To accomplish such a goal, she'd either have to bring in a god with whom she held favor who would assist her or ... gain access to the river of immortality beneath Treoir Castle.

Finished, Dakkar caught his breath, slid over to the side and propped his head, gazing at her. His eyes held so much sensual interest.

She wished she could care for someone the way he seemed to care for her, but she'd left that woman behind long ago. Today's Macha had bigger goals than to gain the love of any man.

"What are you thinking, dove?"

Now was the time to smile and seduce him with her charm so that he would continue to find ways to keep her happy. "Just thinking how it would be nice to keep you forever."

He tried to hide his thrill at that suggestion, but Dakkar's longing sparked at his favorite topic. "Nothing would make me happier than to be the companion you deserve for the rest of eternity. I would do all in my power to give you anything you desired."

Eternity with one man? One who was not even a god?

She managed not to shudder at that thought. A few hundred years perhaps.

She'd wanted one male forever, but he'd taught her that to care so deeply had been a dangerous mistake.

Giving him a treat, she said, "I do love the ways you find to make me happy."

While toying with her hair, Dakkar said, "Like when I took Lorwerth to Atlanta and forced a red dragon into the open?"

That might not be the best thing to remind her of, since he had failed to kill Daegan. "Not the first thing that comes to mind since Daegan still breathes."

"I know, dove, but I told you it would take time. If you'd gift me the ability to teleport, I could do so much more for you now."

She refrained from answering.

Dropping his head down, he covered one of her breasts with his mouth. That gifted tongue sent a sizzle of desire to her womb and dragged a gasp from her.

Lifting his head, he eased over the top of her and pushed inside her, ready to go again. "I am your slave in all ways."

She pointed out, "I have made it simple for you to visit me here. That should be enough."

His smile faltered and so did his erection.

This would be a poor time for her to smile.

Regardless, she would have if not for needing this man to destroy Daegan, as Maeve should have. That stupid cow had allowed Daegan to live all these years, then Macha's own Beladors freed him.

Hard for her to decide which one she wanted to hurt more, Maeve or Daegan.

Poor Dakkar waited for some sign of encouragement.

She had the perfect idea. "Kill the dragon and I'll give you the gift of teleportation."

He turned hard as a chair leg. "Not to sound ungrateful, but would not the dragon's death be worth more?"

Well, wasn't he the confident one? "Such as?"

"We often speak of my becoming immortal," he said.

She silently corrected him. *He* often spoke of joining the ranks of gods, but Dakkar could be the very person to accomplish killing Daegan. She didn't exactly have warriors standing in line who were willing to go after a two-thousand-year-old dragon.

And if Dakkar did succeed, Daegan would be out of the way so that Macha could take control of Treoir again.

She'd never accessed the river of immortality running beneath the castle, simply because King Gruffyn had warned her only a Treoir could summon the river, which remained otherwise invisible. He'd gone on and on about the rules of turning anyone immortal, but she'd glazed over at that point. The fewer immortals around, the better for her.

With access to that river once again in the future, she'd simply hold someone hostage until Brina did her bidding. The one time Macha had seen the river's powers used, Brina's father had summoned the river to give Tzader's father immortality.

Macha had allowed Tzader's father, upon his death, to pass that immortality to his son. All of that had worked perfectly for Macha's plans at the time.

This new plan had true potential and Dakkar was overly motivated. Wouldn't Daegan's death be fun?

It would also mean snatching him from Maeve's reach.

Macha cautioned, "If I agree to gift you immortality—"

"And teleportation," Dakkar interjected, losing points for doing so.

She gave him a withering look and continued, "As I said, if I agree, you must prove you killed him to claim your gift."

His cunning eyes twinkled with delight. "If I bring you an entire dragon body, what would you do with it?"

Lifting a shoulder in dismissal, she said, "I'd create a hundred pairs of red dragon-skin boots."

Throwing back his head, he laughed, then brought that mouth back down to her other breast and stoked a new surge of energy racing over her skin.

Yes, she would keep this one as long as she continued to be entertained.

She did appreciate the level of confidence he showed over the idea of destroying a dragon.

Dakkar lifted his head and said, "Every bit of information will help me to serve you better. Tell me again about the time of dragons and King Gruffyn."

"Not that again."

"Why not?"

"That was when I ruled Treoir with no interference." She hated thinking about good times. She preferred only to experience them.

"Come on, dove. Let's plan your return to Treoir then. When Daegan is gone, no one will ever enter that realm unless you allow it."

She studied him closely. "You seem very sure of yourself."

"I am. You should know me well enough by now to realize I have not been idle when I am not with you."

That sounded as if he already had a plan of action in motion.

What had her arrogant bounty hunter been up to?

Moving his hips to renew her interest in another round of sex, he whispered, "When you take possession of Treoir again, I will be there to help you fill it with your followers and you'll never need to deal with VIPER, Daegan or humans again."

He spoke as a peer, which he would never be, but she would allow him to dream for now. What harm could there be in seeing just what he had to offer?

CHAPTER 14

QUINN WALKED TO THE BALCONY of the midtown condominium in Atlanta that he'd arranged for Reese and Phoedra, his thirteen-year-old daughter.

That wasn't exactly true.

Reese had refused to move the two of them to the luxury unit, which he'd pulled markers to have ready for occupancy in less than a day. She declared she would not aid him in pushing Phoedra to move. He was on his own to explain to his child why they were being forced to make the change.

That's when he'd taken a breath and a step back.

Yes, he'd been angry. Hurt more than anything, but this father business meant not storming in to have his way. He was learning and determined to excel at the most important job of his life.

Once he accepted that Reese would be one of the more difficult opponents he'd ever negotiated with, he'd bowed to her terms. He supplied her and Phoedra with a real estate agent who would chauffer them around to review what was available.

In hindsight, he admitted to himself he had been overbearing. What could he say? His heart had wanted Phoedra with him and overruled his good sense.

He was not happy about his daughter living with Reese instead of him, but she had known his daughter for the past two years. Quinn had just recently met Phoedra for the first time. The girl had been born in secret and watched over by a guardian whose identity neither Reese nor Phoedra would share.

Since Phoedra's mother, Kizira, had been a Medb priestess who had hidden their child from her coven, Quinn had no doubt said guardian was a preternatural.

Phoedra trusted Reese, who had proven she would put her life between his daughter and danger.

Damn, that didn't make him any happier. He didn't want either to be harmed. Once again, Quinn reminded himself he had to be patient and earn his place in Phoedra's life. She'd only recently learned the truth about him and her mother.

He had fallen for Kizira when they were both very young, before he found out Kizira belonged to the Beladors' greatest enemy.

Talk about a clusterfuck relationship between a powerful Belador and a Medb priestess. Failure had been in the stars from the beginning.

Quinn might *never* have known he had a daughter, had Kizira not died in his arms with her last request being that he find the girl. It pained him that he'd missed his daughter's childhood. He could not change the past, only do his best to provide a stable and loving future. It also troubled him that Reese was more a parent to his daughter than he was at this point. Understandable since Phoedra had known Reese when they both lived on the West Coast, and loved Reese. Phoedra barely knew him.

In fact, he'd known Reese longer than he'd known Phoedra. His feelings ran deep for Reese, but they had a complicated relationship, too.

Two screwed up relationships with nonhuman women.

What was the common denominator? Him.

Reese padded out to the balcony and turned to lean her back against the railing. "What's so important you had to bribe Phoedra with a new Xbox game to get her out of the room?"

He took in the city of Atlanta, which stretched beyond this thirty-eighth floor residence like an urban landscape painted with a vibrant mix of green splashes. "I did not bribe my daughter. I want to make her feel like any other thirteen-year-old girl, even though most others have never been through all that she has."

"She's tough and resilient. She's adapting well," Reese said in a consoling voice.

She had a way of making him feel like he was doing right by Phoedra even though he hadn't reached a close bond yet.

As if reading his mind, Reese said, "It takes time, Quinn."

"Seems that's the one commodity I haven't been able to gain and develop."

She gave him an odd look. "Something's wrong, isn't it?"

"Yes. I might as well get to the point. Evalle has been captured."

Reese stood away from the rail. "The Medb grabbed her?"

"Possibly, but they're not the only ones at the top of our list." He explained what he'd learned about the incredible wreck and the planning it had taken to disarm Evalle. "We believe she was teleported away."

"What are we waiting for?" Reese asked, incredulous.

There was the warrior woman who had taken hold of his heart, but that was before he found out she'd been withholding information on Phoedra. They'd had words and were managing a peaceful truce now so Quinn could see his child, but he itched to hold Reese as well.

Pulling his attention from the dazzling blue of her eyes, he said, "Daegan is pulling together a team. We leave very soon."

She walked past him, nibbling on her fingernail.

Quinn turned to follow Reese with his gaze as she moved around. The woman could not be still, but he found the constant motion pleasant to observe.

Angling around, she said, "What do you need? You wouldn't be here if you didn't need something."

Talk about insulting. "That's not true."

She held up a hand to stop him. "Wait. That sounded better in my head, but it was shorthand thinking. I don't mean for Phoedra or me, I mean aren't you here to find out how I can help you with Evalle?"

Explanation accepted, Quinn said, "I would not ask if it were not very important."

"I know that." She gave him a testy look. "What's the plan?"

"I want you to know that I will not think less of you if you refuse my request."

She put her hands on her hips. "I'm a big girl, Quinn. Tell me what you need and I'll make up my mind."

Reese was no girl, but a woman. Not the place to let his mind wander at the moment. He said, "As I mentioned, we're forming a small tactical team. I'd like you to visit the crash site. You've told me your gift of remote viewing doesn't work when someone travels to another world, but if you came with us you might be of aid at a different location along the way. We have no idea where this trip will take us, but if at any moment I feel you are in danger, I would have you teleported home immediately."

Her hands slid down to hang loose. She appeared to be studying hard on his words. "Okay, I'm in, but what about Phoedra?"

His chest eased with her acceptance. "I have a plan for Phoedra."

"Now wait a minute. This isn't some screwed-up way of moving her to your place, is it?"

Don't shout at Reese. Quinn took a moment and spoke slowly to keep from yelling at her. "No. I have not behaved in any underhanded way this entire time."

She looked properly chastised. "I wasn't accusing you—"

"Yes, you were. You're just waiting for me to do something to force Phoedra to live with me. I'd love to have my daughter in my home, but only if she chooses to make that move. Until then, I'm playing by everyone else's rules."

Blowing out a hard breath, she said, "Okay, fine. I admit, I was worried you were going to do that. But you tried to move us out of our first apartment without asking first."

"You two chose this place."

"Only after you forced the issue."

This woman could irritate him if he was in a coma. Straining not to snap at her, he reminded her, "I agreed to this arrangement of Phoedra living with you, but I was not able to sleep at night when I felt my daughter was staying somewhere I considered unsafe and without the level of security I require for myself. You got your way and I am at ease now. The security here is five times greater than where you had her."

"Hold it, bud. I didn't choose that first place."

No, and she refused to tell him who had been pulling strings for Phoedra over the years, which included placing Phoedra and Reese in a substandard location.

To be fair, their first apartment hadn't been the ghetto, but he could not live in finer accommodations while his child did not. With a quick glance, Quinn gave Reese credit for furnishing the new unit in a comfortably casual way, and she'd failed to spend a third of the money he'd made available for their needs.

He told her, "Since you didn't choose that other apartment either, you should be glad for the change. For one thing, you are safer here. I have a contingent of Beladors to protect both of you."

Her eyes fired up. "Hey, I'm not complaining about this place. I was only stating that you have a habit of demanding your way.

Phoedra and I have existed for years in situations that were not of our choosing. We both want the chance to *choose*."

That sounded perfectly fair, but by constantly questioning everything he said or did, Reese had pissed him off after he'd bent to meet her halfway more times than not recently. He said, "You may make any choice you wish, but Phoedra is my child. Until she's capable of protecting herself, I will provide for and protect her in the best way I know how."

"Fine."

That evil female word. It was not fine, but Reese appeared ready to throw in the proverbial towel on this one.

Running a hand through his hair, he said, "I don't want to fight with you, Reese."

"Me neither. So, what's your plan for Phoedra while we're gone?"

He explained how Storm had his building warded for a preternatural apocalypse and that Kit would be staying there. Storm had called to share that new development just before Quinn knocked on Reese's door.

She asked, "Who's Kit?"

"Can I explain that on the way over to Storm's building?"

"Oh. I get it. We need to get rolling." Just like that, Reese went from arguing to action.

Those were the times he took a moment to enjoy the whirlwind of energy known as Reese.

The sound of a microwave running in the kitchen had Quinn turning. He walked over to see what Phoedra was up to and inhaled a deep breath of popcorn.

Had his daughter heard that entire exchange? With her odds at having preternatural hearing, she most likely had.

Reese had taken steps to the right as if to grab something off the sofa, but spun around and raced past him down the hallway.

"Reese?" he called out.

"Packing," she shouted without turning around, and slammed a door.

Phoedra appeared in the entrance to the kitchen with a worried look on her face.

"Something smells good, sweetheart," Quinn started in a happy tone he would always have ready for her. "Do you like your—"

"Oh, uh, sorry, be right back."

He leaned over to watch her run down the same hall to Reese's room. "What's going on, you two?"

Phoedra paused at the door with guilt splashed all over her face. "Helping her pack."

Quinn didn't require Storm's gift of ferreting out a lie to know his daughter had not told the truth.

CHAPTER 15

THE THIRD TIME EVALLE CAME to from a hallucinogenic
dream, she screamed, "*Stop! It!*"

The dream had started as sexy as the last two, but this one
ended with Storm being yanked up on his feet and his head cut
off in front of her. His blood had gushed all over her naked body
and she couldn't get to him.

She'd tried to stay awake, but loss of blood and the inability to
heal had wiped out her endurance. She'd had three dreams in the
same span of hours. The emotional toll was becoming worse than
her physical injuries.

Still shackled to the wall, she called out in a weak, raspy voice,
"Germanus."

No one answered her.

She leaned back against the wall. She couldn't have gotten to
her feet even if she'd been free to do so. Her energy reserve was
nonexistent.

When holding her head up became too much effort, she let it
hang down. Her gaze landed on the dried blood that had seeped
through from her chest wound, but it no longer oozed.

Who cared?

Wind rushed around the room.

She lifted her gaze to Germanus.

He said nothing for probably five minutes. "If you are ready to
speak without shouting, we'll continue our conversation."

Too tired to argue, she just stared at him and let him figure out
what that meant.

Lifting his hands to clasp them, he smiled. "Excellent. First rule
is that I will not induce those images if you do not give me reason
to do so. Next, you should know that I can also bring Storm here.
I have not done so because I can see how this would take longer if

your mate was around to encourage you to fight back even at the risk of losing his life. Also, you would probably make constant attempts at escape."

She struggled not to throw up at the thought of Storm being in this hellhole with her.

"Just because I have not chosen to capture Storm yet, does not mean I don't have the option," Germanus went on. "I know all about your life and have access to everyone in it."

She considered his words. Everyone back in Atlanta from Storm to Tzader, Quinn and Daegan would be hunting her. Storm would keep those in the building safe and the Beladors would protect the others.

What about Adrianna?

Had Germanus captured her, too?

Licking her dry lips, Evalle asked, "Who else is here with me?"

"No one. I need only you."

She allowed herself a moment of relief at that, if he was telling the truth. Forcing words past her parched throat, she asked, "What do you want me to do?"

"Ah, yes. We finally reach the point of cooperation."

Really? He thought this was a voluntary situation?

Evidently so, because he carried on as if she'd agreed. "You will need to continue healing, but only to the point that you are able to shift and function."

Good. Shifting would help her heal faster, but he had to be a fool to allow her the ability to fly away.

Unless he had some crazy-ass power to stop her.

"What exactly do you want from me?" she asked.

"Once you're ready, you'll need to be in gryphon form. I will explain more as you are prepared, but first you must heal further."

Experiencing a moment of hope at the idea of healing, she suggested, "If you let me shift, I'll heal faster and save you time."

He actually seemed pleased at that idea, the fool. He said, "If that is what you wish to do."

Before she could ask anything else, the shackles clicked open.

She slowly brought her arms forward, clenching her eyes shut to stem the tears threatening to pour. It hurt so much she could hardly breathe. When she finally wrapped her good arm across her chest, she moved one leg.

The crooked one wouldn't bend.

Sighing loudly to emphasize his impatience, Germanous held out his hand.

She was not accepting it.

Then he lifted his hand. As he did that, her body rose from the floor until her legs dangled beneath her. The broken one flopped and a stab of pain ran up her leg.

She cursed.

Moving his free hand, he flicked it at one wall and a door appeared.

Had that been there all along but hidden from view? Maybe he hadn't teleported in. Dragging her along kinetically, he stepped out of the room and walked down a long hall.

Where were his guards? Didn't he have any?

It wasn't until he'd ascended three sets of stairs to a much brighter area that Evalle saw any other life form.

But the light was the greater threat. "Germanus, no sunlight unless you want roasted gryphon."

"You will not be harmed. It is twilight."

Two gargoyles, ten feet tall and looking like there'd been a T-Rex somewhere in their background, stood next to an arched opening. They had the same Celtic dragon shape burned into their chests that she'd seen on the clothes Germanus wore.

Ouch.

Just as he'd said, light from post-sunset skies filled the opening. She'd be concerned that since she brought it up, Germanus would now threaten her with death by sunlight, but it seemed he already knew that about her.

He knew too much. Who was this man and what was he doing?

Medieval style weapons decorated the stone walls and vintage rugs covered the slate floors. Windows had no glass. Nothing about this place said twenty-first century.

Germanus lived in a castle.

Was she in Scotland or Germany?

Evalle couldn't wrap her head around any of this.

As their boss approached, the gargoyles quietly studied what Germanus dragged along on an invisible leash.

She could only imagine how vulnerable she had to appear right now. For the time being, she had to button down her urge to snap at him if he was going to allow her to shift and heal.

Let her regain her strength and he'd face a beast unlike anything he could imagine.

Once that happened, she'd figure out what to do next.

Outside the building, lush green land stretched forever toward majestic, snow-capped mountains. She should have spent more time studying geography instead of reading about mythology and watching NASCAR.

No, she cherished her time with Feenix, who was a huge racing fan.

Her heart ached at thinking about Feenix.

He had to know something was up when she hadn't returned by daylight. Storm would keep her baby safe, but he'd have a hard time explaining what was going on without upsetting the little gargoyle.

Germanus would deserve every bit of payback she could come up with once she was free.

The sun was nowhere to be found, but darkness did not seem to be falling. Just a greenish-golden hue to everything. The closer he took her to the edge of the roof, if this area of the castle was called a roof, the more she realized the structure had been built on the side of a mountain.

A thousand feet down, the stone face of the mountain fell away to a valley of grass that swayed in the slightest wind. Beyond that open space, trees filled a stretch that led to a lake in the distance.

A mix of yellow, blue, purple, white and red dotted the valley floor.

Flowers, leafed-out trees and green grass? Would everything be blooming now in northern Europe, or was this castle somewhere closer to the equator? She really had to work on her knowledge of other countries. In her country, the northern states had just suffered a late-spring snowstorm.

What place could she be that was so remote she didn't even see roads?

She had no idea, but this was a perfect spot for someone like Germanus to hide what he was doing, and maybe even let preternatural beasts like those gargoyles fly without being seen. Who tended the castle? Where were people? Maybe he used his majik to prevent humans from coming too close, but ... that was more power than she could wrap her head around.

Looking out over the beautiful land, she felt the first trickle of true belief that she could escape.

Germanus paused near the edge, moving his hands to position her close to it. "You may shift and fly. Do not attempt to fly away. You will not be successful."

Could he have warded an area this massive?

She didn't care what he'd done. She got ready to call up her beast and turn into a gryphon.

Daegan had given her permission to do so when she'd battled alongside him in the human world. If the Tribunal found out that she'd shifted, she had no doubt in her mind that Daegan would back her up and claim she had a right to save herself.

It was nice to have a true ruler who would fight for his people.

Changing shape strained every muscle.

By the time she felt the full extent of her gryphon, she was exhausted. She probably should have healed a bit first before trying to change, but she had no idea if Germanus would allow her to shift again.

Her body would have to keep up.

Now was the time to find out what power she had available.

After the slowest shift in history, she stood, but kept weight off the broken rear leg, which was fairly useless. The crooked leg kept trying to heal ... but it would not mend straight. Lowering it to the ground to take some of her weight, she tested her pain level. Tolerable in this form, but she could only use that limb as a prop. If she had a patch over one eye, she could be a peg-legged gryphon pirate.

She dipped her large eagle-shaped head down to peer at the damaged leg to get a better view of just how crippled her gryphon would be.

When she turned her gryphon gaze to Germanus, he explained, "I could break the bones again to allow that limb to heal properly, but you will be able to move around in human form with one good leg, and it may prevent you from being foolish."

Would he think chomping down on his head was foolish?

She gave serious thought to trying it, but he wouldn't have allowed her to shift if there was any chance of her attacking him successfully. She couldn't speak in this form except telepathically with another Belador, Brina or Daegan, but she could glare her disgust.

Undaunted by a gryphon giving him the evil eye, he said, "If you feel able to fly, you may fly for ... this long." Another hourglass appeared above his open hand and flipped to start timing. "It is half of one human hour. Do not waste your time."

Enough interacting with him.

She had to determine her next move.

Evalle's gryphon hobbled to the edge and looked over the side where the land was way, way down. Could she fly for sure? She moved her wings out and up, then down, testing them. Some bones in one wing were still mending, but the major ones seemed able to function.

He was going to allow her to fly untethered?

She didn't feel any majik wrapped around her neck or legs.

It was now or never. Dropping down on her three strong legs, she shoved up, flapping her wings, and leaped over the side.

Her huge gryphon body dropped like a rock in a pond.

She kept flapping harder until she felt her wings finally catch air. Halfway down, still beating like a crazy, overgrown bird, she lifted slowly and took aim at the clouds.

Air swept across her eagle head and heat left from the sun warmed her feathers. Her aches and pains had not vanished, but diminished beneath the exhilaration of flying.

For that one moment, she enjoyed peace.

Gliding back and forth, she banked and flew as if testing her strength, when in truth each move took her further from Germanus and his castle.

From a distance, the stones used to build it seemed to sparkle as if cut from unusual rock. The gargoyles had joined Germanus at the top of the castle, standing like two deadly guards.

With a return of even limited strength, her mind cleared to calculate her escape. Another man had delivered Evalle to Germanus. She still recalled the kidnapper saying, "He is definitely hunting it."

That *it* had to be her, right?

Dismissing that as unimportant, she came up with one thing that mattered.

If Germanus had to send someone to kidnap her, then he had a weakness of some sort. Otherwise, why had he not gone for her himself?

He'd said she couldn't escape.

What could stop her?

Time to find out.

Evalle continued to fly back and forth, continuing to gradually widen the distance from Germanus and his castle. On the next bank to her right, she looked back to see his tiny form still standing as if unconcerned.

She could taste freedom.

Arrogance had taken down the mighty more than once.

Being preternatural did not equal being intelligent. Germanus could be yet another example of how criminals were often idiots.

Straightening out her flight path, she made up her mind to find out just how much luck she had today. But what felt like longer than a half hour had passed and she had not gotten any closer to the mountains. The distance must be further than she'd estimated.

She had a serious problem. Her stamina was waning.

She couldn't keep flapping at this pace much longer.

Would Germanus expect her to be too weak? Had that been his plan? To let her wear herself out, then recapture her?

She finally turned in a large circle and glided down to where she could land. Normally, she could set down gracefully, but she'd forgotten her damaged limb.

The jar from taking her gryphon weight streaked pain up her right rear leg.

Dropping to the ground to allow all her legs to rest, she searched in every direction beyond the castle.

How could this place be so remote? There had to be locations like this in the world, but traveling had never been an option for her beyond what she could do at night.

She had no idea what else the world offered beyond initially being trained in Alaska and being assigned to the southwest region of the country for a brief stint. Then she'd met Tzader and Quinn, who moved her to Atlanta. Best friends ever.

During her flight, she'd been so busy working her way out from the castle, she hadn't searched for any other sign of life.

Now she noticed the quiet around her. Too quiet.

This was not the time to quit. That flight had drained her, but she had to go on.

Searching all around, she sensed no sign of a ward. Nothing majikal to prevent her escape. Germanus clearly thought to allow her enough freedom to tire herself out, then send his gargoyles after her.

She was ready to take on those gargoyles, who had no similarity to her sweet Feenix.

Sucking in huge breaths, she lifted up and felt every ache and pain from the battering her body had taken. Her poor body was exhausted. She could rest later.

With a couple of limping steps forward, she growled with determination then leaped into the air, flapping fast to gain altitude again.

Her wings were beginning to feel like rubber.

This time she went higher to locate a thermal where she could fly longer without expending so much energy. After becoming a gryphon, she'd studied all she could about birds and flight.

Up high and coasting, she mentally patted herself on the back for a good plan until she took stock of her position. Those mountains in the distance appeared just as far away as they had back at the castle.

It would be nice to ask someone for directions.

Wait a minute! She could use her telepathy to reach Beladors anywhere in the world, maybe even that powerhouse Trey. She called out telepathically, *This is Evalle Kincaid of the American Beladors. If you hear me, please answer.*

Nothing.

Her heart thumped with a rush of excitement. Some Belador had to hear her.

She kept calling out as she glided toward the mountains and started asking for anyone who could hear her to contact Trey McCree via telepathy or the phone number she included. Being the most powerful telepath Evalle knew of made Trey the best choice for contact. She had no idea where Quinn was, but knew he'd be hunting her, and she would hope that Tzader remained on Treoir for the obvious reasons.

A roaring sound broke into her thoughts.

She banked to the left to see behind her.

The sky was dark with flying beasts. Not just gargoyles. There had to be thirty winged creatures. All of them huge and heading for her.

Her stomach dropped. She turned and flapped like a mad gryphon trying to reach the mountains.

Screw it. She swept around to the right and saw miles of grass, trees and maybe a river, but the view in that direction seemed to be infinite. Swinging back the other way, she found the same. The mountains continued in both directions, too.

Deep calls and growls from the flying beasts closed in.

Her heart thumped with a flood of adrenaline.

She turned back for the nearest mountain and doubled down, flying harder.

A shadow fell over her from above.

She looked up to see the underbellies of both gargoyles. Those two were even more gargantuan in flight than standing inside the castle.

She did her best to fly like a fighter pilot, dipping and angling one way, then another.

One of the gargoyles did an impossible turn in midair and dove for her.

She rolled away, but he dragged a claw down her back. Fire raced through the new wounds. Something else hit her from the other side, sending her into a cartwheel spin.

Noise from the rest of the living squadron grew louder. She got smacked again, knocking her out of the roll and sending her spiraling down. Straining, she beat her wings mercilessly and pulled up just before hitting the ground.

But she had nothing left in the engine to fight the many flying beasts now circling her.

Setting her wings, she glided to the ground and made another rough landing. Her gryphon body slid on her chest this time, banging up her wings. Why hadn't she healed more during this flight? Her back felt flayed open. When she finally stopped, she spit out a beak full of dirt and grass, then just stayed flat on the ground, breathing hard.

The thumps of other heavy landings surrounded her.

When she could manage it, she pushed her body up using her wings and had to sit on the ground with her crooked back leg sticking out to the side.

Just beyond the circle of beasts, she noticed a massive carcass. Possibly a wyvern, based on its shape, similar to dragon but with only two legs. The body appeared to be charred black on the inside while the remaining skin was nothing more than a layer of boils. Ew.

Both gargoyles landed as a perfectly trained pair, then one dropped a shoulder and Germanus slid off to the ground.

He walked over to her, shaking his head. "You can't blame me for this. I told you not to try, but figured we had to get this out of the way."

Despair seeped into Evalle's mental fortress, doing its best to knock down defenses that already felt puny as a toothpick structure. She fought back, forcing herself not to give in even if she was defeated for the moment. He had no idea who he was dealing with now that she'd healed a bit.

Of course, her body didn't feel too great at the moment.

"Shift to your human form, Evalle."

She intended to defy him, but her body clearly didn't care what she thought because it started shifting.

How could he make her do that?

Bones, skin and muscle went into action ... everything felt twisted, yanked and pulled through a grinder. As her human shape finished forming, blood ran down her back. She tried calling up her beast to heal it, but all she got was a weak trickle of energy.

Nothing made sense to her anymore.

The pale brown sack dress covered her again. Was that for her benefit? Why would he care?

She swayed in place, depleted of what renewed energy she'd enjoyed for a short time. What happened to having more power as an Alterant and gryphon?

She lifted her hands.

Germanus warned, "No. Use your kinetics against me without my permission and it will strike back at you twofold."

Truth or not? She hadn't intended to attack him out here where she was outnumbered, only to raise her hands in question, but she lowered them now.

Germanus stood there with his thumb and forefinger stroking his chin while he studied her. "That was not bad. Better than I had thought you'd do with the damage you had to repair. This may go more quickly than I'd hoped."

"What do you want, Germanus?" She opened her arms, outward this time so he could not mistake her intention. "It had better be worth bringing down the Beladors and our dragon king on your head, not to mention my mate who will be worse to face than all of them together. Storm *will* find me. When he does, there will be no stopping him from killing you."

She believed that and had to keep reminding herself or she'd go mad.

"You can't leave me, Evalle."

"Was doing a pretty good job of it until I got tired," she quipped, just to tweak his nose.

"If you could teleport out, you would have already tried, but I was told that you do not possess that ability. That should clear up any ideas you have for escape or anyone unwanted showing up."

Despair turned into a cold lump of fear in her stomach. "What are you talking about?"

"I should probably have told you this sooner, but I wanted you to get any rebellious urges out of your blood. You are in the realm of Scamall. You cannot leave. Daegan would be wise to avoid a place where the god who created this realm can destroy that dragon. Never forget that I am the powerful one here. Even if the dragon does come, it will not matter who he brings. If the dragon does not come, not even your Skinwalker mate can track you to this realm."

All hope died with his words.

No one was ever coming for her.

Storm would have no way to find her without the emerald chakra stone, and even that would not work with them in two different realms.

CHAPTER 16

Himalayas north of Nepal

CATHBAD FELT CHILLY AIR BRUSH his skin as his teleportation ended on a cliff overlooking snowcapped mountains of the Himalayas.

Even in the middle of night with not a human light to be seen, snow glowed beneath a full moon shining across the spectacular landscape.

No sign of human life as far as the eye could see.

Some parts of the human world still held pleasure for him. He had always enjoyed his time in this remote area. With his body now properly outfitted with snow boots, thick clothing and a heavy fur cape, he turned from the vista.

Taking in the face of this peak that rose into the clouds, he moved his hand and kinetically forced a huge boulder to grind aside. The massive stone kept any unlikely human who showed up from discovering his secret cavern.

The ward he'd left in place discouraged his guest from leaving.

With the stone displaced far enough to allow him passage, he entered carefully and listened for any sign of life.

Nothing moved.

Strolling down the tunnel as it curved from side to side in its descent, he finally reached the last major arc before his path straightened, ending in a sparkling room fit for a queen, right down to royal seating. It was as though a mythical artist had gathered piles of brilliant sapphires, mixed them with ice to form one piece, then sculpted that into a throne. Elaborately decorated trunks overflowing with gold coins, goblets, furniture, jewelry, more than most people could imagine, stood in a glowing pile. He had to tilt his head back to view it.

A king's treasure.

Or to be more accurate, he should say a queen's.

He noted that everything appeared unharmed, which encouraged him. He'd expected the place to be demolished from a fit of rage.

Perhaps that would bode well for his visit.

Still, nothing made a sound.

He walked slowly toward the center of an area that stretched a hundred feet across and deep. The seventy-foot-wide, half-frozen pond in the very middle lay quiet, with a glass-smooth surface.

Beneath the surface, the water dropped three hundred feet.

The air stilled with a frozen tenseness.

As he lifted his head to peer at the soaring ceiling, fire lashed down from above.

Cathbad teleported away in a blink, before the blaze struck the empty spot he'd vacated. He reappeared on top of the thirty-foot-tall pile of precious metals and spectacular jewels.

Glowing red sparks sizzled where he had been standing.

Adjusting his position until he was comfortable, he sat with his elbows propped on his knees and looked up.

Diaphanous-blue and pearl-white scales covered the silvery skin of a dragon, now clearly evident where she had sucked up against the ceiling.

Cathbad asked, "You miss me, my sweet?"

With a massive flap of her wings, she lunged away from the top of the cavern and swooped down across the pond, dipping a wing to make a tight circle, and landing on the opposite side of the frozen water from him.

Rising fifteen feet tall, with wings open as if ready to attack, the dragon posed as a gigantic, elegant beast. One Cathbad had kept here for the past two thousand years.

She did have reason to take issue with him for locking her underneath the water all these centuries, but she was also alive today because of him.

Everything came with a price.

She would soon learn his.

Rumbling sounded deep inside the dragon before a puff of blue-gray smoke swirled from her nostrils. Diamond pupils in her serpent eyes speared him with anger yet to be released.

"Have you not tried to shift your shape yet?" Cathbad asked.

He'd been hoping she'd figured out how to do that during his absence. He knew from reincarnating into a world unlike the one he'd left two millennia back that she would be disoriented.

Thankfully, her line of dragons had not possessed teleportation ability like Daegan of Treoir. Cathbad had found that flaw disconcerting when he first decided to keep a dragon for himself, but now he was glad for the power he held over her.

She needed to realize he was not her enemy.

Still no response beyond her steely death glare.

He said, "I have something interestin' to tell you, but I wish to talk with you in human form."

Hatred burned so vividly in her gaze, her eyes should be shooting flames.

He kept up the calm discourse. "Surely you must be ready to leave this cave."

Finally, the hatred dropped a notch to mere disgust.

He chuckled. "I have waited as long as you have for this day. The difference is that I can teleport away and wait another thousand years."

That struck home.

Her shoulders lowered and she tucked her wings around her body, but still she remained in dragon form.

He had one last idea that might force her to call up her power to shift.

"When last we met, Brynhild, you regained consciousness for only seconds, but long enough for you to accept my offer of livin'. You did so because you had one goal you wished to fulfill before you died." That was as good a version of the actual events as she needed at the moment.

He continued, "I recently met with the dragon known as Daegan. Ya do recall the only son and dragon heir of King Gruffyn who ruled the Treoir power, don't ya?"

Her eyes filled with interest.

About time. Cathbad explained, "Daegan lives in today's world and rules as a mighty king over Treoir Island with an army of Beladors at his disposal, who jump to fulfill his every wish. Women fall to their knees in front of him. He ... "

The dragon lifted her head and roared in fury. Fire spiked straight up and spread over the ceiling. Stalactites melted and dropped straight down, followed by water from melted ice.

Cathbad pointed his finger up to form an invisible shield over his body.

His patience was rewarded as the fit of anger passed and energy swirled around the glistening wings. She began to shrink. Muscles twisted shorter and bones popped with the first change she'd managed in thousands of years.

He flinched at the crack of one particularly noisy bone as it reshaped.

That had to be painful after so many years.

When it was all said and done, an exotic female beauty stood with silvery-white hair flowing long past her shoulders. Her hair acted much like a glass prism, changing to electric colors as the strands reflected light.

A god of lust had crafted that shapely body.

Cathbad suffered a rare moment of empathy when he realized she had yet to clothe herself. He flicked his fingers at her, though she could do it herself once she remembered. She hadn't been known as the strongest of the ice dragons, but others in her bloodline had possessed the kind of majikal ability required to call up clothing.

A gown of spun gold covered her, hugging the tall shape and sliding erotically over her truly spectacular curves.

Not that he had any qualms about observing a beautiful naked female, but he had more in store for this one than a sexy interlude.

The sooner he managed to calm her, the sooner they could get started. He'd once thought having a dragon when he reincarnated would be of great value. Then he'd awoken to find himself in a modern world where dragons were myths.

He might not have brought Brynhild out of her deep sleep if Maeve had not shown signs of mental deterioration, which was dangerous with someone who possessed her level of power.

The last time Maeve had a meltdown in a Tribunal, he accepted that something would have to change soon.

Having a dragon shifter at his side would make that change smoother for him.

"Feeling better?" he asked Brynhild.

After a sweeping look down her body, she lifted her gaze to him but did not answer. Crossing her arms in front of her chest, she whipped them away with a broad stroke. Her hair immediately shifted into a mass of finger-thick braids that swirled in and out as they covered her head in an attractive pattern.

One long ponytail fell free and swooped over her shoulder, ending just short of her waist. The gown vanished, replaced by black armor with her family's dragon emblem engraved in silver, finished off by silvery-blue and black metallic boots with matching arm gauntlets, no doubt of an impenetrable material.

Same as the rest of her armor.

Black kohl outlined her eyes and thick lashes hovered low, issuing a visual threat. Her lovely mouth remained pursed in a defiant shape.

Strings of silver chains with intermittent jewels of black onyx wrapped her throat in a choker.

Holding her left arm away from her body, she barked out an order in her native tongue.

A shield burst from the piles beneath Cathbad, dumping him sideways. The shield flew over to her, then paused in midair, allowing her to slide her hand and arm through the back side.

Righting himself, he waited for the inevitable.

Holding her right hand out, she spoke again, but as one would to a lover. "Come to me, *Lann Saoirse.*"

No sword arose from the pile.

She stared at her empty hand and snarled at Cathbad in a thick Nordic accent, "Where is Lann Saoirse?"

That was going to be a sticking point for them.

"I don't have your sword, Brynhild. I managed to move as much of your hoard as I could find once you were safe, and I protected all of this. I've taken nothing of yours. I don't need any of your treasures or your sword."

"Safe?" she shouted, moving around the pond that quivered from the force of her anger. "You captured me and locked me in that watery grave!"

Cathbad stood and his power curled around him like a protective armor.

After Brynhild emerged from the pond, he'd allowed her a month to come to her senses and put the past behind them. As he picked his way down the jangling pile of treasure, he reminded her, "I *did* save you. Your father lost his castle and his army in the great Dragani War. Your sisters were trapped and beheaded, or have you forgotten that?"

She stopped, shock riding her gaze. "No, this could not happen."

"It *could* and *did*. Your father was a good king, which was not in his favor when fightin' ruthless enemies." Good equaled weak in Cathbad's world. "Thankfully, your mother was already long dead before the war started."

Lowering her shield until it hung against her side, she shook her head and stared down, muttering to herself. "We were a mighty force. Five dragon children. The most powerful of *all!*"

"I'm sure ya recall life as such, but allow me to refresh your memory. Yes, you and your siblings were born of dragon blood, but there were other powerful dragon families."

Lifting her head, she asked in a thick voice, "What happened to my brothers?"

Could the woman not stay on topic any longer than that?

Cathbad explained, "I don't know for sure, but based on how your sisters died I am inclined to think both men went that way as well, since all was lost when I arrived. That brings me back to savin' you."

"What happened? Why do I not know these things?"

Probably because I used so much power to put you under deep enough to sleep for centuries that I almost didn't recover. He had to be careful how he explained this, especially since most of it he'd have to fabricate as he spoke. "I came to aid your father, but I was too late."

Her words raced out in a long snarl. "Why would a king with five dragon children require anything from a *druid*?"

"We're going to spend another millennia just gettin' this explained if you don't let me finish," he admonished a little more sternly this time.

She waved her hand in an arc. "Talk. Explain."

Beautiful, powerful and deadly. If Cathbad didn't have plans for her, she'd make an excellent diversion for many centuries.

He continued. "Your father sent word that your family had been betrayed. He offered me a daughter to wed if I helped him save his family and people."

She paled at that, but Cathbad said, "I had no use for a wife. I came, thinking I'd have a powerful ally if we were successful.

That's it, plain and simple." Sticking as close to the truth as he could gave his words a ring of sincerity.

Not that it changed her stern demeanor.

Shaking his head a moment, he said, "By the time I arrived, your brothers were off with the army and word began tricklin' in of their imminent defeat. Your father was already ... a bloody corpse, but he'd clearly fought to the end. As I mentioned, your sisters met a sad demise. When I realized I could be of no help, I was about to leave when a woman named Thea ran to me, begging me to save you."

"Thea? My nursemaid?" Pain ruptured the last of Brynhild's anger. She was finally listening.

Nodding, he said, "Yes, a sweet woman. I managed to get her away and find a place for her to live out her days." Those days ended up being a week, but he technically spoke the truth since the woman did live longer. "You were in bad shape. You'd been cut from the throat to the chest in human form. I don't think the warriors you fought realized you were the king's daughter or you would have lost your head."

She stared ahead, looking beyond him. "Why did I not shift into my dragon?"

Good question, and he had prepared for it. "You had been tasked with remaining human to protect the nursery. When the soldiers reached the level before the nursery, you ran out to draw their attention. Thea said you were racing for the battlements so that you could shift and kill the soldiers that followed you, but they had sent someone ahead who surprised you and slashed his sword across your body. You did manage to save the children," he offered as a consolation.

She said nothing.

Continuing to weave truth with his own details, he said, "By the time I arrived, I could help no one but you. You had lost so much blood, I doubted I could save you, but I decided to try. It took a considerable amount of energy to cloak you while doing my best to keep you breathin'. I teleported in short bursts, which cost me a great deal of time, to deliver you here."

"What is this place? It smells of another dragon."

No softening yet in her face, but he would not have wanted a wallflower.

Shrugging, Cathbad looked around, then came back to her. "I knew of this mountain and the deep, frigid pond inside. You are correct. It was once the lair of another dragon that lived and died many centuries before you were born."

Stepping closer every few minutes, he pressed his point. "I spared your life so that you may live again."

"For what reason?" Her eyes were wild with confusion. "How many years have passed since my family died?"

"Two thousand."

That was the last fracture.

Anguish seeped into her face, but this woman was not one to fold in public. She straightened her back. "My family is gone. I wish to join them."

Not today.

Cathbad calmly asked, "Why would you do that when I told you I just came from talkin' to Daegan of King Gruffyn?"

Her eyes flared with life again. "Daegan?"

"Yes. Isn't that what caused you to shift?"

"I thought you only spewed words to make me change."

He admitted, "I was doing that, but they were all true."

She whispered, "Daegan? He lives?"

"Oh yes. Maeve captured him before the great Dragani war. She turned him into her throne." He waited for a reaction.

Sounding confused, Brynhild asked, "Yes. I did hear of that. He is free now and has not killed her?"

"I'm sure he'd like to, but it's not so simple to kill a Medb goddess hidden inside her own realm."

Angling her head in question, Brynhild said, "You speak the truth? This is not some ruse to manipulate me?"

He admitted, "I do have plans for the two of us, but I tell you the truth. Daegan lives. Doesn't it matter that the man you were betrothed to has survived all these years?"

Standing straight, she smiled, "Yes, very much."

Cathbad returned her smile. "Have I not done well by you?"

The pupils in her eyes turned into diamond slits when her gaze narrowed sharply. "You imprisoned me!"

Clearly she was not feeling appreciative yet. "That was yesterday. We're living today. Are you not excited about the chance to see Daegan again?"

Her eyes lit with a renewed excitement. "Very much. I wish to have my hands on Daegan, the beautiful dragon son of the most powerful house. The man ... " She paused on a slow release of breath, then her voice strengthened. "The man who could have saved my entire family by mating me and uniting our families as powerful allies, but he refused me." Her voice took on more power. "I was not good enough for him." She glared at Cathbad as if she saw the dragon she hated. "We fought *two* dragon houses alone in the war. Take me to Daegan right now! *He. Will. Die!*"

The cave trembled with her declaration.

Cathbad rubbed his hands together. "Now we're talkin', but you're not ready to attack Daegan yet."

"*Yes! Now!*"

"Listen, my sweet. Daegan has had the benefit of bein' privy to changes in this world while he was trapped as Maeve's throne for almost the same time you were sleepin'."

"Imprisoned," she corrected.

"Can we not get past that?"

She answered with a mulish expression.

This was going to take some work, but he had known that keeping a dragon for all these years would not be simple.

Cathbad said, "My point is that Daegan has had time on his own to better adapt to the changes you have yet to see, and even more so, he has the aid of his Belador army."

"Beladors? His father's army still lives?"

"The descendants live and they are loyal to Daegan. A lot has happened. Even if you could kill him with one stroke, which you can't yet—"

She growled like the beast she could shift into.

"—would you really be satisfied with merely killin' him?" Cathbad finished. "That seems far too humane for what he deserves."

Her face relaxed into a thoughtful expression. "You make good points."

"I have a lot of good information and I know all the players in this world we now live in. I am your guide through fittin' into your new life and in gainin' retribution."

"What do you want, druid? What is your goal in all of this?"

It had taken her long enough to accept that there were terms to be discussed.

He said, "First I want to train you to be able to move fluidly through the human world, then I'll explain my plan. In the meantime, I promise I will help you pay Daegan back for all he cost you once you do your part to help me gain what I want."

She gave it a long consideration before saying, "I will think on this agreement. It has merit, but I will not wait forever to destroy my family's enemy."

"The time frame depends upon you. I've waited for you to reach the point you're prepared to train and learn what you need to know."

"Open this cave."

He paused at her order. "We are in a remote area, but to go outside you need to realize this is not a world that knows about dragons. Things have changed greatly."

"You said this was once a dragon's lair. Is there no room to fly?"

"There is."

"I have no desire to be seen until I am ready to reveal myself. I will not engage an enemy ill prepared."

That was the attitude he'd been hoping to see emerge.

Cathbad considered cloaking her with a short-range concealment. That would keep her on a tight leash. "I will open the cave, but I want an agreement first. I have told you the truth. You do need me to find Daegan and to succeed in killin' him, but that will happen only as long as my goals are met as well. I want your oath on your family's honor that you agree to stay with me and do as I ask."

She bristled. "I will not stay as your mate."

"No, my dear. You're far too special for mere sex. Besides, even if I wished to mate with you, I do not possess the dragon blood required for a true mating."

"It is good to fear my blood. If a man forced himself on me and was not of dragon blood, I could burn him inside me. I don't know about a druid body, but it would not be wise to challenge me."

Internally, he shuddered to think about getting involved with someone who showed the potential of being more dangerous than Maeve. "You have no issue with me and I believe that ability to injure a man was the very thing that saved your sisters from being raped."

She flinched at the painful reminder of what the war had taken from her, then stared down as if studying the ground. When she lifted her head, she'd made a decision. "Yes, I swear on my family's honor that we have an agreement. You have my word as the first born and last living child of Eógan, the ice dragon king." Then she paused with a strained look. "Am I the last one?"

"As far as I know, but I was not in this world for almost as many years as you. I continue to learn things that surprise me."

"Why were you gone so long?"

"I'll explain how I only recently returned once you've completed your exercise." Looking to keep something of value of hers, he asked, "Will you give me your shield to hold while you fly?"

Rolling her eyes, she handed him the shield. "Yes. Do not be a nagging old woman. We have come to agreement."

Ignoring her, he accepted the shield and walked to the entrance, which was still open. He cleared the ward that had prevented any preternatural being from passing through except him, and moved the boulder further to the side.

Behind him, power pushed out from where she shifted again.

She stepped up to him in her dragon form and nudged him with a flick of her wing. When he didn't step away, she opened her huge jaws and spoke in a deep version of her voice.

"Move, druid."

"First, I need to cloak you, but keep in mind it's only effective for maybe two miles, then you'll have to come back."

The serpent-like eyes that had stared at him in hatred before, now smirked. She lowered her head to eye level with him. "I need no cloaking, druid."

"You don't want to be discovered too soon by accident and let Daegan know you live," he argued.

She stepped to the opening and stood there with her head up in the wind. In the next moment, she became translucent.

She called out, "We inherited my father's dragon blood, but I also received the gift of my mother's blood. She was part dragon, part Jinn. I am the only child with her special gift."

As she'd spoken, her body had completely disappeared.

Flapping sounds followed, then launched away from the mountain. Her laughter rippled through the skies.

How had he never known of her mother's bloodline and that those two women could turn invisible? Because he believed dragon kings would wed only those with pure dragon blood.

Evidently her father had chosen a woman who carried genie blood.

Cathbad cursed to himself. His currency had been information that he could wield faster than kinetics.

For all the money he'd spent researching her family long ago, no one had known any of those dragons possessed that gift.

The king had wisely hidden that secret.

He thought on it for a bit, then realized what bothered him about her cloaking. Why hadn't she used invisibility to escape those who had cut her down?

He grinned. Unlike him, she had a flaw to her gift and he would discover what hampered her turning invisible.

An hour later, he lost all pleasure from this visit.

The dragon had not shown herself.

Brynhild had sworn on her family's honor that she would return ... but not when. If she ran from him, she would face his fury.

CHAPTER 17

Storm and Evalle's Building in Atlanta.

STORM PROWLED FROM SIDE TO side of his conference room as he waited on team members to show up. The hour he'd been waiting for was now a minute past. It was only mid-morning and still Sunday, but every second felt like a day as he waited to get rolling.

If anyone other than Daegan ran late, they'd be left behind.

His patience was nonexistent.

Not after seeing what had happened to Evalle and her bike. His animal howled to be freed to hunt, but these people all cared for Evalle and brought a ton of power and skills to the table.

For her, he'd lock down the need to start shouting orders and accept that he had very little to go on. For his jaguar, he promised blood would be spilled and he would not hold his animal back when the time came.

No one was stopping him from tearing apart those who dared to hurt Evalle. And she was hurt badly. That emerald had been a part of her being, not just a cosmetic rock attached to her body.

Quinn stepped into the room. "Storm, I have Phoedra and Reese with me. I'd like to get Phoedra settled with Lanna, then Reese and I will be back."

Storm nodded.

"Just a moment." Kit, who had been sitting quietly with her hands clasped in front of her, stood up. "I know you don't want me in this meeting, though I'm willing to help any way I can and I'll be monitoring our Nyght resources once you're gone. For now, I'd like to meet Quinn's daughter so she'll be comfortable with me, and then catch up with the boys."

Storm had never cared much for Isak, but he held a high level of respect for Kit and the way she'd raced here to help Evalle in spite of Isak claiming he would never allow nonhumans around his mother again.

That man had to know Kit backed down from no one. Kit would always be welcome in this building.

Storm said, "Thank you, Kit. For everything."

"You're welcome." Kit looked to Quinn, who said, "I think it's a brilliant idea to meet my daughter. Thank you."

She joined Quinn at the door and they walked away.

A security video screen monitoring the garage alerted Storm to a movement in that area. He'd moved vehicles to the outer edges to clear a space in the center. Daegan appeared first with Tristan right behind, both having just teleported in now that Storm had adjusted the ward for certain people.

The sound of those two moving through the building's foyer reached Storm just before they entered the conference room.

Storm asked, "Any news from any front?"

Shaking his head, Daegan said, "No. If this was some form of kidnapping for gain, they have yet to send a demand such as was done when Isak's mother and those twins were captured."

"Speaking of which, Kit is here and I'm allowing her to stay," Storm announced to get Kit's presence out of the way.

Daegan's face tensed. "I thought we agreed no humans."

"We did. Kit showed up and my choice was either hear her out or physically force her to leave."

The dragon king grunted. "I can see why you allowed her entrance, but I still don't understand."

"After listening to her, I realize my only goal is to find Evalle and bring her home. Kit made valid points about her organization's ability to produce intel in ways we sometimes can't in the human world. I'm not passing on any help at this point when we have nowhere to start looking. Evalle and Adrianna are friends today because Evalle got past her prejudice against a Sterling witch and accepted Adrianna's aid to find me when I was beyond anyone's reach. They're now close friends. Isak even helped the two of them back then. I don't like the guy, but that dislike is not going to stop me from doing all within my power to find my mate. If you can't abide having humans involved, I'll understand your withdrawal."

Daegan frowned. "Do you honestly believe I would abandon you?"

"No, I'm just putting everything on the table."

Giving it a moment with a thoughtful expression in his eyes, Daegan declared, "I will trust your judgment on using humans in this."

"Thank you, but do know that I'm limiting involvement to Isak, his mother and their people."

"Understood. Now, what is Isak's mother doing while she is here?"

With one weight off Storm's mind, he said, "Kit will funnel any information her people receive to us and she'll watch over the teens when I leave."

Daegan's face held a curious expression. "You feel that they'll be safe with a human?"

"I'd rather go up against a deranged demon than Kit when she's in protection mode over these kids. Between my ward and her hovering, they'll be safe."

"In that case, her presence here will be valued."

Tristan walked over and grabbed a cold drink from the refrigerator stocked for any meeting. He popped the top and turned to lean back against the cabinets. "I've got some thoughts, but it will save time if we go over this all at once."

Storm tamped down on his urge to rail at anyone who hesitated to share information, but Tristan was right. This would be quicker if they didn't have to repeat everything.

He was all for fast and efficient.

Quinn returned with Reese trailing behind him. Neither took a seat. They were all standing around the table as if sitting would diminish their positions.

The garage door opened, which could only be for one person since she was not present and Storm had not given car access to anyone except the witch. Quinn had traveled via a hired car of some sort and entered through the front door, which Storm had left unsecured for a specific twenty-minute window of time. Kit's fingerprint specialist had come and gone, working as efficiently as he'd expect a Nyght employee.

In the next moment, Adrianna stepped into the room wearing low boots, jeans, button down shirt and a jacket of tough-looking material, which he'd bet was an unusual blend no human would find.

That witch was just as furious as Storm and had her hair pulled back tight in business mode.

She dropped a backpack from her shoulder and looked around. "What's wrong with the chairs?"

"Waiting on the ladies to sit," Daegan answered, sounding as though he spoke for all the men.

Any other time Storm would agree.

He'd always respected women, but Adrianna was a warrior and he'd treat her as one.

She gave her patent half smile, then took a seat.

Reese grabbed a chair and sent a what-are-you-waiting-for glare at those standing. Everyone chose a place at the table, leaving Storm as the only one standing.

He waved a hand and a whiteboard descended from the ceiling behind him. "I know we all want to attack this in the best strategic way, but I intend to find the most direct and quickest path to Evalle. I don't want to mislead any of you. I know you all care deeply for Evalle and I appreciate your being here more than you can know, but I will not allow any human or preternatural to get in my way. Don't expect me to play by anyone's rules or laws. There are none I will heed while Evalle is in danger."

There were no furtive glances indicating any trepidation at the declaration.

No one fidgeted.

Adrianna replied, "What he said. I'm in with Witchlock under the same terms."

Storm gave her a nod of thanks.

One by one, every person in the room gave their vote of confidence in the same way until they came to Daegan.

Daegan leaned back with his arms crossed over the T-shirt he wore. The dragon king apparently found modern clothes to be comfortable for working in the human world. He said, "We will stop at nothing to bring her home alive. You have my word for that and for the future protection of everyone on this team."

Having expected someone to remind him there were laws that couldn't be broken, Storm shouldn't feel so surprised by the unqualified support. But it was indeed humbling.

"Again, thank you all. I've watched Evalle throw herself at danger to protect everyone she loves. You are all worthy of that love." Turning to the whiteboard, Storm started writing as he spoke. "This is what we know about Evalle and Adrianna's wrecks this morning." He listed times and what little information they had, which included an unknown preternatural and two humans he had scented at the scene.

He said, "Reese, I'm not sure you know this, but I found no scent leaving the wreck site that I could track. From that, we've determined Evalle and those two humans must have been teleported away."

Reese said, "Quinn told me and took me to the scene."

All heads swung to the woman with the unusual remote viewing ability, which allowed her to see where someone traveled from a specific spot to their final destination.

Looking around at the group, she said, "Just to be clear. If you don't know, I can't follow a teleportation trail."

Storm's hope took a nosedive.

Reese said, "I ran into a blank wall, which supports your teleportation theory."

Adrianna asked, "Is there any way to power up your viewing ability?"

Lifting her shoulders, Reese said, "Until helping Quinn find Phoedra, I had not used it in many years, and never for serious tracking. I'm sort of learning as I go."

Tristan groaned.

Quinn shot him a look that threatened him if he dissed Reese again, but Reese put her hand on Quinn's arm, which quieted him. She added, "I'm just qualifying that I am willing to help in any way, and while I wasn't able to help there, I might at a different location."

Storm put that note in the back of his mind.

Quinn asked, "Do we have anything on the humans?"

"Kit said her people were searching for them," Storm replied. "She said we'd be given any intel the Nyght Company could produce. They searched the traffic videos and are running the images through facial recognition software."

"Damn," Tristan said. "That's impressive."

"Let's hope so."

Adrianna piped up, "Just before I arrived, Kit called and asked me to be the contact for our team. She said she might have her hands full with all the teens here." The witch didn't sound excited about that, which meant Isak would likely be the one contacting her.

Storm looked to Tristan, who had been with Evalle when they evolved into gryphons. "You said you had an idea about why they took Evalle."

Tristan had been slouching, but now sat up straight and explained, "When Kit and the twins were captured, their captors had left a letter with their demands. But when Evalle was taken to TÅµr Medb, no one sent a request for a payoff because the Medb wanted gryphons for attacking Treoir. I only see one of a couple options. If they wanted to kill Evalle, they could have. If they wanted something in trade, they would have sent word by now. That leaves the last possibility. They want Evalle for her abilities."

Twisting around to him, Adrianna asked, "Why not grab me? Evalle is deadly in her own right, but if they had a shot at gaining Witchlock, wouldn't that be more powerful?"

Storm took in both points and couldn't argue against either one.

Tristan said, "Oh hell yeah, *if* they could make you do what they said."

Her lips curled into an almost smile. "Not in this lifetime."

"Exactly," he agreed. "Now consider Evalle. Why would they be able to force her to do their bidding and not you?"

It took all of a half second for Storm to answer that. "Because Evalle would die fighting a battle on her own to protect me, Feenix, those teens upstairs and Kit, all of you ... the list goes on forever. Not that Adrianna isn't as willing to step up to the plate, but it would be so much easier to force Evalle into a corner." His gut lurched at the thought of what she had to be facing.

"That's my point," Tristan said. "Also, Evalle is directly connected to the Beladors and Daegan. I think we should start with the idea that she was taken for a specific purpose. That's why they pulled her emerald off, which prevented you from tracking her, but they have to know we are all coming for her. Taking that into consideration, they might have something planned soon."

Reese spoke up. "Don't bite my head off, but I'm going to

throw out another possibility. I've spent a lot of my life feeling like a bug under someone's glass jar just for the purpose of their entertainment. That wasn't actually the case," she added with a quick glance at Quinn who had started frowning. Once his face calmed, she said, "What if someone took Evalle just to ... keep?"

That was Storm's greatest nightmare.

He would use all the resources he had, which were extensive, to search this universe and beyond for her, but if someone sent no kidnap payment demand, left no trail or if they left this realm for another one none of them knew about, he'd never find her.

Daegan entered the conversation from the opposite end of the table. "I second Tristan's suggestion."

Tristan managed to not look surprised, but just barely.

Storm waited along with everyone else for Daegan to expound.

The dragon king said, "Many things have changed over the centuries since I was born, but preternaturals are not that complicated when they have a goal. If someone had grabbed Evalle to keep as a pet, for example, the question is, why would that person bring down the wrath of the Beladors." He paused then added, "And that is nothing compared to crossing me, I promise you. Anyone who has been around long enough to reside in another realm has also been around long enough to know who I am and that I am free. No, some being did not wake up this week and decide to start a war for a pet."

Adrianna had been watching Daegan intently. "Then that begs the question, what *do* they want Evalle for?"

Storm actually let out a breath that had bottlenecked at the thought of Evalle being turned into someone's personal entertainment. There was no guarantee that wasn't the case, but he liked the reason Daegan stated, which supported Tristan's hypothesis.

Daegan said, "I don't know the why yet, but I believe once we begin tracking down every lead we'll get that answer."

Quinn asked, "What is it we have to start tracking, though?"

Before Daegan could reply, Adrianna's mobile phone rang.

She lifted her cell phone and answered, "Thought you were going to text me." Her eyes sharpened and she cocked her head in interest. "Where?" After a few seconds, she instructed, "Please do not confront them before we arrive. We're on the way." She paused then added, "Thank you."

Standing up, she said, "Isak's team identified the two men from the traffic video and determined where they live. He said there are lights on in the apartment."

Everyone stood and made noises about being ready to go.

Daegan asked, "Storm, is your building secure so I can teleport us to the location of the men?"

"It will be as soon as we step into the atrium."

A part of Storm couldn't wait to unleash his inner demon to drag intel out of the humans. The other part reminded himself that Evalle would not be happy coming home to a demon after she'd risked her life to keep him from turning completely to the dark side of his blood.

His jaguar snarled and pushed.

Storm gave a silent nod to his animal. This would be a bad time for anyone to test his control by hampering his ability to find Evalle.

CHAPTER 18

HOLDING A CALM CIRCLE AROUND herself and her Witchlock power while teleporting, Adrianna opened her eyes the moment she sensed they had arrived. She stood mere inches from a poor excuse for a streetlight doing its best to offer some illumination against the dark skies. Those lights wouldn't be on this early in the afternoon if not for the bloated rain clouds moving slowly over Atlanta.

Wasn't late May supposed to be nicer than this?

The flowers around her house were blooming and they needed the rain, but this unseasonable cool was just dreary.

The building next to the streetlight had been covered in graffiti.

Almost getting impaled by that steel lamp pole would officially make this the worst Sunday-before-Memorial Day that she'd ever been through.

Opening her hand, she used Witchlock spinning at tennis-ball size to scout the surroundings for any unexpected energy.

"Do you detect anything?" Daegan asked, unbothered by water splashing on his head, face and body.

Turning to Daegan, she closed her fingers and said, "No." Nodding at the post, she said, "Cut the landing a little close, didn't you, dragon?"

He shrugged. "Perhaps you should stand right next to me in the future, witch. I would have destroyed anything in the way of landing."

Was he serious? "How does that work when it's a human being or one of the Beladors?"

"My energy naturally pushes anything living out of the way."

"Of course. What was I thinking to question an arrogant dragon?" she grumbled.

He'd teleported the team to the west side of Atlanta. They stood in a rutted parking lot next to what might have been a garage for car repairs at one time, based on the old-style garage doors. The crumbling metal building had a rusty screen door hanging off the hinges of a walk-in doorway and was fronted by a two-lane road.

Wind swirled the steady rain.

Tristan, Storm, Quinn and Reese stepped close to form a small circle with Adrianna and Daegan. Storm had his arms crossed and his lips tight in a grim line. Water ran off his carved features. That man wouldn't care if he stood in a downpour of acid rain right now.

Quinn asked Adrianna, "What's next?"

"Isak said he'd watch for us and ... " She angled her head to look past Storm. "That's probably him now."

Five dark images emerged from the deepest shadows across the street, taking form as a black ops team with Isak in the lead.

With the night-vision monoculars they wore, each one reminded her of a cross between cyborg and human.

She'd take her chances with a cyborg over Isak in full battle mode. He and his men stopped ten feet away.

Why did her heart hold a dance party at the sight of that human? He was covered in black from head to toe and she could only see one eye.

She reminded her foolish heart that he would never fully accept a nonhuman woman.

Isak began reporting. "I'm thinking you know that my people used facial recognition to track the two humans on traffic video to this location, but we have no live confirmation it is them. They were seen walking the downtown accident location twenty-two hours prior to the collision, which leads me to think they were scouting the site. We normally would have inserted into their apartment building first to confirm the target identities and that both are still inside, but you asked that we not approach until you arrived." He sent a pointed glance at Adrianna when he mentioned being asked to wait.

Fine. She'd give him points for doing as she'd asked, since Isak was not one to take direction from anyone else.

Pausing only to wipe water off his uncovered eye, Isak said, "I want to make one thing clear. Until we have an opportunity to interrogate these men, we can't pin Evalle's kidnapping on them."

Daegan rumbled a noise and Storm growled, both sounds she took as threats if the human didn't move this along.

Adrianna had asked the team to allow her to take the lead in dealing with Isak since she was the most experienced with this particular person, barring Evalle being present. She addressed Isak, explaining, "If you're concerned that we're going to kill a human without determining if they're guilty of anything, we aren't. Interrogating them will be simple as we've brought our own lie detector." She nodded at Storm who stood very still, like an earthquake before it destroyed an entire city.

Adrianna knew better than to take Storm's extreme silence as a good sign.

For that reason, she warned Isak, "Time is of the essence and we will tolerate no one standing in the way. Thank you for locating the humans. Once you point us in the right direction, you would be wise to leave."

Isak's lips curved with an all-knowing smile not meant to be confused with a happy expression. "Not going anywhere. Follow me." He turned and strode down a long alley.

When he reached a building that advertised used vehicle tires, Isak initiated a series of hand signals, sending his men to each end of the building.

Adrianna stayed close to Isak. Too close. She kept catching the scent of him. Not aftershave or cologne. As a black ops soldier, he never wore those when working. No, this was the scent of Isak alone, some deadly combination of unscented soap, shampoo and sexy man. Witchlock seemed to heighten all of her senses at times, just from her connection to it.

Still, how could one tiny smell find its way through all this rain and wind outside?

Shaking off the distraction, she studied a light on inside a room on the second floor.

Isak whispered, "That light was reported illuminated as soon as my men arrived, but we have no traffic cam in this area. We got nothing with our thermal scan, so this could be a bust with no one there."

"I understand," she replied. "But even if it is empty, Storm can track the scent if someone hasn't teleported them away. We need something, a lead, anything that gives us a place to start looking."

Daegan walked up. "I'll teleport in and determine what's going on."

Isak stiffened and swung his gaze to the dragon king. "That's not how we do this."

Just as quickly, Daegan said, "This is how *we* do things. Adrianna suggested you leave. If you stay, you work with us. If anyone gets in my way, I'll teleport them out of my way."

This is why Adrianna had suggested she take the lead.

Could the air get any more polluted than having an overload of human and preternatural testosterone?

She kept her voice soft, but snapped, "Daegan is going in. He's pretty indestructible when only humans are involved. We need intel. He's not going to kill our only chance at getting that intel. Everyone clear?"

Isak's posture eased. He arched an eyebrow above the one exposed eye. "Yes, ma'am."

Daegan snorted. "I'll bring all of my people inside if it's safe." He told Isak, "I assume your team would prefer the steps."

"Yes."

Daegan lifted a hand and vanished.

Quinn walked up, hair dripping with water. "Are you our dragon whisperer, Adrianna?"

She said, "No. I'm more like a dragon irritator."

Quinn cocked his head as if hearing a telepathic message, then told the team, "Prepare to teleport."

She stood outside one moment and after a short blast of energy, she stood inside a squalid room. Sure, it was dry in here, but putrid stench hit her hard. Rotting food sat on the counter and in the sink along with dirty dishes and trash. She didn't want to look too closely at what was littered on the floor. She gagged and covered her mouth.

As Storm, Quinn and Reese appeared in the middle of the same kitchen-living room space, Reese doubled over.

Tristan pinched his nose, but he was too macho to throw up in front of Daegan.

Pigs lived cleaner than this.

But that wasn't the only thing turning her stomach.

It was also the disgusting smell of dried blood and expelled body fluids along with lingering nasty body odors.

Storm's nostrils flared.

Isak and his men pounded through the quiet building and hit the door once, knocking it open. He told his men to stand outside, then flipped up his monocular as he entered. His gaze went first to Adrianna before taking in the macabre scene.

Quinn had Reese turned away from the bodies and was holding her at the waist as she unloaded her stomach. It wasn't as if she could damage the floor.

Daegan studied the two men without seeming to notice the revolting odors. Probably a more common smell back during the days of dragons and battles fought with swords.

Adrianna peeked. Both men they'd come to interrogate had their throats sliced and their abdomens had been cut open.

Once she breathed through her mouth, Adrianna asked, "If this was done by a preternatural, why kill them that way?"

Storm walked over to take a closer look, which had to be even more repulsive with his strong sense of smell. He said, "That was to hide any majikal signature and probably to make it appear to be a human crime. Whoever did this is still masking their scent, but that takes energy just like any other supernatural action. We need to find a place where the killer was comfortable enough not to expend the energy to mask his smell." He raked a hand over his hair. "Damn. We're at another dead end."

Reese coughed and stood up as Daegan produced a glass of water out of thin air to hand her. She pinched her nose to drink.

Adrianna had to give him his due. That dragon shifter had some kind of old majik.

Isak said, "These men match the images my people used to identify them." His blue eyes moved past everyone to reach Adrianna, then he said, "I'm sorry. I want Evalle found, too."

Storm turned raw eyes toward Isak at the mention of his mate.

Isak said, "Any resource I have is yours to help you find her."

Storm managed to say, "Thanks." Then he stepped out of the room into the hallway.

Ever the smart mouth, Tristan said, "Those two speaking? Brace for an apocalypse next."

Adrianna gave the Alterant a sharp look. "You're not helping, Tristan."

Reese was arguing with Quinn in terse whispers over something and finally said out loud, "*I can do this!*"

They all turned to her.

Reese's face had turned the color of a faded paper doll. Standing straighter, she kept her nose pinched and sounded as if she had a cold when she spoke. "I want to try my remote viewing to see if I can figure out if the killer went somewhere next, but I won't see anything if he teleported again."

Storm returned. "The only trail I found belonged to these two and is almost a day old. No preternatural scent trail."

Nodding, Daegan turned to Reese and asked, "What do you need to try your remote viewing?"

She grumbled, "Killing the smell would help, but not if it's going to block my access to the energy left behind."

Daegan took a hard look at the two dead guys as if he hadn't realized that had been an issue. He lifted a hand, his lips moved with a silent word and a film formed over each body. Next, he did the same thing to block the sink, counters and most of the floor debris.

Adrianna's next breath drew in cleaner air. The room still stank, but without the nasty taint from the bodies.

Everyone made a sound of appreciation.

Reese sniffed a little and let out a big sigh. "Thank you, Daegan. That knocked down the smell significantly."

"You're welcome."

She walked toward the bodies with Quinn dogging her heels.

Adrianna wasn't the only one to notice Quinn's attention. On the other hand, his daughter did live with Reese. Everything about that situation seemed odd, but Adrianna didn't pry into other people's affairs.

She respected everyone's privacy because she was guarded about her own.

Turning her back on the gory scene, Reese closed her eyes and lifted her fingers to her temples. In a matter of seconds, she was moving her head a little this way, a little that way, and then she stilled.

When she lowered her hands and opened her eyes, she seemed to still be looking at something.

Storm cautiously asked, "Did you see anything?"

Reese chewed on her lip then released it. "Maybe."

"He didn't teleport away?"

Her face closed down as she pondered that. "I don't think so, but I didn't see anyone in particular. Based on what I've encountered in the past, I shouldn't be able to see anything once he teleported away, but this time I followed a path, which makes me think he might have taken off on foot."

Storm swallowed. "Can you explain?"

She raked a handful of wavy hair off her face. "I saw a *path* from here to the trolley. Then I was inside the trolley going from this direction back into downtown. When the trolley stopped at Peachtree Center, the path pulled my attention off the train to the sidewalk and I followed along as it kept moving until everything stopped in the middle of some funky painted art."

Quinn asked, "Did you notice a street sign?"

"No." Scratching her head, Reese said, "I've never been trained to use my gift, so it's a surprise to me any time it works even that much."

"Thanks for trying, Reese," Storm murmured. "If he didn't leave a trail from here to the trolley, I doubt he left one once he exited the trolley."

"Hey, don't quit so fast," she ordered. "It's not over 'til it's over."

Storm's mouth opened, then closed without a word.

Clearly, he didn't know what to say to that verbal yank on his attention. Even Quinn gave Reese a wide-eyed look.

Adrianna nudged Reese with, "What else did you see?"

Scrunching her face, Reese grumbled, "That art thing ... I've seen it, but I haven't lived here in a long time."

Daegan asked, "Where do you think it might be?"

"I can't put my finger on the street."

Prodding a little, Tristan asked, "What's the first thing that comes to mind when you think about that art?"

Reese closed her eyes. "Seems like it's at an overpass to the interstate in downtown." Her eyes popped open. "I do remember that spot. I could find it if you put me close."

Storm's eyes sharpened with a thought. He snapped his fingers. "I bet it's at Ralph McGill Boulevard and—"

"Courtland Street," Quinn supplied. "It's the overpass with folk art on display at different times during the year."

Grinning, Tristan told Adrianna, "See? I'm very helpful, witch."

Isak glowered at Tristan.

Adrianna quickly replied, "Whatever, Alterant." That snarky comment calmed Isak, but why would he get upset over her being called a witch?

She would never understand that man. In hindsight, she'd been wrong to tell Daegan she should lead this outing, because Isak confused her more than ever, and she needed her attention on finding Evalle.

The man acted as if he cared.

She'd been there, gotten her heart trampled and had no desire for the T-shirt.

Daegan said, "We have to deal with these bodies before we leave."

Storm had that ready-to-explode look on his face. He said, "Fine. I can get there on my own before you finish dealing with this."

Isak stepped in. "I'm not teleporting with anyone. We'll handle the cleanup. That way, you can all leave together."

Adrianna wanted to hug Isak for the offer. It allowed them all to stay together when she feared letting Storm take off alone.

Evalle should be here to see Storm's look of surprise. He stood there a moment, then seemed to come to a decision and extended his hand to Isak. "Thank you. I'll repay the debt someday."

Isak took his hand for a brief shake. "You don't have to pay a debt when something is offered freely. I can't help in your world, but we'll keep looking for any lead to pass along."

Daegan said, "You are an unusual human. You stepped in to give aid when your offer was first turned down. I never forget when help is given. If you ever need assistance from our people, all you have to do is ask. It will be known that you are a friend of the Beladors."

Isak gave him a sincere sounding, "Thanks."

Adrianna should be taking notes for Evalle. That was as close to being knighted as a human could get in the world of Beladors.

Quinn and Reese were in another quiet argument where she had her arms crossed and was shaking her head. Quinn had the frustrated expression of a man up against an immovable object.

Daegan, Tristan and Storm had decided to take one more look around just to be sure there was no additional evidence.

Isak walked up to Adrianna.

Her back turned rigid as a steel rod, but she schooled her features to show no outward change, maintaining her mildly interested expression.

When he stopped in front of her, Isak drew in a deep breath that expanded his massive chest before he exhaled slowly. "When this is done, I'd still like to talk with you."

She wanted to lash out at him for hurting her, but her conscience evidently played for Team Isak because it quickly pointed out how he'd given them aid.

Where was the man who had told her and Evalle he never wanted his mother to be around nonhumans again after they'd all battled to save Kit and the twins in Blairsville?

Knowing Kit, she'd laid into her son as soon as she caught her breath from being captured by preternatural predators. No doubt she reminded Isak how the Beladors had lived here secretly for many years, protecting humans.

Even if that had happened, it would not change the fact that Isak did exactly what Adrianna had feared at the first hint of trouble. He'd declared nonhumans the enemy.

Yet he stood here among nonhumans in a roomful of carnage, waiting for her reply.

She swallowed the angry words that had filled her heart since they parted ways in Blairsville that rainy night. "Thank you for your help in finding these men."

Isak said nothing. He was going to make her answer him.

She added, "Like the Beladors, I also consider you a friend."

He arched one eyebrow at that.

Infuriating man. "I do not wish to repeat past mistakes, Isak. I told you before we got ... involved, that it was a bad idea. I was correct."

Finally, he said something. "I'm willing to admit you were right at that moment, but it doesn't mean you're right about the future."

Steeling herself, she stuck to her decision. "I am not willing to go through what happened again."

At that, he looked at the ceiling, apparently searching for the right words. When his gaze came back to her, he admitted, "I screwed up. Big time. I just want a chance to talk about it."

No way should she agree to that.

To be the most powerful witch of all that she knew, she had a disappointing lack of discipline around this man. Just hearing his voice curled her toes. Blast him. The only thing that had hurt her more than losing her sister—who'd had her majik cooked by a crazy witch—was being rejected so coldly by Isak.

Her conscience weighed in again. *What could be the harm in hearing him out?*

Where was Evalle, who would be all up in Isak's face right now?

Adrianna could fight her own battles, but she did not show explosive emotions in public. Evalle did and this is one of those times she'd love to have her friend here.

Without that support, she folded to her conscience. But as Adrianna started saying, "I have considered your words and I will—"

Daegan boomed, "Everyone ready? Let's go!"

Isak had been hanging on her words like a condemned man expecting a reprieve from the guillotine.

Shaking her head, she said, "Sorry. I have to go."

As she stepped past, Isak gently clasped her arm.

All it took was that one touch to stop her.

The rest of the team had ceased talking and turned where they stood in a group in the middle of the room. Every pair of eyes watched her.

She whispered, "Please, Isak."

He immediately released her arm.

She couldn't leave without him knowing one thing. "Kit came to Storm's building and refuses to leave until we return. She's heavily protected by a ward, but I wanted you to know."

Isak said nothing, but one look at his face shouted how upset he was for his mother to be there.

Storm offered, "She's in the safest place from nonhumans and humans alike right now, Isak. Plus, Lanna is a miniature supernatural Terminator when anyone she cares about is threatened. Lanna has taken Kit as one of hers to watch over."

Isak said, "Copy that, but I'm still sending three teams and snipers to watch over your building."

Everyone waited for Storm to argue, but he said, "If that gives you a comfort level about her safety, that's fine by me."

When Adrianna took her place in the group for teleportation, she turned to look at Isak.

He'd walked out of the room and was talking to his men.

Was he so angry he couldn't look at her?

Maybe she'd be glad later that she hadn't folded and accepted the olive branch he'd extended just now, when he hadn't tried to find her at all before today.

But he's willing to talk now.

She told her conscience, *You don't get a vote.*

The room blurred and they were off again. She appreciated the ease of traveling with Daegan, but even with his power, constant teleportation was exhausting. She hadn't expected to feel the drain on her body.

Thinking back, she had more appreciation for how Tristan had teleported the team in and out of the TÅµr Medb realm, then from North Georgia to downtown Atlanta. Unlike Daegan, Tristan had not been born with the gift. He'd gained it from a powerful drink he'd been given, which allowed him limited ability to teleport.

Tristan had ended up with blood pouring from his eyes and nose during that adventure to rescue Daegan from TÅµr Medb.

A busy breeze lifted Adrianna's hair as the team landed at the overpass Reese had described.

Humans walked around a display of folk art spread over a wide area on the southeast corner where Ralph McGill Boulevard and Courtland Street crossed.

Adrianna lifted her hands to form a cloaking, but Daegan said, "We're safe. They can't see us. We just need to not bump into one of them and knock someone over the wall into traffic."

The dragon must have cloaked everyone as they arrived. She said, "Got you."

Daegan said, "Storm, can you scent inside this cloaking?"

"Yes, but it's not as distinct in my human form. I'm going to shift."

Peeling out of his clothes, Storm wasn't the least bit self-conscious about exposing all that bronze-colored skin. Out of consideration for Evalle, Adrianna didn't watch.

Reese, on the other hand, hadn't been expecting a naked man in the group. Her eyes widened for an instant before Quinn stepped in front of her.

Adrianna could swear she heard him say, "If you want to ogle someone, you can look at me."

"I've seen *you*," Reese quipped.

Quinn rubbed his forehead. "I will not survive this operation with you."

Power rushed through the cloaked area as Storm shifted.

Ignoring the domestic squabble, Adrianna watched as Storm's jaguar stood eye level to her. He growled a deadly sound.

Daegan said, "I will keep you hidden, Storm. We'll stand out of the way."

Nodding, the jaguar started padding around, avoiding humans, but keeping his nose to the ground. The breeze ruffled his fur.

His huge head lifted sharply. His chest expanded on a deep inhale. Swinging around, he took three long strides and stuck his nose to the ground behind one of the larger displays.

When he lifted up and turned to the group, his eyes glowed yellow ... then red. Oh, no. Evalle would not want him to go demon mad.

Hurrying back to where his clothes were piled, Storm shifted so fast Adrianna couldn't believe it didn't hurt.

As he stepped into his jeans and yanked them up, Storm said, "He must have dropped his cloaking right before he teleported this time. I got a scent."

"So you can identify him if you smell him again?" Quinn asked.

Pulling the T-shirt over his head, Storm said, "Yes. In fact, I've smelled it before, but it's one of thousands I catch any time I'm out."

Studying Storm, Daegan asked, "Are you able to identify multiple scents?"

Without a hint of hesitation, Storm said, "I can catalogue and recall thousands at any time. It surprises me that I'm not pulling up a mental image to go with this scent, though. I might figure it out now or weeks from now, but I have more than that scent to go on. I smelled Noirre majik."

Daegan said, "Truly? That actually surprises me."

Storm had dropped to the ground to put his boots on. "Why?"

"I considered both Macha and Maeve for this. Macha is not one to do something so rash. As for Maeve, I would have thought Cathbad would show more forethought. When last we spoke, he did not want a war or for us to invade TÅμr Medb."

Standing up and sounding excited, Storm said, "Don't know what to tell you, but it's definitely Noirre. I smelled more of it in that one tiny spot than any Noirre I've ever scented before. It was crazy strong."

Shifting his attention to the place where Storm had found the scent, Daegan said, "Let me get us out of this cloaking so I can smell it as well."

Nodding, Storm said, "I can wait another minute."

Quinn pointed out a spot not far from the art exhibit where they could shed the cloaking unnoticed by humans. Once they moved there and Daegan dropped the protective shield, they hurried back to the current folk art on display.

Storm led the way to the place he'd detected the odor. He jerked his head back. "Man, I didn't realize how much the cloaking dulled the scent. That smell is even more powerful now."

Bending down to sniff, Tristan stood up quickly. "That's the worst Noirre funk I've ever inhaled."

Daegan squatted down, ran his hand a few inches above the spot, then stood up. He took in the group and said, "It may not be Maeve."

Storm's face ruptured with fury, clearly ready to argue.

"Ya'll just now findin' this place?" a deep voice asked.

Reese jumped around. "What the heck are you?"

Quinn quietly said, "Let me introduce you to Grady, Evalle's favorite Nightstalker." Then he told everyone to circle Grady to protect him from view by humans in case his image began to solidify on its own.

Grady gave Quinn a look. "What you talkin' 'bout."

"Don't worry," Quinn said. "I've seen you and Evalle. I don't know how it happened, but I do know you occasionally take corporeal form without a handshake."

The old guy had a fierce attitude for someone wearing dirty clothes that were two sizes too big. The clothes he'd worn when he died.

Evalle had told Adrianna more than once that she believed Grady had been a highly educated man when alive, maybe even a professor. But he was also a cantankerous old ghoul that Evalle would protect just as avidly as one of the living beings in this group.

Grady told Quinn, "I'm not just her favorite, I'm the best one of the bunch. She knows it. So does her mate. Right, Storm?"

"You're right. Have you got anything to share?"

"I do."

Storm extended his hand.

Grady looked at it with a foul expression then told Storm, "Don't go insultin' me. You'll just upset Evalle."

Storm pulled his hand back in apology and crossed his arms.

That pushed Grady to start talking. His voice reminded Adrianna of Morgan Freeman. "My contacts said two men helped one of your kind kidnap Evalle. The ghouls saw those two men a day before the wreck. Sounds like they were snoopin' around the location."

"That fits with what we've learned," Storm confirmed.

"Different ghouls saw those men within minutes of the wreck, but in the Old Fourth Ward. Somebody had to be movin' them around fast to cover that distance."

"We found their bodies tonight," Quinn interjected. "We've come to realize the kidnapper is teleporting, which is hampering our ability to catch a trail."

Deep wrinkles covered Grady's old face when he seemed to chew on that. "They dead, you say? You didn't get no intel from those two?"

"No," murmured through the group, but Storm said, "It did lead us here."

"We gotta find her," Grady muttered, irritated. "This is all I got. The Nightstalkers around the wreck when it happened said the power guy wearing a hood stank of Noirre, *bad* stink like they never smelled, then the odor disappeared like he cloaked it."

Daegan said, "That also fits with what we've just discovered."

Scrunching up his face, Grady looked at Daegan. "You shoulda found that girl by now."

Showing no sign of offense at Grady's words, Daegan said, "We're working on it."

"You better hurry up and git to it. Humans took videos of the wreck and that hooded guy disappearing with those two humans and Evalle. Shit is hittin' the fan. Word is VIPER's havin' a fit and blamin' Evalle. I ain't standin' for that."

Storm said, "She is *not* facing VIPER for any of this."

At the same time Quinn said, "They'll have to face all of us," and Tristan harrumphed in agreement.

Daegan lifted a hand, asking for silence. When he spoke it was to everyone. "Evalle will answer to no one over this. If VIPER has an issue, they will face me. End of discussion."

Rubbing her stomach unconsciously, Reese said, "Back to the hunt. Why would someone powerful enough to teleport need humans?"

Grady held his arms out with his hands open. "Somebody gonna do that when they got no team or followers. Whoever it is needed humans to drive the trucks, then he killed 'em. That stinkin' Noirre might be sloppy or maybe someone usin' it to point us at the Medb."

Adrianna added, "Or, the Noirre use is so obvious that it could actually be the Medb behind this and they intend to claim they're being framed."

Daegan's gaze bounced to each of the team as they spoke. He seemed to be allowing them to figure out something on their own.

Adrianna asked him, "What are you thinking, Daegan?"

"This particular Noirre scent is key to finding Evalle."

"You just said you didn't think it was Queen Maeve," Storm pointed out with suspicion in his voice.

"I don't. This scent is of *pure* Noirre."

Grady's form floated around in one spot. "Say what?"

Adrianna said, "Grady. Down, please."

"Oh." He floated back to eye level with the other men.

Daegan explained, "Pure, as in the original form of Noirre majik."

Agreeing, Storm said, "That makes sense and it's enough to convince me where we go next. I've been at a lot of supernatural crime scenes since coming here and have never smelled any Noirre this strong. Queen Maeve and Cathbad have to be behind this."

"Not necessarily," Daegan argued gently. "This Noirre is full strength. When I said pure, I meant that it was straight from the plant."

"What plant?" echoed around the group.

Daegan looked fairly shocked. "None of you know where

Noirre originated?"

Adrianna noted every headshake.

The dragon king explained, "Back during my time, prior to my being captured by Queen Maeve, she sent half her warlock army to bring her a section of the plant that grew in a cave where the bodies of over a thousand innocent women and children had died. The cave was in Ossory. When Vikings raided the nearby village, women and children ran to hide in the cave because of its narrow entrance. The Vikings thought they were clever and tried to burn them out."

Quinn picked up the thread, saying, "The entire group was asphyxiated. It was Dunmore Cave. The area once known as Ossory is now Kilkenny or maybe County Kilkenny, now that I think about it."

Tristan scrunched up his face. "Where's that?"

"Ireland."

Giving a short nod of agreement, Daegan continued. "Yes, that's the cave. All of the Medb army sent was lost except a warlock left near the entrance as a lookout. He returned to the queen, claiming he would accept any death rather than ever go back to the cave. He was terrified after hearing the screams of dying warriors. Next, she sent a mage, who also died."

Grady had his arms crossed and remained a few inches above ground in his translucent form. "That Maeve a greedy bitch. Killin' people just to get majik to kill more people."

"What was in the cave that attacked the soldiers and mage?" Tristan asked.

Daegan said, "The Noirre plants."

Adrianna couldn't have heard him correctly. "A *plant* was that deadly?"

"Yes. The plants are said to be not just deadly, but sentient. The Vikings believed a mother to a child lost in that cave had been a witch and that she cursed the Vikings. The plants grew from that curse."

Reese said, "Never cross a powerful mother."

"No truer words have been spoken," Daegan agreed, then continued explaining. "Maeve must have offered Cathbad whatever he wanted, because after the mage died, the druid went to the cave and Maeve joined him, though she remained outside.

He survived long enough to teleport out, but he was badly injured. She poured a load of power into the druid to keep him alive."

Tristan asked, "So Maeve is definitely behind this?"

Shaking his head, Daegan said, "Not necessarily. Macha knows the history of the Noirre plant as well. To be honest, it could be either one. Maeve would have knowledge of how to battle the plants, but Macha is willing to go to any length to kill me and get Treoir back. That's why I said the pure Noirre is key to finding Evalle if we can determine who gained the most recent plant."

Moving back and forth, Grady said, "Now you talkin'. Sounds like that bunch of spirits controllin' those plants. You take me with you, I'll git to 'em and make 'em talk to me."

Adrianna admired the Nightstalker's loyalty to Evalle, but Grady might be in danger if he entered a hostile spirit's area.

Turning a warm expression to Grady, Daegan said, "I am not sure you could teleport away from this place, and even if you could, Evalle would never forgive me for putting you at risk when you do not have powers to protect yourself. You could be of far more benefit by continuing to monitor this area and inform our Beladors of any threats from humans exposing our existence."

Grumbling under his breath, Grady finally said, "Word is VIPER might be your biggest threat. They upset about more humans coming out with videos of other supernatural activity. Every paranormal researcher and demon hunter outside of Atlanta be showin' up before you know it."

Reese asked, "Speaking of demons, have you seen any in the city recently?"

"Naw. Not since the last one."

That's right. Adrianna now recalled that Reese had energy that turned her into a demon magnet. Maybe that was the reason Quinn wanted Reese out of here, away from a potential threat.

Heaving a deep sigh, Grady told Daegan, "Okay. I'll stay here, but I ain't forgivin' no one if she don't come back."

"Understood." After appeasing the ghoul, Daegan looked to Storm. "Do you now see why I say this scent is the key?"

The Skinwalker nodded and said, "The kidnapper might have left his scent around the plants, and even a trail if he thought no one would suspect his gaining pure Noirre. How do we get to the plants?"

Everyone except Daegan stared at Storm as if he'd lost his mind after that story of hideous deaths in the cave.

The dragon king answered, "I'll show you. Let's teleport."

CHAPTER 19

Realm of Scamall

E VALLE HAD LOST COUNT OF days.
Germanus explained that days ran at a different pace in his realm. If she wanted to entertain herself by keeping track, she could figure approximately five days in here for every one in the human world.

Had she been here five or maybe six realm days?

Her gryphon had suffered wounds on top of wounds the entire time. The best healing she could manage was to merely stop the bleeding, which left thick scars.

Germanus had to be behind that. He held all the power in this realm ... other than the god who created this, whom he had yet to name.

She would not have voluntarily fought any of the beasts in his little kingdom, but he continued to throw her into a pit with ferocious adversaries who looked at her like dinner.

In fact, she'd bet Germanus kept them starving.

He fed her only once a day and even at that it was some disgusting gruel. She ate it and fought every threat for one reason—to remain alive long enough for Storm to find her. Her mother's voice pushed her to show her inner strength.

Evalle sucked it up time and again to do her best, but she rarely slept for fear of watching Storm die in multiple ways. Surviving became more difficult with every new realm day.

Shift after shift, her human body still reflected the damage inflicted on it from battling a wyvern. She'd been sure she was battling a dragon at first until she took in the wyvern's reptilian body with an arrow-shaped tip on its tail. Fortunately for her, it had no fire-breathing capability like a dragon. Then she'd fought a bird the size of a house known as a roc. That one had ripped one of her wings loose, which took everything she could call up to heal.

Germanus would announce each new creature with fanfare. The last one had been a cockatrice, which also resembled a two-legged dragon but with the head of a rooster. After killing that one, she'd limped away with her hind legs chewed up.

She was past the point of caring about how the scars looked or the damage to her body. She could only put one foot in front of the other and keep moving forward.

Darkness crept into her mind, constantly telling her if Storm could have found her, he'd be here by now.

When her mother's voice argued to stay in the moment, Evalle pushed harder, determined to survive and find a way out of this realm. But if she couldn't get out, she believed Storm, Daegan, Adrianna, Tzader and Quinn would find her.

She blinked her eyes and realized once again she was in the fighting pit in her gryphon form. The single benefit she'd found was that the realm sunlight did not affect her. She hadn't had her glasses since waking up in this hellhole, but neither was she blind outside the castle.

"Ready to face the kwane, Evalle?" Germanus called from his throne high above a round amphitheater much like the Colosseum. Maybe that's where he got the inspiration.

Had Germanus been around when that Roman structure was being built?

"Evalle?"

Standing awkwardly on her crooked, but now stronger, rear leg, she looked up at him and just stared.

She'd faced every creature he'd thrown at her.

Now he expected her to fight a kwane. What was that?

She finally nodded her gryphon head, indicating she was ready.

When the gate opened, a black bird the size of a human walked into the arena. All those black feathers and one spot of color, a dark gold beak with large nostril holes.

Birds tended to have fragile bones compared to a gryphon, no matter the size.

She started shaking her head, telling Germanus she would not kill some creature in cold blood. Even if that bird breathed fire, it wouldn't go one round with her. Every other flying critter had attacked Evalle's gryphon with intent to kill.

Her gryphon stood ten feet tall and seriously outweighed that bird.

"I'm waiting, Evalle."

Instead of answering, she shifted to her human form, hoping the damn bird wouldn't attack her. She'd had occasional use of her kinetics, again controlled by the whims of Germanus. When she stood barefooted in her usual sack dress, she looked up to find Germanus seething.

Score.

He stood up and yelled, "I did not bring you here to use as a sacrificial offering."

Maybe she was feeling stronger or maybe she was losing her mind, but she yelled back, "I still don't know why I'm here, but I'm not killing something that much smaller than my gryphon. If this is all for your sport, you need to raise your expectations."

He mounted one of his gargoyles, and it flew him down to the arena. He gave the kwane a command and it backed up ten steps to stand near the gate.

Walking over to Evalle, he said, "You will regret testing my limits."

"I doubt it. On the other hand, if I knew what you wanted and why I'm here other than to prove I will survive, this would be simpler."

"Very well, I'll tell you. I had hoped to get you better trained first, but—"

"Better trained?" she asked with no small amount of sarcasm. "I've killed a wyvern, a roc, a cockatrice and I would have smashed this bird if I sat on it."

He allowed her to interrupt, then continued. "As I was saying, you are dragging your feet in training. These first battle opponents have been nothing compared to what I have in this realm. My goal is not for you to kill all of the beasts, only to cull out the weak ones. If I wanted you destroyed, I would have done so long ago, but you will play an important role when Daegan does arrive."

She didn't want to ask, but she needed to know. "What role?"

"You will help kill the dragon, of course."

Her mouth opened, then closed, in shock. This guy was freaking delusional. "First of all, I'm not even that powerful. Second, I am not attacking the dragon king of the Beladors."

"You *will* be strong enough with the aid of my army, which you will lead," he argued.

"Even if I were to consider doing that, which I'm not, what do you need with me? Why not fight him with your army? In fact, why would Daegan even care to come bother you if you had not grabbed me?"

"You will do as I say and battle whatever and whomever I point you toward."

She crossed her arms. "No. I've been fighting to survive and I'll kick anyone's butt who tries to hurt me, but you can't make me do anything you say like this bunch of flying sheep who jump when you snap your fingers."

He sighed. "I keep trying to do this the simple way, but you are stubborn."

"It's a character flaw I fail to see the harm in."

Turning, Germanus looked at the other side of the arena, which looked big enough to play two football games side by side.

Germanus waved a hand toward one of the four gates.

Screaming reached her ears. It came from deep inside the building on the other side of the fighting pit.

Evalle froze.

That had sounded human. She hadn't seen any humans except Germanus and he wasn't worthy of a place in the food chain.

The gate opened and an eight-foot-tall gargoyle she hadn't seen before walked out, dragging the person still screaming. A young, human-looking guy.

Jerking back and forth, the guy yelled, "Let me go!" His voice sounded full of tears.

Growling, the gargoyle grabbed the young man by his shoulders and lifted him off the ground then turned him to face Germanus.

Evalle went still with shock.

No. That couldn't be ...

"*E-valllle! Save me!*" Kardos cried out.

She lunged forward and was pinned in place. Her arms were locked to her side. She pleaded, "Let him go. Don't hurt him."

Germanus said, "Unfortunately, you keep forcing me to prove that I do rule this place and everyone here will do as I say, including you." He turned to the kwane and quietly ordered, "Attack."

The gargoyle released Kardos, who started for Evalle. Tears spilled down his face.

She yelled, "*Runnnn!*"

Kardos looked all around. The gate behind him closed.

"Don't do this," she begged. "Please don't do this. I'll do whatever you want."

Germanus said nothing as the kwane opened its wings wide. Lightning shot down from a clear blue sky to strike the bird. Blue veins of electricity raced across its wings and body.

Then the bird's beak opened and two fangs dropped down.

Kardos took one look at the bird, spun and ran for the gate that was shut tight. He flipped back around with terror streaking his young face.

The black vampire bird began herding Kardos from one side to the other.

Evalle's heart banged her chest like fists beating to get out. She screamed at Germanus. "*Stop it!* You made your point. *Stop it!*"

He ignored her.

With a flick of its wing, the bird sent a lightning bolt of energy at Kardos that hit him so hard he lifted into the air, howling in pain.

The bird flew up and hovered as it stabbed those sharp fangs into the vulnerable teenage body.

Kardos and Evalle screamed at the same time.

Blood ran down the floating body and poured to the ground as the bird fed.

Evalle couldn't feel her legs or hands. How could she have let them do that to Kardos? She yelled curses at Germanus between tears. "You miserable bastard. That boy did nothing to you. What kind of monster are you?"

Germanus calmly turned to her. "One you should not test again. I can bring the other twin, Lanna, that little pet gargoyle ... even Storm in here next. My friend who brought you here filled me in on all of them. He knew I would need that knowledge to deal with you. Are we finally clear on who is in charge?"

She couldn't answer him. She drew shuddering breaths as she stared at the limp body now lying on the ground and no longer making a sound or moving. Her mind could not accept the image, but she smelled the fresh blood on her next strangled breath.

Germanus gave an order and his gargoyle scooped up the body.

"What are you doing with him?" Evalle said, her voice a broken sound even to her ears.

"I had intended to burn the remains."

"No." She cried the sad word.

"There is nothing you can do for him. If I don't burn it, my army will use what is left for food."

She wasn't going to survive this after all. Her gaze locked on the gargoyle lumbering out of the arena. She would kill every creature in this place. There was nothing but evil here.

Germanus thought she'd lead his army?

Not if she managed to rip apart all of them.

Then she could help Daegan if he did find her, but something told her that Germanus had a trick up his sleeve he had yet to share with her.

Maybe she'd die here after all.

She could no longer regenerate from death like the other gryphons currently on Treoir Island. They all started with three regenerations and the others had used at least one.

The invisible clamp holding her in place vanished.

Germanus walked back to his gargoyle ride and climbed on. He said, "Are you ready to face the kwane now?"

With that, the gargoyle pushed off the ground, flying too easily for something his size with wings that small.

She turned to the black megabird, now bulked up after having fed on someone she loved.

She cracked her neck and called up her gryphon fast. Power surged in a flash flood through her body. The physical pain that shift caused was nothing compared to how her heart suffered.

I will destroy this one for you, Kardos, she vowed silently.

Then she would do her best to either take down every other creature here, including every fucking gargoyle, or draw her last breath trying.

Now she was glad she had not bonded with Storm or she could only wonder what fate he would face by being connected to her.

The kwane opened its winged arms.

New lightning bolts struck each wing. That miserable black

bird made a high, keening noise of delight, then its fangs dropped. Evalle lifted her gryphon head and roared in fury.

Bring it.

CHAPTER 20

Himalayas north of Nepal

ICY STALACTITES HAD BEGUN REFORMING above Cathbad's head by the time he heard Brynhild return in dragon form to the remote lair he'd provided for her.

He eyed the shield at his side.

Would she call it to her again?

Power rushed in from the cave opening, alerting him that she'd just changed shape.

When she entered, she was in human form once more, and still wore gear suited to a medieval battle.

She would be a tenacious one for sure.

He stood with his hands in his pockets. "Enjoy your flight?"

"Yes. I did." She walked over and lifted the shield, letting him know just how confident she was to gain it at any time. "Where is Daegan?"

"If you're ready to begin training, I'll show you."

She gave him a flat stare. "I asked about Daegan."

Cathbad could not allow her free reign if she was going to destroy his plans before he got started. "If you think to attack Daegan the first time you see him, then I will not help you."

Sighing with anger, she spit out, "You are an old woman to nag me."

Enough was enough.

Stepping close, he powered up his energy so that she would know he was not her lackey. "Take heed, Brynhild. I am *not* an old woman. I am a druid who has survived many things more dangerous than you. There is a limit to my patience. You would be wise not to reach it or to continue testing me."

She took a step back and tossed her shield away. "You would

threaten an ice dragon?"

"Only if you continue to be unreasonable."

She lifted her arms above her head and shoved her hands down in front of her while yelling a battle cry.

He saw the attack coming and didn't move.

Fire rained down on him in a shower.

His clothes disintegrated. His hair, close-trimmed beard and eyelashes burned away. Once the flagrant assault was over, he stepped calmly from the spot where embers continued glowing across the floor.

That surprised her.

Her face twisted in rage. Flipping her hands around, she slammed him with a load of power.

His naked body flew across the room backwards. At the last second before he would have splattered against the wall, he could have teleported, but he didn't.

Inches from the jagged wall, he stopped in midair and remained suspended. As he floated there, he called up a new set of clothing, then replaced his hair, eyelashes and beard.

Floating down to floor level, but stopping two inches above the ground, he moved toward her until they had ten feet separating them.

The room stank of singed hair and burned clothes.

He might have made a mistake in keeping this one.

Maybe he'd have done better to go find one of her brothers before both princes had died. Surely a male dragon would be more suited to strategizing a battle plan, and less emotional about the goal.

Straightening the collar of his shirt and smoothing his hands over the new suit, Cathbad gave her a weighty look. "What else do you have?"

She'd become deathly silent, probably just realizing she'd stepped into a majikal pile of shit up to her neck.

When she said nothing, Cathbad told her, "In that case, I think we need a little more time apart."

Her eyes turned reptilian, a sure sign she prepared for a battle.

He flicked a hand to the side and pointed at the pond.

Ice ruptured and burst into the air.

Her gaze left his to follow the explosion.

With the chunks of ice suspended above the churning water, Cathbad said, "I will not battle you every inch of the way. If you are not prepared to do your part and follow my lead, then perhaps you need another fifty or sixty years underwater ... but you shall be conscious this time."

Shaking her head back and forth, she said, "You would not." Then she glared at him. *"Do not dare!"*

She began shifting into a dragon.

Cathbad pulled a bracelet out of his pocket. The wide silver band had the Celtic braided outline of her family's dragon emblem and glowed from being so close to Brynhild.

He lifted the band and ordered, "Return to human form, Brynhild."

She was halfway shifted.

Her body stopped expanding and started shrinking. The gut wrenching sounds coming from her blasted through the room and echoed back.

In seconds, she had returned to human form, now naked after ripping out of her battle gear. But she had to also be exhausted from shifting so many times close together.

She began shivering and wrapped her arms over her breasts. Pushing an evil look at him, she snarled, "That bracelet is mine! Give it to me."

"And still, you've learned nothing," he chided. "I hope you enjoy your next time out of this world." He lifted his empty hand.

Her eyes flared wide. "No. Do not. Wait. I will ... talk more. Do not send me—"

With a flick of his wrist, her naked body lifted up and dove head first into the water. He pointed at the still-suspended ice then down at the pond.

Chunks flew back together like a movie scene shot in reverse.

He powered up his hearing.

Brynhild screamed curses at him.

She might find her way out of there. If so, she would be ready to kill him when he returned for her again.

Or she could become an ally with better manners if she was still beneath the surface next time. He couldn't give her fifty or sixty years.

He didn't have that kind of time to waste while stalking Daegan.

CHAPTER 21

County Kilkenny, Ireland

STORM'S OLFACTORY SENSE PICKED UP the scent of Noirre the moment he landed in Ireland near Dunmore Cave. Having a teleporting dragon on hand made all the difference in this hunt.

He didn't want to push anyone to enter a cave known as a death trap, but he had no qualms about going in on his own.

Tristan walked up with his gaze on the sinking sun. "Think it's the same day here, right?"

Quinn confirmed, "Still Sunday, but four hours later. That puts local time around just after five in the afternoon."

Time had no relevance to Storm while Evalle was missing. As the team assembled again, he asked, "What do we know about this place today?"

Quinn said, "The cave is a tourist location. I can't recall everything, but I do remember reading that bodies were recovered from the site during archaeological excavations at one time. Once those were removed, this cave was turned into a museum of sorts." He asked Daegan, "Will the plant be growing where those removed bodies are buried?"

"Not the Noirre plant. It grows only deep inside this cave, which means some remains were missed. Maybe the spirits had a way of shielding those. I have no idea where the plants and bodies are exactly, other than inside the cave."

Stepping into the conversation, Tristan mused, "How can something that deadly be in a cave where humans have survived visiting? Why haven't those plants been discovered?"

Reese had been staring out over the rugged landscape covered in patches of grass, rock and dirt. She suggested, "Plants are living things. Daegan said the plants were thought to be sentient. If this is the case, the plants could have moved the bodies to a secure location inside the cave."

"I smelled Noirre out here," Storm announced to the group. "If the plant only grows inside, then it's been brought outside."

"Can you pinpoint an actual spot for the scent?" Daegan asked.

Lifting his nose to determine a direction, Storm took off, moving quickly. If they wanted to go with him, they had to keep up. After hiking over a knoll and down the backside of the hill, Storm noticed a sign off to his left that indicated the entrance of Dunmore Cave. They had to keep an eye out for human visitors and staff. Daegan might need to drop a cloak over them again.

Storm stopped short and leaned down.

When he straightened, all of the team had caught up. He pointed at the ground. "The Noirre scent is right here. I'm picking up the scent of the same being from the art park in Atlanta in this spot as well."

"Have you figured out who the scent belongs to?" Tristan asked.

"No, but I've smelled it around Atlanta on occasion. No matter how hard I try to connect it to a face, I can't, which means I haven't *seen* this person's face."

"We're close to the cave," Quinn said, turning to nod. "That fits what I've read about the entrance being at the bottom of a gulley." He told Daegan, "As we crested the hill, I climbed a bit further and saw two cars leaving. There's only one in the parking lot, which probably belongs to staff. The cave exhibit closing at five local time would make sense."

Reese moved forward. "Let me see if I can pick up anything from here."

Evalle had shared with Storm that she picked up more going on between Reese and Quinn than just their joint interest in Phoedra. Evalle had seen them kiss once and said Quinn looked at Reese like a woman he cared about. His mate had been anxious to grab Quinn alone to ask what was up.

Out of consideration for Quinn right now, Storm sent the Belador a questioning look about Reese using her gift.

Quinn gave him a let-her-do-what-she-wants shrug.

Storm understood Quinn's frustration.

He'd experienced that many times while trying to do the right thing by allowing Evalle the space she needed to function, but constantly worrying about her being in danger.

More than anything, Storm hated to be proven justified for what she called overprotectiveness.

He didn't know how they'd move forward from this, but he never wanted to lose her again.

First, he had to get her back.

When no one argued with her, Reese planted her butt on the exact spot where Storm had located the scent. She muttered, "Just remember that if he teleported from here, I won't find anything."

"We understand, Reese," Quinn told her. "But please don't go beyond what you can do safely."

"Since I don't even know my limits with this, guess I'll stop when it hurts," she tossed back at him.

Quinn muttered a Slavic curse.

At least it sounded Slavic to Storm. Then Quinn went over and knelt behind Reese with his hands on her shoulders. "Perhaps my energy will aid you."

She smiled slightly.

Storm noted an almost intimate connection between those two and felt certain others on the team had noticed it as well. Evalle had good reason to be curious about that relationship.

Reese closed her eyes and all expression fell away as she started whispering words that had a familiar ring to Storm.

Evalle said Reese had a connection to the Haida tribe of western Canada. Her words held an inflection similar to the Navajo language Storm sometimes used for chanting.

When she stopped whispering, creases formed in her forehead and at the corner of her closed eyes as her attention was drawn to something. She'd been leaning forward as if trying to see further, then she jerked backwards, knocking Quinn on his butt as well as breaking his connection to her.

"Reese?" Quinn scrambled to check on her.

Her eyes flew open. She smiled and started to speak, then wrenched to the side and threw up.

"Dammit, Reese," Quinn complained, as he held her shoulders for the brief sickness.

Once again, Daegan supplied a glass of water along with a cloth this time, which Quinn accepted.

Reese took the water, wiped her mouth with the cloth and pushed to her feet, then handed the water back to Daegan.

The dragon king frowned and the glass vanished.

Quinn said, "I told you back in the building with the bodies that you shouldn't use your gift until you figure out why it's making you sick."

"Remote viewing didn't make me sick."

Storm started to confirm that as truth, but before he had a chance, Quinn demanded, "Then what *is* making you sick?"

Reese shot right back, "None of your business."

The fact that she lied must have been written all over Storm's face. Quinn had shoved a fast look his way before Storm could hide his reaction.

That had to be why Quinn told Reese, "You're lying."

Lifting her hands in a back-off motion, Reese said, "Not talking about it here and now. Stuff it." Then she told the group, "When I was hunting for Phoedra ... " She paused to glare at Quinn and inserted, "Before *you* came along ... I could see Phoedra in real time being kidnapped."

Storm frowned. What did that kidnapping have to do with this one?

Rubbing her hands together in a nervous manner, Reese said, "But when I was at the dead body place we just left in Atlanta, I traced the path without seeing anyone actually *on* the path. That was a little new. This time, I also traced a path, but I could see a hooded guy who stood up from this spot with a plant in his hand and walked until he found transportation. He traveled to a town, then vanished. I think my remote viewing is evolving and I might have seen our kidnapper leaving this spot on foot even though he is clearly already gone."

"Why not teleport from here?" Adrianna mused out loud.

Tristan snapped his fingers. "Maybe he's like me and teleporting isn't a natural gift. He may be limited."

"That's good information, Reese," Storm complimented. "Thank you for doing that, but please don't do anything else to disturb your ... health." He had an idea what might be going on with Reese, but it was not his place to interfere with those two.

Her eyes widened at his hesitation right before he finished his comment.

She gave him a little thank-you smile, then raked her wild hair off her face and asked, "What are we going to do? Is there any point in going inside that death trap?"

"Actually, there is," Daegan replied. "As Grady suggested, there must be spirits of some sort in there who can shed some light on the being behind this."

"I agree, Daegan. If you'll teleport me inside, I'll start searching the place," Storm said, ready to face whatever waited in there.

"I shall teleport both of us," the dragon king announced, making it clear he would not stand back from any battle. He followed up by telling the others, "There's no point in putting all of you at risk. If for any reason we don't return, Tristan will teleport you home."

"Not to argue with you, boss, but wouldn't it make more sense for me to teleport Storm inside? We can replace me, but not you."

Damn. Storm had wanted to rip Tristan apart more than once in the past when the hardheaded Alterant had dragged Evalle into trouble.

Now he was willing to enter that cave?

"You are valuable as well, Tristan," Daegan admonished, but with no heat. "I am the stronger teleporter of the two of us. I am the best hope for getting us out."

"Yeah, but I'll teleport his ass out if it looks like we're going to lose, where you'll probably stay and fight if he refuses to leave."

Ah, there was the person Storm had known, but in fairness to Tristan, the Alterant was here and willing to help. Storm wouldn't criticize Tristan's strategy.

Quinn offered, "Why don't I join you two in case I can use mind lock?"

"I don't care who goes as long as we do this soon," Storm said, shutting down further offers. He'd rather go alone than have the death of another person on his conscience.

"This discussion is tabled," Daegan ordered. "If Cathbad survived this, I am easily as powerful." He turned to Quinn, "If one, or both, of us returns injured, your powers will be needed most at that time. If something occurs out here and you can't reach me using telepathy, then Tristan will come to find us."

Reese inquired, "Are you also as powerful as that druid, Storm?"

Storm simply replied, "We're about to find out. Ready, Daegan?"

With the group left to watch their backs, Storm and Daegan entered the cave silently, their bodies taking form again in the middle of a display area.

Daegan grumbled, "Your world is cluttered with useless things."

"Looks like this place is empty, but we need to avoid security footage."

"Where would that be?" Daegan asked.

"I see a few cameras, but there may be some I don't see."

"I'll cloak us."

Storm would rather not dull his ability to scent, but after sniffing the hundreds who had passed through here recently, he agreed with Daegan's security solution.

Informing Daegan, "I smell the being who had the Noirre plant outside," Storm took off, following the scent trail. His nose led him through public areas of the cave illuminated with subtle lighting appropriate for a place where so many innocent beings had died.

The scent trail continued past a NO ENTRANCE sign.

Daegan stayed close as Storm bypassed the warning and entered a tunnel.

When the tunnel split, Storm followed their kidnapper's trail. Eventually the passage narrowed to a spot where they'd have to crawl to continue, and he doubted their bodies could squeeze through the opening.

Daegan put a hand on Storm's shoulder.

"What?" Storm asked softly when he turned to face the dragon king.

"That is a dangerous place. A perfect spot for being attacked."

"You're stopping now?"

"No, I suggest we teleport to the other side, but the spirits associated with those remains that lie here may know a preternatural is nearby. I have no information on exactly how Cathbad was attacked or what he did to survive."

"Send me in first." Storm had wanted to keep the dragon king out of this anyhow.

Daegan said, "Prepare to teleport through that small opening. We're both going in."

So much for keeping the casualties low in this operation.

"Let's stand back to back," Storm suggested for the strongest defensive position.

"Good thinking." Daegan turned.

As soon as Storm's back touched Daegan's they were teleporting.

Insertion was instantaneous.

So was the Noirre attack.

CHAPTER 22

Realm of Scamall

CLOSING IN ON A WEEK of residence in the strange realm Germanus ruled, Evalle snuck through the castle. Germanus had granted her two hours to rest.

She didn't trust him enough to lie down and sleep. Instead, she took quick naps while standing so she'd wake as soon as her body went limp and dropped to the floor.

That bastard was not screwing with her dreams again.

Inhaling a deep breath, she looked around the central area of the castle, saw no Germanus or gargoyles, and entered the stairwell that descended to the lower levels.

She'd expected to smell mildew from dampness.

Oddly, this structure showed no signs of being here for hundreds of years.

Or maybe a couple thousand years.

She rubbed her arm where a nasty gash tried to heal.

Different day, nothing new.

She'd come to realize the Noirre majik that had been shoved into her chest wound after she arrived here had interfered with her normal ability to call up her beast energy. Or it could be that the guy who stuck all that dark majik in her body had placed a spell, which allowed Germanus to control her healing via the Noirre majik. She'd heal somewhat each time she shifted into her Gryphon form, only to immediately face the next flying creature Germanus sent to attack her.

Being fully healed was a thing of the past.

To her credit, she was gaining more ability at air battles, but to her detriment she was losing the desire to keep fighting.

Daegan, Storm and the Beladors might never find her.

How would they know if she was here?

Germanus claimed he'd made a blood pact with her kidnapper that they would shield each other's identity, but the kidnapper would alert Germanus the minute Daegan was on the way to attack.

Nothing had been said about sending a message to Daegan. Germanus was not telling her everything. No surprise there. She had her doubts about the sanity of a human living alone inside a realm for two thousand years.

Was the dragon king supposed to figure all this out on his own without a tip? If the kidnapper vowed not to share anything about Germanus or this place, did he have some sly way to send Daegan here? If so, Daegan had to suspect a trap.

Her dragon king would still come for her.

Storm and the rest of her friends would, too. At one time, she'd felt like the poster child for Evalle-against-the-whole-world, but that had changed. Reminding herself of that had warmed her heart and raised the urge to fight on at first, but that urge had begun to wane more with each passing realm day.

In her mind, she wished everyone would appear right now.

In her heart, she did not want anyone she loved to die in this place.

Would their spirits ever rest or just stay here? Who knew, but ... again, she was glad Storm had not tied himself to her.

What is with all this whining? Evalle asked herself before her mother's voice got a chance to do it. The woman's spirit had said little recently, though. Maybe time moved faster here than in her mother's world, too.

The constant mental drain and lack of decent sleep had Evalle dancing close to insanity.

She could not give in. She was alive to fight another day, which would happen sooner rather than later, unfortunately. Storm was hunting her. They could defeat anything together.

That dragon would be leading with her Skinwalker keeping stride. Actually, knowing Storm, he might take off on his own, but she hoped not. Daegan would need to bring backup with him, because he'd be at serious risk in Scamall if Germanus had a powerful god—or more—ready to attack him. Even if he knew what awaited, that dragon would still come after her, and deserved for her to show enough faith to hang tight.

Figuring her way out of here was about more than just her. People needed her. She had to keep telling herself that so she wouldn't give up.

She'd gone from being so very alone to having Tzader and Quinn at her back.

Now, she needed an extra set of hands to count the people in her life she could depend on, and who also knew they could depend on her.

That cheered her and stomped her moment of weakness. This was the time to be tough and believe in her mate. Storm had always found a way to locate her in the past.

Maybe the cavalry would show up, too.

Oh, yeah, maybe Macha and Maeve will team up to save you.

Evalle blew out a long breath. *Shut up, mind. It's my fantasy.*

Descending deeper into the bowels of the castle with each carefully placed step, and avoiding the area where she thought the dungeon was located, she constantly listened for any sign of an enormous gargoyle coming for her. She'd had true affection for gargoyles before coming here.

The ones in this realm were monsters.

Not like her little Feenix. It hurt to think how confused and stressed he'd be right now, but he was tough, too. Storm, Lanna and the boys would watch over her sweet gargoyle and keep him safe.

Evalle kept her mind on her task, which was to uncover as much information as she could about Germanus. She might just find a way out of this mess or at least a weakness in his armor.

She'd been taking step after step, heading down stone stairs, but stopped at the first sign of light below.

Her ragged heart kicked into gear, pumping hard, but still nothing like when she was in the pit. In there, where adrenaline and the will to live kept her fighting, one day ran into the next, blending into one endless stretch of battles followed by misery.

Now was the time to calm down and not alert anyone to her presence.

Once her breathing slowed, she continued toward the light. At the last step down, she reached a wide landing where she poked her head past the arched opening.

Now she knew where the glow had originated.

The sight of gold goblets, silver plates, gold figures, dazzling jewels, ancient weapons polished to a shine and ... there was too much to mentally catalog.

This should be next to *hoard* in the dictionary, or *king's ransom.* Germanus said a god made this realm and moved all her captor's belongings here. Had Germanus been a king? He wasn't a dragon or he'd have shown her that side by now.

Tiptoeing as if someone two floors up in a stone structure might hear her barefooted steps, Evalle limped her way through the room. She rubbed her arms against the chilly air.

Four torches were mounted to the walls, their light reflecting off the mountain of treasure that peaked thirty feet in the air. It sprawled at least forty feet in diameter. What all was in that pile?

Stepping closer, she knelt to touch a plate large enough to hold a Thanksgiving turkey and more. The metal work was beautiful. Someone had spent hours shaping this and engraving the design of grapes and vines around the edges.

"Exceptional collection, isn't it?"

Evalle flinched and shoved up to her feet, turning quickly to face Germanus. "I was ... just finding my way around and got lost."

"Liar," he accused, then cut loose a deep belly laugh. "I expected you to go off on your own at some point. You found it, but then it's not like I have to hide it in my own realm."

She fought the urge to yell at him that there was nothing funny about any of this. But if she wanted intel, she wouldn't get it by antagonizing a lunatic. Every bit of information she could squeeze out of him would help if she discovered a way to leave.

Not if, but when. *Never, ever think escape is impossible.*

The minute she lost all hope, she might as well be dead.

She had too much to live for to give in. Time to pretend she was getting accustomed to being here.

Breathing deeply as if relieved, she lifted a shoulder. "You caught me. If I'm going to spend a lot of time here I'd like to know more about this place."

"Oh? So you concede that you will never leave Scamall?" he taunted.

To agree would not be believable.

She scoffed at that. "Not even. I'm only conceding that I'm bored as hell and curious. This isn't exactly a vacation spot for me."

He laughed again. "I like that about you. You speak your mind. In my time, it was frowned upon when a woman acted so boldly, but you are a warrior. But be very clear on this, you *will* be here forever."

Keep thinking that, dick breath. She waved off his comment as inconsequential. Then she waved the same hand to indicate the pile of treasure. "Is this what you did before you landed in this realm? Spent your life stealing gold and jewels, then ratholing it here?"

He bragged, "Oh, no. I gained this all at one time."

She gave him a dramatic look of disbelief that upped his arrogant smile. Her acting skills might not be as lacking as she thought. "This is ... this is incredible. It looks like some kind of dragon hoard," she joked, hoping he'd take the bait.

Germanus strolled past her to stand at the opposite side of the extraordinary pile, gazing at it with admiration.

Was he not going to answer?

"It is a hoard," Germanus murmured. Sending his gaze back to her, he admitted, "It was mine for the taking once the king's defenses fell."

She had a bad feeling that she knew exactly what he was going to say when she asked, "Where did you take it from?"

"Galway."

"Huh?" Did he think she knew all the geographic locations in the world?

Annoyed, he said, "Has Daegan told you nothing of where he was born?"

"Uh, no, it hasn't come up in any discussion. You stole this from *him*?"

"Of course not."

She was actually glad to hear that. Otherwise, this would definitely turn into a war if Daegan showed up.

Germanus explained, "All of this belonged to King Gruffyn."

"His father?"

"The very one."

This man had been insane centuries ago.

He was so far beyond that now.

She'd found a thread of information and would not let go until she'd unraveled one of his secrets. "How did you manage to get away with that much treasure from a king who had a dragon? That's hard to imagine."

"You doubt me?" His happy little mental party turned into annoyance at her questioning his ability.

Time to stroke his ego. "Hey, I'm sitting in a realm in who-knows-what dimension with you and an army of flying beasts. I know you're capable of what you claim, because ... hello. The evidence is staring me in the face. I just want to know how someone pulls off something this fantastical."

Using fantastical should stroke his swollen ego, right?

He walked across the room, snagging a torch on the way.

She had no option except to follow if she wanted more answers.

He entered an alcove on the side that hadn't been evident earlier. Probably shielded by majik. Shoving the torch in a new holder, he stood there as light filled the smaller room with an orange glow that brushed over a throne fit for a king.

Germanus had stolen the king's throne, too?

Daegan would slaughter the enemy of today's Belador to protect his people.

She tried to imagine how much more deadly the dragon king would be to someone who dared to possess his father's throne, especially when the king probably hadn't survived this incident.

To be sure, she asked, "What happened to the king?"

"What do you think happens when a king is dethroned?"

Yeah, just as she'd thought. "Was he a bad king?"

"Gruffyn was a weak king, always putting his people ahead of building a true dynasty with an army capable of raiding for more gold. In his place, I would have ruled the world. Should have, in fact."

Settling into the enormous chair covered in gold gilding and with plush cushions of a deep red material that appeared downy soft, Germanus had the face of a content man.

Would he still have that calm expression in death?

He lifted a jeweled crown of gold from a small table at the side of the throne and placed the exquisite piece on his head.

If Daegan stood here, he'd torture Germanus before beheading him.

She'd hand the sword to her dragon king and offer pointers.

Sounded like Daegan's father had been a good and decent ruler, which would be easy to believe after the time she'd spent with Daegan. He'd had a solid role model.

She warned Germanus, "Daegan will not let you keep all of this."

"He's not taking *any* of this from me. I've been here for centuries." Leaning back with his crown half-cocked, Germanus said, "I can't believe Queen Maeve was stupid enough to keep Daegan alive all these years. She should have killed him and saved all of us a lot of trouble."

Poor baby. Should Evalle apologize for imposing on his life as well by having to be kidnapped?

She doubted he'd answer her question, but it was worth a try. "So Queen Maeve is behind kidnapping me?"

Germanus gave her a smile of tolerance, but no reply.

Returning to his comment about Queen Maeve keeping Daegan alive, she told Germanus, "Daegan said the queen doesn't want him dead. She kept him all that time because she wanted to torture him by making him spend eternity in the shape of her throne."

After saying that out loud, it made her question Queen Maeve's involvement, since Germanus definitely wanted the dragon dead.

Germanus sat up. "A dragon throne you say? I only heard she'd captured Daegan." That tiny piece of information brightened his day. "I like the way she thinks, but she still should not have allowed Daegan to escape."

Evalle had played a part in Daegan's escape, which had involved taking him out of TÅμr Medb in the form of said throne, but sharing that might put a damper on the light mood.

Thinking back over her conversation with Germanus, she pulled on her lower lip until she returned to the one question that had badgered her mind since showing up here.

Why was this happening and why now?

Could she be standing in the middle of the answer? She asked, "Are you concerned that Daegan will come for that hoard?"

"Of course he will. I'm not concerned, but anticipating it." He looked at her as if she'd asked if breathing clean air was healthy. He bent forward, propping a hand on one knee. "Every dragon needs a hoard. Daegan will settle for nothing less than his father's treasure."

"Why would he even think you had this stash? Did you know his father?"

"For many years. I was his steward."

Evalle mentally dug through historical novels she'd read. "Wasn't a steward some kind of accountant back then?"

"Exactly. I oversaw the finances of his entire kingdom. The king was not prepared for a war or he'd still have all this treasure. Or at least, Daegan might."

"What war?"

"The great Dragani War. Have you studied no history?" Germanus seemed genuinely disappointed in her lack of dragon-era education.

"Hey, I knew what a steward was," she snapped. Pointing at herself, she said, "I haven't been alive even thirty years yet. I'm just now finding out about things that happened over the past one hundred years in our world, much less something that happened two thousand years ago."

"Your education is sorely lacking. Once you battle Daegan and he's gone forever, I'll ensure you have plenty of history to study."

She walked to one side and turned to start back, using Tzader's motion of pacing to think. Seemed to work for him, but he didn't walk with a limp.

She missed Tzader. And Quinn.

Pushing that away, she addressed this ridiculous battle Germanus expected her to have with Daegan. "You do realize Daegan is a dragon shifter and I'm only a gryphon. You also said all I had to do was lead your creatures into battle with him, not kill him." If Daegan did show up, she hoped he would fight back because she'd have to really battle. If she didn't give her best attempt at fighting Daegan's dragon, Germanus would harm someone else she loved.

Her options sucked, because she would not be the reason the Beladors lost a true leader.

Right now she should be wishing she'd been born human, but she tossed that wish right out the window. If that had happened, she would never have met Storm. She'd never regret whatever it took to have him in her life.

Her heart ached from the pain of Noirre permeating the organ, but it hurt worse from losing Kardos. She'd never be able to heal from that. She was not letting this monster kill anyone else she loved.

She only hoped the kidnapper got what he deserved somewhere down the road for doing that to an innocent person. If he ever showed his face here, she'd find a way to gut him.

If protecting all she held dear meant battling Daegan, she'd apologize and do it, but she was banking on Daegan teleporting her out.

Germanus had said it wouldn't be possible, as though he controlled all activity in and out of the realm. But if that kidnapper had managed to enter on his own, that would mean someone else could pass both ways, right?

Was his threat of her not being able to leave just a bluff to keep her from trying to escape again? She'd like to think so, but anything was possible in the world of preternaturals.

Not the most comforting thought.

Pausing in her barefooted limping, she leveled with Germanus. "Even if I wanted to kill Daegan, which I don't, he'd burn me into a lump of charcoal before I got off even a kinetic shot ... and that's *if* you allow me to use all powers." Not to mention her bum leg that was strong enough to stand on, but not much use for anything else. She had a sick feeling the Noirre plugged into her chest would never allow those hideous scars to heal or her chest to stop hurting.

"Daegan won't kill you," Germanus argued.

She stuck her hands on her hips. "Not if he has a choice. I'm one of his closest advisors and I know he does not want to harm me, but he is not going to stand by and let me take him apart."

"I never expected him to do any such thing. But I know Daegan, because he's more disgusting than his father. Daegan is the last of the white knights and you're a woman, which he would never raise a hand to harm. Besides, as I explained, you only have to battle him. While he's busy trying not to harm you, my army will take care of the rest."

This delusional jerk was living in a fantasy world.

She chuckled. "The seven critters you have left are not going to take down Daegan even if he fights them alone."

"Don't laugh as if I am the fool here," he warned in a booming voice that vibrated the walls.

She was not cut out to be a spy. Undercover operators had to maintain their cover at all times and never show what they were thinking or feeling.

With her anger boiling over at everything from getting kidnapped, to not being allowed to heal, to watching Kardos die, she snarled, "I don't get you at all. You're safe here. You can sit here and count your money every day forever. Why bring Daegan's wrath down on your head?"

He stood. "Safe? I've been stuck in this realm for centuries with nothing but my imagination to keep me company. I can't conjure a woman or touch you. If I do, my dick will shrivel and I will be without even manual entertainment."

So that was why he had not tried to force himself on her. She'd thought it was her repulsive image. She'd also thought he was favored by the god who put him here, but it didn't sound that way.

Germanus must have pissed off that powerful being. With her captor on a rant, she stifled her anger and tried for an understanding tone. "What? Why would your god do that? You must be one of his followers who worshipped him."

Staring at his shiny pile of goodies, Germanus groused, "I did worship Abandinu in spite of risking a lashing if the king had found out. Abandinu was everything to me. When I asked my god for a safe place to stash this hoard and somewhere Daegan couldn't harm me, I thought he would put me in a castle far from King Gruffyn. But no," Germanus scowled.

Evalle didn't breathe. *Don't interrupt the mad man.*

"Instead, Abandinu built this realm for his favorite winged beasts, then teleported me here with all my possessions. He said the day Daegan died that he would free me. Then he disappeared. The bastard."

Part of that story had to be missing.

Evalle had nothing but disdain for gods and goddesses she'd faced in Tribunals, but she had learned they did little without a reason. Basically, they were lazy and self-serving.

What had Germanus done to be treated this way by Abandinu?

Probably hadn't been wise of Germanus to curse a deity, but she had no qualms about watching him get smoked if his god heard that.

They'd both wronged Daegan and his father.

Tired of listening to the rant of someone who didn't deserve any consideration, she muttered, "Sympathy is between shit and syphilis in the dictionary, Germanus."

"Dictionary?"

"Argh. Can't even insult you, because you've been isolated forever."

Sitting back down with a glum look on his face, Germanus said, "My god abandoned me long ago. Now I find out Daegan is free and still immortal. What am I supposed to do? Just sit here for eternity with a dragon after my ass? That is not happening. I will have a new protector once I leave here. She will reward me just for killing Daegan."

Evalle's ears perked up. "Who?"

Germanus would not answer.

"Let me get this straight. You're preparing for a battle with a dragon and you don't even know the name of your new benefactor?"

Speaking through clenched teeth, he said, "I *do* know her name. I promised to not speak her name until she gives me permission."

Dead end there. Evalle switched gears, acting uninterested. "Whatever. So who kidnapped me? I know it wasn't a woman."

"You keep asking the same questions."

"If you'd answer them, I'd stop asking. See how that works?"

Gifting her with a smirk, he said, "How about this? I will give you the names you ask for before I leave."

Hold everything. "You're really leaving me here?"

"It will not be possible to take you with me." He said that as if it was obvious. Nothing was obvious.

This might be her only chance to find out everything she could. "You made this deal with my kidnapper, right?"

Germanus frowned. "Correct."

"He said he'd get you out of here if you kill Daegan, is that the deal? What about your pile of treasure?"

Giving her a look that questioned her IQ level, he said, "Once I have Daegan's head on a platter, I will escape this miserable realm with my treasure and live forever."

She only knew one way to live forever. "My kidnapper promised you immortality, too? And you trust this guy? Why?"

For just a second, doubt dimmed his confidence, but it disappeared as quickly. He sat up, placing the crown to the side and explained, "This man had the power to harvest pure Noirre when others died attempting it."

Pure Noirre? Was that why the majik used on Evalle smelled so strong? Noirre got traded secretly among preternaturals, but Noirre majik was believed to have always come from the Medb. A pure form had Evalle again thinking Queen Maeve had to be behind this.

Germanus kept listing evidence to support his trust in the kidnapper. "When someone can enter a Celtic realm through a bolthole, shield his trail and show up with the purest form of Noirre in his hand, then deliver a Belador who shifts into a gryphon, I have a hard time arguing."

He had her there. "Where did this guy find pure Noirre?"

"Ha! You do not know where Norrie originates, do you?" he scorned. "I am stuck in this realm and still I know more than you!"

She hated to admit it, but Germanus was correct on that point. She said, "I'll give you that. So where did Noirre come from?"

"Dunmore Cave in Ossory," Germanus replied, full of smug arrogance.

"Where is Ossory?"

"Listen closely and learn something," he snapped. "The Vikings of Dublin were raiding—"

"Dublin? As in Ireland? I thought Vikings were Swedish or Nordic or something like that."

Shaking his head in disgust, he said, "There were three groups of Vikings in Dublin, Limerick and Waterford at one time. Those in Dublin were going after the Waterford bunch when they raided Ossory. Fearing capture as slaves, the women and children hid inside Dunmore cave because it had a narrow opening they could defend. The Vikings decided to burn them out, but—"

Evalle snapped her fingers. "They asphyxiated those innocent people instead. Damn."

Germanus narrowed his eyes at her with irritation. Or was he confused?

Did he not know what asphyxiated meant? Rather than poke

back at him about having a better vocabulary, she focused on keeping him talking and said, "They suffocated, right?"

"Yes. I knew of Noirre in my time, but my friend shared more details. He said some remains were recovered, but a small number of skeletons were hidden deep in the cave."

Evalle had this comical vision of skeletons creeping into a dark corner to hide. Yep, her mind was going.

Undeterred, Germanus kept explaining. "The mother of one little girl was not present when the women herded the children to the cave. That mother was captured trying to save her child. She cursed the raiders and swore she'd have vengeance."

Evalle mentally nodded her approval over the mother getting back at those murderers any way she could.

Germanus continued, "The Vikings soon realized they had captured a witch, which was why someone probably allowed her to escape when they invaded Spain and fought the Moors. She was taken in by a man who found her almost dead. He used his powers to heal her and realized she also had powers. He convinced her to stay with him. They had seven children who inherited various abilities and gifts. My friend who kidnapped you is a descendant of that impressive power. He grew up being told of the cave that hid his ancestor's remains and how the original Noirre plant grows from the skeletons of those killed."

She had to close her gaping mouth. Noirre was a *plant*? "When did all that happen?"

"Not that long ago. I believe in early 900."

Eleven hundred years ago was recent? Guess time was relative when you lived in this realm. She forced her sleep-deprived mind to think what was bugging her about all that. She questioned, "Who first used Noirre?"

"Queen Maeve, of course."

She was growing tired of his you're-an-idiot tone and argued, "But she and Cathbad the Druid went to sleep or whatever for two thousand years, then recently reincarnated."

"I heard as much."

That's when she realized what didn't fit in her mind. Waving her hands, she said, "Whoa. Hold everything. I'm no genius—"

"Quite true," he interjected.

She sent him a scathing look and finished her thought. "Well you're no Einstein either, because the math doesn't work. How could Queen Maeve do anything in 900 if she supposedly went into this deep slumber a thousand years earlier?" Evalle considered everything. Maybe that slumber and reincarnation bit was all a big lie. Not that much of a stretch when considering that queen and druid.

Germanus sighed with great satisfaction at knowing things Evalle did not. He taunted, "I told you that Queen Maeve used Noirre majik during my time."

"Not possible. I … this makes no sense."

Grinning now, he said, "I should make you wonder for the next thousand years you spend in here alone and unable to hold a conversation with another person."

The light bulb flashed on in Evalle's head. Germanus was talking to her now because he hadn't been able to do this for two thousand years.

Her heart hit her feet at the possibility of repeating his life here.

Germanus must not have realized how bad that thought shook her, because he never paused, chattering on. "I find that I am not ready to end this conversation, so I will fill in the gaps in your sad education. Queen Maeve had a seer who told her of a powerful majik to be found in a cave in the future. The queen was unwilling to wait a thousand years and wanted it immediately. Perhaps because of the slumber you say she and the druid had planned. The queen brought in Cathbad, who said he could open a time portal to one spot, but he could not leave it open long due to the power and majik needed. She sent part of her army to retrieve the Noirre majik from the cave."

That sounded incredible, but possible.

What was she saying? What *wasn't* possible when preternaturals were involved?

After all, Queen Maeve and Cathbad planned a way to spend two thousand years out of pocket, then reincarnate at a time to coincide with forcing Alterants to evolve into gryphons. Who saw that coming?

Yeah, she could see how that crazy queen would risk so many lives to travel through a time portal and battle deadly plants.

Evalle mused aloud, "Huh, so the queen's men grabbed the Noirre and jumped back to her world?"

"Not exactly. She lost half her army. One warrior barely entered the portal to return before it closed and was able to report what happened. She next sent a mage who died, then Cathbad agreed to go with her to gain the Noirre. My friend said Cathbad almost perished retrieving the plant and his majik was so damaged from creating those portals he was believed unable to perform that majik ever again."

Could be or ... maybe Cathbad told the queen he couldn't open a time portal like that one again to prevent that crazy goddess from sending him places he didn't want to go.

Would any of today's Beladors know about this?

She doubted it, because Tzader or Quinn would have told her during the many hours they'd spent filling in her education. Daegan would probably know.

She said, "Okay, let's say that I accept that my kidnapper gained Noirre, but I'm not sold that he has such easy access to immortality. Is he immortal?"

Germanus had opened his mouth to argue, but said, "Not yet. He will become immortal at the same time that I do. This way, everyone is invested."

How easy was it to make someone immortal?

Evalle had a sick feeling the kidnapper's offer to Germanus was based upon reaching the river that ran beneath Treoir Castle. This new information pointed at Macha being behind the kidnapping, as much as the Noirre pointed at Queen Maeve.

No clear winner in the villain race.

Based on Germanus' story, the kidnapper was of Celtic ancestry, but descended of a Spanish Moor as well. What was he? A Medb warlock? What other power or ability did he possess that would help her figure out his identity? She'd like to know who hated her enough to do this.

She thought back on how she'd sensed someone or something following her where she met up with Adrianna in the woods. Could the guy be Fae? She asked, "Can the kidnapper fly?"

Germanus cocked his head in a odd way. "I do not think so. Why?"

"Just wondering if he had a way to follow someone who was very fast."

Sitting back with a smug look, Germanus nodded. "He had a

pet peregrine falcon that was dying. Once dead, the bird became his eyes."

"What do you mean?"

"He performed a necromantic spell on the falcon to allow him to control its movements, plus see through its eyes."

"The kidnapper is a necromancer?"

"No. He does not possess that gift, which was why he said he needed the pure Noirre to perform the spell. He also used it to hide his trail and to keep you alive once he removed the stone from your chest."

Worse than having Noirre in her chest, she had *pure* Noirre stuck in there.

"You're insane, you know that?" That popped out of her mouth before she thought it through.

Bright yellow rolled over his eyes. "Careful with your words, Alterant. While I do miss conversation, and find your desire to speak your mind entertaining to a degree, I can always bring the other twin to kill."

She hated to cower in front of anyone, but she would not be the reason anyone else died. She quietly explained, "In my shoes, you'd want to know what was happening. Maybe if you gave me a better idea of what's going on, I could help you more than you realize."

"I've answered all your questions with the exception of withholding names."

She scrambled for an idea of how to keep him from shutting down on her. "Not all of them. I have one more question."

"Very well, what?"

"Would any Alterant have sufficed, or was I the target?"

"You were. Not that I cared which one he captured, but of all the Belador gryphons, you had the most to lose. I had to agree when he explained how that would make keeping you in line easier as compared to someone with little to lose."

She hoped Tristan found out the truth and didn't carry guilt over swapping with her the night before she was taken.

He observed her quietly for a long moment. "You said if you knew more, you could help. I'm always interested in a deal. Do not ask me for names, but what else do you wish to know?"

Relieved he had calmed down in the face of her anger, she took him up on his offer. "You never answered me about why you're doing this. Daegan doesn't bother anyone unless they poke him first. Why start trouble with him now?"

"Me?" Germanus snapped forward and gripped the arms of his throne. "I didn't start this. He did."

She kept her voice calm, but still pointed out, "I'm not seeing how he did this. *You* had me kidnapped. From what I can see, that's the catalyst to all of this."

His forehead creased with true confusion. "Why would I do that unless I had to?"

What was with this guy? "I'd ask if that was a trick question, but I'm not sure you'd grasp my meaning," she said dryly.

"I'll make this simple, because women in today's human world must be more dense than they were in my time."

She would not let Daegan kill Germanus.

He'd have to wait his turn behind her.

Germanus spoke as if instructing an idiot. "If Daegan were not so bloody greedy, you would not be in this situation and he would not be facing death here. He could have stayed in the human realm or on Treoir and left me alone. Understand now? Although, I will admit that a part of me is glad he started this conflict. Once he is gone forever, I get my life back."

At the risk of being slammed again as a simple-minded woman, Evalle asked, "Greedy? Does Daegan even *know* that you have his father's treasure?"

"He does not know where it is yet, but he *is* hunting for his hoard. He might not show up for fifty human years, but with so many people willing to do his bidding, I do not expect it to take long."

Evalle grabbed all the disjointed pieces floating around in her mind and pushed them together. She gave this maniac an incredulous look. "Before I was captured, no one, not even Daegan, was hunting for this gold. Where did you get that wild idea?" She paused, remembering what Germanus had said when he first found her down here. "Is that why you said I found it first? You meant *I* found this treasure before Daegan, who is not even hunting it?"

Her head spun at the gravity of this entire situation.

Her whole life and world had been yanked away, loved ones

harmed, her mate and dragon king now at risk plus who knew how many more because of this crazy man being played.

His giddiness dissolved into anger. He accused, "You lie."

She opened her arms out wide. "Why should I lie? I have nothing to gain by lying. You said yourself that I speak my mind."

"You're trying to trick me, but it won't work."

Her head hurt as all of this made sense in a sick way. "Not me, but someone else has sold you a line of crap." She recalled the conversation she'd heard Germanus and the kidnapper having when she was still half conscious.

She snapped her fingers. "That's what you two were talking about when he delivered me, wasn't it?"

Germanus had been staring off, lost in thought. He glared at her. "What?"

"When your buddy, the kidnapper, dropped me in here. One of the moments I was conscious, you asked if he was sure someone was hunting *it* and he said yes. I thought you were talking about me, but *it* was referencing this treasure. The kidnapper told you Daegan was hunting that pile over there." She pointed over her shoulder with her thumb.

Germanus went from an angry warlord to sounding like a petulant child trying to convince someone he was right. "It is Daegan's hoard. He has to have it!"

"Stereotype much?"

"Stop spouting stupid words!"

She wanted to howl at this idiot. He didn't send someone to kidnap her. He was the patsy here.

The kidnapper had an ulterior motive to snatch her and set up this trap for Daegan. And he'd used pure Noirre. Had to be crazy Queen Maeve. Who else would be so bold knowing Daegan would rain more than fire down on someone for doing all this?

It felt good to know she had a leader she could depend on and who put his people first, but she hated the danger he'd be facing here.

Evalle said, "No, Daegan doesn't need a hoard. He's not some cartoon dragon from medieval stories. He's real and has the heart of a king. He would never put any of us at risk for any treasure."

Those words settled in her heart.

She was right. Daegan had never acted like a self-centered

dragon.

Damn Germanus and whoever had discovered that this lunatic could be manipulated. She wouldn't go so far as to say Daegan would not come for the treasure if he knew it was here, but he was someone who would go alone and not risk losing even one warrior for something that could be replaced.

She repeated, "I am in Daegan's inner circle. I can say without question that prior to your grabbing me, not *one* of Daegan's people had been hunting any gold. And Daegan has had too much on his plate to run around treasure hunting. You have been played for a fool."

Getting her say in and watching Germanus have a meltdown felt good. Seeing a chink in his plan emboldened her to stick to her resolve and survive.

She added, "In fact, regardless of some oath, your kidnapper buddy is very likely spreading the word that you are holding Daegan's hoard ... and me. You won't have to wait long. He's coming and so is my mate. Those seven flying creatures who survived battling me will *never* stop Daegan in dragon form."

Her heart surged at the taste of imminent victory.

Daegan and Storm would survive and she'd get out of here yet.

This was what a rush of hope felt like after being at the bottom of her emotional barrel. She couldn't wipe the smile from her face if she tried.

Seriously pissed, Germanus stood and walked over to a wall next to his throne. He sneered at her. "Those seven and you are only intended to slow him down. These are my army." Germanus lifted his arm and called out, "*Nunc aperta.* You're too stupid to know *those* words, but that is Latin for *open now.*"

She ignored his dig at her vocabulary as shock blasted her happiness to pieces.

The wall turned foggy then cleared, much like peering into a scrying bowl.

Twenty huge beasts meandered through a field. His menagerie held everything from massive wyverns, much larger than the one that had survived fighting her, to manticores to things she couldn't name to ...

A dragon?

There were *two* dragons alive today?

Plus, this bunch appeared well fed.

Germanus bragged, "These will not be defeated." Turning to her, he broke out a huge smile. "I only wanted to cull the weak ones and use those that survived to show me how it looks when you really battle so you can't pretend. If you don't battle, I will send word to your kidnapper to bring me the rest of your friends ... *and* your mate if he doesn't come here first. When he does arrive, I will send my two gargoyles out to tear him apart."

He walked out, pausing at the entrance and turning to her. "You lie about Daegan hunting the gold. No dragon can stand to lose a hoard such as this one. A dragon is nothing without a pile of treasure that rivals all others."

Her mind screamed with rage at his ancient thinking, but she wouldn't break down in front of this monster and give him one more second of enjoyment.

That didn't stop her from shouting, "Think what you want, Germanus, but you'll see my mate for sure and he'll be the one tearing your monsters apart. He'll come with Daegan. They'll defeat your army." She hoped like hell they could. "When they do, we'll all teleport out of here."

Clenching a fist, he said, "They might. You won't."

What did that mean? "They won't leave without me."

His hand relaxed along with his face. "I thought you heard us talking when you first arrived. Evidently you missed some of our conversation."

She waited for more. Germanus would talk to an empty room.

He said, "Remember seeing the wyvern carcass in the field the day you tried to fly away? That was a demonstration for me. The kidnapper spelled the wyvern as he fed it a tiny bit of the Noirre majik, then he tried to take the beast out of this realm. Majik created in here cannot leave. That beast screamed when it tried to pass through the limits of the realm. My friend held it there long enough for the majik to boil inside the animal. Then he dropped the writhing body back to the ground. If you recall, he also shoved Noirre into your chest to close the wound. He spelled that too. Had he not, you would have died. If you try to leave, you will suffer much more, but you will probably die faster."

He turned and climbed the stairs.

Her skin felt clammy and her stomach churned.

She'd thought ... she always had a chance to escape. She screamed out loud this time.

His laughter floated down.

CHAPTER 23

County Kilkenny, Ireland

A VINE AS THICK AS HIS arm wrapped Storm's neck. His claws had extended the second he was attacked.

Daegan fought off his own rabid plant.

Storm was desperate for information, but it would do him no good if they didn't both survive. He wasn't sure he could get out of here without Daegan.

Spirits with open mouths filled with sharp teeth screamed loud as banshees. He saw only fifteen or twenty.

Sounded like a hundred.

Maybe these *were* banshees.

This place reeked of Noirre majik, like one big, disgusting cloud of it.

More vines wrapped Storm's chest and began squeezing like a massive green python. Two new vines curled around his ankles.

Sharp spikes stabbed his chest.

He snarled and began shifting into his jaguar.

Daegan roared at the spirits, "Cease or I will destroy you!"

The attack continued.

As Storm's jaguar came forward, he clawed at the vine cutting off his air.

In the next second, Daegan's power exploded as he shifted into a dragon, allowing fire to boil around his own fangs.

Everything stopped at once.

The spirits quieted.

Weeds stilled.

But Storm finished his shift and slashed his way free.

Vines whimpered and withdrew, coiling back to the host bodies stretched over the floor from one side to the other of this cavern.

While Storm could smell the Noirre, there were no other odors such as a preternatural scent he could match to the one he'd found outside and in the Atlanta Folk Art Park.

His jaguar roared, just as ready as Storm to attack out of pure frustration, but Storm had gained more control after returning from the demon underworld. He was forced to hold that control in a tight fist now.

He'd wait to see what Daegan had in mind, since the dragon had staked its claim as the alpha in the room.

The stalemate might not last long once the spirits and plants figured out they actually had the upper hand here. There was enough Noirre here to blow this cave out of the ground and take out miles of land.

It wasn't as if the spirits could die.

Daegan's dragon mouth opened and words spoken in a deep voice suited to a creature his size said, "We did not come to steal Noirre or to harm your resting place. If you will answer our questions, we will leave you alone and never return."

No one offered a reply.

Storm's jaguar panted, not from being out of breath, but a sign he did not want to be held back. The plants were covered in long thorns and bright red flowers.

Beautiful in a strange way. Deadly in a real way.

The puncture wounds on his chest stung like crazy.

A small, female child spirit floated forward, away from what appeared to be her skeletal remains. Her spirit form was missing a hand, as was her skeleton.

Even if someone chopped that off before she died, wouldn't she have it back now as a spirit?

For such a small thing, she had a voice right out of a horror movie. "Who are you to ask anything of us?"

Daegan's dragon said, "I am the dragon king of Treoir, son of King Gruffyn. I am two thousand years old and know of your murders. Had we been allies then, I would have flown here to protect you."

Her head tilted in a confused dog look. "Why?"

"Because I had two sisters. I would have destroyed the world to protect them."

Way to go, Daegan. Storm hoped that won them a few points.

Vines curled and slowly moved forward.

Maybe not.

Storm growled low at the vines. They quickly retreated, but this standoff would not last forever.

The female looked around and every spirit focused on her. Were they communicating silently?

When the spirits returned their blank stares to Daegan and Storm, the young girl slowly floated back around to face them, too. "What do you wish to know?"

Since Storm could not speak in animal form, Daegan had to handle the negotiation. "We are looking for one of ours who has been taken. We wish to know who was the last person to visit this cave and ask for a Noirre plant."

She kept moving her head as she pondered her answer. "Family."

Storm wanted to growl at them to be more specific, but Daegan's patience was paying off.

"That explains one thing then," Daegan commented.

"What would that be?" she asked, genuine curiosity in her question.

Daegan said, "That explains how someone entered your domain and left with his life and a plant."

She said nothing to counter Daegan's words, which in Storm's mind confirmed that it was indeed a male.

Gently pressing her, Daegan said, "I would like his name."

"Do you wish to kill him?"

Storm lifted his jaguar head to meet Daegan's reptilian gaze. Hoping the dragon understood, Storm nodded his head up and down. He avoided lying to spirits. That never went well even if the consequences came years later.

Swinging his big head back to eye level with the young girl, Daegan explained, "That depends on whether the man has harmed this jaguar's mate."

The smooth skin on her forehead furrowed. She stared at Storm's jaguar for a long moment. "Why would he hurt your mate?"

This was too difficult in animal form.

Storm shifted back to human shape and Daegan immediately covered his body in jeans and a T-shirt. Even in this young girl's time, speaking to a naked man at her age was not appropriate.

Nodding at the dragon, Storm squatted so that he would not be standing above her. "I'm not sure yet exactly what your relative has done, but I believe he was involved because pure Noirre has been discovered where my mate was attacked and kidnapped. I'm desperate for any help in finding her."

The girl's eyes swelled as if she was about to cry, which would be a trick for a spirit. "No. This descendant swore he would use Noirre to avenge our deaths and harm no female or child."

Storm realized she was telling the truth and she must have made it clear about not hurting a female or child because of what had happened to those who died in this cave.

This sucked, but he had to tell her. "He lied."

She floated backwards slowly.

Uh oh.

Daegan said, "She doesn't believe us."

Storm asked, "Please don't attack. Tell me how we can prove to you that we're telling the truth."

She conferred with her spirit family once again. After the stretched silence, the girl came forward, but only halfway.

What did that mean?

Daegan lifted his head, wings back and ready.

But the girl said to Storm, "Swear on your family's blood that you tell the truth. If you give that oath in here and fail to tell the truth, you will regret it."

Daegan rumbled a noise, but Storm couldn't look up and lose the tiny connection with this spirit. There were many reasons why he shouldn't consider giving that oath, the first of which was that he had no absolute evidence that the kidnapper was her relative.

His gut said it was. He was going with that, but he still wanted to make an educated guess with something this important. "Can I ask one question first?"

She cocked her head, which he took as a yes.

"When was the last plant taken from here?"

"I have no sense of time, but it has not been long."

Daegan picked up Storm's line of questioning and asked, "When was the last plant taken from this cave before that?"

Energy rippled through the room.

Spirits moaned and swayed.

The female clenched her little fist, looking ready to put a beatdown on someone. Her voice went two octaves lower. "Was a very long time ago. A goddess sent her army, then her mage and then a druid who stole from us."

Lifting a hand to ask for peace, Storm said, "I'm ready to give my oath."

When silence descended again, he gave his oath. "I swear on the blood of my ancestors who were honorable Navajos in a new world you would not know about. And I swear on my own blood that you are welcome to take my life if I lie, because I am willing to give my life to save my mate."

Whispers erupted behind her. The little girl lifted her only hand without turning, and all spirits quieted.

Storm continued, "I ask only that regardless of what you determine, I be allowed to save my mate before you claim my life. A person used pure Noirre only one day ago where we live in another land. I don't know if the person who wielded the pure Noirre majik was the descendant of your family, but if that is the only person to visit you recently and leave with a plant, then it is possible. He is either the one who attacked my mate and kidnapped her or he gave the Noirre to someone else who did. I had placed an emerald chakra stone on my mate's chest using majik so that I could always find her. The person who took her from me clawed the stone out of her body and left the bloody emerald on the ground, then teleported away."

The female gasped at that. She shook like a volcano on the edge of erupting.

She screamed a high-pitched wail that doubled anything they'd first heard.

Daegan shifted back to his human form with his clothes on, and clamped big hands over his ears.

Storm covered his, but he was still alive, which he took as an encouraging sign.

When the spirit finished her fit of anger, she trembled, still a child at heart. "He lied to us." She pointed to the skeleton that matched her size. "I gave him my own hand, which became a single plant once it was removed."

Storm cringed at the child giving up a hand even if it was from her bones. Spirits were energy and her spirit had suffered for a long time. She shouldn't have to sacrifice even more.

He offered, "If we return your plant, will that replace your hand?"

"No. It cannot be replaced, just as half of that body cannot be returned." She pointed to a spirit with only an upper body. "The druid stole that."

That would be Cathbad the Druid. Storm sensed that he and Daegan had stayed past the point of remaining safe. "Will you now please share the name of the descendant you gave the plant?"

The girl's spirit still shook. She floated back and forth in an agitated state. The others mirrored her movements.

Storm glanced at Daegan, who looked just as concerned. They were losing her.

Still angry, she stopped abruptly as if realizing Storm and Daegan were still present. "He is called La Cuchilla."

Daegan gave a small shake of his head. He didn't recognize the name. Neither did Storm, and his stomach dropped. He could translate the Spanish words that meant "The Blade," but La Cuchilla was not a Celtic name or any name he'd ever heard.

But it was another lead. Something instead of nothing.

Storm addressed the girl and her group. "Thank you for sparing our lives and sharing that information. What can we do for you in return?"

Her face softened. "Why would you offer us anything when a descendant of my blood has harmed your mate?"

Storm smiled a little. "I would give you eternal peace if I had that power. None of you harmed my mate and should not be held responsible. Also, if you knew my mate, you'd know that she would be disappointed in me if I did not offer what I could. I'm sorry for what happened to you and your people. I wish we had not needed to disturb you."

Swirling around in a blur of motion, she consulted silently with the other spirits. All heads nodded to her, then the girl returned to address Storm and Daegan. "We wish to never be disturbed again. If we are, we will move throughout the cave to bring others in to be with us."

That threatened human lives of the cave exhibition staff and visitors.

Giving their situation thought first, Storm admitted, "I can't guarantee another descendant will not attempt to come here in the future."

Her face fell.

Why did he feel like he'd stomped a puppy when he was trying to be honest? He quickly continued, "But this dragon shifter and I can create a blood ward outside the entrance to your place of rest to prevent any other supernatural beings from entering, and possibly even a descendant. You should know that it will also prevent you from leaving as well."

Sounding more like a spirit who had been around for centuries now, she said, "This is where we will all remain forever. We have no wish to leave. We want the ward."

Daegan asked, "What do you wish done with your descendant when we find him?"

Storm growled at possibly being prevented from making the kidnapper pay for harming Evalle.

Daegan shot him a work-with-me look.

The female didn't smile, but her voice lightened to that of a child this time. "You may do as you please. It will not prevent him from paying his debt to us for breaking his oath." She paused. "And he did not teleport here to visit."

Storm started asking, "What is the consequence of ... "

She pointed to the wall. "Leave now."

Daegan didn't hesitate. He teleported them to the tunnel where Storm and Daegan placed a ward that would require the both of them working together to break.

Storm said, "That will protect the humans who remain in the public area of the cave, but that won't stop the Medb and others from wielding Noirre majik that is currently out in the world."

"This is true, but that is not our concern at this moment."

"You don't know anything about La Cuchilla, do you?"

"Sadly, no, but we have the largest force of warriors in the world. We will find him."

Storm believed that, but would it be soon enough for Evalle?

Daegan asked, "Did you catch that last part?"

"What specifically?"

"When she said, 'He did not teleport here to visit'."

"That's right," Storm murmured. "Wonder what she meant? He has to be teleporting to get around from continent to continent and inside here."

"It is curious, but he does walk or use other transportation on occasion based on what Reese discovered. He may have entered a different way than we did."

Daegan teleported them outside to join the group.

Quinn immediately asked Daegan, "Please teleport Reese home."

"How many times do I have to tell you that you do not make my decisions?" Reese said, shoving her face up at his face.

Unperturbed by her bulldog spunk, Quinn said, "You're sick and you won't tell me why."

Stepping back, she crossed her arms. "Are we looking for Evalle or not?"

Tristan asked, "Did you two find the Noirre? You don't stink of dark majik."

Daegan filled them in, drawing a lot of horrified looks. As he wrapped it up, he said, "As for the Noirre smell, I think it comes from wielding the majik or ripping a plant from the skeleton, though it was said they grew originally from the remains. We slashed vines to break free, but they immediately reformed back to the host skeleton."

Walking back and forth as Daegan spoke, Storm waited for the dragon to finish before he jumped ahead to his next concern. He asked, "Anyone ever heard of La Cuchilla?"

No one spoke up.

He asked, "Got any idea how to find him?"

Adrianna said, "I have an idea."

CHAPTER 24

B ACK IN ATLANTA MOMENTS LATER, Adrianna felt sympathy for Evalle, who often suffered motion sickness when she teleported. Adrianna normally didn't, but her stomach argued that hurling could be in her future if she did this much more today.

She'd asked Daegan to drop them in Piedmont Park where the skies were still dark, but that was due to being early evening as much as the rain continuing to fall. The dragon king had told her to envision the specific spot she wanted and he landed them exactly where she'd chosen.

That's why they could now emerge from the shadows with no humans being the wiser.

Thankfully, one human passed out against a tree with a beer bottle inches from his outstretched hand had seen nothing. Soaked from head to foot, he slept on.

She'd almost dried out in Ireland, but this drizzle seeped in, drenching everyone. At this point, she welcomed the weather that kept more people inside than out in the park right now. A few humans in raincoats were out in the large field, walking dogs that didn't care about the wet weather. None of them had been close enough to see her group appear out of thin air.

Still, Daegan and the team were going to get caught with so much teleporting.

"What is your idea?" Daegan asked, snapping her back to the moment.

Storm stepped up and said, "Probably Isak. Am I right, Adrianna?"

"You two don't need me if you can answer your own question," she said with a gentle tease in her voice to beat down the tension that had ridden Storm for so long. "Yes, Isak can find almost anything, human or preternatural, and you know he wants to help."

"Call your soldier while we move toward the road to meet him," Daegan said, prompting Adrianna to pull out her phone and send a text while they walked.

When Isak didn't reply immediately, her stomach clenched.

Then his text came through, asking what she knew about this La Cuchilla. She told him they were back in Atlanta and believed that was the kidnapper's name. Also, that in spite of his Latin sounding name, he could possibly be of Celtic descent.

Isak sent back a simple, *Copy that.*

Storm and Daegan had avoided the overhead lights, opting to gather the group in a dark area near the tree line close to the road.

She'd just closed her phone and turned to join the others when Grady's translucent shape took form. Poor guy. "Grady?"

He floated over to her.

She suggested, "Step over to the tree with me." When he did, she extended her hand. "Evalle would want you to have this."

She waited, giving him time to think it through, then Grady accepted her handshake for only about five seconds, then he let go.

"Uhm, Grady, you should have shaken with me for a full ten seconds to stay solid for ten minutes," she gently told him. Surely he knew that.

He took corporeal form quickly and kept his voice low. "You heard what Quinn said in that art park."

She recalled Quinn commenting about observing Grady and Evalle, but he hadn't elaborated. "Yes. What was he talking about?"

"I can make my body solid by myself sometimes. Cain't tell you why 'cause it's a secret, but I'm good for a while now. I 'bout had to give that Quinn a smack when he started sayin' too much."

"I'm not sharing anything," she assured Grady.

"I know. You a good friend to Evalle. What ya'll find out?"

Funny how a ghoul could lift her spirits with his knowing she was a friend. She suggested, "Let's go talk with Daegan and Storm. They were attacked in the Noirre cave, but they survived and have more information." As she led the way back to the group, most of which had been watching her, Adrianna said, "I sent Isak a name we discovered and he's using his network to trace it."

When they reached the group of weary teleporters, Grady asked, "You don't know where Evalle is yet?" His voice broke.

"We're working on it and got a lead," Storm said, patting the old guy on the shoulder. The Skinwalker looked as if he couldn't believe he was comforting a ghoul.

Adrianna smiled inside. That was life with Evalle's surrogate family.

Grady said, "I been pushin' every ghoul I know for anything. One thing I found out is that the guy who took Evalle shielded his face whenever he was seen walkin' around the city."

Reese asked, "Anything else, Grady?"

"Hold on," Grady said and faded.

"What have you got, Grady?" Storm asked when the ghoul became visible again.

"That hooded guy ain't been teleportin'."

Tristan held his hands out in confusion. "He *had* to teleport to move Evalle out of here without leaving a trail. Otherwise, Storm could track him or Reese could find him with her gift."

"You callin' me a liar, Alterant?"

"No, Grady," Tristan groused. "I'm just pointing out facts so we can figure this out."

"Grady might be on to something," Reese said, grabbing everyone's attention. "I've been working under the impression that we knew for sure Evalle was teleported away."

Adrianna kept her eyes on Daegan, whom she considered a barometer of whether they were getting close with a lead. He was locked on Reese's words as if he could tell she was on to something.

Storm brought up a point. "The little spirit in the cave actually said La Cuchilla had not teleported in to see them."

"La who?" Grady asked.

"The kidnapper related to the spirits," Daegan provided.

"Oh."

Reese said, "If everyone will let me finish, I'll explain where I was going with this." Once they all quieted, Reese asked Quinn, "Do you remember when we had to go to New Orleans to find Phoedra?"

"Yes."

"The kidnappers didn't teleport when they vanished. They

opened a bolthole. The only way I knew that at the time was because both in Seattle and in Oklahoma, I actually saw the bolthole open and swallow them."

"That's right. In fact, the van dragged you into that bloody hole at one point."

Reese waved her hands. "Forget about that. I'm saying that if the kidnapper is using a bolthole and I can't see that, he could be using something to shield his action each time. Maybe that's why he went after the pure Noirre. If that's the case, the reason I could follow the kidnapper's path in Atlanta and Kilkenny had to be due to him walking. Though why would he have walked away after murdering those guys?" She shook her head, "Maybe he was saving energy for some reason. Anyway, bottom line is he could very well be using a bolthole, but if that's his trick, he's got some extra juice to cloak his bolthole departures."

Daegan's eyes widened briefly, just enough to support Adrianna's suspicion that Reese might have hit on the key to tracking the kidnapper.

Storm cursed. "That only expands the possibilities of who could have taken Evalle. We still don't know why she was kidnapped, either."

"That reminds me. That ain't all I found out," Grady said, jumping in. He gave Daegan the evil eye. "Word on the street is this all started 'cause you huntin' your hoard. You put my baby girl in danger for money?" Grady balled his bony fists, ready to take on the dragon king.

Daegan immediately said, "I assure you I am not searching for any treasure, and if I ever did, I would not put one of my people at risk to do so. Never one of my circle of seven advisors."

Adrianna's gaze went from the dragon king to Grady. "Who in the world put out that rumor?" And how was that information connected?

Storm jumped in and told Grady, "Daegan speaks the truth. But *someone* is lying. Not you or your Nightstalker friends, but the kidnapper probably planted that lie."

Grady crossed his arms and got a stubborn look that Evalle had told Adrianna about more than once. "I'm gonna go back and dig around some more. That better be the truth. But you all need to know that VIPER is losin' it over the humans now seeing trolls on top of disappearin' hooded guys."

Tristan wondered aloud, "Why would trolls expose their existence unnecessarily? That makes no sense. It puts them on VIPER's radar."

"I don't know," Grady said. "But VIPER been lookin' for all of you to pull into a Tribunal for answers. You best be usin' that cloakin' stuff and stay free so you can find Evalle."

Had that Nightstalker threatened the dragon king yet again?

Adrianna could understand Evalle's affection for the old guy. Good thing Daegan had a high level of tolerance for someone sincerely worried about Evalle.

A Hummer rolled up to the curb near them and parked. Isak stepped out alone, which was odd for him.

Adrianna thought he traveled with a full black ops team at all times. She noticed Grady fading and sent him a wink before he blinked out. That Nightstalker probably avoided humans when they might be able to see him.

Isak let his gaze dance over Adrianna prior to addressing everyone. "I wasn't able to identify La Cuchilla."

Storm grabbed his head and walked off cursing. He turned around and came back, but his eyes were that of a man fighting for his last breath.

Adrianna's heart thumped a sad beat. "Thanks for trying, Isak."

The soldier frowned at her then passed his irritation around to everyone else. "Don't sound so disappointed. I did get some intel. La Cuchilla has popped up as a code name for someone gathering intel, but he has not exposed his face. If I had a day, I could hand you an identity."

Storm quietly said, "That would be nice, but we might not have a day. Before we teleported away from the building, Lanna told me she sensed Evalle's energy was fading."

From the surprise on every face, that was news to the entire group.

Isak repeated what they all believed. "They won't kill her if they didn't do it here, Storm. They need to keep her alive for something."

"I realize that, but it doesn't mean she isn't suffering." He raked his hand over his head as if trying to jar some brain cells. "We found out this guy La Cuchilla was related to someone killed in

Ireland during Celtic Viking raids."

Reese shook her head. "That's confusing."

Quinn asked, "Why?"

"I know people interbreed with different races, but remember how I told you I saw the vision of the hooded guy holding the plant outside that cave just now in Ireland?"

In an awestruck voice, Isak said, "All of you just zapped over to Ireland and back?"

"Yes," Storm snapped. "Go ahead, Reese."

"The hand I saw sticking out of that robe was a dark-toned skin color. He might be of Celtic descent, but I wouldn't have guessed that. Do you think he lied to the spirits?"

"I doubt they would have allowed him to leave alive if they had not confirmed his blood relation," Daegan said. "If he is using a bolthole, the question is how he came by that ability." He asked Reese and Quinn, "Do you know the origin of the bolthole majik you encountered while hunting Phoedra?"

Reese angled her head in Quinn's direction. "It was *his* friend."

Quinn quickly clarified, "It was not a friend, but an associate. I know the family, but they would not share this gift with anyone. After our meeting in New Orleans and observing the punishment for using a bolthole to kidnap my daughter, I feel confident in saying no other family member has gone off the reservation since then."

Giving a shudder, Reese muttered, "You're right. Nobody would repeat that mistake."

"Huh, okay, I have a little more," Isak continued in his briefing voice. "What I did find out was a rumor that the kidnapper is under the protection of a powerful goddess. That's why contacts were hard to locate when I put my people on the street to get a name."

Adrianna was astonished at how quickly he got what he did.

Daegan's entire demeanor shifted to action mode. "That's all the information we need. Thank you, Isak, for your help. It is greatly appreciated." Turning to Reese, Daegan said, "Thank you, also, Reese. Figuring out it could be a bolthole is what I needed to pinpoint who is behind this."

"Glad I could help in spite of being told to go home," Reese said, sweeping her gaze from Daegan to Quinn at the end.

Storm crossed his arms. "How is that going to help, Daegan?"

"I now know it *has* to be Maeve or Macha."

"We've suspected both of them since the beginning, but that's when we thought the kidnapper could teleport or had someone else who could. If this guy has been opening boltholes, he could be working for anyone. What have you come up with that we aren't seeing?"

"Boltholes are not easy to gain. They often come from a family with that gift, but some have been opened using a majikal instrument. To bestow that ability on someone requires significant power and there are particular requirements. I now have a way to pin down Macha and Maeve to get the truth. I'm going to a Tribunal."

"*We're* going to the Tribunal," Storm announced.

Daegan said, "Agreed. I need a moment to contact Sen to have a Tribunal ready when we arrive."

Tristan grumbled under his breath.

Daegan turned to him. "Problem?"

After a little hesitation, Tristan said, "Yes. I do have a problem with that. You already faced off with a Tribunal who did nothing to drag either goddess in, and you just heard that VIPER is on a tear about the humans witnessing paranormal activity. In fact, it sounds like someone made an announcement urging preternaturals to show off to humans. Going to a Tribunal right now is a risky idea. You'll be walking into a new fight. Can I go to the Tribunal in your place?"

"No. While I respect your opinion, this is something only I can do with Storm's help," Daegan clarified for his second in command. "I need our team teleported to Treoir. Are you up for that?"

Sounding exhausted, Tristan said, "Yes. I just hope Sen doesn't get an attitude from that first meeting and pull some crap."

Daegan could sound so deadly when he spoke low. "Sen will know the minute we meet that to delay us even a second could be risky for him."

"Ditto," Storm added.

Quinn announced, "Reese is not going with us."

She grabbed her head. "That is *it!* I've had it with you."

"I feel pretty much the same since you refuse to tell me what is making you sick."

Tristan sighed. "I'll take Adrianna to Treoir. You two figure out your domestic issues by the time I come back. I'm only doing this twice."

Quinn snarled, "It's not a domestic issue."

"What makes you think there's anything domestic about *him*?" Reese asked with plenty of sarcasm.

Giving them both a glare that was short on patience, Tristan turned to Adrianna. "Ready?"

"Give me a moment, please."

Muttering something about late night soap operas, Tristan headed over to stand with Storm and Daegan.

Isak's gaze hadn't moved from Adrianna since the last time those blue orbs had settled on her. With everyone stepped away, he asked her, "Do you have to go?"

Why did he sound as if losing her would matter?

He'd walked off in Blairsville without a look back. He did not get to play this card when *he* felt like it.

She answered, "Yes, I have to go. I don't know what we'll be up against, but they'll probably need my Witchlock power, too."

A muscle flicked in his jaw, but he didn't make some snide comment. "Okay. Be safe."

Isak walked toward his truck, not looking like any of this was okay at all.

She must have been up too long and her mind had lost the ability to see her next move as a bad idea, but she followed him. "Isak."

He paused in opening his door and turned back.

"Thank you. Everything you've done today has been a help and very much appreciated."

Poor guy looked as if he wanted to make everyone disappear, but he just said, "You're welcome."

A thousand words raced around in her head. None of them made sense. She knew better than to make any decision right now. This was a time to pull her emotions in tight and prepare for whatever they were about to do, because sending them to Treoir meant Daegan had a plan.

Knowing this could be the last time she saw Isak, she struggled not to step into his arms and let him hold her.

After an extended gazing match, he said, "I'm going back to

watch over Storm's building. There's a limit to how long I'm leaving Kit in there with preternaturals running wild around the city. Something is up with the nonhumans in Atlanta. Some of them definitely want to be seen. This city is going to erupt, and I want her safe before that happens."

That was all Adrianna needed to pull up her emotional stakes and pack her heart away. She and Isak would always be of two different worlds.

Also, that meant as exposure to Adrianna's world spread, they'd be on opposite sides of the battle.

Isak would never be happy with the strange and unusual anywhere around Kit.

Adrianna still wanted to reassure him. "The minute we know something specific, someone will come to inform you."

"Someone?"

Don't touch that, she warned herself. "If I can do it, I will be the one."

Clearly her warnings worked on everyone but her.

Isak drove off.

When she returned to Tristan, Quinn and Reese were standing six feet apart, not speaking. Oh, boy.

Daegan said, "Sen knows we're coming. Ready, Storm?"

The Skinwalker nodded. "We can't get there fast enough if your idea means we can locate Evalle."

"We'll soon find out."

With one look around, probably for humans, Daegan and Storm vanished.

Adrianna told Tristan, "Let's go, if you're ready."

"I'm ready to take you. Not so much for dealing with those two when I get back."

She took in Quinn's grim face and glanced at Reese who had shifted even farther away from Quinn. That woman had a hand over her stomach again.

Adrianna said to Tristan, "They have things to work out, but I have a feeling you'll only be teleporting Quinn to Treoir."

Tristan said, "They need to get a room."

Adrianna caught herself before she said it looked as though they already had.

CHAPTER 25

STORM MARVELED AT DAEGAN, WHO hadn't hesitated to enter a realm where he was at his most vulnerable for a woman he had only recently met. Storm had originally agreed to be one of Daegan's circle of seven advisors for no other reason than it allowed him to be available to watch Evalle's back.

But after this, Storm had a whole different sense of his role with Daegan.

He would stand with this dragon shifter in any battle. No other powerful being had ever gone to bat for Evalle. Most of them had misused her or treated her and the other gryphons as livestock.

Sen stood to one side, glowering as usual while they all waited.

Storm whispered to Daegan, "I just remembered one place I *know* I've smelled the kidnapper's scent."

"Oh? Where?"

"The night we battled Lorwerth and his bunch."

"They all died."

Storm said, "That's right, which means the person behind that attack had been there, but was not present when we showed up."

"Interesting."

In dragon talk, that probably meant Daegan was even more anxious to find the kidnapper.

Justitia, Hermes and Loki took shape on the raised dais.

Evalle had told Storm how every time she got stuck dealing with Loki he spent the entire time playing with some majikal gadget or poking fun at someone at his victim's expense.

This wasn't the jovial prankster god facing them now.

Loki spoke in a dark tone. "Interesting seeing you again, Daegan, and especially now. I thought the Beladors and Medb had figured out how to get along. Evidently not because I've been informed that humans have recorded evidence of preternatural activity in Atlanta. Media is having quite a time with it. Have you come up with a plan for fixing that?"

"I didn't create that problem, so no, that is not why I am here. I want the Tribunal to mediate an issue."

"Perhaps you haven't realized that this is not a good time to joke."

Daegan's voice boomed. "Do I sound as though I'm joking?"

"Dare you raise your voice to me?" Loki said in a savage tone.

Shit. Storm hoped Daegan's plan had some safety valves.

Daegan had a staring match with Loki, then said, "Oh, I do dare. I am furious. My people are being attacked. Part of the fault lies with you and the rest of the Tribunal deities."

Storm managed to hold a blank face, but it was an effort when he wanted to yank Daegan aside to remind him they needed the Tribunal's help ... right?

Wasn't that why they were here?

The dragon king getting zapped by three deities would not further his goal.

In the tense silence that followed as Daegan and Loki did battle with their eyes, Justitia asked, "What is your grievance, dragon?"

When Daegan moved his gaze to her, he was more respectful. "When you allowed the Medb to join VIPER and to begin sending their warlocks to the human world, in spite of all the Belador deaths they have caused for centuries, our people had the additional duty of watching our own backs while still trying to protect humans. I've heard the stories, so I'm sure you know them."

Loki gave an exaggerated sigh. "That's it? Queen Maeve is no longer part of VIPER. Macha has pulled out as well. Problem solved."

"Problem not solved. When we were losing children to Medb warlocks and trolls, you did nothing."

Justitia asked, "Is that why you are here?"

"No. I'm merely making it clear that the Tribunal owes the Beladors. I have a simple request."

Loki barked out, "No. You do not come in here and insult a Tribunal, then ask for our help."

Hermes paused in strumming his instrument, cast a curious glance over everyone, then continued playing.

Storm wished now that he'd asked Daegan for more details of his idea so Storm could help get them back on track.

Daegan said, "You will not keep the humans in the dark forever. As they learn that we exist, you will need the Belador force more than ever, especially since we have people blended into every line of work and in the human governments. You have no other allies of VIPER who can boast the same." He took a deep breath, during which no one countered his comment. "We can all work together and survive, or we can fight each other and see who has the biggest sword."

Justitia said, "Your point is valid. We have worked with preternaturals who are not preying on humans and we will continue to do so as long as it meets our needs."

Looking over at her, Loki said, "Speak for yourself, Justitia."

"I was doing just that, Loki. If you wish to go to war with a dragon whose mother is an unknown power, that is your choice as well. I intend to build alliances."

Daegan encouraged her by saying, "A wise woman. What about you, Loki? Are we going to share resources or do I withdraw my Beladors and allow the rest of you to figure out the human issues on your own?"

Crossing his arms, Loki ignored the question and instead said, "My patience is running out. State what you want and we'll decide if we will award your request."

Storm almost rolled his eyes at the irritating god. No wonder Evalle hated the bastard.

Daegan said, "I again request that you call in both Queen Maeve and Macha so I can question them."

That quieted the trio on the dais.

They turned to speak quietly. When Loki turned back, he said, "You do realize both of those goddesses have already refused that request and want to kill you, right?"

"Yes."

"We can't guarantee that we can stop them if they join forces."

"I'll worry about that." Daegan sent a look at Storm that said to hang in there.

"What reason do I give them for coming here?"

"Tell them I will give them one chance to clear their names. If they are guilty of kidnapping Evalle Kincaid, I will bring an army to their realms and I will not leave until everyone is destroyed ... even if it requires calling in my mother."

Out of the corner of his eye, Storm caught Sen's jaw drop.

Laughing, Loki asked, "You would threaten those two for an *Alterant*?"

Daegan murmured, "Not yet," to Storm.

That's when Storm realized he'd been growling under his breath.

Instead of replying to Loki's question, Daegan asked, "If you are losing patience, Loki, why are you dragging this out?"

"You will get what you asked for, dragon," Loki said, with a load of warning boosting his voice. Then he was silent and still for a long moment. When his eyes moved again, he said, "I've informed both goddesses of your threat and guaranteed they will not be harmed by anyone while in this Tribunal meeting."

Daegan's eyes took on a dangerous glint. "I see. You've given them the opportunity to attack me with no recourse from the Tribunal, but that does not protect them from me. If I am attacked, be prepared to suffer the consequences since you will be standing too close to them and I can't guarantee your safety either, at that point."

The surly Loki returned.

Energy flushed through the room on a rogue wind.

Macha appeared on the left side of the dais and Queen Maeve took form on the right side.

Both swung furious gazes at Daegan, affecting the dragon king not one bit.

Macha started, "I did not come here out of any concern about you showing up in my realm. I'm here only because Loki agreed to not stop me from ending your miserable life, dragon."

Daegan moved his attention from her to Queen Maeve, who looked rough for a goddess, in Storm's opinion. He'd heard that the queen had lost her shit the last time she attended a Tribunal and her body had warped out of shape.

"Miss me, Daegan?" Queen Maeve asked the dragon king, as one would taunt a tortured prisoner. "I will have you back where you belong."

Macha glanced over at her codefendant. "You're an idiot for keeping him so long. You could have killed him in your realm, but no, you had to play wicked queen."

Queen Maeve's head grew and twisted.

Ugh. Storm might never wipe that image from his mind.

Loki warned, "Maeve."

She seemed to catch herself and shrank back to normal size.

Justitia said, "Ask your questions, dragon."

Daegan started with, "Which one of you has kidnapped Evalle Kincaid?"

The queen gave him a dumbfounded look and rolled her eyes without replying.

Macha smiled. "Still haven't found your Alterant?"

Daegan said, "Answer the question."

Her head now back to normal size, Maeve said, "If I had Evalle, do you think I'd be stupid enough to come here?"

Macha piped up, "Of course. You were stupid enough to let that dragon live."

Justitia said, "Macha, please do not create additional conflict here."

"I don't have your Alterant, Daegan," Maeve snapped. "If you can't keep up with your livestock, that's your problem."

Storm went from furious to insane in two seconds.

All five deities stared at him.

Daegan softly said, "Your eyes are red, Storm. I need your control."

Closing his eyes, Storm drew in a deep breath and pulled his demon back down.

Daegan asked the Medb queen, "What about Cathbad? Would he have her?"

"No. I just saw him and mentioned this. In fact he was quite put out, thinking I had something to do with any kidnapping, which I don't."

The dragon king turned to Storm. "Truth?"

"Yes."

Justitia gave Daegan a confused look. "Anyone who lies here will light up red, dragon."

"I know that, but I also know it's possible to shade the truth and not trigger that consequence."

The goddess of justice didn't care for that truth.

Storm thought back over all the problems they'd had with

Queen Maeve. He suggested, "Let me ask a question."

Daegan said, "Storm wishes to aid me in questioning the goddesses." He hadn't asked, but posed that as a statement.

The deities must either be enjoying this interrogation or wanting to hurry it up, because no one denied Storm.

He asked the queen, "Do you know of anyone who might be involved in Evalle's kidnapping or anyone who would be presently setting a trap for Daegan?"

Maeve lost her humor. She stared at Storm as if she could shoot blades from her eyes and stab him, but she had not been given permission to attack Storm.

Storm felt Daegan's energy spin up. The dragon must sense that Storm was on to something.

Queen Maeve said, "I am done with questions."

Daegan suggested, "I will not attack you or your realm if you have someone to hand over, Maeve. Is that person worth a battle in TÅµr Medb with my mother?"

Tense silence reigned for seconds, then Maeve raised her hand and whipped it in a fast circle.

A man appeared wearing his boxer shorts and bedhead. "What ... what's going on, Maeve?"

"This is a Tribunal, Perth."

"Really." Then he twisted to look up at Loki and the other deities. "Oh, shit. How could you bring me here?"

Daegan asked the new guy, "Are you currently working on a way to kill or capture me?"

Perth had total confusion written all over his face. "No, where'd you get that idea?"

Groaning, Queen Maeve said, "You shouldn't ... " She quit talking as Perth's body turned bright red.

Justitia finished Maeve's sentence. "You should not lie here or you will turn red."

Perth yelled, "Hey, this is bullshit. What are you all up to?"

Daegan ignored Perth's frantic outburst and pressed on. "Did you kidnap Evalle Kincaid?"

"No!"

Storm hated to admit it, but he said, "Truth."

Daegan jerked around to face him. "It is?"

"Yes. Also, he does not have the skin tone Reese described."

Turning back to Maeve, he said, "Is that the only person in your group who is actively working on killing me?"

"Of course not. Every warlock out there would bring me your head to please me." She pushed a disgusted look at Perth. "This one is no longer of value to me. Do with him as you wish."

Evidently realizing he stood to lose his life, Perth turned a furious face to the queen. "You bitch! I had a brilliant plan going. I paid the trolls to show off to humans and I was giving humans access to one preternatural event after another. They're tagging the videos with the word Belador. I had teams ready to back me up when the dragon showed. I ... you have no idea what you screwed up by exposing me."

Loki boomed, "You are intentionally exposing preternaturals to humans?"

Queen Maeve looked up at Loki and quickly clarified, "I had nothing to do with his planning. He offends me with this tirade."

Loki pointed at Perth and Maeve's servant exploded into a miniature, body-shaped fire that lasted only seconds, then left a pile of ashes. The god waved a hand without looking and the ashes vanished.

Maeve grinned like the lunatic she was.

Daegan turned to Macha, "One down, one to go. Yes or no, Macha. Do you have Evalle?"

"I wish I did have her. I would enjoy watching your face as I stand here protected. No, I don't have your little half-breed. Are we done?"

Loki had perked up after killing Perth. Evidently he just needed to murder someone.

Storm's insides were churning with the lack of information forthcoming.

Daegan boomed one more question. "Do either of you know someone who goes by the name La Cuchilla or uses that for a code when dealing in intelligence gathering?"

Queen Maeve laughed. "No. You are pathetic."

Storm realized Daegan had not moved a muscle. That man's gaze was locked on Macha, who had also gone completely motionless.

The whole room quieted.

Storm normally controlled his pulse around preternaturals, but his jaguar sensed a hunt. His nostrils flared.

"What about you, Macha?" Daegan prodded. "Are you harboring the man we're hunting?"

All three Tribunal members on the dais turned to Macha, even the musician.

That bitch goddess knew who had Evalle.

Storm clenched and unclenched his hands to force his jaguar to sit tight.

Macha finally said, "I know who La Cuchilla is. What proof do you have of his committing a crime?"

Daegan declared, "I will show you and this Tribunal my proof once you bring him here."

Storm considered all that the team had found out. Neither he nor Daegan had any tangible proof.

When Macha showed no sign of bringing the kidnapper to the meeting, Daegan continued, "If you refuse to deliver this man, then I can only assume you are willing to accept responsibility for what he has done. That would be strange when you've proven you are not one to fight battles for others, particularly if you are not directly responsible for the kidnapping. Before you choose to fight this battle, know that I am at wit's end with my people being attacked. I intend to make those responsible for harming and capturing Evalle wish they had never drawn their first breaths."

Storm wouldn't have put what he had in mind for the kidnapper in such civil terms.

"How much could someone harm an Alterant while kidnapping her?" Macha argued.

Storm couldn't take this any more. "Evalle is my mate. She had a chakra stone fused to her chest by majik. The monster who kidnapped her first crashed her body into a building, then dug the emerald stone out with a claw, which wouldn't have left so much blood at the crash site if she'd been able to heal. He mutilated her body to remove the one sure way I could track her, but I *will* find her and everyone involved is going to pay."

Justitia turned to Macha and said, "You surprise me, Macha, to associate with such a disgusting animal."

Daegan said, "Storm tells the truth, as you can see. I do as well. What will it be, Macha? Who will stand beside you if we go to war?"

She was trapped.

Her face said she hated being in this position and, in that instant, it was clear that this La Cuchilla had screwed his deal with her.

Lifting her arms, she called out, *"La Cuchilla, come to me!"*

In a flash of energy and light, a man appeared, but not in a robe. He wore black cargo pants, a gray long-sleeved knit shirt, boots and a bandanna around his neck. His curly black hair was damp and his cocoa-brown skin covered in perspiration.

He blinked and looked at Macha. "I was busy. Why would you ... " He finally noticed the rest of the room. "What the hell?"

Daegan muttered, "He does not appear to be Celtic, but his skin matches."

"I don't care," Storm said then took a deep inhale. He told Daegan, "The scent we have been hunting is his."

"Who is this man?" Daegan asked.

Storm spoke to La Cuchilla. "Oh, wait. I know you. You're Dakkar. You run the bounty hunters."

"So?" But Dakkar's gaze jumped all over the place then went back to Macha. "What's going on, Macha?"

She wouldn't acknowledge him.

Loki asked, "Are you also known as La Cuchilla?"

Dakkar jerked his head around to snarl at Macha. "How could you share that?"

Shifting her eyes slowly, she met his gaze with a stony one. "Do not speak to me in that tone."

That was the look of a man kicked squarely in the nuts, which had to hurt more when a goddess did it. Storm couldn't wish that misery on a more deserving person, but Dakkar would suffer far worse before this was over.

Daegan asked, "Did you use *pure* Noirre to kidnap Evalle?"

Macha eyed Dakkar with revulsion. She said, "You deal in Noirre? Why can't I smell it?"

Storm volunteered, "He's a mage who can mask odors. He went to Ireland for the specific purpose of taking pure Noirre from where it originates."

Queen Maeve interjected, "How did he gain pure Noirre and live to use it?" The longer she looked at him, the more amazed her face became.

What color had been in Dakkar's face flushed away. "What ...

what are you talking about?"

Still confused, Macha said to Dakkar, "You are Moor, not Celtic."

Now appearing intrigued, Loki said, "You have to answer the questions, Dakkar. All of them."

The bounty hunter swallowed and kept his eyes on Daegan, but asked the Tribunal deities, "Are you going to let that dragon kill me?"

Daegan shrugged and replied before Loki could. "I am only looking for Evalle. I have no plans to kill you."

Storm allowed that since he and Daegan had an agreement. The person who had hurt Evalle belonged to Storm. He'd give Dakkar a fighting chance and it might not go his way, but Storm could not walk away from this with Dakkar still breathing.

"Dakkar seems overwhelmed," Justitia said, stating the obvious. "It is very simple, Dakkar. The dragon king accuses you of kidnapping Evalle Kincaid, the Alterant. I think most of us would like to know how you managed to gain the pure Noirre since the dragon king claims you used this dark majik in capturing Evalle. Wielding any form of Noirre is forbidden."

Queen Maeve scoffed at that and Justitia swung her laser gaze at the crazy goddess, who composed herself.

"What proof do you have?" Dakkar shot back at Daegan.

"Only your answers."

Macha twisted up her mouth, just realizing she'd walked Dakkar into a trap.

Justitia persisted, "Time to answer, Dakkar. Do you have Evalle?"

"No." Nothing happened to Dakkar.

Storm snarled, "Truth, but he still lies. He kidnapped her for someone else."

Daegan asked Dakkar, "Did you kidnap Evalle and hand her to someone else?"

"No." Dakkar's body turned sunburned red. That made the whites of his rounded eyes stand out even more.

Justitia turned her blindfolded face to Dakkar. "Back to this pure Noirre, which I understand grows in a cave in Ireland and is deadly to retrieve. How did you gain the Noirre?"

Sweat pebbled Dakkar's forehead and streamed down his face.

His wild gaze flicked around in search of any help. There was none. Turning to Justitia, he said, "My ancestor was a woman whose child died in that cave while trying to escape the Vikings that attacked their village. The child's mother was captured and later escaped, then married a Moor. Noirre plants grew from my ancestor cursing the Vikings for the death of her daughter. When I went for the Noirre, that child's spirit allowed me to live only because I was a relative. She gifted me a plant."

Daegan clarified, "That child's spirit gave you her hand, which turned into a plant and cannot be replaced."

Macha's jaw dropped more. "You are disgusting. I have never allowed Noirre around me."

Storm shook his head mentally at her. Of course, that bitch was only concerned about Noirre around *her* and not the little spirit who lost a hand.

Ready to get moving, Storm asked Dakkar, "Who did you give Evalle to and did you use a bolthole?"

Dakkar started shaking his head as if he feared replying.

Macha snarled at Dakkar, "This is what you were doing when you said you wanted to earn your place with me? I gave you a bolthole so you could come and go in my realm. Not for your whims. You expected immortality for this debacle?"

"I only wanted to be with you."

His body turned brighter and brighter red until he looked like a neon tomato.

She shook her head and looked away in disgust.

Justitia asked Macha, "You gave him a *bolthole* that would access a Celtic realm *and* offered him immortality?"

Storm realized the Tribunal goddess was calling out Macha for breaking some kind of entity rule.

Really unhappy now, Macha said, "Yes, he had a bolthole, but specifically for visiting *my* realm. No, I was not going to make him immortal."

Macha did not change color, but Storm murmured to Daegan, "She's jading the truth a bit."

Daegan nodded his understanding.

Loki snarled, "How dare you give him access to the realm of any Celtic deity?"

Whipping her head around to face Loki, Macha ranted, "Do not make it sound as if he could go anywhere. He could only use the bolthole to enter *my* realm. The only way he could enter another realm was if ... " Her voice faltered.

Justitia finished the sentence for her. "If he was of Celtic descent, which Dakkar is. Bad mistake, Macha. One that could bring many in your pantheon down on your head."

Dakkar had been staring in horror. He roared at her. *"You lied to me! You said you would make me immortal!"*

Macha told him, "Oh, please. I do not answer to you or anyone else. For that matter, do not think to make my lie worse than yours."

Daegan said, "I am not finished questioning this man."

"I've got nothing else to say to you," Dakkar shot back.

Sounding as if he found this entirely too entertaining, Loki said, "Listen up, Dakkar. Unfortunately, once you lie in here, you must reply to *all* questions and answer truthfully. To lie again will result in your losing a body part each time. Refusal to reply is the same as lying. It's quite sad to watch when a man's most prized part is the first to go."

Tears leaked from Dakkar's eyes. "No, please. I can't. I gave a blood pact."

Loki said, "That doesn't matter in here. A blood pact agreed to outside this realm can't harm you in this realm."

"Okay, okay." Dakkar started mumbling to himself.

Storm mentally shook his head at this slime. Dakkar had to be too panicked to realize that while the broken pact might not affect him in here, it would come calling the moment Dakkar left the Tribunal.

Luckily for Dakkar, Storm had no intention of letting that man leave here alive. He asked the bounty hunter, "Who did you give my mate to?"

"I, uh ... I gave her to Germanus."

Daegan dropped his crossed arms and asked in a voice filled with disbelief. "Germanus? The man who was my father's steward?"

"That one."

"How is he still alive? He was not immortal."

Dakkar's face turned a deep red, much like a thumb slammed with a hammer. "You know of Abandinu?"

"Yes. He was a god tossed out of the Celtic pantheon."

Shuddering through each breath, Dakkar said, "Abandinu created a realm where Germanus could live forever."

Storm didn't need his empathic gift to know this Germanus guy being alive was a major issue for Daegan.

"What does he want with Evalle?" Daegan asked in a voice so deep it sounded similar to his dragon voice.

Storm hadn't been the only one to pick up on Daegan edging closer to shifting.

All five of the other deities stared at him. Hermes stopped playing and ordered in a shaky voice, "Answer the dragon!"

Dakkar choked out the words. "Germanus is using her as bait, waiting for you."

Daegan asked, "Why would he think I even knew he was alive?"

"I ... I told him you were hunting your hoard. He's got your father's treasure and doesn't want to give it up."

Storm saw red, literally. He had no doubt his eyes were glowing just as bright as Dakkar's body.

Somebody was hurting Evalle for *money*? Grady had been right. He'd just had the wrong person when he thought this had happened because of the dragon king hunting his hoard.

Past the point of showing any of this group beyond Daegan respect, Storm said, "Why would you do this and put my mate in the middle of it?"

When Dakkar hesitated again, Loki said, "You should answer."

Dakkar looked over at Macha with pleading in his eyes, but she ignored him with cold determination.

With a worried glance at his crotch, Dakkar faced Daegan and Storm. Resignation pulsed through his misery. "Regardless of what she admits, I promised Macha I'd bring her the dragon's head in exchange for immortality and the ability to teleport."

Macha had shown little emotion until that point, but her head swiveled to face Dakkar's glowing body. "You are a liar."

"No, Macha, he did not lie," Loki corrected. "He would have lost a body part right away. You are not glowing because you technically did not say that his words were a lie. You should take care what you say next."

Macha lifted an icy gaze to Loki. "I would warn you not to cross me. I do not have to be here."

"This is true, but it sounds as if you were going to grant someone immortality in exchange for killing a VIPER ally in addition to giving him the ability to move around with a bolthole." Loki's tone had shifted to one of censure with no indication that her warning fazed him in the least.

"I will not be held accountable for what a minion chose to do on his own."

Daegan asked, "Dakkar, did she offer you immortality if you arranged for my death?"

Macha's eyes slashed a look of hate at Daegan. "Do not challenge me in a realm where you are at risk."

Justitia admonished, "This is the Tribunal realm, Macha. You do not hold the power here."

"Oh? Who do you think helped create this realm? I was one of the original three Tribunal members. I and the other two hold the greatest power here."

Storm held his breath. This bunch had better not have a throwdown until he and Daegan got all the information they needed.

Justitia instructed Dakkar, "Answer the last question."

Dakkar tried to stand up straighter, probably sensing the turning tide against Macha. "Yes, she did offer me those things."

There it was—absolute evidence of Macha attacking Daegan.

Tension pushed air from the room.

Loki observed everyone for a moment and suggested, "It is in no one's best interest for you to war with Daegan, Macha."

"I am not starting a war."

"You did the minute you supported anything Dakkar did against me and my people," Daegan argued. "You gave him the ability to enter a Celtic realm, which was how he got into Abandinu's." Daegan shifted his attention to Dakkar, "Am I correct?"

"Yes."

Daegan asked Macha, "What do you think Abandinu will do when he finds out what you've done? You can deny it all you want, but one deity will always hold another guilty of anything their followers do that they consider an act of aggression."

Storm wanted to support Daegan, but he'd rather not get busy with a war any time soon. He whispered to Daegan, "I'm with you if there is a war, but is there a way to settle this so we don't have to fight one right now?"

Daegan had been locked in fury while he spoke, but when he turned to Storm his dark face eased. He nodded, "I have an idea for preventing a war."

"I'm all for it," Storm said.

Crossing his arms, Daegan said, "I would ask the Tribunal for a chance to make peace with Macha."

The trio on the dais turned shocked faces to Daegan.

Macha's face registered suspicion.

Dakkar said, "Can I—"

Loki snapped his fingers and the bounty hunter turned mute. The prankster god asked Daegan, "What would appease you, since you were the one she intended to kill?"

Storm pondered this strange interaction. Why would Loki care if Daegan died or not?

Daegan said, "I understand that Queen Maeve called in *Dlí Fola,* the rule of the Blood Law, to demand the return of Kizira's body."

Macha's face locked down to show nothing beyond contempt when she countered, "So? From what I understand, Maeve did not receive the body."

Queen Maeve hissed and Justitia shushed her.

"That's beside the point," Daegan said. "I'm calling in the same rule of Blood Law."

"For what?" she asked, almost laughing.

Daegan's deep voice boomed. "My sister's body. She was left in your safeguard, then you went to war with my king. I demand the return of my sister's body."

Macha took her time replying and exposed a sly smile. "Is she dead?"

Storm had never heard about Daegan's family. This had to be vitally important to Daegan for him to use that as a bargaining chip.

All and good as long as Storm and Daegan left here with Evalle's location.

Daegan said, "If my sister is not dead, then where is she?"

Macha taunted Daegan. "You're the one who called up the Blood Law, which references only a dead body. It is not a living law. I don't have to answer if she's living, do I, Loki?"

Exuberant at the exchange, Loki said, "No, you don't."

Daegan pressed on. "But if my sister is dead, you do *have* to hand over the body. Is that not correct, Loki?"

Looking serious for a tiny moment, Loki said, "That is also true."

Everyone stared at each other until Loki asked, "Macha? Do you have a body to hand over?"

Surprisingly, she looked disappointed to say, "No."

Storm felt hope rush off Daegan in a wave, but then it dissipated, replaced by disappointment. Why?

"I believe we have all we need," Daegan announced in a deadly quiet voice.

Storm said, "Wait, what about ... " The question died on his lips when Daegan looked over and shook his head. Storm had trusted the dragon to this point and couldn't stop halfway.

Daegan must know how to find Evalle, so Storm would wait until they released Dakkar.

That bounty hunter had to die. Painfully.

Loki looked over at Dakkar and shook his head. He snapped his fingers again.

Dakkar's body trembled violently. He could barely speak. "I answered all the questions. Can I go now?" he pleaded, pointing the question at Loki.

Loki asked Macha, "Would you prefer to stay or leave?"

Lifting her arms, Macha said, "I am done with this." With that action, light burst from her in a radiant glow and winked out when she teleported away.

"*Macha!*" Dakkar shouted. "No, come back."

Queen Maeve laughed wildly and vanished before anyone could address her. That goddess was certifiable.

Dakkar focused on Daegan. "You said you wouldn't kill me."

The dragon observed Dakkar with the same distaste as encountering a nasty pile of human waste. He told the bounty hunter, "I spoke to your ancestors in Dunmore cave."

"Wh-what?"

"They know you broke your vow. I don't think you need to worry about the blood oath you gave Germanus," Daegan said.

Loki mused, "He has a point, Dakkar. Dying is not going to be fun for you."

"Wait." Dakkar's frantic gaze went to Loki. "Isn't what Daegan says in here like law or something?"

Striking a thoughtful pose, Loki said, "You are correct."

Storm growled low, preparing to unleash his jaguar.

Sounding slightly relieved, Dakkar remind Loki, "Well, Daegan said he wouldn't kill me."

Loki nodded with understanding. "True. But I never said I wouldn't."

Dakkar's mouth fell open. "No! I'll be stuck in Dunmore Cave forever. Don't do this."

"You should thank me. That will be the next best thing to immortality, which was your goal, evidently," Loki quipped and pointed at Dakkar.

The bounty hunter's body exploded into a fireball so strong Storm and Daegan took a step back and shielded their faces. It was over as quickly as it started. When the fire ended, nothing was left but a pile of ashes.

Addressing Daegan, Loki said, "I hope you remember that we did aid you today."

Lowering his arm from his face, Daegan said, "I'll remember. I hope you keep in mind that Dakkar wanted to be an immortal and he had the makings of a serial killer. That means I helped you remove a danger to all preternaturals today as well."

He got a smirk from Loki in reply. "What do you plan to do about Germanus and Abandinu?"

"Make a statement for all who dare to do this in the future."

"You would enter a hostile realm to fight where you are vulnerable to attack?"

Daegan offered, "Why would that matter to you? If I fail, it will solve many of your problems."

"True, but it would not reveal who your mother is," Loki pointed out. "Will she offer aid with Abandinu?"

Offering all three deities of the Tribunal a confident expression, Daegan said, "I don't need her help for this."

That quieted even Loki.

Storm only hoped that exchange meant Daegan absolutely knew where they were headed next.

Daegan turned to Storm. "Can you live with that justice for Dakkar's part in this?"

Storm wouldn't lose another second going after vengeance when he had a far greater goal. "Yes. I just want to find Evalle. You do know where she is, right?"

Daegan said, "Yes."

Storm was ready to tackle Germanus and Abandinu. He and the dragon had survived this Tribunal. Storm would destroy anything left standing in his way and Daegan would teleport Evalle home.

Finally, this nightmare was coming to an end. He couldn't wait to see his mate.

CHAPTER 26

Treoir Island realm hidden above the Irish Sea

STORM GRITTED HIS TEETH AND hung tight as Daegan zapped them from the Tribunal to the Treoir Island realm in a teleporting blast. He had no complaints though and welcomed anything that kept him moving quickly.

The dragon king landed the two of them on the grounds leading up to the castle, where Belador guards could see who had arrived.

The minute Daegan sent a hand signal to his guards that all was fine, Storm asked, "Okay, where is Evalle?"

"She's in a realm created by Abandinu, a god who was cast out of the Tuatha Dé Danann. Dakkar's bolthole functioned for any Celtic realm as well as in the human realm. Macha had better hope none of the other deities in her pantheon find out about what she did."

Storm wouldn't lose sleep over Macha getting piled on by her peers.

"Where is the realm and how do we break in?"

"I don't know—" Daegan started.

Hell. Would this get any easier? "Are you kidding me? We could have drained every drop of information from Dakkar before Loki torched him."

"Let me finish, Storm."

"Sorry. Go ahead."

"I am not overly familiar with Abandinu as we were forbidden from any association with that god, but Garwyli should be able to give me enough details for me to teleport into the realm Abandinu created."

Blowing out a stream of air did little to lower Storm's need to reach Evalle. He pulled himself together. "I understand, but it's killing me to know where she is and not be on the way there."

Daegan missed nothing. "I realize being this close to finding Evalle is testing your limits. It would test mine if I were fortunate enough to have a mate such as yours. Believe me when I say we will not squander any time in preparing to invade the realm and take her back. But if we jump in without a plan and into a place where someone is expecting me, we may all die in front of her."

Growling in discontent, Storm made his jaguar a silent promise that their time would come soon. His animal shoved and snarled, sensing they were close to finding her.

Storm would love nothing better than to unleash his black beast, but Daegan was right.

Rushing into a trap would solve nothing and leave Evalle at the mercy of others forever if they failed.

"I'm good," Storm said, stretching his neck to loosen tight muscles. "Let's do this."

With a short nod of agreement, Daegan turned toward the castle where his guards stood at attention. As the dragon king approached the steps leading up to the entrance, he told the men and women who watched over the Treoirs, "At ease."

Inside, Tristan, Adrianna and Quinn were waiting and looked up as Storm and Daegan entered.

Quinn must have won the argument with Reese.

That made sense to Storm. Unless they were facing a wall of demons, Reese could not help at this point. He left it up to those two to know what was best for her, but Quinn had been right to prevent Reese from joining them if Storm was correct about what he sensed was going on with Reese.

Reese didn't hit him as a woman who would leave Quinn in the dark for long.

"We know who has Evalle," Daegan announced as he strode up to the rest of the team.

Everyone started asking where, who and other related questions.

Daegan held up his hand for silence. "Evalle is in a realm created by a god named Abandinu."

Tzader came striding in with powerful steps. "A god has her? What the hell?"

"Not exactly," Daegan clarified. "A man named Germanus resides in this particular realm. He has her. He was also my father's steward, but after being captured by Queen Maeve I have no history of what happened to my father, his people ... or my siblings beyond bits and pieces I heard spoken while I was in TÅµr Medb."

That was news to Storm. Eyebrows lifted around the room at the mention of siblings.

All except Tristan, who calmly listened as though he knew some of this. As the dragon king's right-hand man, Tristan having more knowledge of Daegan's past would not surprise Storm.

Quinn asked, "Is Germanus a nonhuman?"

"No. He was human when I knew him at my father's castle," Daegan replied.

Tzader scowled. "Then how did he capture Evalle? And why the hell did he do it?"

Daegan gave the group a quick rundown of all that had transpired, explaining about Perth and Dakkar.

It boggled the mind to think how Daegan was under constant attack, which meant his followers were targets as well. Storm thought back on a warning Daegan had made in the Tribunal that he intended to make a statement when he found Evalle's captor.

Storm took that to mean Daegan wanted others to think twice about attacking him or his people. Storm would lend everything he possessed as a nonhuman to support that statement.

As Daegan explained how Germanus was setting a trap for the dragon king, Tristan's expression underwent an immediate change from interested to concerned.

Tristan asked, "Can you just teleport us in?"

Daegan scowled at the Alterant. "No. You have heard me say more than once that I lead from the front, and always will."

"Just sayin' that we can handle this."

Adrianna's gaze had bounced back and forth, watching the byplay between those two. She asked, "Aren't you most vulnerable in someone else's realm, Daegan?"

That sent Daegan's fierce glare her way, which had no effect on the witch. He said, "This is true, which I expect all of you to keep private. Some deities know this, but the less it's repeated the better."

"We know," Tristan confirmed for the group. "But we're your closest advisors. I'm sure I'm not the only one concerned. We need you, your power and your leadership. Losing you in that realm would leave the entire Belador organization and Treoir vulnerable."

Much as Storm wanted to dislike Tristan, he had a grudging respect for the guy saying he'd sacrifice his life in place of Daegan's for the greater good. From all that Storm could see, Daegan's presence had really made a difference with that Alterant.

Daegan shut down the debate by saying, "I appreciate everyone's concern, but getting into and out of this realm safely with Evalle will require a select group with specific abilities. Tristan, you are extremely capable, but you don't have the teleporting ability that I do. You could get the team in, but you don't know for sure you could teleport all of them and Evalle out, especially if you have to battle other beings first. We will need all of our powers."

Quinn grunted in agreement.

Daegan called out, "Garwyli? I need your presence."

Storm turned with the group as they waited for the old druid, who came ambling down from one of the long hallways leading to the entrance.

When Garwyli finally made it to them, he said, "What news, dragon? Have ya found our Evalle?"

With another brief rundown, Daegan explained what had gone down at the Tribunal. The old druid's face flipped from a frown to surprise to anger.

As he wrapped up the details, Daegan said to everyone, "I've been asking Garwyli to look into the history of my father's time. After the attack by Lorwerth and the Laochra Fola, I realized that until I know what happened during that time, everyone associated with me could be at risk from directions I would not expect. I do not want to make it easy for my enemies to harm my followers." Daegan asked Garwyli, "What can you tell me about Germanus being in a realm created by Abandinu?"

Stroking his long, white beard, Garwyli asked, "Who is Germanus?"

"He was my father's steward."

"Germanus would have been human."

"Yes, and we were forbidden from worshipping Abandinu when my father lived. It appears that Germanus worshipped him in secret."

"That makes sense about your father's rule. As I recall, Abandinu was banished from the Celtic pantheon."

"Yes, he was."

"I see." More fooling with his beard, then Garwyli said, "It does not make sense for Abandinu to bring someone like Evalle to his realm."

Storm argued, "Evidently he would, because that's where she is right now."

Lifting a wrinkled hand to request quiet, Garwyli said, "That is not my meaning. You see, Abandinu created more than one realm."

What? Storm looked to Daegan, who seem unconcerned at the possibility of searching multiple realms.

Continuing, Garwyli said, "This is the first I've heard of Abandinu sending any human to a realm."

"So you can't help us?" Storm sighed, at the very end of his mental rope.

Storm saw his question reflected in the faces of the team.

Garwyli laid a hand on his shoulder. "Do not distress, Storm. Germanus will be in a specific realm, so you will not have to hunt to locate the correct one."

This whole trip had been an emotional roller coaster from the start. Storm said, "That's encouraging, Garwyli. It's just ... you, of all people, know she is everything to me."

"I know, son," Garwyli said, patting Storm's shoulder.

After Evalle brought Storm home from a demonic underworld, she forced him to overcome the influence of demonic blood he'd inherited.

Garwyli had been so impressed by the way Evalle fought for Storm, in the face of Macha's anger among other things, that Garwyli called in a marker a thousand years old and had Storm's soul returned to him.

The druid had cited Evalle as Storm's champion.

She was far more than that to him.

She was his next breath. He had no life or any desire for this life without her.

"I understand your impatience. Give an old man a moment to explain and you can be on your way." Garwyli winked to soften the reprimand.

"Yes, sir," Storm answered in deference.

Turning to the entire group, Garwyli said, "As I mentioned, Abandinu created more than one realm. It seemed to be his hobby. He collected things that interested him such as majikal creatures."

Adrianna sent Storm an apologetic glance before she suggested, "Wouldn't Evalle fit that description?"

Little could bother Storm at this point and she was right to push for any details that might help them.

"Yes, but Evalle shifts into a human form. That did not interest Abandinu. He did enjoy flying beasts such as manticores, wyverns, gryphons and the like, but he had a particular interest in dragons." Garwyli scratched his beard-covered chin. "I could be wrong on the not shifting part."

Pushing the druid to move along, Daegan said, "What else?"

"My point is that taking Evalle would still not make sense. Abandinu had no interest in battling other gods or goddesses. He merely liked to be entertained, but not if he had to face an angry adversary. That's what is so odd about putting Germanus in any of his realms. I have never heard of any other humans being taken for that reason."

"Why would a human even want to live in a realm if he was alone?" Tristan asked. "Feels like we're missing something in all this."

"It's hard to say, but a human living in a realm such as one Abandinu created would remain forever without aging. Perhaps when Germanus worshipped Abandinu, he asked for eternal life. If Abandinu heard that often enough he might have gifted Germanus with the god's version of that by spending eternity in a place where the steward would not age, but I still find that odd. I wonder if it was done as a punishment, since it would be a very sad existence for Germanus."

Moving ahead, Daegan told Tristan, "I need you to go immediately to the gryphons to ask for volunteers. With this god's affinity for dragons and any other flying creature, there could be all kinds of ancient predators to battle in there. I will fully understand if your sister does not join us."

Tristan said, "Thanks. I wouldn't be happy to have her there."

Storm blinked and the Alterant had teleported away.

Tzader asked Daegan, "Why are you taking so many when you might be more effective with a smaller team for inserting and snatching her?"

After witnessing what happened in the Tribunal, Storm had an idea why the dragon king wanted a larger show of force.

"This is not just a retrieval," Daegan said. "I weary of my people being targeted and harmed. Those who know me have no doubt I will come for one of mine, but that isn't enough. My enemies need to know that to touch one loyal to me is to bring the wrath of a dangerous dragon, the Treoir power, the entire Belador force and our allies." Daegan gave a nod to Adrianna with that, then continued. "We are going in to save Evalle first and foremost. Once we are successful, I intend to make a statement that will spread throughout the preternatural community."

Adrianna asked, "What is that statement?"

"For every one of mine who is harmed, prepare to lose a hundredfold if it is within my power."

She gave him a thoughtful look. "I like that. Make a show of force and make others think about what they have to lose if they start a conflict."

"With the exception of those who will war no matter what, a show of force will deter others who prefer life over attacking my kingdom."

Storm asked Daegan, "How many are we taking with us?"

"Everyone standing here, except Tzader, and all of the gryphons that agree to join us."

Tzader scowled, but he had his own job of protecting Brina and Treoir. No one thought any less of him for remaining behind, but that warrior and Quinn had been Evalle's closest friends before Storm met her. To be more accurate, Tzader and Quinn treated Evalle as a younger sister.

Why the gryphons? Storm wouldn't ask. Daegan had a plan in mind. Not that Storm would refuse the additional fighters, but did Daegan believe they had to be airborne to battle inside the realm?

Where would that leave Storm's jaguar?

If they had to fly, Storm mentally counted Daegan, Tristan and what? One or two more of the seven gryphons who currently resided on Treoir Island?

How many creatures had Abandinu collected over centuries of

playing with his realms?

It didn't matter. Storm would go alone if that was his only option, but he was thankful for the bonds Evalle had built with all of these people.

Once Tristan had departed, Daegan asked, "How do I locate the realm with Germanus?"

Garwyli sighed. "As far as anyone knows, Abandinu created three realms for his entertainment."

Daegan sounded just as impatient when he said, "He can have as many as he wishes, but how do we find *this* one?"

Garwyli frowned hard at the dragon king, but explained, "It was said that one realm had been created entirely under water and a second one was full of nothing but constant sunrises and sunsets. That would leave only one." Turning to speak pointedly to Daegan, he said, "Keep in mind that if Abandinu is behind all of this, he will be undefeatable in his own realm, even by you, dragon."

"I know my chances," Daegan said, dismissing any more concerns raised about him. Then he asked the druid, "If you think she can only be in one realm, I need a way to locate it."

"There is a very quick way in by offering your dragon to Abandinu, but—"

Everyone groaned.

"If that's what it takes, that's what I'll do," Daegan stated firmly.

"Bad idea," Tzader broke in. "That would completely destroy any advantage you would have from the element of surprise."

"That's what I was about to say, Tzader," Garwyli groused. "I do have another idea. It might not work if—"

Daegan growled like his dragon. "Druid, *please* do not waste time on what might not work. Just give me enough information to locate the correct realm."

"I'm tryin' to do just that, dragon. The way I see it, there is a simple path. Envision winged beasts around Germanus. Follow that to teleport in, but there is risk of being attacked as you arrive if you land too close."

Storm had to admit that Garwyli had a point. He said, "Listen everyone. I know you're all ready to go in there and battle. I'll never be able to repay this debt, so thank you. But I'm the one who should be teleported in first. I not only shift into my jaguar, but I have majik as well. Give me time to distract any threat if we are landing in the middle of them, then follow thirty seconds later."

Quinn said, "No."

His reply was followed by the same response around the room, ending with Daegan saying, "Nice try, Storm, but I'm not facing Evalle if you died doing that. Let's go."

"One more thing, dragon."

"Yes, druid?" Daegan said, sounding as if one more question strained what patience he had left.

"It is hard to imagine Abandinu allowing any activity in his realm without his knowledge. If Abandinu put Evalle into the realm, then he must be the one to take her out."

Fuck, fuck, fuck. Storm ran a hand over his head in exasperation. "I don't give a damn at this point. I'm going for her."

"Me, too," echoed around the room.

"Let's see how many gryphons we have and get moving," Daegan ordered and strode toward the double doors leading outside.

"Finally." Storm and the others followed Daegan outside where ... seven members of the gryphon pack stood in human form. That was all of them with the exception of Evalle. Tristan didn't look a bit happy about his sister being in the group. That was up to Tristan and his sister.

Storm wished for Evalle to see the support of her peers. That would make for one hell of an air attack.

Garwyli stepped up next to Storm. "I have complete faith in you bringing your mate home."

While that was a nice vote of confidence to hear, Storm prepared for a one-way trip. If Abandinu would not release her, he was not leaving her in another realm forever.

Tristan stepped forward. "I have an idea."

Quinn groaned loudly.

CHAPTER 27

Realm of Scamall

EVALLE STOOD ON THE TOP of the castle and stared at the landscape Germanus had changed to multicolored hills of sand. No green grass or mountains in the distance today.

She took his desolate landscape to mirror his morose frame of mind over the past day.

She'd pissed him off by suggesting that he was being played. The kidnapper had tricked Germanus.

In his shoes, she'd be roaring mad.

Had it made a difference to Germanus? No.

He'd sent a manticore that outweighed her gryphon by five hundred pounds in to battle with her earlier. The beast had to have come from his private stock.

She was so angry, her gryphon had stomped the monstrous beast in five minutes. She shifted back and yelled at Germanus to send the other ones he kept hidden.

After watching her trash the manticore like it was nothing, the two attack gargoyles lost their usual I-can-kill-you-with-one-wing-tied-behind-my-back expressions and turned to look at their boss.

Germanus had smoldered in furious silence.

Evidently none of the handful of winged creatures kept around to intimidate her had known their boss hid more like them. The beasts listening might not shift into humans, but they understood when she yelled through busted lips, "Stop destroying these creatures, you bloodthirsty bastard. Send out your *dragon!*"

That had done it. Germanus leaped to his feet, yelled curses at her and stomped away.

After that, his gargoyles watched her with wary eyes, as though they suddenly realized they might not be at the top of the realm food chain.

She didn't care. *Hard to care about anything in this place when you're doomed.*

Running a hand over the sack she wore for clothing, she could feel the hideous crater in her chest. Heavily scarred skin surrounding it would never heal. Her face, arms and legs had been ripped open over and over again. Some of the wounds had managed to heal, but most left a ragged scar a half-inch thick.

Her mouth bled every time she tried to talk around the gash she'd gotten in her last battle.

The pure Noirre in her system played nice with her Medb blood to keep her alive, but whatever spell the kidnapper had used prevented her body from fully repairing itself.

She hadn't slept soundly after those first nightmares of being with Storm. But Germanus had been so furious with her after their meeting in his treasure room that she hadn't dared to sleep at all. She'd moved constantly, never sitting down, even putting weight on her bad leg and causing pain on purpose, just to stay awake. She was reaching the stage of seeing things she doubted were actually there, like ghosts of people she'd known.

At one point earlier today, she'd started talking to Adrianna, then stopped when the ghostly face didn't answer.

Germanus had laughed and said, "You have to sleep sometime, Evalle."

Not until she died.

She hoped Daegan was up to the task of killing her. She hated to put him in that position, but she'd rather die by his dragon than for Storm to spend his life trying to get her out of here. And he would.

A tear slipped out.

She swiped it away with a vicious slap of her hand.

Germanus would not see her break.

Speaking of the hemorrhoid on the ass of a demon, Germanus stepped out on the roof, accompanied by his pair of hulking gargoyles, and walked over to her.

When she ignored him, he asked, "What? No mouthy comments?"

"Nope, just another day with you, dickless." She sent a sharp look to his groin. Yes, she was feeling mean today and what better target than Germanus? She fought his stinking battles and suffered slow recovery that would never truly heal. He didn't dare attack her for fear of losing all evidence of manhood.

If only he would end up stuck in here for an eternity.

She'd have someone to verbally torture.

Coming up with nasty barbs would keep her busy. Wasn't that what she heard some humans talk about? Keep your mind active as you age.

Germanus must have decided this conversation would be better without his guards. A wave of his hand apparently gave the two gargoyles leave, because they took off over the side of the castle wall. "I look forward to leaving you in this place when I escape, Evalle."

"I have a feeling you're going to be right here with me, oh great leader."

"Why do you keep trying to feed me that lie?"

She finally turned, a feral smile in place. "I seem to be the only person in Scamall who can handle the truth. I've accepted my future. Why is it so hard for you to accept yours?"

"Perhaps I need to give you another demonstration with the other twin."

Good one, Germanus. She'd spent the last two realm days dazed from total lack of sleep, blood loss and a corrupted mental state. She knew not to aggravate Germanus, but sometimes the words spilled out without any thought. Then he made a threat that slashed right through the pain in her chest and bludgeoned her heart.

But he would only use those threats as long as he thought they would hurt her emotionally.

Turning to him, she tried to spin the tables. "I have made friends with your beasts, Germanus. They know I'll shield them from harm if I can. Their greatest threat is you sending them to their deaths and they're starting to realize it. I have also realized you can't kill a beast in this realm, not by your hand, can you?"

His surprise was all the answer she needed to continue. "If you were someone special to Abandinu, he would not have punished you by leaving you in here with no humans for company. I salute him for taking away your ability to try to rape me, key word being *try*. Abandinu clearly likes winged creatures, especially majikal flying ones. What's he going to say when he realizes how many of his pets you've smashed?"

Germanus said nothing, but his eyes told how much he wanted to kill her.

Looked like she had found a nerve.

In that case, she would see what it would take to snap that nerve. She took a step toward him and lowered her voice. "Bring another teenager, or anyone else from my former life, to this miserable place to harm them and I will show you what happens when I turn one of your favorite beasts against you."

"You can't do that," Germanus mumbled. No conviction in that statement.

"Really? You sure about that? Did you not find out exactly what you were bringing into your sick little zoo when you made a deal for me? Let me clue you in just in case the kidnapper who has played you perfectly to this point failed to share everything. I have Medb *and* Belador blood. I'm a gryphon who shifts to human and ... wait for it ... I talk to other flying creatures mind to mind."

Not exactly true since she hadn't been able to communicate with the others here, but back home she could speak telepathically to other Belador gryphons and a dragon.

Germanus failed to fold and start pissing his pants, which would have confirmed a direct strike.

Damn. She'd so hoped for a loss of control on his part.

But neither did he boast that he would show her how wrong she was and bring the other twin.

For now, he seemed to at least be thinking about her words.

That wouldn't last long.

She had been figuring out how to screw with Germanus, but it only lasted for a short time until his pea-sized brain realized she sometimes bluffed.

She wasn't sure how she'd stop him next time her lie didn't work and he decided to drag someone she loved in here again.

Of course, if she stayed here long enough she *might* find a way to communicate with the other creatures. The small group she hadn't killed when she'd been forced to fight were wary of her, as they should be. She would have killed them, too, if she hadn't figured out how to use her kinetics to pin them down until they quit fighting. Then she'd walk away in her gryphon form and they'd struggle back to standing.

More than once, she'd glanced back to find the creature staring at her in confusion.

The only person she wanted to maul and dismember at this point was Germanus. She'd never use her powers against a human, but he had given up that status in this place.

Inside the castle, he'd found an effective way to hold her emotions hostage.

Instead of burning the body after killing Kardos, Germanus had suspended the remains in the center of the castle. No scent of death lingered, just the balled-up, lifeless body inside an impossibly small cage. Every time she saw it, her mind replayed the vision of Kardos being killed … with sound.

For all the times she'd protected the twins, one had faced a brutal death because of her.

The first time she'd seen the macabre chandelier, she'd stopped to stare at it. She couldn't even see his beautiful face.

The fucking gargoyle that took him away had destroyed anything recognizable.

If the day ever came for her to see Storm again, he would know the minute he opened his empathic senses that she was empty inside. Germanus had managed to annihilate her soul.

Yet again, she was glad she had not bonded to Storm.

What would he be going through right now if they had?

Both gargoyle guards that had appeared with Germanus had flown over the castle wall. Now they started making their signature loud noises below her.

She leaned over to see what was going on. They were pounding on the castle walls. What could have upset that pair?

"You will regret all you have said," Germanus called from behind her.

When she looked around, he was grinning like he'd won the preternatural lottery. "The time has come for my escape to freedom."

"What are you talking about?" she asked the maniac.

"We have an uninvited guest in the realm. It has to be Daegan."

Whipping around to search the horizon, she found nothing,

nothing, nothing ... wait.

There.

Giant wings flapped against the stark background.

Germanus was wrong.

That was not just Daegan and she was sick about it. "Oh, Daegan, why did you bring my gryphon pack?" she whispered.

Germanus walked up and spoke softly in her ear. "You will battle now and fight with all your might."

"No." She would send everyone home where they would be safe. She trusted Storm and the Beladors to protect those she loved.

This time Germanus gloated. "Look back down to the steps at the entrance."

When she leaned over the two-foot-thick parapet again, she saw the terrified face of Kellman. His mouth had a rag tied around it. One of the gargoyles lifted a claw that was longer than her hand and held it above the twin's chest.

She screamed, "Noooo." As she yelled, she leaped up on the wall and jumped.

Germanus shouted, "Stop her!"

Her gryphon exploded out of her body. She was beyond feeling pain. Her wings flexed out and she banked away just before smashing into the stones below.

Turning in the air, she headed back to dive-bomb the gargoyle holding Kellman, who kicked and fought.

The second gargoyle appeared and stepped in front of his sidekick to launch himself at Evalle's gryphon, hitting her hard and knocking her sideways.

Spinning in the air, she tucked her wings and landed in a slide. Sand blew up in a blast.

Germanus yelled down, "I give you my word he will live if you battle the dragon, Evalle."

When the dust cleared, the gargoyles and Kellman were gone.

The seven flying creatures she'd battled were perched along the top edge of the castle staring down at her.

They all wore faces of her friends who were gryphons.

She shook her head.

The hallucination vanished, but her flying army still waited for her to lead them. Taking a running start that wobbled with her crooked leg, she pushed up, catching air as she flapped to lift off.

She circled the castle and on the second time around, she swooped across the top of the parapets, screeching at the creatures.

They must have understood that as a battle cry.

Every one of them lifted off behind her.

She had no choice but to battle her dragon king.

If Daegan was with them, she had to convince him to get everyone out of here before Germanus unleashed his own dragon, which would have to be more powerful in this realm.

If Germanus had convinced her of anything, it was that he did rule this realm.

Her mind replayed what to tell Daegan and … it hit her. She could use telepathy. Not yet. She'd been able to access her kinetics more than once when she flew further from the castle. Germanus had ultimate power here, but he'd clearly never practiced enough with it to know his limitations.

But she'd never spoken to anyone telepathically here either.

Looked like a learning curve coming up for everyone.

CHAPTER 28

Realm of Scamall

STORM FLEW THROUGH A STRANGE realm on the back of Ixxter, one of the gryphons who'd volunteered to join the team. Miles and miles of sand. Who would want to live in a place surrounded by only aqua, orange, mint green, pink, yellow, red and silver sand for terrain?

How did Abandinu keep any creature alive here?

Daegan had said he would try to envision the winged beasts and Germanus at a distance in hopes of landing the attack team in a safe place. That had worked. Now for the next step.

Adrianna rode on Daegan's back, and they flew in the center of the pack. Tristan had suggested they hide the dragon until the last minute as a surprise weapon. Also, keeping Daegan and Storm out of view would prevent Evalle giving away their presence. Daegan agreed and told Tristan to initiate telepathic contact if Evalle came to them first.

Quinn rode on the back of Tristan's gryphon.

Initially, Adrianna had cloaked all of them, but the moment they took off for the castle in the distance, Daegan had shouted that their cloaking had not held.

One weapon down plus the loss of a surprise attack.

The sight of seven gryphons flying in tight formation with a dragon tucked in the middle was one Storm would never forget, but he wished it could be eight gryphons with Evalle in the lead and they were all far away from here.

Daegan called out, "They're coming out to meet us."

Storm straightened to see wings flapping toward them. It appeared those creatures were flying from the castle that spread across half the horizon, but that flying division had no sense of formation. Just lots of huge wings whipping up and down.

Silky energy slid over Storm's body. This was some creepy realm.

When Storm looked again, his heart lurched.

Leading that flock of mismatched flying beasts was a golden-headed gryphon with aqua-blue wings.

His throat tightened.

Evalle's gryphon was coming in hot. Did she even recognize her pack flying toward her?

All at once, Ixxter set his wings to land.

Storm looked around at the rest of them and Daegan's dragon. They were all landing. Must have been a telepathic order.

As soon as Ixxter stopped moving, Storm was off his back and heading for Evalle.

Adrianna slid down next to him and grabbed his arm. "Wait."

He jerked around. "Let go, Adrianna. The last thing I want to do is harm you, but I have waited and waited on everything and everyone. I'm going to Evalle."

The witch removed her hand, but said, "What if she's been compelled to kill everyone? Even you."

Power flushed around them, drawing Storm's attention to Daegan, who had quietly shifted to his human form. The dragon king walked over and whispered, "Give Tristan a chance to reach Evalle using our telepathy."

Dressed in his medieval attire, Daegan pulled his sword over his shoulder and turned, preparing to battle.

When Storm stepped up beside him, Daegan asked, "Do you want a sword?"

"No. It would only get in my jaguar's way."

Adrianna was right. Storm had learned patience in gaining Evalle as his mate, a prize worthy of giving up everything he owned. He would show that same patience to prevent putting her in a position to fight him.

She'd win.

He'd never lift a claw against her.

CHAPTER 29

E VALLE'S HEART HAD CLIMBED UP her throat and almost strangled her as she'd neared her gryphon pack. When they set their wings and landed, she drew a shaky breath of air.

She mirrored Tristan's action to land.

He was clearly in the lead.

As she slowed and set her wings, so did her small army that would die quickly beneath the Belador gryphon claws.

But Tristan and company was no match for some of the massive beasts Germanus had shown her yesterday.

On the ground, she turned to give her group a stay-put stare. They remained still.

Hmm. Who knew obedience training worked with a look?

Surprisingly, Storm and Daegan weren't with the gryphons. She was glad she didn't have to face Storm, but shocked that Daegan would send Tristan and the pack on their own.

Or had Tristan figured out where she was and took it on himself to come here? That sounded like Tristan, but she couldn't fault him for keeping their dragon king safe.

It was her job to send the gryphons back alive.

Stepping forward just enough to break out of her group, she sent a telepathic message to Tristan. *Thank you for coming. Please go home. This is a death trap.*

Tristan replied, *We know. No fun if this was easy, right? What the hell happened to you? Why aren't you healing?*

She'd missed him. *Long story and you don't have time to hear it. You have to teleport out of here, all of you, right now. If you don't, I have to battle you. I don't have a choice. The guy in charge is called—*

Germanus, Tristan said. *We know that, too.*

What you don't know is that he's holding a teenager he intends to kill if I don't battle, she shouted mind to mind. *He's seen me fight others like the ones behind me. He'll know if I don't fight hard.*

Tristan muttered, *Shit on a stick. We planned to teleport you out of here.*

She attempted a sad smile around her ripped beak. *You can't. I get that now. We have to find the kid first.*

She didn't want to go into the whole explanation about the Noirre in her chest. She would bet that Germanus had stuck some in Kellman by now, just so he had to stay here, too.

Did Abandinu even notice the population growth here?

Tristan said, *Daegan wants to know where the boy is being held.*

Evalle held her breath. *Daegan is here?*

Hell, yes. So is the tomcat.

Her heart did a backflip. She couldn't decide whether to jump around and celebrate or start crying at the idea of seeing Storm one more time.

She did neither, because Tristan warned, *Don't show any reaction, Evalle. That's why we wanted you to see the gryphons first and why I'm talking to you instead of Daegan, but he can hear us. Also, we know about Abandinu and that he has a soft spot for flying creatures. We figured he might not smoke the gryphons.*

She admitted, *I haven't seen Abandinu since I arrived and Germanus thinks the god has abandoned him.*

Daegan's voice boomed in Evalle's head. *That's good. Abandinu may not care if we destroy that castle and Germanus.*

She implored Daegan, *Please get everyone out of here. This bunch behind me is not the entire army. Germanus intends for me to fight you as a distraction, then while your guard is down he will send the real army. Daegan ... he has a dragon.*

When Daegan said nothing, Evalle said, *Please tell Storm I love him and there is no way to teleport me out of here. Just take him and leave.*

Daegan said, *We heard that I could not teleport you out, but this battle is not over yet. As for Storm, Adrianna would have to put a Witchlock spell on your mate to get him out of here right now and she would no sooner do that than the rest of us would.*

Adrianna was here, too?

Daegan said, *About the boy Germanus is holding ...*

The sound of thunderous wings reached her ears as every Treoir gryphon lifted its head at the sound.

She swept her eagle-shaped head to look as well.

Germanus must have realized she was communicating ... or this was exactly what he'd planned.

His two gargoyles flew in the lead with Germanus on the back of one.

The time had come for her to choose.

Battle her friends to protect Kellman?

Or fight beside her friends, knowing the boy would die?

CHAPTER 30

STANDING NEXT TO THE DRAGON king, Storm ordered, "Tell me what's going on."

Daegan said, "Evalle has to battle us, me in particular, or a boy will be killed."

"You are *not* hurting her." Storm couldn't take his eyes off of Evalle, and he bled for how badly her gryphon had been damaged.

Why hadn't she healed? She could normally heal fast in gryphon form. The spot on her chest where the emerald had been was now caved in and surrounded by ragged gray skin, half-healed.

"What did they do to her?" Storm said more to himself than anyone else.

"I don't know, but she *will* battle me," Daegan confirmed.

"No. Attack the others. Don't. Touch. Her."

Daegan sounded heartsick when he said, "Germanus has seen her battle hard. He'll know if she doesn't and he holds a person's life in the balance. Do you think Evalle wants the death of anyone, especially a young one, on her conscience? Trust me when I say I can do this."

"What the hell is that sound?" Storm pushed to the side to see through all the massive gryphons, wyverns and the rest of the preternatural bodies sitting behind Evalle's gryphon.

Two huge gargoyles flew point, ahead of a pack with a lot of muscle on the wing.

Daegan said, "That's the real enemy."

"There's a dragon in that bunch, too."

"I saw, but Evalle warned me about it. I have no idea who the dragon is, but if possible I don't want to kill that one."

"Why?"

Daegan turned a snarl on him. "Because that might be someone from my past who needs us just as I needed *your* help getting out of TÅµr Medb. I won't allow the dragon to harm any of my people, but I'm pretty sure his orders are specifically to kill me."

"Fine. Fight the damn dragon."

"Not until I engage Evalle."

Fuck this crap. Storm burst into the open, running to his mate.

Evalle's gryphon looked down at him, obviously horrified.

Why? Did she not expect him to come for her? He'd have been here sooner if they'd bonded.

She lifted a wing and used it to hide her face and chest.

"Oh, sweetheart." He slowed and walked over to her gryphon, opening his arms to hug as much as he could reach around her chest. "Don't ever hide from me. I love you."

When he looked up, a fat tear rolled down her eagle face.

Then her head jerked up and she pushed off the ground.

"Evalle, don't!"

Fifty feet away, the pair of attack gargoyles slowed to land while the rest of the enemy air brigade split off, climbing high into the air.

Wings flapped behind him as the gryphons ... and Daegan in dragon form, lifted off.

Storm ripped his shirt apart and shifted into his jaguar.

He caught sight of Adrianna and Quinn on the backs of gryphons as they flew past him.

He'd gladly take on the gargoyles, but those two hadn't even approached.

Their attention was locked on the screeching battles in the air. Storm didn't want to look, but he did.

Evalle flew at Daegan's dragon, slamming him, but then Daegan pushed her away. She flapped around and came back for the next lunge. The dragon could fly faster and had far more wingspan. He whipped back and forth, moving quickly for something his size.

She picked up speed, shot up in the air a quarter mile, did a fast spin and came down, heading for the dragon.

The guy Storm assumed was Germanus yelled, "You are not fighting hard enough, Evalle! *The boy dies!*"

Fucking bastard. Storm stretched his neck to watch Evalle and Daegan.

She jerked her head toward Germanus just before impact with Daegan.

They crashed in a blast of aqua feathers, red scales and her squawking in pain. Her gryphon tumbled through the air until Daegan's dragon made a crazy sharp turn and dove, snatching her up by the wing just before she would have hit the ground head first.

Speaking of the damn ground, it was no longer sand, but now hard as stone.

Had Germanus just done that to watch her splatter?

As Daegan's dragon pulled Evalle's gryphon up, her eagle head was staring at Germanus and shaking from side to side. Was she telling Germanus no?

Storm's jaguar turned to the gargoyles.

One was gone, flying for the castle with Germanus on his back.

Now Storm understood that Evalle was trying to tell Germanus no. That bastard had hurt her enough. He was not making Evalle responsible for the death of that boy. Evalle would champion and protect even a stranger she considered an innocent.

Storm turned his jaguar loose, racing for the castle.

The gargoyle left behind lunged at him.

Storm's jaguar leaped to the right, ruining the gargoyle's timing. The winged beast landed hard on its face. Storm gave his jaguar free reign to jump on the gargoyle and tear through its neck with his claws and fangs.

As soon as the head flopped to the side, his jaguar roared a deafening sound then looked around to find Evalle. She flew high above him with the dragon.

Storm couldn't help her by standing here. He ripped away, racing hell-bent to reach that boy before Germanus did.

Daegan had better be good for his word on keeping Evalle safe.

CHAPTER 31

E VALLE'S GRYPHON HAD SOME BROKEN bones in one wing and no way to heal it fast. Her bad leg had taken days to strengthen and had a bend in it.

She hoped her wings would hold up and she could still fly.

Once Daegan had lifted her gryphon a mile in the air, he released her. His voice came into her mind. *Sorry, Evalle. I intended to make the battle appear genuine, but not to the point of harming you.*

My fault, Daegan. Germanus pulled my attention away. I don't care. Germanus left. He didn't believe the battle.

The dragon swept around to face the castle.

So did Evalle's gryphon.

That's when she saw Storm's jaguar far ahead of them, streaking toward the castle. *No! Daegan, please stop Storm. Germanus threatened to kill him, too, if I failed.*

This was worse than any nightmare she'd had here.

She abandoned the battle still raging between the Treoir gryphons and the realm army. White flashes of energy shot out from Adrianna's hand and Quinn was probably using mind lock.

Flying hard, she looked to her right.

Daegan's dragon stayed with her when he could easily outpace her. He was doing that to protect her, but she wanted him to go ahead and help Storm.

Before she could send him on, a flash of silver yanked her attention up. *Daegan, look out above!*

The realm dragon that had flown high into the clouds was executing the same attack that Evalle had attempted in her effort to show she really was fighting Daegan.

Daegan's red dragon banked hard just before the silver dragon collided with him.

But when the silver one pulled up, he arced to the left, slamming into Evalle's gryphon.

She had the presence of mind this time to dig her claws into the dragon's chest upon impact. If she was going down, so was he.

His claws raked the insides of her wings. *Ow. Ow. Ow.*

Why had he not blowtorched her yet?

Why couldn't she thank her lucky stars for one thing in her favor and not look for more trouble?

They tangled with flapping wings and slashing claws. Where was Daegan? He could kill this dragon right now with the silver one so vulnerable.

Daegan's claws closed around the silver dragon's neck, then he flapped backwards hard, yanking the realm dragon off Evalle. She fluttered to the ground, landing hard and rolling.

Her poor wing hung loose.

Clenching her beak tight, she forced the wing back in place and called up her healing. A tiny push of energy went to the wing.

Boom. The ground shook beneath her.

She hobbled around. Daegan and the silver dragon had landed hard and were battling. Why was Daegan not killing that dragon?

Please tell her that Storm saved Kellman and himself as well. She couldn't leave Daegan when he was at the mercy of anything Germanus threw at him.

She started hobbling toward the battling dragons.

That would be an incredible view if not for Daegan's life at risk. She called out telepathically. *Pin the dragon down, Daegan, and I'll rip out his throat.*

No. Do not touch him.

Evalle's gryphon stopped. What?

The red dragon flapped up, lifting the silver one off the ground, then he dropped the realm dragon hard enough to knock him senseless.

When the silver dragon stopped moving, she said, *You did it, Daegan. You killed him.*

His red dragon banked around to face her. *No, I didn't. I want to take him back with us.*

You can't take anything out of here.

I will take you both.

She was not arguing with a dragon that had lost its mind. *I'm going after Storm.*

Without waiting on an answer, because the dragon king could reach her telepathically, she pushed off, groaning in pain. When she reached the castle, she found large patches of blood.

No! That gargoyle had better not have hurt Storm.

She shifted back to her human form. She wasn't as powerful in this form, but she could get around inside far better as a woman than as a huge gryphon.

Inside she listened for ... Kellman screaming, the sound of a jaguar fighting ... anything to give her a tip.

The silence frightened her more than the noises she'd anticipated.

Her heart thumped like mad. Which way should she go?

Up or down?

What about the arena? Would Germanus be there with Kellman? The arena was behind the castle, but accessed through a lower level.

Padding around on her bare feet and wearing the sack that automatically clothed her every time she was in human form, she peeked at the mangled body suspended above her head.

No second body yet.

Germanus would have hung the second one by now. He was just that sick. She had a chance to save Kellman, but she also had to find Storm.

Her gut said to go downstairs. If Germanus was not there, then she'd check the arena next. Tiptoeing quietly down every step, she listened for any hint of a gargoyle attack.

She'd never seen the gargoyles down here, so maybe they couldn't navigate these steps?

She paused to look into the treasure room where the hoard glowed innocently. What could be worth more than life?

Nothing.

She started to bypass it and head to the arena when she heard a weak, "Evalle, help."

Kellman?

Catching herself, she stepped into the room and moved deeper past the pile of treasure until she saw Germanus in his special alcove with one hand around Kellman's throat, holding him above the ground.

Kellman had his back to her.

"Let him go, Germanus. I did as you wanted. I fought the dragon."

"No, you didn't." A gold and silver sword stood next to his throne. His *stolen* throne. He was no leader.

"Yes," she argued. "Daegan is dead. Go outside to see for yourself." That would give her a chance to grab Kellman. She didn't know what she'd do then, but she would fight everything Germanus threw at her to save that boy.

"Take another sword from the pile and bring me the dragon's head."

Well, shit. "I am too busted up to drag a head that big in here. I need time to heal." So true. Her battered arm fell loose on one side. She could feel blood seeping through the sack dress and down her legs. "Let's go to the roof so you can see for yourself."

"I am not leaving here."

Why? Was he worried someone would steal his booty?

A loud and vicious roar echoed through the building.

The sound of Storm's jaguar was music to her ears, but she didn't want him in here.

Now that she thought about it, Germanus had brought no gargoyles in here either time she'd been in this space with him.

Did that mean Germanus was more powerful in here?

She felt Storm's energy enter the room behind her. Her heart squeezed with the need to turn around and hug her black jaguar, but that would only put him at further risk. Without moving, she pleaded, "Please leave Storm. He wants to kill you and Kellman."

Did her mate leave?

No. Storm shifted back to human. She'd been around him enough to recognize the power shift when he changed forms.

He walked over to her, but didn't touch her. She didn't blame him.

She looked like an abomination even in human form, and she had to be filthy since Germanus had given her no way to bathe. She didn't look at Storm for fear of seeing how awful she appeared reflected in his eyes, but she would never forget him hugging her gryphon and saying he loved her.

Storm told her, "Not going anywhere without you."

She opened her mouth to make him understand that she couldn't leave here.

Germanus yelled, "This one dies!"

"No!" Evalle lunged, but Storm held her back.

Germanus had a crazy look in his eyes. He grabbed the sword and shoved it through Kellman, then dropped him.

Evalle screamed and fought against Storm's hold.

Kellman made a painful noise and doubled over, falling to the side.

Storm was saying, "Stop!"

She fought to get to Germanus. "No! He killed Kellman."

"No, he didn't." Storm was holding her carefully, but he was not turning her loose. "Stop, Evalle, or I'm going to hurt you by accident."

She begged, "Let me kill him. Please, let me kill him."

Germanus smiled, "Your mate knows I'm safe here."

Energy burst into the room. Daegan stood there a second later looking like a deadly warlord from a time long past. "You son of a bitch."

That deflated the arrogance that had been growing in the face of that monster.

Evalle didn't care who showed up. She kept pleading, "Let me go, Storm!"

Daegan said, "You can't harm Germanus in here, Evalle. This is a sanctuary room for him. To attack him would hurt you."

She folded at the knees, which took her to the floor. Living with those two deaths on her conscience was more than she could do.

Storm kept his hands on her.

She cried for the twins she'd loved so long. Her voice broke. "I have to kill him. Please," came out in a whisper.

Daegan said, "That is my father's throne and his treasure, Germanus."

The bastard lifted his chin. "It's all mine now, dragon. Just wait until I call *my* dragon in to thrash you."

"Your dragon tried. He failed."

"Not possible. You can't kill my dragon in this realm. He's more powerful than you."

Daegan said, "He recognized my power. He's the second son of the ice dragon house. You put him in here for two thousand years!"

"Not me. Abandinu."

Daegan accused, "That god would not have brought a dragon from my time when we were all born of powerful dragon houses. Not without *everyone* believing that dragon was dead. Abandinu would not do such a thing knowing it would start a war with all the dragon houses for that insult."

Guilt spread across Germanus from his eyes to his shaking hands. But that didn't stop him from spewing more garbage. "You don't know what happened. You were in Queen Maeve's tender care when the war started."

"Why is that dragon here?" Daegan demanded.

Evalle heaved hard breaths in and out, watching as Germanus began to squirm. Now, right now, she could rip him apart.

Storm knelt behind her with his arms loosely wrapped around her. Any touch hurt, but she would not give up this moment with him.

Germanus warned, "Do not anger Abandinu. I know your mother was a goddess, but this is not her realm, which means she would be vulnerable here."

"No, it is not her realm, but only a fool would assume anything about a powerful being of which they know nothing. *You* are a fool. Abandinu is not. What would make you do something so stupid, Germanus?"

"Do not call me stupid." Germanus stood up shouting, "I am the one holding all the power right now. You will eventually die. When you do, I am free of this place. I still do not believe you killed my dragon. When he kills you, I will escape and be given immortality by Macha. You cannot defeat her in her realm."

Storm said, "You miserable piece of flesh. Dakkar, or La Cuchilla, whatever you call him, is dead. Daegan sent Macha home with her tail between her legs. How do you think we found you?"

That struck home like nothing else said to this point.

Germanus shook his head. "No, La Cuchilla sent you here to die. We have a blood pact."

Evalle finally put it together and turned to Storm. "Dakkar? The bounty hunter? He's the one who did this?"

Storm tightened his arms around her. "Yes. He was using you as bait. He knew we would come for you and he believed that bitch, Macha, would grant him immortality if Germanus killed

Daegan."

Evalle laughed even though it hurt with her mouth screwed up. "Warranty on blood pacts must be void if one of you dies."

She looked around and up at Daegan with tears in her eyes. "I have to kill him."

Nodding calmly, Daegan said, "I had thought to deal with him myself, but I would not take that from you."

When she looked back at Germanus, the crazy guy stared at them as if she and Daegan had spoken a strange language.

The dragon king moved his arms out and around.

They all teleported onto the windy roof.

Germanus twisted one way then the next. "You can't do this. I hold all the power." His voice trembled this time when he said those words. He caught himself and slowly turned to look out over the battlefield.

Seven Treoir gryphons and one silver dragon stood together.

Daegan said, "My magic is older than this realm. You *assumed* you held all the power here."

Evalle smiled in spite of her busted lip opening up and bleeding. Then she said to Storm, "Let me go. I have to avenge the twins' deaths."

"You think that was one of the twins?" Storm asked.

She turned slowly to him. "Yes. It was."

"No. I swear to you they're both safe in Atlanta."

She shook her head, unable to accept his words over what her eyes had shown her. "Germanus sent someone ... Dakkar probably ... to kidnap them. I watched both of them die."

"The twins are not dead, Evalle. I had a ward set that would alert me to any breach. I saw Dakkar die with my own eyes and no breach had happened by that point. I don't know who the bodies belonged to, but Dakkar probably brought two homeless kids and Germanus used the realm majik to convince you they were your twins." Storm swallowed, then his face turned murderous. "I am so sorry he did that, but I'm going to make him pay."

She lifted her fists in the air, shrieking with rage over the torment Germanus had put her through.

Shaking her head at Storm, she declared, "No. *I* will make him pay!" She pushed away. Calling up the change felt like having her body rammed into this stone structure over and over. Adrenaline surged through her gryphon as it screeched with fury, then turned to Germanus.

He backed away with his hands out in front of him, ready to wield his power.

He had killed two boys the age of the twins.

He had tortured her from the inside out.

She turned her gryphon loose on the man who had sent one flying creature after another to its death, leaving their blood on Evalle's hands.

Time lost all meaning as she attacked and Germanus threw his energy at her. She batted strike after strike aside, glad that Storm was not jumping in to take this from her. He deserved to rip Germanus apart, but she needed this and her mate would understand. When she finally broke through the last strike, she opened her beak above his head, ripped it off, then tossed away the miserable face she never wanted to see again.

Lifting her head, she called to her pack and heard their screeching cries in return.

Evalle?

It took her a minute to realize Daegan was trying to reach her telepathically. *What?*

Shift back.

Hurts.

I know, but you're strong. You can do it.

She wanted to argue. She'd shifted and fought to the point that she could barely stand now that the adrenaline was wearing off. But her dragon king had given an order.

The change took time and energy. When it was done, she sat on the ground, but surrounded by soft cloth this time. Running her hands over the material, she realized she now wore a deep blue robe.

Storm reached down with open hands. "Can you stand?"

She took his hands and struggled to her feet.

That's when she realized Tristan and the other gryphons had arrived and shifted to their human forms, all clothed. Daegan often handled that part just to save time. They stood in a circle around them. Even the realm dragon was here, but not changed.

Could that one shift to human, or not?

Quinn hovered nearby with fear riding his gaze.

Adrianna's normally no-expression face filled with horror as she took in Evalle.

Tristan stepped up. His voice sounded sad when he asked, "You ready to leave, badass?"

Storm had a gentle, but firm hold on her elbow as if he was afraid to touch any other part. She shook off the mental fog from changing. Her heart filled with love for this bunch.

It was time to send them home.

Her mother's voice came into her head. *Trust your friends who came for you.*

Evalle told her mother, *I do, but even Storm can't fix this. I can't talk to you right now. I need this moment with Storm.*

Seeing them for the last time hurt. She would not cry and make this harder for Storm. Swallowing the lump in her throat, she said, "I can't leave here."

Daegan said, "Garwyli told us that anyone put in here by Abandinu must be removed by the god. Did Abandinu put you in here, or Dakkar?"

"I have not met the god. From what you've said, Dakkar kidnapped me?"

"Yes," Storm said, now stroking his fingers lightly over her head. "That bounty hunting bastard. So the god didn't put you in here. Finally one thing in our favor." He let out a breath of relief.

She said, "That's not why I can't leave."

Quinn came over to her. "Why not?"

She placed a hand on her chest. "I know you all saw the hideous wound where my emerald was torn out."

Storm's chest rumbled with a low growling. He paused to say, "I'll heal you."

Turning to him, she gave her crooked smile that would probably never return to normal. "Not this wound, sweetheart. I was dying by the time he got me here so they shoved Noirre majik into the wound. Dakkar placed a spell as he used the Noirre. That saved me probably because of my Medb blood. Germanus showed me what happened to a wyvern Dakkar tried to take out of this realm after feeding it Noirre and placing a spell on the creature. The transition of exiting the realm boundaries attacked the Noirre."

Adrianna said, "Let me pull it out of you."

"I would, but it's wrapped inside my heart and running through my blood stream. That's why I haven't been able to heal here. I'm guessing that Dakkar spelled the Noirre to attack my Belador blood so that I would not regain all my power. He wanted to ensure that I stayed here for eternity."

Storm said, "If that's the case, I'm staying with you."

"Go home, Storm." She hurt saying that, but he would not survive. "Abandinu only likes winged creatures. He'll probably kill you."

Her mate was adamant. "We leave together or stay together."

She put a hand covered in wounds and scars on his face. "You would make me watch you die?"

The look on his face crushed her and his words came out thick with emotion. "I am not alive without you."

Rumbling started in the distance.

She swung her head to determine if a thunderstorm had started. There were no mountains or multi-colored desert landscape now, just gray ground.

The sky had jagged lines spreading across it like an egg cracking.

Tristan yelled over the noise. "What's happening, Daegan?"

"I don't know."

The farthest point she could see inside the realm seemed to be folding in. This had to be what the inside of a toothpaste tube looked like when it was being squeezed.

Air blasted past them.

Bodies of the dead creatures burst into gray clouds of dust.

A voice louder than all of them speaking at one time shouted, *"You destroyed my sanctuary!"*

Adrianna asked, "That wouldn't happen to be Abandinu, would it?"

"That's exactly who it is," Daegan confirmed. Then he powered up his voice almost as loud as the angry god's. "We did not come here to harm your sanctuary, but to rescue one of mine stolen by Germanus."

"You entered without permission. You must pay a price. I want the gryphons!"

More of the landscape slowly imploded, pushing strong winds at them. Evalle's hair batted around her face.

Storm pulled her into his embrace, still careful as he held her close.

Daegan yelled back, "No. The gryphons are my people. I have no argument with you. Allow us to leave and I will not call in another god or goddess."

The world around them kept collapsing.

The castle trembled.

Tristan said, "I'm guessing we have less than a minute."

"Abandinu!" Daegan shouted. "Let my people leave or this will be a war with more than one pantheon. This was not your fault. Do not make it your problem."

Evalle looked at Daegan's face to see if he was bluffing.

She had no idea.

Note to self. Never play cards with Daegan. That wouldn't be an issue since they would all have to leave and she would stay, but at this point she wondered what her eternal home was going to look like.

Abandinu's voice finally boomed down from the heavens, *"You may leave. I no longer wish to power this realm."*

Evalle said, "He can't destroy this place."

"Yes, he can," Daegan said. "Time for all of us to go."

"What about Evalle?" Storm shouted, because Abandinu went into full demolition mode.

"We got seconds," Tristan shouted.

Daegan ordered, "We're teleporting."

Evalle argued, "No, let me stay. Don't make Storm watch the Noirre boil inside of me. I look awful, but that ... " She twisted to Storm and begged, "I can't let that be your last vision of me."

Tristan grabbed one of her hands.

She flinched.

Storm snarled, "Get your hand off her."

Daegan had everyone pulling in close around them.

Still holding her hand, Tristan shouted at Storm, "She dies if she stays. She dies if she leaves."

In the second it took Storm to process that, Tristan dropped his head to Evalle's ear. "Do you trust me?"

"Yes, but ... "

An explosion rocked the realm that sounded as if an atom bomb had just gone off.

The world shifted and blurred. *No, Daegan, don't teleport me,* she called to him.

Evalle screamed. Her chest felt pulled in ten directions.
Fire burned her from the inside out.

She heard a mash of voices yelling and felt hands grabbing at
her ... then she lost touch with all of them.

Then, it was blessedly silent.

CHAPTER 32

E VALLE CLAWED AT THE AIR.
Agony flooded her body for what seemed an eternity. She didn't understand why dying took so long. She gave up fighting and ... the pain eased until she could breathe.

In fact, it disappeared completely.

That could only mean one thing. She was truly dead.

Where was Storm?

She wanted one last kiss, just a chance to say goodbye. Just ... more time with him, but she floated in a sea of murky darkness. Black would be a color next to this. She had no sense of having a body.

Time stretched into no time. No place. Nothing.

Where was her mother's spirit now? Wouldn't she at least be around to welcome Evalle into the afterlife?

Go back, Evalle, her mother said from far away. *Do not follow me.* Her mother's voice faded to nothing at the end.

I don't think I get a choice, Evalle answered and floated some more.

The next voice in her mind was male and whispered, *Evalle?*

Her eyelids fluttered enough for her to see a tiny light flickering far away.

Could that be Storm trying to reach her? Was his spirit guide bringing Evalle into that private realm so she could see her mate one more time?

Her fingers touched nothing. Did she even have hands? Maybe she was too far gone into the next world for him to connect with her. See? She'd been right to be glad she hadn't completed the bonding with Storm or ... he might have died, too. He'd said they would be linked forever.

Her thoughts faded ...

Evalle, listen to me, dammit!
The words dragged her back from where she'd drifted off.
But ... that was not Storm's voice. In fact, it sounded like Tristan.
Why would he be able to talk to her and not Storm?
Dammit, Evalle, where are you?
I'm right here, she replied in her mind. *How can you talk to me when Storm can't? Wait, did you die, too? Oh, Tristan, I'm sorry.*
He made an odd sound. Was he laughing? The bastard. *What's funny about dying, asshole?*
Tristan said, *Nothing. It hurts like the devil, but you have to come back to us.*
I can't.
Don't quit now, Tristan ordered her. *Remember how Tzader only survived because of you dying with him in Treoir Castle? He trusted you when you forced a link open between the two of you, then you brought him back to life with you the third time you died?*
Tristan paused and said in a quiet voice, *I'm not Tzader, but you can trust me. I grabbed your hand as we blasted out of the realm and I'm not letting go.*
Now she could feel his fingers squeezing hers.
Her heart made a faint thump. Then it thumped again.
Was this happening? She said, *Tristan, I trust you. I have for a long time. I feel your energy.* Hope jumped all over the place in her heart, but the organ wasn't really doing its part yet.
His fingers squeezed hers again. He said, *Get ready, because you're only feeling the leading edge of my regeneration, and the rest is gonna seriously suck.*
More energy seeped into her.
She opened her mouth to draw in a breath, but a wave of power poured into her body, stealing that breath. Power surged so fast and hard it felt as if she'd been stabbed with a handful of lightning bolts. She arched and yelled in her head, because she had no breath or voice, no way to stop the searing pain coursing through her.
She lost touch with parts of her body.
Worse than that, she couldn't feel Tristan's hand any more.
But ... she could hear him yelling, *"It's not working! I lost the connection!"*

She wanted to tell him not to feel bad, that he'd tried, but she couldn't talk. Her body spun wildly like being sucked into the vortex of a physical tornado.

In her mind, she called out, *Storm! I love you.*

Strong hands yanked her into a hard embrace. Then she heard it, the one sound she longed for ... Storm's voice.

He was chanting a swift rush of words in his native language. When he paused, he whispered gut-wrenching words of love and need that flowed through her mind, blending with the chaotic power surge.

More chanting, plus now she could hear Adrianna's voice. And maybe Garwyli's, too.

The spiraling energy her body had turned into began to slow down.

Storm begged in a hoarse voice, "Please come back, sweetheart. I can't lose you."

The furious energy finally dissipated and her body calmed. Every muscle felt limp as cooked noodles. She inhaled and ... smelled her mate.

Her eyes fluttered open, but speaking was difficult. She squeezed out, "Storm?"

He stilled and asked in an incredulous voice, "Evalle?"

Talking was beyond her so she smiled.

Loud cheering erupted. Storm clamped her body to his trembling one. "Thank you for not leaving me."

Licking her lips, she croaked, "Never."

Content that he was nearby, she let go and drifted asleep.

Time moved in slow waves that occasionally woke her. She couldn't force her eyes to open or her mind to reach for full consciousness, but she recalled the sensation of being held as she teleported again. Then she fell deep asleep.

When she finally roused, she moved to stretch. Huh. Her arms worked.

Warm fingers brushed over her face.

She might not be a Skinwalker, but she knew the scent of her man.

Wait. Her brain fog continued to clear.

She was alive?

Evalle opened her eyes and squinted against the blurry image.

Please, no more nightmares of losing Storm.

When the world came into focus, she saw the face of the man she would cross a river of fire for if that was the cost of just one more minute with him.

His beautiful teak-brown body was stretched out beside her, with his head propped up by his bent arm. Straight black hair fell loose over powerful shoulders. Those brown eyes kept sweeping across her face as if he didn't believe she was there.

His smile didn't quite reach his gaze, telling her how difficult this had been for him. "Hi, sweetheart."

She opened her mouth, but no words came out.

Moving around, Storm came back with a glass of water he held to her lips while lifting her up to drink. When he put the glass away, he came back to kiss her. Not one of his let's-get-naked kisses, but a sweet, I-need-you-more-than-life kiss.

She smiled against his lips. "I missed you, too."

He doubled down on the next kiss, growling with pleasure.

When he lifted up, he said, "I missed you more." Drawing in a long breath, he said, "There was no way I would have left you there, but much as it pains me to admit this, you wouldn't be alive right now without Tristan."

So she hadn't hallucinated all of that. "Is he okay?"

"Yes."

"He linked with me, didn't he?"

"That's what Tzader said happened."

She considered that and asked, "Why would Tzader explain? Why didn't Tristan tell you?"

"Tristan thought he'd lost you while he regenerated, that he'd done something wrong. As soon as it was clear that you did survive, he just teleported away. Daegan went after him, then came back and said Tristan needed some time."

"We have to thank him," she said, hoping this mended the rift that had driven friction between Tristan and Storm for a long time.

"No, I'm the one who has to thank him, which I will figure out how to do as soon as he surfaces again. I owe him anything he asks for at this point."

Her smile turned into a grin.

Storm finally smiled for real. "What?"

"Tristan will probably never let you pay that debt. He'll love having it to hold over you forever."

Rolling his beautiful brown eyes, Storm muttered, "Probably true. I'll still thank the jerk."

Her gaze tripped past Storm to take in the room. She appreciated the soft lighting. Their building in Atlanta was incredible, but it did not have thirty-foot ceilings with gold-framed paintings that looked as if someone had paid the equivalent of buying a house for each one. Nor were their walls at home shiny marble. Leaning a little, she took in the massive bed that appeared to be three feet off the polished stone floor.

Pulling her gaze back to him, she asked, "Where are we?"

"In a private suite in Treoir Castle."

Her eyes widened. "No kidding?"

"It's the truth. Daegan teleported us to the grounds outside the castle where we all tackled saving you. Once it was clear you were going to make it, he ordered you brought inside and kept here where he said your energy would rebuild faster. The minute we showed up and Brina found out what had happened to you, she started spouting orders. She had everyone in this place jumping, including Daegan."

"No."

"Yes." Storm pecked a kiss on her forehead and kept toying with her hair. "She used her powers to clean and clothe you, then she ordered Garwyli to continue healing you ... "

Evalle reached up to touch her face. Her fingers ran over a scar that ran across her neck. She cringed at realizing how she must look.

Storm clasped her hand and his voice turned serious. "Don't."

"I'm hideous."

His eyes darkened above a fierce frown. "You are gorgeous. That old druid healed about eighty percent of the wounds and scars. He's letting you rest and waiting to see if your beast can heal the rest, but I want you to hear me. I. Love. You. I don't give a damn if you still had all the scars you had in Abandinu's realm." Storm watched her as what he said sank in. Then he growled and added, "You're not going to be happy until the scars are gone, are you?"

"No. I'm not particularly vain, but I don't want to look at a reminder of that place for the rest of my life if I have a choice."

He nodded with understanding.

That was her man. He understood.

She did an internal check to see if she could even feel her beast. Her insides had never been this quiet. No energy swirled. "Storm ... I can't feel my gryphon."

Squeezing her hand, he said, "Your body has been through so much trauma in the past days, then you died and came back to life. Give yourself a chance to heal. Don't try to do too much yet. Can you do that for me?"

"Sure." She would not admit the idea of losing touch with her gryphon upset her far more than the scars. But Storm had been through a lot in recent days as well.

His heart needed a break from so much stress and misery.

Hers did, too.

She would be thankful for being alive and with Storm. If she couldn't heal her scars, so be it. She would learn to live with the way she looked and put that realm behind her.

If she never shifted into a gryphon again ... she'd figure that out as well.

Right now, it hurt too much to consider.

CHAPTER 33

Treoir Island realm hidden above the Irish Sea

"DO NOT OVERDO IT, EVALLE!" Brina ordered.

Evalle sighed and said, "I'm fine. I'm getting more power back every day. It's been three days. Now, are you getting married or dragging this out for another month?"

Brina smiled at her. "That's the first time you've snapped at me. Such a fine gift on my weddin' day."

All of her friends were certifiable.

They had to be to enter the realm of a god who could have wrapped up that place around them like celestial trash and poofed it out of existence.

Two arms came around her waist.

She smiled. After the past days of heavy-duty healing by Garwyli, the scar on her lip was fading and it didn't pull the skin when she smiled.

Teasing him, she said, "Better not be grabbing me. Storm might see you."

Her Skinwalker nuzzled her neck and said, "If anyone except me dared to stand this close to you he would already be on his ass. I love you, sweetheart."

She closed her eyes and let those words sink in. She never expected to be here or anywhere with Storm again. Lifting one of his hands so she could kiss the palm, she murmured, "I love you more."

As happy as she was to be right here right now with him, her heart still ached. She'd been working up the nerve to tell Storm something important, but she could not bear to see his reaction.

Not yet. They had time.

"Evalle!"

At the sound of Lanna's voice, Evalle twisted to the side and identified the voice. She yelled, "Lanna!"

Storm let her go to embrace the young woman. Evalle said, "How are you?"

"I am good." Lanna stood back and gave Evalle a weighty observation. "You will be, too. You are strong and Storm's love is all you need to heal."

Evalle started to argue that she was almost there, but this young woman would have heard the lie in her voice. Lanna knew Evalle's outside would be fine. She was talking about her internal scars.

"I know," was all Evalle could say, then changed the subject. Her throat tightened when she asked, "How are the twins?"

"They are happy, but miss you. They are with Kit for a visit."

How many times would Evalle relive their deaths? Storm had told her how Kit had stormed the building. Pun intended. "That's great."

"*Evalle, Evalle, Evalle*," chortled behind Lanna, who was all smiles when she stepped out of the way.

"Feenix?" Damn it. She did not want to cry.

Evalle's baby gargoyle flew into her arms. She clutched him to her and buried her face into his little neck.

Tears stung her eyes, but if she cried everyone would freak out, even at happy tears. "I missed you, baby. Love you."

He patted her face and smiled a toothy grin. "Love you. Mine." Barely touching her, he tapped her cheek with the side of his claw. "Ow."

"It's okay. I'm tough and I'm healing."

She spent the next few minutes in a blaze of happiness.

Then Feenix asked, "Thorm?"

What a way to touch her heart by asking about her mate. Now that she thought about it, Storm had probably orchestrated bringing Lanna and Feenix here.

She turned her gargoyle to see Storm a short ways behind her. "He's here, too. He brought me home."

Feenix made a move like he was going to fly, so she opened her arms. Her little gargoyle fluttered up and then down to the ground. When he tucked his wings, he waddled over to Storm, who watched him.

They stared at each other for a long moment.

Feenix took another step and wrapped a chubby arm around Storm's leg as he said, "Mine."

She thought her heart was going to explode.

Storm's brown eyes filled with the look of a man who had everything he wanted.

Almost everything.

He wanted her bonded to him.

———

Daegan kept watching for Tristan and the gryphon pack. His second in command had sent word he'd be at the pack village unless Daegan needed him.

Saving Evalle had taken a load of power from Tristan, but almost losing her had been the most difficult part. It might be the first time Tristan had ever held the power over someone's life in his hands, which was humbling for anyone.

Garwyli had been wandering around the grounds, taking in all the decorations and plans for the wedding. Over a hundred chairs were set up in a half circle for wedding attendees.

The old druid paused next to Daegan and stared out over the vast Treoir realm, which was fifty times larger than the one Germanus had been in.

"I have been thinkin' on your problem, dragon."

Daegan was coming to realize the old guy liked to poke at him because he was comfortable with having a dragon king. "Which problem, druid? I have a list as long as the day."

Scowling at him, Garwyli said, "Your family history."

Daegan might have found the answer to that with the silver dragon if he could convince that one to shift, but he wanted to hear the druid out. "What have you to tell me?"

"Every dragon family had dragon squires. Is that not true?"

"True."

"That would be the place to start then," Garwyli declared, as if Daegan could visit one today.

Frowning at the druid, Daegan said, "If I am unable to find my missing, and possibly dead, sisters, then how am I going to find today's descendants of dragon squires?"

The druid snarled, "I will not spend my time helpin' you if you intend to allow every little thing to slow you down."

What did you say to a cantankerous old druid? "I will take that advice to heart."

"'Tis time for the ceremony soon. Where be your gryphons?"

"They will arrive in time." Daegan knew that Brina had sent an invitation to each gryphon and both Rías living on Treoir Island, making it clear they were all important to her and Tzader.

She'd also invited the entire guard regiment and castle staff plus particular Beladors she and Tzader had befriended over the years.

Quinn had asked that Phoedra and Reese join them, which Brina snapped at him was expected. Quinn just smiled and muttered something about the moods of expectant women.

In the distance, what appeared to be a flock of birds took shape as they neared, then a mix of gryphon colors became evident. Some had golden heads, but Daegan would treat them all the same with the exception of Tristan.

His second-in-command had no golden head, but he had stepped in to be the gryphon pack leader when Evalle had relinquished the role.

Daegan squinted his eyes.

The entire pack dropped out of sight behind trees in the first line of forest at the end of the field, which was now littered with preparations for a Treoir wedding.

He smiled, recalling when he'd used the term "littered." He'd heard that while in Atlanta and liked the way the word sounded.

Brina had not. She set him straight that her extensive decorating was not litter.

Twilight settled over the landscape only because Brina had requested that lighting for her wedding.

As a doting uncle, he would give her all that she asked for, and thankfully, she was a sweet queen without a selfish bone in her body. This child would be the first he'd see born in many, many years.

While it was sad to have lost so much family, he counted himself a fortunate dragon shifter to have Brina, Tzader and their child, plus a mixed bag of beings he was proud to stand beside.

From the tree line, nine people emerged—seven Alterants and the two Rías who must have ridden on the gryphons and carried clothing for the pack—heading quickly toward him.

As expected, Tristan was in the lead.

A blur streaked past Daegan on his left when the gryphons were forty feet out. That blur had been Evalle using her Belador speed, a good sign she continued to regain her powers.

Right behind her came Storm, who stopped next to Daegan.

Evalle slowed to a walk and dropped down on a knee.

Storm asked, "What the hell?"

"Your mate is telling Tristan he has earned his place as leader of the gryphons and she is willing to follow him." Daegan cut his eyes at the consternation on Storm's face. "That's a very good thing, Storm. She does not want to be here when her place is with you and Feenix."

"You're right." Storm stood with his arms crossed and respect in his voice. "I owe Tristan more than I can ever repay to have her here. He came up with a way to save her when I had none."

"Tristan is a little overwhelmed by what happened. I think he feared he had taken on responsibility for her wellbeing then couldn't pull her all the way through."

"I can appreciate that. I thought I'd lost her myself. That's why having all of us work together is stronger than one alone," the Skinwalker admitted while he waited on his mate to return.

Daegan understood how it felt to learn a tough lesson. Storm had struggled not to go after Evalle on his own, but he'd done the right thing.

When Daegan faced Abandinu in the realm, he'd had his own concerns about saving his people. His last offer would have been to hand himself to Abandinu if that was what it took to send them home.

He was glad to have everyone safe.

Evalle should not leave until she felt strong enough. Storm had been forced to make a quick trip back to the human world while she rested. Trey had reached Tzader by telepathy to inform them Storm's building had a contingent of guards and firepower surrounding it and that was drawing human attention he didn't think Storm wanted. Trey offered to handle it if Storm gave him instructions. When Garwyli assured Storm that Evalle would sleep possibly for an entire day, Daegan teleported Storm to his building.

Storm dealt with the Nyght group and requested to be teleported back in less than ten minutes.

Daegan asked Storm, "Did all go well when you returned to open the ward for that Isak fellow's mother?"

"Nothing is ever simple with Isak, but he did help us when we needed intel. I opened the ward for Kit to leave, but she refused when the twins chose not to teleport back with me. They're street kids and barely comfortable around me, much less coming to a place like this. Kit would not leave without them. Isak loaded everyone up to take home." Storm smiled at something.

"What?" Daegan asked.

"They were almost packed up and out, when Kit stopped to remind me about asking Tristan to train her Rías friend, Jasper."

"I thought Isak did not care for nonhumans around his mother?"

"He about popped a blood vessel when she admitted she'd been training Jasper in the woods alone."

Daegan grinned. "I could use a warrior like her."

"Not unless you intend to let her run everything. She's like a miniature general. If she had our power ... hard to image how scary she would be." Storm kept smiling.

"When you see her next, tell her the Rías will be welcome to train with our other two."

"I'll let Evalle tell her when I take her home," Storm said. "I almost had to ask you to teleport Kit here when she found out Evalle was alive, but she decided to take the twins home and wait until Evalle was ... back to normal."

Hearing the worry in Storm's last words, Daegan said, "Evalle will shift when her gryphon has healed."

"I know. I keep telling her that." Storm asked, "Speaking of shifters healing, how's that silver dragon?"

"I have had to place him in a space beneath the castle," Daegan said, not pleased about that. "I have never known a dragon that did not shift into a human form, but he may have been in that realm so long his body has forgotten how. I consider it a good sign that he was aware enough to realize I was the more powerful and bow down in deference. That told me he could be saved. Garwyli and I will work with him."

"I still don't understand how you saved that dragon by feeding him your blood after we teleported out, but you didn't step in when Evalle was in distress." Storm looked over. "Don't get me wrong. I'm not criticizing. I just want to understand. So many things in our world can mean the difference in life and death. The more we know, the better prepared we are."

"I'm not insulted. Your question is valid. I would have killed Evalle with dragon blood. I wasn't sure I wouldn't do that to the silver dragon to be honest, but he took his last breath and his heart stopped beating as we arrived. I had nothing to lose by pouring dragon blood down his throat."

"How do you think he ended up in the realm?"

"Abandinu enjoyed dragon battles. I think Germanus might have been at fault for bringing the dragon into the realm and Abandinu decided if no one searched for the dragon there was no problem."

Tristan walked up, cheeks red with embarrassment. "I'm back."

Before Daegan could speak, Storm extended his hand. "Thank you for saving Evalle. If you ever need anything, all you have to do is ask."

Having followed Tristan, Evalle stood to the side, watching them with a big grin.

Tristan's eyebrows lifted. He took Storm's hand and shook. "No big deal."

Evalle muttered, "Jerk thing to say," but she was laughing so Tristan smirked.

"'Tis time for a weddin'," Garwyli called out.

Daegan waited until everyone except Tristan had walked past him, heading to the chairs set up around a dais covered in flowers and butterflies.

With his gaze on the activity, Tristan said, "Sorry I bailed on you."

"Had I required your presence, I would have called," Daegan told him. "We have problems in the human realm. It will take both of us to handle them."

A muscle in Tristan's jaw clenched. "I'm ready. I just don't want to hold someone's life in my hands again."

"That is a request I have to deny."

Tristan's gaze cut to Daegan, but he said nothing.

Daegan explained, "We have thousands of Beladors across the world under the command of Maistirs, but ultimately their direction and safety falls to our shoulders. You have proven you are strong and capable. I have ultimate faith in every decision you make, but you must always remember that even as we fight hard for our own, we will lose some. It's a difficult thing to watch the light go out of the eyes of those we care for. When it happens, we must allow time to grieve, then move forward with the knowledge we have done all that we can."

"I understand. I guess I just have to let that sink in."

Daegan turned and slapped Tristan on the back. "For now, we celebrate. Time to join the party."

Garwyli presided over a ceremony Daegan wished his sister, Jennyver, whose blood Brina carried, could witness.

Brina wore his sister's smile and intense green eyes. With a gown of gold trimmed in green that flowed over her rounded middle, Brina might be the most gorgeous Treoir bride ever. Tzader faced her wearing a deep-forest-green suit. Daegan commended her on choosing a husband any uncle would want for his niece.

Garwyli could be annoying at times, but as the old druid spoke clearly and with warmth in his words, his voice reminded Daegan of people and times he'd never see again. He'd always accepted his lot in life, even when he'd landed in Maeve's trap. But with this new freedom, he, too, wanted a life.

To have a lasting bond with a woman, she had to carry dragon blood.

Not likely to find such a woman in this era.

His gaze moved to Evalle, who sat with Storm and her tiny gargoyle between them. Quinn's daughter, Phoedra, had been thrilled to teleport here with Reese, but Reese had not fared so well. Perhaps, like Evalle, she suffered motion illness when she teleported.

Lanna and Phoedra whispered and laughed together. Lanna would watch over her young cousin.

As the ceremony came to an end, a collective sigh went up as Tzader and Brina kissed.

Daegan still couldn't believe anyone would keep those two apart for four years, standing on opposite sides of a ward.

Afterward, the castle staff rushed inside to begin setting out a feast upon the many tables arranged so there would be little delay in eating. In his day, there would have been fresh kill, perhaps a wild boar, but he could appreciate the more civilized offerings as well.

When it came time for gifts, Brina and Tzader smiled over the multitude of thoughtful presents for them and their baby. Some had been handcrafted, which Daegan gave a silent nod of appreciation for—those made by hand carried an extra touch of love.

He walked up last as the final gift had been unwrapped, the guest thanked profusely and the item placed to the side where a young woman kept track of names and gifts. Brina wanted to write a personal note of thanks to each and every one.

Clearing his throat, Daegan said, "Brina and Tzader."

When the happy couple stood, Daegan took two steps away to the side of the dais so that he could see everyone and not have his back to the crowd.

His action drew curious looks.

He said, "I find this as fine a time as any to announce that when I called all of mine to me in Abandinu's realm and teleported, my father's treasure made the trip as well."

That had been a pleasant surprise.

"That's great, Daegan," Tzader said. "Your father would have wanted you to inherit it. Besides, every dragon needs a hoard, right?"

The crowd chuckled at that.

Brina had a hand on her growing middle. "I am glad for you, uncle. 'Tis nice to have somethin' from your past and I'm sure there are items you'll recognize."

"I do, niece. Thank you both, but that is not my treasure to keep."

"Why not?" Tzader sounded ready to fight whoever dared to threaten their dragon king's hoard.

"I had my own hoard at one time, but I have not bothered to hunt for it, because that treasure pales in comparison to the one I now possess."

The couple looked at each other.

Murmurs rumbled in confusion.

Brina asked, "What hoard, uncle?"

Sending his gaze out over the many faces who looked to him to be their leader, he then turned to Brina and Tzader. "You are all my treasure. You've opened your arms to welcome me and have accepted me as your dragon king to watch over you. My father had intended to divide his treasure between his daughters once they were ready to receive it. I was not there when he died, but I knew him well. He would want me to carry out his wishes. For that reason, this treasure belongs to Brina and Tzader." Lifting his voice, he said, "To hold our enemies at bay, I will still be known as the dragon king of Treoir, but to you I am the ruling patriarch to watch over my flock. That is why I now present to you the true king and queen of Treoir."

A cheer went up.

Tzader's mouth fell open. Brina smiled through tears and touched her husband's chin to close his mouth.

Daegan lifted a hand and all fell silent. He whispered the words of his family's language, a blessing on this couple.

More tears sprang from Brina's eyes. She sniffed. "Look what you've done, uncle."

"What?"

"Embarrassin' me in front of our people."

"That's not me, niece. That's the bairn makin' you weepy."

"I am not weepy," she snapped at him.

Garwyli said, "Two."

Daegan had something he wished to say if everyone would pay attention. He sighed. "What two, druid?"

"Bairns. I been meanin' to tell everyone she'll be havin' two heirs."

Brina's face turned white.

Tzader sat her down. "Take it easy, muirnin." Once she was sitting, Tzader growled at the druid, "Next time a little warning, Garwyli?"

Garwyli's bushy white eyebrows lowered in confusion. "Ya want to know when she be carryin' again?" the old druid asked.

Brina shouted, "No! I would like to get through this one."

"Two. Just told ya that."

Everyone laughed.

Daegan was growing old waiting for quiet again. "Back to what I was telling you. The treasure is yours, but there is one thing in particular that I wish to gift you."

Lifting his hands in front of him, Daegan whispered again.

A horizontal disc of gold, the size of a dining table for four, appeared at waist level. Turning slowly in midair, a library of thick tomes standing side by side appeared on the surface. Many of the volumes had hand-tooled leather bindings that had been well used over the years.

"What is this, uncle?" Brina asked with awe.

"These are the chronicles I've spoken of before, that have been kept for many centuries, since the first dragon blood of our line. All the dragon families maintained records of their own families, plus allies and enemies. These are the ones from my father's archives. The years after my father's death will be missing, as my father would have passed this to me at that time, but Garwyli is helping me fill those in, as best we can."

Still off to the side, the druid said, "You need a squire."

Adrianna quipped, "I feel like I've fallen back in time with words like bairn, carryin' and squire."

"'Tis the language of all ages," Garwyli told the witch.

She sent him a nod of appreciation for his instruction.

Daegan asked the druid, "Can we have that discussion again later?"

"Aye."

Returning to the tomes, Daegan said, "I have only had time to review the last entries, which shed some light on the Dragani Wars. In my father's treasure pile was a sword that may point toward those behind the greatest bloodshed of his time."

Tzader asked, "What sword?"

"It's called Lann Saoirse and belonged to an ice dragon. That sword should still be with her family."

"Her," murmured through the crowd.

To end the immediate speculation, Daegan said, "Sadly, the dragons are all dead now."

"You be livin'," Garwyli argued.

Every gaze watched for Daegan's reaction.

He told Garwyli, "I was captured in a realm."

"What of that silver one?"

Don't teleport the druid away from here, Daegan told himself. "Again, we will discuss this later."

"Aye."

That's what the druid said last time.

Returning to his point, which was not to make everyone sad about no potential mate for him, Daegan told Brina, "This is the history of your family. When you have need to access it, you must simply call up this library by name, but always keep that name secret until you are ready to share with your own children."

Silence fell gently over the crowd as Daegan telepathically gave the ancient name to Brina and Tzader.

Brina smiled and stood to hug him.

Family was everything.

He gave thanks again to have what he'd gained since leaving Maeve's clutches. He could have escaped to be more alone in today's world than in her tower realm.

Once Brina sat again, Daegan explained, "The history of our family is written in the Treoir language, which you should have been taught just so you could read these books. It's similar to Gaelic, but with changes intended to protect details about family treasure, for example. Garwyli and I have spoken of this language. He understands enough to help you read these tomes when I am not available."

Daegan pointed at the turning disc and it paused. Then he gave a finger crook to a specific one that looked new and had no writing on the spine. The thick book had been covered in rich green leather. Gold trim floated above the cover in a three-dimensional design.

Daegan angled the book back so that it opened to the middle with blank pages.

Placing his hands under the open book, he carried it to Brina, who accepted the offering. Daegan explained, "Once this library is passed down, a blank tome appears for the next line of descendants to record their history. This one is yours and Tzader's. I don't know how much we'll recover from the missing years when I was imprisoned, but Garwyli and I will do our best to record information in a separate volume."

A tome in the library trembled.

Brina said, "Uncle, one is shakin'."

Daegan turned to reach for the volume he had not noticed the first time he'd found the library.

The tome jumped into his hands before he could grasp it. Pages flipped fast, fanning his face, until pausing on the last page covered in images and text.

"This is in my father's writing," Daegan said, murmuring to

himself, then he read out loud. "The day you read this, you will know I am gone. I fear I've made errors in trust even within my own kingdom. I placed a spell upon this library to open only for you. You will have the power to make it available to others, if you survive as I pray you will. I had hoped to mount an attack against the Medb and gain your freedom, but I have failed. We have a traitor who started the Dragani War, placing all dragons in conflict. I feel I can no longer depend upon the squire family we have relied upon for generations, as they grow more afraid each day that I cannot protect them. I leave you with the only name I trust and pray that you will find her or her descendants."

Daegan read the last sentence silently to himself.

Her family name is Luigsech.

CHAPTER 34

County Galway, Ireland

CASIDHE STRETCHED TO PUT BACK the heavy book of records she'd been reading. She'd been hunting a thread of connection for a customer from Scotland who had too much money. She intended to give him good reason to spend some with her family.

Those customers were fun for her. Tracking their ancestries turned up fascinating trivia and sharing that information brought smiles all around.

Who wouldn't love her job?

The bell on the shop door tinkled, but she didn't go running to see who might be their next customer.

Fenella handled the front desk. She had the perfect personality, where Casidhe preferred working behind the scenes. Her expertise lay in digging up details not often found in the usual genealogical searches.

She had a gift for it.

When a smooth male voice began speaking with a mild Irish lilt, Casidhe's sixth sense nudged her to listen in. Another of her gifts was being an exceptionally talented snoop.

He said to Fenella, "I understand you are a historian of County Galway families."

Moving down a long aisle, then hanging a right into another one that headed toward the front of the building, Casidhe found her favorite spot for observation. Now she was in line with Fenella's desk. Casidhe moved the book that allowed her a nice view from where she hid in a dark space. She made less noise than a shadow when need be.

A sweet, round-faced woman with shamrock green eyes and a

pleasant disposition, Fenella smiled up at the attractive couple. "Aye, we keep a fair number of records, but not for all who have lived here. For that, you might need to be lookin' to Connemara Heritage and History Centre. If I can help ya, I will. My name is Fenella. Who might you be?"

"We are the Cavans," the man said.

Having an Irish surname did not constitute Irish heritage any more than did a lilt to his words. Casidhe had heard many versions, some of which were bogus, but this man had sharp eyes and a handsome face that looked to have some true Irish blood. He wore a fine suit that had cost a few pennies at a posh shop. His gray beard had been perfectly trimmed, and some might put him in his forties, but she didn't think so.

Yes, she had a suspicious streak about every stranger, but it had served her well more than once.

Her gaze moved to the woman at his side, who was almost as tall as he. She wore dark sunglasses, electric-blue gloves, black pants, black boots and a white, knee-length wool coat with a silver scarf over her head.

Why did it seem she was hiding her identity?

All Casidhe could make out about the woman's face were beautifully shaped cheeks and a fairly nice mouth, though it appeared to have no idea how to smile.

"So nice to meet you, Mr. and Mrs. Cavan. Would that be the family name you're lookin' to trace to ancestors?"

"No. I have my family tree, but I have been hired to locate the history of a family that lived in this area many centuries ago."

"Oh. There is not so much of the very ancient history to be found sometimes, but I will find out what I can, dependin' upon what you can tell me. Let's have the family name and we'll start there."

Casidhe stifled a snort.

That Fenella could lie and no one would question her. She had that gift, but it was more that she looked to be someone's plump grandmother.

The Cavan guy smiled, "Wonderful. I'm interested in the Treoirs. They lived here a very long time ago."

The spit dried up in Casidhe's mouth. She waited to see how Fenella would handle it.

Fenella sat back. "But you are not a Treoir descendant?"

"Sadly, no. What little I've heard of them sounds truly fascinating, though."

"What would that be?"

Cavan paused as if he hesitated to share anything, but he said, "As I understand it, they lived during the time of a King named Gruffyn. My client was told as a child that his family hailed from that lineage and the records were kept by ... squires. He hopes, if nothing else, that you might point us toward the names of squire families of that era."

Now, Fenella took her time answering. When she did, she no longer sounded like anyone's sweet grandmother, but more the guardian she could be. "Your client must know that families of squires who kept records of royal families from two thousand years ago are not so simple to trace."

Casidhe watched the couple more closely.

If Cavan's client were truly related to the Treoirs ... forget about it. That wasn't possible. But just to play devil's advocate, if he *were*, that client would know he couldn't just send a stranger here to ask about such things.

Cavan tilted his head as if he found Fenella's words hard to comprehend. "Are you sayin' you aren't interested in my inquiry?"

Sitting forward again, Fenella replied in a sugary voice that hid her razor-sharp mind, "Oh, no. We never turn down good coin. I am only sayin' it takes a while to reach a squire family. They're a reclusive lot. I will be happy to send word once proper incentive is provided."

Mrs. Cavan finally said something. "An incentive?"

She asked the question with a bite in her voice. Her husband reached over and patted her hand, as if telling her not to speak.

What had the wife so jacked up?

Fenella gave the couple a wary frown. "Surely ya know I don't speak of money. I suggest ya talk to your client. He, or she, should know what is required to approach those families."

"You don't possess any records here?" Cavan pressed on.

Fenella's eyes twinkled. "Your client should know much of that history be spoken rather than written."

"I see," Mr. Cavan said and did not sound surprised. "This Treoir family intrigues me more and more. I shall contact my client tonight to convey our conversation. I will surely be in touch soon."

Smiling as if she'd made every wish they had come true, Fenella said, "That would be wonderful. Top of the day to you both."

Mrs. Cavan's lips had yet to change from the stern line.

Casidhe waited until the couple had been gone a full minute before exiting her hiding place. When she made it to the front, Fenella had closed the door and pulled the shade down over the window. The heavy furniture crafted by hand had been placed in here over seventy years ago, and only to update the furnishings then. Casidhe's family preferred to remain a bit in the past, surrounded by the wonderful scent of aged tomes she loved like children.

Walking to her desk and sitting down, Fenella asked, "What do you think, Cas?"

Casidhe carefully moved a small stack of books, and sat. She leaned back, thinking. "The man is old ... and powerful."

"How old?"

"To be honest, I have no idea, but he is not what he presented to you."

"I suspected as much," Fenella mused. "What of the woman?"

"She bothers me more than he does. She is old and powerful, too, but not in the same way."

"What do you mean?"

Casidhe lifted a foot to the bench and wrapped her arms around her bent leg. "It may not make sense, but she stood too still for my likin'. That she did not know what incentive was expected did surprise me, but Cavan clearly knew what you meant. He seemed to be keepin' her calm, but why? Her two words came out with the force of an order, not a simple question."

"Foolish woman to think she could order me to do anything'," Fenella muttered.

Laughing to agree, Casidhe said, "But it has been a long time since we've encountered anythin' like that pair. It does prick my curiosity."

Fenella swung a serious face to her. "Doona go lookin' for trouble."

Casidhe loved to tweak Fenella's nose. It brought out her brogue. "I did not open the door and call them in."

"What will you do?"

"We must inform the others."

Fenella suggested, "You may want to wait. They did not ask about King Eógan's family."

"Askin' about the Treoirs could be sincere ... or a ruse to find information on the other families." Casidhe shook her head. "No. Those two were here to snoop around for more than harmless ancestral information, because there is no such thing when diggin' into these families. Mark my word, they have a greater plan afoot."

"For one not even thirty, you've a good eye and ear for these things even without your gifts," Fenella admitted. "Keep me informed and I will send word if I learn more."

"Good. I doubt the man is truly a Cavan any more than that couple bein' human as they pretended. We both have our duties and now is the time for me to do mine." Casidhe considered just who the Cavans could be. Friend or foe?

If they be friend, they would have given a sign, which she and Fenella would have recognized. That put them clearly as the enemy. Casidhe curled her hands into fists, feeling the heat of anger pour into them at the potential threat to the family.

"Casidhe! Your eyes are glowin'!"

Shaking off the moment of anger, Casidhe calmed her energy. "I am fine."

"Not so fine if you lose control. How am I to keep ya hidden if anyone senses your power?"

"No one has discovered me since I came to be with ya," Casidhe said to keep Fenella calm. In truth, she had serious concerns about those two returning, because Cavan had a wily look to his eyes.

If she was correct about how old he might be, and she knew better than to doubt her instincts, he could pick up on her presence.

Standing, Casidhe said, "I believe they'll be back soon. I can't be here when they do show up again, not until I have more information. I will return when I do."

"I will do my best to keep them busy until then, but the family needs to consider moving again."

That pissed her off. Casidhe was the first line of defense for her family. She would not let some old being come in here and upend her people.

"Casidhe," Fenella said in a warning tone.

"I know." Casidhe closed her eyes, gave it a minute then opened them again. "Better now?"

"Ya canna make a mistake. Not now."

"I will not allow anyone to harm the family," Casidhe vowed and walked off. She wove her way to the rear of the building and down a set of stairs to a musty smelling basement cluttered with crooked piles of books and boxes.

Careful not to disturb cobwebs, she squeezed between two stacks and pushed a book that slid into the stone wall with no resistance. Once she entered the tunnel, she moved a rock with her foot and the entrance vanished. How long had it been since she made this walk?

Counting mentally, she came up with ten months. The last time she'd come this way had been only to visit for her own benefit after sending word to expect her.

Showing up unexpectedly would put everyone on edge.

It couldn't be avoided. They had known this day might come.

When she found the ladder to the surface, she climbed up until she reached the inside of a tree older than most living things in the human world. Once inside the tree, she had enough room to move her arms straight out away from her body.

Light flashed from the silver and metallic-blue sword standing against the curved inside wall.

That sword had been created for a female warrior her size.

There had been two others made of similar design.

One had belonged to Brynhild, the first daughter of King Eógan.

That sword had been named *Lann Saoirse*, Blade of Freedom.

The third daughter's sword carried the name *Lann na Fírinne*, Blade of Truth.

The sword now flashing with energy in front of her was hers by right, or so she'd believed her entire life. The *Lann an Cheartais*, Blade of Justice, had been made for the king's second daughter, his favorite.

Her heart raced.

There was only one reason this sword would be churning with power. It sensed her need to protect the family and stood ready to do its duty as it had two thousand years ago.

Or ... it sensed an enemy coming to claim it.

Her father had told her this day might come, though he hoped it would not. She lifted the worn leather scabbard lying on the ground and fitted the harness onto her back. She had another sheath for battle, but this one would lie closer to her body, and be easier to conceal as she traveled.

With her gear in place, she stepped back and crooned, "Come to me *Lann an Cheartais* so we may do our duty."

If the sword did not come to her, she had failed to prove worthy. Her father had warned her to never call it to her unless she was prepared to take control of its power.

The sword quivered, then slowly lifted upward. Turning in the air, the blade glided up and over her shoulder, where she waited for it to swing around and insert smoothly into the scabbard.

Or stab through her heart if it found her lacking.

Hard to know what something that old would do when she had never truly known if this was her sword to wield.

Until now, she'd been only the caretaker.

Deep in her heart, she'd always questioned whether she deserved the position she'd been given as a child, but she never doubted her commitment to the family.

When the sword slipped into place on her back, Casidhe released a sigh of relief and reached over her shoulder to feel the hilt. A hum of energy flowed through her arm and buzzed her body with a soft vibration she welcomed.

Patting the jeweled handle, she said, "We will train soon, but for now we must travel to see my father and the family."

Lann an Cheartais sizzled with a push of energy.

Her sword knew she was not talking about the wonderful Luigsech family, which had raised her.

———

Cathbad walked Brynhild down the street toward a park in County Galway. So much had changed since his last visit.

How many centuries ago had that been? He didn't want to add up the years. Instead he said, "That was an interestin' visit."

"Yes."

This woman had much to learn. She'd come close to snarling at the historian. When he'd returned to Brynhild's cave this last time, she had emerged from her ice bath prepared to play nice.

She said all the right things and showed no sign of conflict.

He had lived too long to easily accept her docile attitude when it surely hid a homicidal fantasy involving him, but for now Brynhild walked calmly alongside him. She'd accepted his disguise to hide anything that might give her, or her power, away.

Unfortunately, it may not have been enough shielding.

Cathbad asked softly, "Did ya feel the power in the shop?"

Finally, a smile from the ice dragon.

She answered in a smug tone, "Oh, aye. If Daegan knew of the squire for his family, he would have been here already. Whoever hid from us in that shop was no human."

"Exactly, my sweet. We shall pretend we did not notice the one hiding. With a wee bit of luck, that one will alert those we hunt and we shall be a step ahead of Daegan. All the while, I will continue to train you."

Offering a full smile, she agreed, "I will be the best of students. When the time comes, I will destroy the red dragon and all that he holds dear."

She might be difficult, but this ice dragon would accomplish what Maeve lacked the vision to even imagine.

With this ice dragon, Cathbad would rule Treoir ... and the world.

Thank you for reading my books. If you enjoyed this story, please help other readers find this book by posting a review.

———

Join my newsletter list (I NEVER share emails) at www. AuthorDiannaLove.com to be notified first about the new Belador spinoff series, **TREOIR DRAGON CHRONICLES.**

(If the link does not work, because technology sometimes gets a migraine, email assistant@authordiannalove.com with **BELADOR LIST** in the *subject line* to receive the link.)

For **SIGNED & PERSONALIZED PRINT** copies of Dianna's books visit *www.DiannaLoveSignedBooks.com* where you can preorder new books.

———

The Belador series is an ongoing story line, so you may want to read the books in order. Available in ebook/print/audio.

Book 1: Blood Trinity
Book 2: Alterant
Book 3: The Curse
Book 4: Rise Of The Gryphon
Book 5: Demon Storm
Book 6: Witchlock
Book 7: Rogue Belador
Book 8: Dragon King Of Treoir
Book 9: Belador Cosaint
Book 10: Treoir Dragon Hoard
Book 10.5: Evalle and Storm
Tristan's Escape: A Belador Novella

———

While you're waiting on the next Belador adventure, take a look at Dianna's new League of Gallize Shifters series.
GRAY WOLF MATE is book one in this exciting new

paranormal series. Shifters came out seven years back and, since then, the world has never been the same for many.

Tess Janver and Cole Cavanaugh fell deeply in love in college ... then he disappeared without a word. She'd feared the worst, or thought she had. After six years, he returns as a beefed-up version of his former self. That's not the only thing different. As someone working in a preternatural criminal investigation unit and the daughter of a senator determined to rid the world of dangerous shifters, Tess is caught between performing her duty to humans, protecting the only family she has left and risking her heart to a man who once destroyed it.

Cole had no choice in becoming a Gallize shifter and now he's facing the end of his days from a fatal mating curse he can't stop. He never planned on Tess finding out he shared his body with a wolf, but she's in danger from a rogue wolf pack. He's not leaving until she's safe ... and he has a chance to redeem himself in her eyes before his time is up.

———◆———

Gray Wolf Mate
Mating A Grizzly
Stalking His Mate (2018)

REVIEWS ON BELADOR BOOKS:

"...non-stop tense action, filled with twists, betrayals, danger, and a beautiful sensual romance. As always with Dianna Love, I was on the edge of my seat, unable to pull myself away."
~~Barb, The Reading Cafe

"...shocking developments and a whopper of an ending... and I may have exclaimed aloud more than once...Bottom line: I really kind of loved it."
~~Jen, top 500 Reviewer

"DEMON STORM leaves you breathless on countless occasions."
~~Amelia Richard, SingleTitles

"...Its been a very long time since I've felt this passionate about getting the next installment in a series. Even J. K. Rowling's Harry Potter books."
~~Bryonna Nobles, Demons, Dreams and Dragon Wings

Belador novels are released in print, e-book and audio.

BLOOD TRINITY

– Belador Book 1

Atlanta has become the battlefield between human and demon.

As an outcast among her own people, Evalle Kincaid has walked the line between human and beast her whole life as a half-blood Belador. An Alterant. Her true origins unknown, she searches to learn more about her past before it kills her, but when a demon claims a young woman in a terrifying attack and there's no one else to blame, Evalle comes under suspicion.

The one person who can help her is Storm, the sexy new agent brought in to catch her in a lie, just one of his gifts besides being a Skinwalker. On a deadly quest for her own survival, Evalle is forced to work with the mysterious stranger who has the power to unravel her world. Through the sordid underbelly of an alternate Atlanta where nothing is as it seems to the front lines of the city where former allies now hunt her, Evalle must prove her innocence or pay the ultimate price. But saving herself is the least of her problems if she doesn't stop the coming apocalypse. The clock is ticking and Atlanta is about to ignite.

"BLOOD TRINITY is an ingenious urban fantasy ... Book One in the Belador series will enthrall you during every compellingly entertaining scene." **Amelia Richards, Single Titles**

"...a well written book that will take you out of your everyday life and transport you to an exciting new world..." **Heated Steve**

ALTERANT

– Belador Book 2

Evalle must hunt her own kind...or die with them.

In this explosive new world of betrayals and shaky alliances, as the only Alterant not incarcerated, Evalle faces an impossible task — recapture three dangerous, escaped creatures before they slaughter more humans...or her.

When words uttered in the heat of combat are twisted against her, Evalle is blamed for the prison break of three dangerous Alterants and forced to recapture the escapees. Deals with gods and goddesses are tricky at best, and now the lives of all Beladors, and the safety of innocent humans, rides on Evalle's success. Her Skinwalker partner, Storm, is determined to plant all four of his black jaguar paws in the middle of her world, but Evalle has no time for a love life. Not present when a Tribunal sends her to the last place she wants to show her face.

The only person she can ask for help is the one man who wants to see her dead.

———

"There are SO many things in this series that I want to learn more about; there's no way I could list them all." **Lily, Romance Junkies Reviews**

THE CURSE

– Belador book 3

Troll powered gang wars explode in cemeteries and no one in Atlanta is safe.

Demonic Svart Trolls have invaded Atlanta and Evalle suddenly has little hope of fulfilling a promise with the freedom of an entire race hanging in the balance, even if she had more than two days. She takes a leap of faith, seeking help from Isak, the Black Ops specialist who recently put Evalle in his cross hairs and has a personal vendetta against Alterants who killed his best friend.

Bloody troll led gang wars force Evalle into unwittingly exposing a secret that endangers all she holds dear, and complicates her already tumultuous love life with the mysterious Skinwalker, Storm. But it's when the entire Medb coven comes after her that Evalle is forced to make a game- changing decision with no time left on the clock.

———

"Evalle, continues to be one of my favorite female warriors in paranormal/urban fantasy... I loved The Curse... This was a great story from start to finish, super fun, lots of action, couples to root for, and a fantastic heroine." **Barb, The Reading Café**

RISE OF THE GRYPHON

– Belador Book 4

If dying is the cost of protecting those you love... bring it.

Evalle has a chance to find out her true origin, and give all Alterants a place in the world. To do so, she'll have to take down the Belador traitor and bring home a captured friend, which means infiltrating the dangerous Medb coven. To do that, she'll have to turn her back on her vows and enter a vicious game to the death. What she does discover about Alterants is not good, especially for the Beladors.

Her best friends, Tzader and Quinn, face unthinkable choices, as relationships with the women they love grow twisted. With time ticking down on a decision that will compel allies to become deadly enemies, Evalle turns to Storm and takes a major step in their relationship, but the witchdoctor he's been hunting now stalks Evalle. Now Evalle is forced to embrace her destiny . . . but at what price?

———

"Longtime fans of the Belador series will have much to celebrate in the fearless Evalle Kincaid's fourth outing...with such heart and investment, each scene has an intensity that will quicken the pulse and capture the imagination..." **RT Book Reviews**

DEMON STORM

– Belador book 5

We all have demons... some are more real than others.

With Treoir Island in shambles after a Medb attack that left the survival of the missing Belador warrior queen in question and Belador powers compromised, there is one hope for her return and their future – Evalle Kincaid, whose recent transformation has turned her into an even more formidable warrior. First she has to locate Storm, the Skinwalker she's bonded with who she believes can find the Belador queen, but Storm stalks the witch doctor who's threatening Evalle's life. When he finally corners the witch doctor, she throws Storm a curve that may cost him everything, including Evalle. The hunter becomes the hunted, and Evalle must face her greatest nightmare to save Storm and the Beladors or watch the future of mankind fall to deadly preternatural predators.

DEMON STORM includes a **Bonus Short Story** - DEADLY FIXATION, from the Belador world.

———

"There is so much action in this book I feel like I've burned calories just reading it." **D Antonio**

"...nonstop adventures overflowing with danger and heartfelt emotions. DEMON STORM leaves you breathless on countless occasions." **Amelia Richard, Single Titles**

WITCHLOCK

– Belador Book 6

Witchlock vanished in the 13th century ... or did it?

If Atlanta falls, Witchlock will sweep the country in a bloodbath. After finally earning her place among the Beladors, Evalle is navigating the ups and downs of her new life with Storm when she's sucked into a power play between her Belador tribe and the Medb coven. Both groups claim possession of the
Alterant gryphons, especially Evalle, the gryphon leader. But an influx of demons and dark witches into Atlanta threatens to unleash war between covens, pitting allies against each other as a legendary majik known as Witchlock invades the city and attacks powerful beings. Evalle has one hope for stopping the invasion, but the cost may be her sanity and having to choose which friend to save.

———

"Evalle and friends are back in another high energy, pulse pounding adventure...Fans of Rachel Caine's Weather Warden series will enjoy this series. I surely do." **In My Humble Opinion Blogspot**

ROGUE BELADOR

– Belador Book 7

Immortals fear little ... except a secret in the wrong hands.

While searching for a way to save Brina of Treoir's failing memories, Tzader Burke discovers someone who can help her if he is willing to sneak into the heart of his enemy's stronghold—TÅµr Medb. He'll do anything to protect the woman he loves from becoming a mindless empty shell, but his decision could be the catalyst for an apocalyptic war. The deeper he digs for the truth, the more lies he uncovers that shake the very foundation of being a Belador and the future of his clan.

While battling on every front, a secret is exposed that two immortal powers have spent thousands of years keeping buried. Tzader and his team have no choice but to fight for what they believe in, because the world as they know it is never going to be the same again.

DRAGON KING OF TREOIR

- Belador Book 8

The Treoir dragon holds the fate of the Beladors in one hand …
and his own in the other.

The Beladors finally have a true leader in Daegan, their new
dragon king, but life is far from secure now that they've inherited
his enemies. As their Maistir, Vladimir Quinn played a risky role
in freeing the dragon from the lair of their enemy, the Medb.
Quinn now faces a heavy price for his part. The Medb queen
is out for blood. Vigilante killings erupt among Atlanta's secret
preternatural community and all fingers point to the Beladors.
The dragon king has his first real test as a ruler when he has
to choose between protecting his people and entering a hostile
realm full of deities capable of killing a dragon. But as a two-
thousand-year-old warrior, Daegan has never shied away from
any battle. Quinn, Evalle, Storm and friends race to discover who
is trying to turn the entire VIPER coalition against the Beladors
before war breaks out. With the clock also ticking down for
Quinn, who has been ordered to hand over Kizira's body to the
Medb queen, Daegan reveals an even greater reason the Beladors
have to prevent the queen from any chance to use necromancy on
that body than secrets Quinn protects.

Freedom is never free. Not when the powerful gods and
goddesses poised to decide Quinn's fate see an opportunity to
also destroy a threat to their existence – the last dragon shifter.

———

*"...fantastic, exciting, edge of your seat suspenseful story that
flows so well from one book to the next."*
—The Reading Cafe

BELADOR COSAINT

- Belador Book 9

Belador Maistir, Vladimir Quinn, has yet to locate his daughter and now his worst fears have come to fruition. A vicious enemy hot on her trail plans to turn his child into an apocalyptic weapon. Quinn doesn't even know what the young girl looks like or where her deceased mother hid her. He knows of only one woman—a remote viewer—who might be able to help, but Reese O'Rinn has vanished into thin air, literally. Quinn has even less chance of finding that fiery female and no time to search for her. A powerful entity is determined to push the Belador dragon king, Daegan, and the entire preternatural world into the open, starting with the city of Atlanta. Chaos sends Quinn and all the Beladors running hard around the clock. When their innocent families come under attack and the VIPER coalition refuses to send aid, Daegan invokes the ancient rule of cosaint to protect his people, but will that backfire on him and the Beladors? Alliances are tested. Secrets are exposed. Battle lines are drawn in blood. It all comes down to who lives and who dies as Quinn faces an unimaginable sacrifice to save his child.

———

"The Belador series is beloved and intricate."
—*USA Today*

TREOIR DRAGON HOARD

-Belador Book 10

Two thousand years ago, someone stole the king's treasure from Daegan's father. An unexpected enemy uses this hoard to set Daegan on a path to his ultimate demise by dangling the one bait everyone knows the dragon king can't ignore—protecting one of his own.

While racing to help a friend, Evalle lands in a trap where she's given the unimaginable choice to either destroy her dragon king or condemn everyone she loves to die. Even her Skinwalker mate, Storm, has no way to track her this time.

Friendships and allies are tested as Atlanta erupts with preternatural exposure. Who will join Storm and Daegan to go where, even for a dragon, the chance of survival is nil? With the enemy willing to gamble everything to take down her dragon king, Evalle makes up her mind to accept her destiny, but on her terms. She never wants anyone to see what she's become, especially Storm.

Destiny is not a choice, but a summons. The hourglass favors no one.

"The Belador series is beloved and intricate."
—USA Today

OTHER BOOKS BY DIANNA

If you like the Beladors, then you might enjoy Dianna's new League of Gallize Shifters paranormal romance (stand alone) written with urban fantasy world building.

Gray Wolf Mate
Mating A Grizzly
Stalking His Mate

Complete Slye Temp romantic thriller Series
Last Chance To Run
Nowhere Safe
Honeymoon To Die For
Kiss The Enemy
Deceptive Treasures
Stolen Vengeance
Fatal Promise

Micah Caida young adult Trilogy
Time Trap Time Return
Time Lock
The Complete Red Moon Trilogy hardback

*Signed and personalized Red Moon books available at www. **MicahCaidaSignedBooks**.com for that special reader.

(Micah Caida is the collaborative name of New York Times Bestseller Dianna Love and USA Today bestseller Mary Buckham)

AUTHOR'S BIO

NEW YORK TIMES **BESTSELLER DIANNA** Love once dangled over a hundred feet in the air to create unusual marketing projects for Fortune 500 companies. She now writes high-octane romantic thrillers, young adult and urban fantasy. Fans of the bestselling Belador urban fantasy series will be thrilled to know more books are coming after soon with the new Treoir Dragon Chronicles. Dianna's Slye Temp sexy romantic thriller series wrapped up with Gage and Sabrina's book–Fatal Promise–perfect for bingers! She has new League of Gallize Shifters paranormal romance series. Look for her books in print, e-book and audio. On the rare occasions Dianna is out of her writing cave, she tours the country on her BMW motorcycle searching for new story locations. Dianna lives in the Atlanta, GA area with her husband, who is a motorcycle instructor, and with a tank full of unruly saltwater critters.

Visit her website at *www.AuthorDiannaLove.com* or Join her **Dianna Love Reader Community** group page on Facebook and get in on the fun!

A WORD FROM DIANNA...

Thank you for reading book 10 in the Belador series. Wow, it's just amazing to think we're at ten books and I still have so many stories to tell. You might have noticed that I'm working on the TREOIR DRAGON CHRONICLES. There is a lot of story yet to tell about the dragons so it only made sense to allow the time and page space to do it justice. I will still be continuing the Belador stories. Daegan will continue to have a role in those books just as the Beladors will appear in the dragon chronicles. That's all I can tell you right now without giving up spoilers.

As always, I have to thank my wonderful husband, Karl, first. You would have no books without all that he does to allow me the time in my cave. We've been together many years and I cherish every day with him.

A special thank you to Jennifer Cazares, Sherry Arnold and Stacey Krug for being *very* early super readers who did a wonderful job and caught those small things that might have interrupted a reader's journey through the story. Their help is so very valuable.

Many of you know Cassondra, my assistant who has been my first reader for many years. She does a terrific job of catching continuity issues and keeping me on the right path. In addition, her husband, Steve, often reviews pages and catches things neither of us see. They've been a huge support for many years and are dear friends. Judy Carney brings a smile and great attitude every time she's asked to catch edits and reading bumps to insure a smooth flow, too. I can never release a full novel without it being in audio for all my wonderful audio book fans! For that to happen, Stephen R. Thorne steps in to do a terrific production of narrating the Belador books, then Joyce Ann McLaughlin is a superb audio editor, and good friend, who catches those few things I'm sure I would not in spite of Stephen's really clean read every time. Thank you both for helping me to hand the fans a high quality audio production.

I am blessed to have made wonderful friendships with readers such as Kimber Mirabella and Sharon Livingston Griffiths, who are always willing to help at any time. Candace Fox has been giving me a hand with events on the Reader Community Facebook page, which I always appreciate. A big thanks to Leiha Mann for all she does to help me promote my books.

A very SPECIAL THANK YOU to all of my awesome early review team who just keeps on bringing it!

No book goes out without a awesome Kim Killion cover – she's an artistic genius – or being formatted professionally by Jennifer Litteken (she's a goddess) and crew who I owe a few martinis to for going above and beyond.

Sending hugs and love to Karen Marie Moning, a good friend as well as a talented author who I thank also for the healthy life change she initiated in my life.

Thank you again to my peeps on the Dianna Love Reader Group on Facebook. You make every day wonderful.

Dianna